strange
attractors

Ana K. Wrenn

Dedication

To Kathleen, Howard, David, Cary, Katie, and my
big, beautiful, and messy family of choice.

Chapter 1

Rose Red

PROFESSOR SONJA J. STOREY LOOKED at her watch. The Gucci bracelet usually glowed, but it looked dull under the fluorescent light of the dingy corridor. That was precisely what Western Highlands State University did: it took the shine off everything.

She had arrived on campus early that morning, as was her practice, and ignoring the rigid two-cup rule she had on teaching days, she had foolishly permitted herself a third cup of jasmine tea. Even more foolishly, she had neglected to use the department restroom before walking across campus to her classroom.

With only minutes to go before her lecture started, Sonja needed to use the restroom—very likely a filthy restroom and one of the many reasons she rarely visited any but the ones in her building.

Last night's dream is to blame for this disruption.

Images flashed across her brain, drawing her into a mental chase, but the images wouldn't settle long enough for her to make sense of them, leaving her uneasy. *What did I even dream?*

Shit! Sonja stood in the doorway of the restroom, her shoulder against the door, her mouth hanging open. A full-bodied statuesque woman held what looked like a pose from the *Kama Sutra*: standing at the sink, folding over the rusty porcelain, lips close to kissing the murky mirror, and maintaining a reverse leg lift.

"Sorry. I'm in your way," the woman said, glancing in Sonja's direction while blotting a tear-stained face with a paper towel. "Come in, come in." She straightened and lowered her leg, giving Sonja space to get by.

"I'll be quick." Sonja's bladder pressed her forward, past the weeping stranger and toward the line of metal stalls. Her tone was cool. The last thing she needed was to get sucked into a whirlpool of human drama.

At the door of the end stall, she glanced back at the younger woman. Under different circumstances, she might have complimented the smart outfit on display: silky red blouse paired with fitted gingham slacks and the quirky but attractive bourbon leather boots. The ensemble complemented the woman's golden-brown skin. But there wasn't time, and she slipped inside.

"Sorry if I frightened you," the woman's voice cracked out just as Sonja lifted her skirt, pulled down her body shaper, and hovered over the toilet to relieve herself. "I'm Crystal. Crystal Byrd. That's Byrd with a Y, by the way. People misspell— Never mind."

"Department?" Sonja asked perfunctorily after flushing. She lifted her Coach tote off the door hook, stepped out of the stall, and approached the sink next to where the woman stood. "Your answer, I did not catch it," she said surreptitiously taking in the stranger's long legs, rounded hips, and broad back, deciding that the outfit wouldn't flatter her own slight frame, particularly her flat buttocks.

"You didn't catch what?" the woman asked, lowering the paper towel to reveal puffy eyes.

"Your department."

"Gender Studies."

"Faculty?" *Too fresh to be an administrator.* Sonja quickly washed her hands and, standing on her tiptoes, pushed the towel lever with her elbow, producing a puddle of cheap, mud-colored paper towels. She snatched the towels and crab-walked toward the door.

"Assistant professor. One of those baby PhDs." The woman chuckled and fixed her amber eyes on Sonja and leaned against the sink. "Came here to develop my department's online curriculum."

Sonja nodded and waved her hand in the air as she left, severing the interaction.

She looked at her watch again and realized she would be on time for class, but her lecture would be delayed as she set up her presentation slides and took attendance.

"Sorry about the public weeping."

Rubber soles squeaked against the flooring behind her, and Sonja realized that the woman had followed her out.

"I thought getting the doctorate was the hardest part of becoming a professor."

"It will get easier." Sonja tossed the lie over her shoulder but kept walking.

The leggy woman easily caught up and matched her stride with Sonja's.

"Will it really get easier? This first semester is kicking my ass, and we're not even—what?—a month in."

Sonja turned the corner and saw her classroom, the door open. The seated students chattered and fidgeted with nervous energy.

Sonja pivoted toward her unwanted companion. "Not to be rude, Kirsten—"

"Crystal. And your name?"

Sonja overlooked the unexpected sparkle in Crystal's swollen eyes and the faint smile. The stranger was poking fun at her. And few poked at Sonja without consequences.

"I am Dr. Sonja J. Storey," she said, stating her name as if reading it off her CV "This is my classroom. You are delaying my lecture." And with that, she turned and walked into the room and shut the door behind her.

Sonja passed the front row seat where Jacob Randalls had once sat and an image from last night's dream flashed into her mind.

Jacob diving into the ocean, disappearing under crashing waves.

As suddenly as the dreamy images appeared, they dissipated, releasing her to face rows of students, their eyes filled with fear and resentment.

These students hate you already. And they have yet to take the first exam. You will never have another student like Jacob. He wanted to learn, wanted to improve his station in life.

Overcome by unexpected longing, she missed her step but managed to grasp the raised edge of the media console and twisted to face the class, striking a pose akin to a stork sunning with its wings splayed. Since the class seemed unaware of her blunder, she righted herself and stepped up beside the console.

"A meeting detained me," she said crisply, each word snapping like an icy branch. "While I record attendance, review your syllabus. Ensure you are aware of upcoming deadlines."

She retrieved the seating chart and reached for the media control pad to wake up the computer and overhead projector. Her hands knew the classroom's technology better than any lover's body—not that she'd had that many lovers or classrooms. So, when she touched a slip of paper instead of the cool control pad, she paused. She looked down at the sticky note that was a red-rose hue—a dead rose, that is.

Let's Play a Game!

Sonja ripped the sticky paper off the control pad and stared at the four words, the black, skeletal letters stirring something in her. Queasiness, perhaps, or something deeper, darker.

"To whom does this belong?" she asked the class, holding up the note. She kept her voice steady, her enunciation precise, to cover the emotional debris threatening to surface.

She studied the students' faces in the harsh lighting, assessing their blank catfish eyes and grouper mouths. Only mid-September, and already she couldn't wait to be done with this batch. Again, she thought of Jacob. She hadn't allowed herself to think about him for some time, but after last night's dream, he seemed to be haunting her.

Because you destroyed him.

"This note," she said, shaking the red square as if that would help her shake off the voice clinging to her brain like a barnacle. "Is anyone here capable of speech?"

"Don't know."

Sonja leveled her gaze at the disheveled student wearing a worn hooded sweatshirt. "Pardon?"

"Don't know." The student cringed under Sonja's glare.

"Well, thank you, Ms.— Your name?"

"Ronnie."

"Your *full* name."

"Staller, ma'am. Ronnie Staller."

4

Sonja stepped out from behind the console, a synthetic black block out from which emerged various cables that drove to the floor and swam across it like silvery eels. She stood before the class. The sand-colored walls curling around rows of tan chairs reminded her of a conch shell filled with rotting meat.

"Class, a brief reminder on this Tuesday morning: I am not ma'am or missus. Address me as Dr. Storey or Professor Storey."

She bit back the urge to add, "I earned every bit of my Ph.D." There would be another opportunity. There always was.

Sonja crumpled the sticky note and dropped it in the trash can, releasing it from her thoughts at the same time. Returning to the console, she finished attendance, then squared her shoulders and prepared to reclaim her day.

"If you did not read the article, do not speak. Listen. Take notes. I do not repeat myself."

Someone snickered in the back of the room, perhaps the boy with the baseball cap pulled low over his face or the girl wearing the childish pink shirt spattered with purple unicorns. The snickering was familiar commentary on her professorial style and reminded her of her mother's derision.

Sonja held the class in a cold gaze. "*If* you graduate," she said, launching into her lecture, "you may gain employment. Therefore, keep this in mind: chaos. As your reading contends, collapses in an organization's order often originate from a small, unknown variance. Over time, that variance produces large, dramatic, and unanticipated outcomes."

She paused. Most of the students were slumping in their seats, their eyes not on her. Sonja narrowed her stance and placed her hands across her lower belly, feathering her fingers. She liked to imagine that her long, red-coated nails made her hands look like the blood-tipped wings of a snowy owl after a kill. When she had the class's attention again, she continued.

"The fundamental challenge of organizational leaders, then, is to adapt in the face of chaos. Leaders must adapt or risk being obliterated."

Staller threw up her hand.

"Ma'am!"

Sonja glared at the student to silence the interruption, but Staller blundered ahead.

"I'm thinking… You mean to say that when things go bad at work, you don't really know why. That the thing that caused things to go bad might be real tiny. Then POW!" Staller punched her fist into her other hand. "Everything goes wonky. All 'cause of that small thing."

"Class, this is an important lesson. Utilize the language of your reading. Let the experts inform how you speak. You will be tested on your understanding of that language. Additionally, you will not be taken seriously in this world unless you speak properly," Sonja said, then turned toward Staller without really seeing the student's face. "Your answer contained minor accuracies. Reread the material. Refine your knowledge, and reconsider how you express yourself."

She dimmed the lights and returned to the media console, her private island in a hostile sea. She brought up her slides and clicked the remote. Large scarlet letters lit up the screen, making student faces appear to have been bloodied.

CHAOS THEORY

"This semester is about chaos. You will master chaos theory, or you will fail. Now for a review of key terms."

An hour later, the students filed out. She logged off the computer, collected her personal items, and exited the classroom, confident that she had left the morning's messiness behind her.

––––––––

Sonja knew the route from Walker Hall to Terrell Center so well that she could take her eyes off the sidewalk and survey the campus, her body programmed to avoid crumbling sections. With each step, she grew more determined. Soon, she would visit President Maxwell Knowles and deliver her second unsolicited report about the pathetic state of WHSU. The campus consisted of outdated buildings and uninspired green spaces.

Just as she had last November, on her next unannounced visit, she would sweep past the open-mouthed secretary, and, uninvited, enter the President's office to rebuke him for his lack of leadership. During that previous meeting with him, she had been escorted out of his office, him murmuring promises about placing her on a planning committee. But before her compulsory exit, she had berated him over the numerous beautification awards given to peer institutions. Their campus had never earned a single award.

She hadn't heard from the president since, and the committee seat had never materialized. But another assignment had, an assignment that put her in the crosshairs of a certain lunatic professor, Dr. Horace Watson. Sonja knew from the start that the Faculty Termination Inquiry Committee—a committee that considered stripping a professor's tenure—would have consequences, and not the kind she relished.

"Hiya!"

Sonja jumped at the loud greeting behind her, and she stepped up her pace as quickly as her three-inch red Fluevog pumps would let her, but it was to no avail. The junior professor from this morning's encounter jogged up next to her, grinning.

"Sorry for startling you, Sonja." The peals of laughter further vexed Sonja. "I thought you heard me call you." The Assistant Professor smiled down like they were on friendly terms.

"Look, Kristen," Sonja began, prepared to deliver a lecture about etiquette in academia.

"Crystal. As in crystal clear. And Byrd. As in flapping wings, but spelled with a Y." Crystal laughed, her delight unrestrained. "You're awful with names, huh?" Without waiting for an answer, she continued. "I wanted to apologize for crying in the bathroom, then keeping you from your class. And now for scaring you. Sorry."

"You did not scare me," Sonja said sharply.

"If I were in your shoes, I'd be irritated. I've stepped all over your boundaries, and in such a short time," Crystal said. "So please accept my apology for annoying you."

"Which time?" Sonja switched her tote to her other shoulder, as if that could keep Byrd out of her personal space.

Crystal snorted. "That's funny. You have a funny streak. You would get along with my mom. On second thought—" She laughed again, then trailed off. "When you came into the bathroom... Well, I had just had an upsetting experience. I'm still reeling."

7

Finally, Terrell Center came into view. The square brick building housed unpopular departments away from the rest of the campus, but at least Sonja could take refuge in her office.

"What you said earlier, Sonja…"

"It is Dr. St—"

"I hope you're right about things getting easier. Because I just got threatened. Anonymously, of course. Bastard left it on my campus voicemail."

"It happens." Sonja was approaching the rear entrance of her building, the unsightly path to her office through the bowels of Terrell Center, but, today, it would be her route to freedom.

"Wait! Sonja, are you serious?" Byrd tugged on Sonja's designer bag. "Have you been threatened?"

"Of course," Sonja replied. She pointedly raised her forearm and looked at her watch. "Look, this must end. I am pressed for time."

"You walk, I'll keep up. Do you ever get used to the threats, the harassment?"

"How you react is entirely up to you." Sonja bumped her tote into her unwanted companion without effect.

"That call… It was horrible." Byrd shuddered. "And I've had nasty crap hurled at me all my life. But this asshole says, 'Let's you and me play a game. I rape you. You scream and—'"

Sonja halted abruptly and faced Crystal. "What did you say?"

"He threatened to rape—"

"No, not that. The other part."

"What other part?" Crystal knit her eyebrows and stared down at Sonja.

"The game," Sonja said, suddenly distracted by how the morning sun played against the streaks of auburn and gold in Crystal's hair. "The game," she said again, urgently needing to get the information and get away.

"'Let's you and me play a game.' Is that what you mean?"

"Yes," Sonja said dispassionately, though her stomach was roiling. "Threats are an unfortunate consequence of our profession, particularly for females. Now I must go." Sonja hurried to the heavy door and opened it with trembling fingers.

"Okay. Well, bye. Maybe we'll run into one another again soon—" The door closed, cutting off Professor Byrd's words.

8

Chapter 2

Bends Head

SAFELY INSIDE TERRELL CENTER, SONJA stared at the grungy floor, slowly inhaling and exhaling, trying to push down the image of the red sticky note.

It's happening again, girlie. This time—

"Shut up," she told the voice in her head. "It is a coincidence. Do not see a pattern where there is none."

She ordered herself to move, but her pumps remained frozen to the floor. "You're running out of time," she muttered to herself, but her words sounded more prophetic than chastising, so she added, "Go. Prepare for class. No time to dawdle."

The ancient cooling system blasted her with air, reminding her that this was a problem she could solve. Fired up with fresh indignation, she headed for the department office.

"It's September, Harmony," Sonja peered at the department secretary over the wooden privacy panel.

The secretary looked up. "Oh. Dr. Storey. What is it now?" Harmony Singh looked like a fifty-something pixie in both size and hairstyle. Her sunny disposition matched her bright floral cardigan. But Sonja knew there was a stinger under the cheeriness.

"It's September," Sonja repeated. "And yet the AC blasts cold air. I have asked you to address this with Facilities."

Harmony pressed her lips together. "Dr. Storey, I've told you before, I don't control Facilities Management. I report your concerns. What happens after that…" She shrugged and adjusted her cardigan, the fat woolen blooms wilted over bony shoulders. "Maybe they should hear it from you."

"It seems I have two jobs, yours and mine." Without waiting for a response, Sonja stormed off in the direction of her office.

But then she slipped, barely catching herself on the doorjamb. One pump sailed across the floor. The other lay on its side, a single toe still inside.

As she regained her balance, she felt something cold and slippery seep through her pantyhose to the bottom of her foot. She retrieved her flyaway pump but didn't put it back on. Instead, she limped back toward her office. That's when she saw the oily puddle on the floor.

"What the hell is that?" she yelled.

Harmony called out from the other end of the lobby, "You okay, Dr. Storey?"

"Come here," Sonja demanded.

The secretary made her way toward Sonja. "Dr. Storey, I'm going to have to insist on you not talking like—"

"Look there. Outside my door. What is that?" Her index finger formed an exclamation point for her barked exasperation.

Harmony squatted to get a closer look. Sonja studied the older woman's sculpted thighs, which made Sonja only too aware of the way her own muscles sagged beneath her expensive clothes.

You're above such pettiness, Sonja reminded herself, and returned her gaze to the puddle.

"Smells…fishy." Harmony stood up. "How did it get here?"

"How am I supposed to know? I've been in class."

"I'll call down to Bob. He'll be here lickety-split."

"Well, tell this Bill person that I want the mess gone before I leave for my next class in an hour." Then she hobbled off to clean up.

"His name's Bob," Harmony called after her. "Our hardworking custodian. A good soul too."

Sonja didn't reply, her mind on bringing to heel the morning's disorder before her day got completely out of hand.

———————

Sonja sank into her Italian leather chair, a gift she had given herself following her promotion to full professor a few years earlier. She had found the masterpiece in a high-end Manhattan showroom. When she gave her Foxboro shipping address to the well-dressed sales associate with long, glossy hair, it was like an embarrassing public confession that she lived in North Carolina's hillbilly country.

Today, though, the soft leather cushioned her aching back and absorbed her anxieties.

With a sigh, Sonja sat up and reached for her mouse. She entered her password and watched the background image of her published books materialize: *Crisis and Conflict: Elevating Your Game*; *Fighting Emotional Ninjas in the Workplace and Beyond*; and *Stop Whining—Win!* All three had been released by a small independent publisher. None had earned much in the way of sales or accolades.

Unlike Ashley's book, girlie.

She swatted away the stinging taunt about her half-sister who deserved not a second more of her life.

Bitch has already stolen so much.

"Enough. I will never see her again. She is behind me."

Putting aside her resentment, Sonja began going through her inbox. As she deleted spam and university updates, she was soothed by the monotonous clicking of her mouse. It made her feel like she was accomplishing something, no matter how insignificant.

She stopped scrolling when she saw the next subject line.

Something Big Headed Your Way

Sonja opened the email. It contained only white space that framed a blue link.

She immediately deleted it, as instructed by the campus IT nerds, then emptied her trash folder. Next, she checked her voicemail. Three missed calls, no messages. By then it was time to leave for her afternoon class.

She stood up and smoothed her sheath dress and matching blazer, taking pleasure in the feel of the expensive onyx fabric that she had lucked into at Nordstrom Rack. She winced as she forced her swollen feet into her suede pumps. The feet of her pantyhose were still damp from trying to rinse out the foul scent of fish oil.

As she combed her hair, she reminded herself to check for any gray strands later. She liked wearing her black hair like a helmet; it caused people to give her a wide berth. Besides, only the Gray Hairs—the older male professors—got more respect as they grew older. Sonja's student evaluations would suffer if she allowed her hair to silver. *Hag. Ugly bitch.* Those were only a few of the names that students had called her over the years. The insults were trite, but they reminded her that male and female professors might work on the same campus, but they taught in different worlds.

Smoothing her hair and suit one last time, Sonja grabbed her tote and opened the door. She jumped at the sight of an old man leaning over a mop in the doorway, his baggy jeans hanging low to reveal what his T-shirt did not cover.

"What the hell—"

He stood up and turned around, smiling broadly. "Sorry if I gave you a fright. Just cleaning up this here mess, ma'am."

"Dr. Storey," she corrected automatically. "Good to see you are sorting this out. It has been an inconvenience."

"Yes, ma'am. Looks like Dr.—"

"You will need to move. I must pass," she said, shouldering her bag.

"All rightie-tightie," he said agreeably. Returning the mop to the large yellow bucket, he rolled it out of the way. Gray water sloshed in her direction.

"Easy! You're splashing my Fluevogs. They cost a fortune." She hadn't clawed her way out of the black mold of her childhood to have her achievements ruined.

"Sorry, ma'am. Did I get your flu dogs wet?"

"No, Flue—never mind." She hurried down the hall, intent on reaching her classroom before the students did.

"You have a good day, ma'am," the janitor called after her.

For a moment, Sonja regretted her hostility. He seemed genuinely kind.

Enough sentimentality. You must be tough as nails. You know what happens when you're not.

She threw back her shoulders and headed to the main office.

"Where's Harmony?" Sonja asked a student worker sitting at the desk and scrolling on his phone. An open can of tuna balanced on the edge.

The young man didn't look up. "Don't know," he mumbled.

"Repeat that," Sonja said with enough command in her voice that he finally looked up, pushed his unkempt hair off his forehead, and stared at her vacantly.

"Don't know where Harm is," he said.

If that head bends over that phone one more time, I'll scream.

He returned his eyes to the screen, his hair falling over his brow as he bent his head and ignored her.

Seething with anger over the rude and incompetent treatment, Sonja slammed the door shut, and strode out of Terrell Center.

Five minutes later, mounting the stairs of Walker Hall, each click of her heels a rebuke of WHSU and everyone associated with it, she entered her dark classroom and looked up to see the projector hanging from the ceiling like an albino bat.

"Only the best at Western Hillbilly State University," she grumbled, flipping on the lights. The projector would need to be rebooted, wasting precious preparation time.

Still looking at the hovering projector, she set her Coach on the chair adjacent to the media console. Then feeling for the control pad, she looked down in disbelief at another sticky, same faded-rose color, same scrawled message.

Let's Play a Game!

The words practically squeaked in her head like the disembodied voice of a half-sister she hadn't seen in person for decades.

For the second time that day, Sonja ripped off the sticky note and marched to the trash can to retrieve the matching one she had discarded that morning. She tucked both notes inside her attendance folder and set the matter aside.

For now.

Sonja had a pretty good idea about how today's office hours would go as soon as the student entered through the open door without knocking and collapsed into the chair next to her desk.

"I'm freaking out."

"Good afternoon. Do come in," Sonja said coldly, her freshly painted lips curling into a tight smile.

"Yeah, sure," the student mumbled, and stuffed her hands into the pockets of her WHSU hoodie. The front was stained with what looked like dribbles of coffee—or maybe it was dried blood.

Sonja looked at the student, noting the nervous tics, the labored breathing. "Your name and the reason for your visit?"

"Ronnie Staller. Told you in class. And I just told you why I'm here. I'm freaking out."

"What is the exact nature of your concern, Ms. Staller?"

"You're making no sense in class. I thought I knew what you was saying at first. Then you started in on that other stuff, and I'm back to what the hell?"

Sonja swallowed the harsh retort on her tongue, and, instead, she said, "You mean, 'I knew what you *were* saying, Dr. Storey.'" More than ever, Sonja missed the loss of intellectually curious students like Jacob.

Before he fell apart. Or more accurately, before you tore him apart.

She crossed her arms and secretly pinched the tender flesh of her elbow creases, a technique that helped her keep her emotions in check.

"Whatever," Staller mumbled. "Like I was saying, I try, but I'm not getting it."

"Ms. Staller, what is your goal in coming here?"

The young woman shrank into the chair as if wordlessly asking permission to exist. "Already told you. I'm freaking out."

"I am neither a counselor nor do I have an EdD."

"A what?" came more of a bray than a question.

"An EdD. A doctorate in education. Meaning I am not a specialist in *how* people learn. If you need that kind of help, I recommend visiting our university learning center—"

"I've already been there. Lots of times. Them people don't know what the fuck they're doing."

"If you cannot conduct yourself in a professional manner, this meeting will end." Sonja glared.

Staller balled up in the chair, legs up, head down on her knees. "Yes, ma'am," she mumbled.

"Ms. Staller, sit so that I can see your face."

The student's body unspooled.

"That's better. Now, we have only had a handful of lectures so far. This morning, you demonstrated a small degree of understanding, but you must acquire a more sophisticated vocabulary. Nevertheless, you were the only student who contributed to the discussion. So I am not sure why you are freaking out, as you call it."

Staller opened her mouth to respond, but Sonja held up her hand. "I will finish my point. Uninterrupted. Without graded assignments, it is too soon to assess your academic progress." She picked up a slip of blue paper from the desk. "Here is the number to the learning center. On the back is contact information for Student Health Services. They have counselors. Call them."

"But this chaotic thing, I get bits. But then it's gone. I read lots too!" Staller slapped the side of her head. "I remember something 'bout butterflies...and fact...fact talls—"

"Fractals."

"Yeah, that. The patterns. And how no one sees 'em. That makes no sense. I see patterns everywhere, sometimes so much I want to scream."

Sonja responded evenly, though her pulse was pounding in her neck. "Those core concepts are in your readings. Review them. Once you have done that, come to me with specific questions. Do you?"

"What?" Staller looked blankly at Sonja.

"Do you have specific questions?"

"How am I supposed to ask questions if I don't remember enough to ask?"

Sonja crossed and recrossed her legs. It was time to conclude this fruitless interaction. "If you are that concerned, withdraw from the class."

"I can't. I'm needing it to graduate. I don't have no one to help."

"Then review your course material, take notes, attend class. Bring specific questions to me during office hours. And call those numbers on the card." Sonja waited for Staller to respond, then rolled her chair closer to her computer. "Is that it, Ms. Staller?"

"Yes, ma'am." With a heavy sigh, Staller stood up and moved to the doorway. "Door open or closed?" she asked.

Sonja flashed on another day. A hulking male body stood over her, her face pressed against the rough carpet.

She blinked away the memory. "Open," she said. "And Ms. Staller."

The young woman turned, hope rising in her eyes. "Yes?"

"It is Dr. Storey, not ma'am."

"Yeah, sure," Staller said, then lowered her head and mumbled something.

"What did you say?" Sonja barked.

"I said, see you on Thursday." Staller slung her backpack over her shoulder and left.

Sonja could have sworn that Staller had spelled out, "C.U.N.T." Of course, it wouldn't be the first time someone called her that. Her own mother had that honor.

Thirty minutes later, Sonja uploaded her latest edits to the termination inquiry report to the cloud and prepared to go home.

A glass of pinot, an evening with my laptop. Sounds perfect.

She closed down her computer, picked up her tote, and locked her office door. On her way out, she stopped at the main office.

"Harmony."

"Yes?" the secretary responded with a honeysuckle smile and wasp eyes that stung.

"Have that janitor—"

"Bob."

Sonja waved her hand dismissively. "Have *Bob* go back over that spot. It still smells fishy."

Instead of responding, Harmony turned toward the female student worker sitting nearby. "Sarah, do me a favor," she said, her voice tinkling like windchimes. "See the book on the copier? Would you please run it over to Dr. Waters? Looks like he forgot it again."

"Sure thing, Harm." The student worker hopped up, grabbed the book, and turned to the doorway, stopping in front of Sonja.

"Yes?" Sonja asked.

The young woman glowered in silence.

"You're blocking the door, Dr. Storey," Harmony said. "Go on, Sarah. Dr. Storey will let you by now."

Sonja stepped aside and watched the young woman walk away, noting the bargain basement sweatshirt and worn jeans, the same kind of cheap, ill-fitting clothing she had once worn.

She turned back to the secretary. "Harmony, the janitor," she nudged insistently. "I am relying on you to handle matters with...Bob."

"Sure," Harmony replied. The tinkle of windchimes was gone.

Her directive delivered, Sonja left the building and headed toward her BMW, affectionately dubbed Bimmer. She was looking forward to that glass of pinot.

But when she reached home, her mood darkened again.

She blamed it on the mangled carcass in her driveway.

Chapter 3

Hellish Thing

As her car idled, Sonja studied the carcass, mentally spitting out scenarios about how such a hellish thing came to be there.

Do not be tempted by faulty logic. This incident is unrelated to the notes or the fish oil. A predator probably dragged it here. Maybe that skinny fox that skulks around.

But that conclusion failed to satisfy her need for certainty. She screamed with fury and frustration, the sound filling Bimmer's interior. Her beautiful house spoiled, as if some force was trying to pull her back into the chaos of her youth.

She tried to regain her slipping composure by tethering it to her well-maintained property. The walkway of 747 Summit Street was like a spotless beige ribbon winding from the road's edge, through the front yard, and ending at the curved steps. A package awaited her on the top step, likely the Yves Saint Laurent tote she had recently ordered from a designer goods reseller. The door, navy with vanilla trim, was covered with a wrought iron security door, its steel embellishments swirling like thick *crème pâtissière.*

"Everything is in order," she announced to no one in particular.

She could have sworn her house smiled in response, the wide windows twinkling, the brick blushing a reddish hue.

"Everything is in order," she repeated, then looked again at the thing in her driveway that disputed her confident statement.

You sure? Things seem to be falling apart. Or getting back to normal, girlie. She heard her mother's voice followed by grotesque laughter, a mix of hoggish snorting and phlegmy coughing.

Sonja cut the engine and climbed out of her BMW to investigate this latest mess.

Bloody clumps of fur dotted the smushed carcass. "What were you?" Sonja asked it. "Rabbit? Raccoon? Well, you're dead now, and I don't have time for this."

She returned to her car and sat, pondering the best way to deal with this latest episode. Suddenly, she regretted hiding the key to her locked security door in her bedside nightstand, a habit she had picked up after her nasty ex. This situation could be more easily resolved if she entered through the front and changed clothes before taking the interior stairs down to the garage; there was no way she was going to deal with a dead animal in her expensive attire. She could drive down her steep driveway into the garage one story below street level as she normally did, but that ran the risk of running over the carcass, making cleanup even messier. On the other hand, the driveway was too steep to walk down in her heels, and she wasn't about to ruin her pantyhose by taking her shoes off.

She slammed her hand onto Bimmer's horn in an automotive protest, releasing her frustration. The sharp honk gave her a moment of satisfaction, and with a smug smile, she drove forward, avoiding the carcass as best she could but swearing she heard the crunch of tiny bones.

She rushed upstairs and changed into her expensive designer leggings—LNDR, to be exact—and the matching jacket. Silently, she reprimanded herself for not having kept at least one or two sets of casual clothes when she overhauled her wardrobe after her last promotion. Now she had nothing suitable to wear, not even a cheap pair of shoes. Her spotless Gucci sneakers would have to do.

Returning to the garage, Sonja grabbed a shovel, hiked up the driveway, and scraped up the fleshy mound. Without looking for oncoming traffic, she crossed the deserted street to the vacant lot and dumped the mess in the withered leaves and twisted vines. The faded *For Sale by Owner* sign nailed to a scrawny tree caught her eye, and she hoped the lot would never sell, thus preserving her solitude atop Summit Street.

As she trotted back to her house, she looked for any witnesses to how this latest mess might've come to be. She thought she saw movement in one window of the hermit's house, but she decided she had imagined it. When she inspected her driveway, she was pleased to see that there was barely a trace of the carcass. But what pleased her more was opening the package that waited for her on the porch.

———————————

An hour later, Sonja had inspected her new tote and stored it with her voluminous collection of bags and purses, poured herself a glass of pinot, and retreated to her office. She opened her laptop and clicked on the committee report she had coauthored with Mary Ann Russel, a professor out of Health Sciences who Sonja did not detest.

Sonja started her latest—and hopefully last—review, determined to cross this work off her to-do list.

During the period beginning November 16 of the last academic year, Dr. Horace Watson, Full Professor in the Department of Economics, pursued a sexual relationship with Ms. Cindy Franklin, an undergraduate major in his department. Ms. Franklin alleges that she declined Watson's requests for dates. When she enrolled in his Macroeconomics Theory course, Franklin alleges that Watson again pursued her for a romantic relationship and that she agreed to go on a date with him on January 18. They were romantically involved until February 17.

A second Economics major, Ms. Wanda Dobbs, alleges that Watson began pursuing her for a sexual relationship on February 8 while she, too, was enrolled in his Macroeconomics Theory course. His relationship with her continued until March 16.

Both Franklin and Dodd allege that after Watson ended his relationships with them, Watson created a hostile environment in the department by sharing defamatory information about them with students, faculty, and staff, referring to the two students as "sluts" and "deranged feminazis."

Franklin and Dodd reported Watson's behavior to the chair of the Economics Department on April 19 (See timeline, Appendix A.),

20

alleging that Watson began a campaign of retaliation. According to the plaintiffs, Watson posted to social media false information about them under the name "Professor Chaos."

Sonja's heart began pounding; her eye twitched. She whipped her head toward the door, half expecting to see her ex, his lips curled into a cruel smile.

Avery is gone. Out of your life for good.

Yet the images continued. She still saw Avery Bruce rounding the corner, the cuffs of his white dress shirt neatly turned up, the silvery hair on his forearms catching the light.

"Pillows." That's what he used to call her in that rich baritone that he used when gaslighting her, back when bruises still mapped his possession of her body.

She forced herself to turn back to her laptop. "Put that matter behind you. Writing about Watson's behavior is provoking you to dwell on the past," she said out loud, sounding stronger than she felt.

The members of the committee, headed by University Assistant Counsel Jodi Jenkins, had been reviewing the allegations against Dr. Watson for weeks, a review that necessitated Sonja's repeated reading of unpleasant details. For one, there was the report by Title IX investigators with hundreds of pages of evidence, including social media posts by someone called "Professor Chaos."

It was when she had first read Professor Chaos's posts that her eye spasms returned, a relentless twitching that had dissipated years ago when she rid herself of her ex. Every word in those foul posts reminded her of the wounds she kept hidden under her designer clothes.

A chill ran up her arms, and she rubbed them vigorously, wondering if her effort to create a safe fortress for herself would turn out to be futile.

"Stop sabotaging your progress. Finalize revisions. End this pathetically unproductive day on a productive note."

She gritted her teeth and tightened her face into a painful scowl. But as she returned her fingers to the keyboard, she found that she enjoyed the ache. It felt like a fitting price to pay for accomplishing such a noxious task.

Chapter 4

Growled and Cracked

SONJA STOOD LOOKING OUT THE glass door leading out to her deck that she had named the Floating Perch. She wouldn't allow herself to step outside until the report was finished, as if Horace Watson's grotesque behavior might sully the beautiful decking and taint her outdoor sanctuary.

She took another sip from her second glass of pinot, trying to disguise the bile erupting from her stomach.

"Finish that report," she chided herself, sloshing the wine around the glass. She worked to steady her hands but failed.

She had tried rereading some of Professor Chaos's posts, but after her day, she couldn't get past the first one. Gulping down the rest of the pinot, she placed the empty glass on her dining room table and returned to her office.

"After today, I will not have to read this filth again." But she didn't trust her own reassurance. Vileness seemed determined to find her, regardless of her actions or advancements.

Reluctantly returning to the pages on the screen, she read through the next section of the committee report that cited some of the social media posts, her pulse racing as erratically as a drunk hummingbird in a storm.

WHSU Girls sit in my classes. Legs spred. Gates of hell wid open. Try Worthless Hore Slut University.

Freaky Cindy franklin loves to be choaked and spanked the dirty slut cries butt she lovs it.

Wanda WantsIT Dods got TITTIES that juggle when smacked than bitchs men WanTIts.

As long as Sonja had been dealing with this case, she still couldn't fully reconcile the image of Horace Watson, full professor with thirty years of teaching under his belt, with Professor Chaos, an illiterate misogynist. But she had seen the evidence, including the email provided by the department chair detailing an admission by Watson that he was Professor Chaos.

Once she finished reviewing the posts, she relaxed a little, but the pain of gritted teeth and a scowled brow kept her laser-focused on the task at hand.

Sonja moved on to the section of the report where the committee had met with Watson. Her heartrate returned to normal, and she reminded herself that she only had a few edits remaining.

Through his attorney, Watson initially declined to be interviewed by the inquiry committee. The committee scheduled a meeting on August 19 with Watson; however, he failed to attend. The Office of University Counsel contacted Watson's attorney and rescheduled.

On that date, Watson and his attorney met with the committee from 9:10 a.m. to 9:32 a.m., with Watson arriving ten minutes passed the agreed-upon start time. He made the following statement: "This is a First Amendment violation. I'll sue everyone on this kangaroo court. I'll uncover your sickest secrets if you fuck with me." Then he turned his chair around to face the wall, keeping his back to the committee.

During the remainder of the meeting, Watson's attorney had the opportunity to make statements, offer evidence, and answer committee members' questions. The attorney made the following statement: "As Dr. Watson said, this is a First Amendment issue. But there's something else. Love. Dr. Watson fell in love with two different students in the same semester. It's not ideal, but let's not end the career of an esteemed educator over matters of the heart. Dr. Watson has served this institution for thirty years."

The meeting between Watson and the committee ended following a second statement by Watson, "This is a witch hunt. There will be consequences for this injustice." Watson and his attorney left the meeting at 9:32 a.m.

The committee met again on September 4 to review available evidence. Following a unanimous vote by members, the informal inquiry committee recommends that Dr. Horace Watson be suspended with pay and that his case be advanced to a formal hearing committee, per the WHSU Faculty Handbook.

Sonja stopped reading. Dr. Horace Watson had occupied enough of her time. She logged onto her university account and typed an email:

Mary Ann:

My edits are attached. If the report is revised further, I require an additional review prior to signing. Otherwise, I am prepared to sign the report as written. I assume Samson and Andy have already provided you with feedback on our previous version. Due to the significance of this committee's responsibilities, it is essential that all members have a hand in producing this report.

—SJS

Sonja hit Send, shut down her laptop, and closed the door to her office. She was done for the day with all penis-related problems.

She retrieved her empty wineglass and refilled it for a third time. Raising the glass, she toasted. "Cheers, asshole. May you die in poverty and obscurity." She drained half the glass. The mental image of Horace Watson transmuted into the face of her ex. She raised her glass a second time. "Dr. Avery Bruce, I wish you much worse."

Sonja moved onto the deck and leaned against the thin metal railing. This floating perch was the reason she had written an earnest check the first time she had set foot inside the place.

The house was second from the end of Summit Street. The raised deck stood above the others in the neighborhood, except for the cottage next

24

door that was occupied by an elderly recluse she had only ever seen from a distance. The L-shaped deck was Sonja's refuge most of the year, the place she relaxed with a glass of wine and gazed at the stars.

The deck's longest section ran along the back of her home, two stories above the steep slope that was her backyard. Here, she had the most privacy, the view being the wild area below, a place of towering trees, snaring shrubs, and veiling vines that belonged to someone else. Her own yard was cultivated, maintained by a lawn crew that never disturbed her, and it contrasted with the darker, uncultivated space like a suburban yin-yang.

The shortest part of the deck sharply cornered the side of her house and ended near the edge of the front yard, allowing a peekaboo view of Summit Street. Fortunately, though, the builder had ended that section before it merged with the lawn, leaving the entire deck suspended above everything and helping her remain disconnected from the rest of the neighborhood. She usually only walked this part of the deck to inspect her property.

Which is where Sonja was when she saw a strange man standing in the middle of Summit Street, waving at her as if he knew her. Only when a child emerged from behind the man's legs did Sonja's pulse return to normal.

"Is it cookie season already? Come to take my order and money," she grumbled to herself. "Uninterested," she called out in a voice that growled and cracked.

She retreated to the rear deck. It seemed the wrong time of year for cookie orders, but she easily convinced herself that the pair was only intent on making a sale and disturbing her well-earned peace.

Leaning against the cool metal railing, Sonja nursed her wine. She stared dreamily down into the wooded area, watching the shadows shift, but the longer she stared, the more she saw things creep and slither in the wild place near her tidy home.

She drained her glass and stumbled back a bit, inhaling sharply at the catch in her lower back. Right now, it was only a twinge, but she knew her back problem could become worse, given the right (or wrong) circumstances. And recently, she seemed to be encountering mainly wrong circumstances.

Worry fluttered in her, moth-like, a delicate but repeated ramming of her mind: both her back ache and eye spasm had revisited her. But true to form, Sonja flipped off the disturbing thoughts like she would an outdoor light that buzzed with insects. She assured herself that the ticks and twitches that had departed when Dr. Avery Bruce went away would vanish once more after the committee report on Dr. Horace Watson was finalized.

She went inside to get a muscle relaxer and heard a strange noise reverberating throughout the house. She froze. It stopped and began again, a two-toned bell atop a lower-pitched buzzing.

Her doorbell.

She hadn't heard it in so long that she had forgotten what it sounded like, and now it wouldn't stop. It was probably the father-daughter sales team. If she ignored them long enough, they would go away, and they did eventually.

She ate a simple dinner of salad topped with sautéed shrimp, then picked up Star Dancer, her telescope, from the corner in the dining room, returned to the deck, and removed the black cover. Like a woman wearing stilettos, the crimson telescope wobbled from time to time on its slender tripod as if close to tipping over, but it was a sleek beauty that provided Sonja with escape when she needed it most. After a challenging day like today, she eagerly left the Earth behind to survey the celestial diamonds against the night's black velvet. Losing herself in the starry night restored her equanimity, and, finally, she was ready for bed.

Sonja woke with a start. She had heard a sound, perhaps.

Tink.

There it was again. She lay still, listening, but the noise didn't repeat, and she wondered if she had actually heard it. It was too late, though. She was wide awake.

Let's Play a Game!

The words loomed in her mind and cast sinister shadows across her psyche. She threw the covers off, turned on the bedside lamp, and padded over to her tote to dig out the sticky notes. Placing them on the marble top of her Etienne nightstand, she studied the handwriting. The letters were shaky but uniform, right down to the exclamation point.

It was time to face the question she had tabled earlier:

Messages on red stickies. Fish oil. The carcass in the driveway. The Byrd woman's reported threat of rape. Could they be connected?

"This is silly," she scoffed, but the quaking of her voice belied her words. She spoke again, sounding more certain. "You are making causal connections that do not exist. *Post hoc ergo propter hoc.* And even if those notes are threats, they were written by a coward."

You have defeated worse enemies. Like the Gray Hairs.

She had outlasted that dangerous group of male professors, save one. And Professor Lewis Waters wasn't long for Sonja's academic world.

"Remember all you have achieved, everyone you have defeated. An amateur stalker has no chance against you."

Oh, everything's connected. A big, messy tangle, cackled the voice in her head. *You can talk big and fancy like your daddy, trying to make sense out of nonsense. But, girlie, you know it's all going to hell.*

"Silence. I will consider this matter tomorrow," she told herself, then went to her office to fetch a folder, added the two sticky notes, and returned it to her tote, alongside her attendance records.

She crawled back into bed and pulled the covers up to her chin. She needed to sleep. If she looked tired, if she had bags under her eyes, students would comment about her appearance on teaching evaluations.

She squeezed her eyes shut, but they popped open again.

I left Star Dancer outside. Uncovered, exposed to the elements.

"It will be fine for one night," she promised herself, suddenly nervous about going into the darkness outside, especially after the day's events.

Chapter 5

Bloody Sun

Sonja pulled into campus parking and shut off her headlights and engine. She remained inside Bimmer, trying to shake off the uneasiness and exhaustion that had plagued her since waking up. Those same feelings drove her from her house even earlier than usual, and now, she sat staring at the charcoal shadows and black sky.

"Damn." It dawned on her that she had forgotten to bring Star Dancer inside. It wasn't even a month into the semester, and Sonja's concentration was already slipping.

She got out of the car and hitched her Valentino tote to her shoulder, a bag that had probably cost more than her mother's entire wardrobe and apartment furnishings combined. Sonja viewed it as an investment in her future, a reminder of where she was going rather than where she had come from.

"Let's collect some heads." Sonja took a deep breath and straightened her spine, and as she did, her back caught, then released almost immediately. She would have to take another muscle relaxer when she got home.

She walked toward Terrell Center, slowing when the sidewalk slipped between two buildings. Something crashed, a metallic sound, and Sonja stumbled, catching the toe of her Calvin Kleins on the uneven sidewalk and further tweaking her back, but she turned in the direction of the noise, seeing nothing except the nearby residence hall.

Anxiety crawled and skittered in her gut, but before it could take hold, she continued walking toward Terrell. Once inside, she flipped on the lights and inspected her heels. There was a barely noticeable nick in the brandy-hued leather. She had half a mind to complain during today's Faculty Senate meeting about the deteriorating campus.

As she climbed the stairs to the main lobby, she noticed something white flapping on the bulletin board. She moved to look closer.

It was *her* flier, the one advertising an upcoming seminar. Someone had ripped through her photo.

Snatching the torn flier off the board, she headed to the department's main lobby and into shadows laced with red from the *EXIT* sign. Running her hand down the pimpled wall, she flipped on the light switch. *Toughen up. It's a torn flier.*

Even Mary Ann Russel had been targeted by vandals in the past, and most of her students loved her. Last spring, a flier she posted had been defaced with the words *FAGGY CUNT*.

Then there were the incidents from the previous fall. Someone had covered the Multicultural Center's display of Frank X. Walker and other Affrilachian writers with white paper, *YOU WILL NOT ERASE US* written in large, black letters. And around that same time, racist messages were found on restroom walls.

"We will rise above the filth in this place," Sonja decreed, but her words sounded empty.

She was determined not to let the flier incident derail her day, so when she got to her office, she added the torn paper to the folder in her tote, sticking the two red notes to it, and labeled it *GAME?*

She switched on the electric kettle and checked her email while she waited for the water to boil. The first subject line jumped out at her.

HELP!

It was an email from Ronnie Staller. Instead of reading it, Sonja saved it for later and worked through the rest of her inbox. Then she made her tea, gratefully breathing in the scent of jasmine.

Remember when you met with Jacob?

She glanced at the empty visitor chair where Jacob had sat during their discussions about chaos theory.

"Too few students delight in wrestling with the ontological underpinnings of theory," she said to a man not there. "You detested that you never arrived at a conclusion. Does chaos theory account for free will? Or are we doomed to be buffeted by countless tiny variances over which we have little control?"

The memories floated up, and she smiled. She looked again at the visitor chair, halfway expecting to see Jacob.

With a sigh, Sonja opened Staller's email.

It's Ronnie. From class.

I can't sleep, Prof Story. Im freeking out. Been up all night trying to read but Im not getting any of this. Im terrified. Am I going to fail. I can't fail. I'm paying for school myself. Im all alone. PLEASE HELP?

Sonja breathed in the aroma from her teacup before typing her response.

Ms. Staller:

When corresponding with me, send a proofread email about class material. After you generate a list of specific questions, you may see me during office hours. Also, see the link below for Student Health Services. They have counselors.

—Dr. Sonja J. Storey, Professor

After sending her reply, Sonja pulled up the Student Affairs webpage and clicked on *Report a Concern.*

"The university expects us to be social workers, counselors, and parents," she mumbled as she completed the report, her fingers flying across the keyboard. Before she hit the Submit button, she said, "If a student needs special care, you do it, Dean Lu. You get paid four times what I do."

That task accomplished, she sat quietly sipping her tea and watched the dawn break through her window.

Red skies in morning...

She couldn't remember the rest of the saying. It was something her mom had said.

"A bloody sun means a storm's coming. Better keep you home from school. You stay with your mommy. We'll have an extra fun day, girlie."

But those days had been far from fun.

Shaking off the memories of her childhood, Sonja retrieved *Emotional Ninjas* from the shelf. The book had been her biggest seller.

Biggest seller. She snickered as she opened the cover and saw the dedication.

For Dr. Storey

That was it, and it didn't specify which Dr. Storey: her father, her half-sister, or herself.

She had, in fact, dedicated the book to herself. She was the one who had clawed her way out of her miserable upbringing. Unfortunately, even this book hadn't sold well. None of hers had.

Ashley's debut book did. Do one of your online searches, girlie. Find that press release. See how your little sister stole your life.

"Enough," she hissed. She opened the book to her favorite chapter, *"Handling Losers, Liars, and Lepers Like a Boss!"* Years ago, she had written a note in the margins in small letters.

Follow-up book?? Managing toxic colleagues. E.g., AB? Gray Hairs?

Curiosity shifted into excitement, and she considered whether to write a fourth book, one that would succeed where the others had failed.

There you go, girlie, forgetting all those empty chairs. Go home and look inside that box of books you keep hidden in the garage.

"Shut up," she snarled.

But memories hooked her, dragging her back to the campus bookstore at her first book signing. Her *only* signing. Even her colleagues had failed to show up to the sparsely attended event. Except for Lewis Waters, and while he had purchased a book and congratulated her, Sonja had seen the mockery in his eyes.

Another person had come too.

"Dr. Sonja J. Storey," Bruce Avery had said, his voice as smooth as Kentucky bourbon, his lips curled like Lucifer's tail. "What a sad turnout.

I expected better, given your reputation on campus." He tossed his copy of *Emotional Ninjas* at her.

"Write something nice for me. Sign it 'Pillows.'"

Soon after, the camera flashed, producing the only photo that appeared in the university newspaper and the local press. She kept the unframed photo in her barrister bookcase at home. Whenever she felt the urge to do something bold and foolish, she removed it and forced herself to study the image and to see the sneer on Avery's lips, the condescension in his eyes, the fear and yearning in her own, reminding her of the cost of her naivety.

"You aren't that young fool any longer." Sonja now held the title of full professor, the rank that Avery had achieved during their brief relationship. "You have"—she paused, tasting the word before she said it—"evolved."

She leaned back in her chair, resting the book on her stomach.

"If you write another book, it will be successful. Failure is not an option." She looked out the window and watched the reds bleeding into the cornflower blue as the sun ascended in the sky. She felt heat on her right breast and glanced down in horror. But it was only the sun's rays, not Avery's fingers. Or teeth.

She snaked her arm across her torso, as if to shield herself from a man no longer on campus. Then she returned her book to its assigned place and tidied her desk. She smiled, confident that she had made a decision that would advance her professionally. It felt like the smile of a queen surveying her domain. Or would be once she gathered her courage.

Chapter 6

Day After Day

By the time the Faculty Senate session started, Sonja felt and looked put together in her Anne Klein black crepe suit. Soon, though, her poor night's sleep caught up with her and her attention lagged, along with her patience.

The session had devolved into a barnyard filled with strutting roosters. The chair of the Grades Appeal Committee struggled to be heard above the commotion.

"At the request of the provost, our committee has been looking into restructuring the Grades Appeals Committee," Senator Cynthia Walden began. "The specific question posed to us is whether there should be a seat for a representative from the administration, two seats for representatives from student government, three tenure-track faculty, and—"

"I protest," Faculty Senator Douglas Christopher shouted, leaping up and interrupting a stunned Senator Walden. "We sit like docile sheep while this administration systematically erodes faculty governance. We were elected by our constituents, and we have a duty to safeguard faculty governance with the ferocity of Cerberus."

Sonja, who had been staring at her cell phone, looked up in time to see Senator Christopher roll up his sleeves as if he were preparing to slug it out with someone. Sonja shook her head and returned her attention to her phone, searching for an article she had read last semester.

"Point of order!" someone shouted. "Dr. Walden was speaking—"

"I'm not stopping anyone from speaking. As you know, I'm committed to giving voice to those marginalized on our campus," Douglas responded, evidently indignant that his own interruption had been interrupted.

"I believe *I was* speaking, Senator Christopher," Walden protested, but Douglas barreled ahead.

"While I appreciate Cindy's work on restructuring the Grades Appeals Committee, I'm incensed." Melodramatically, Douglas pointed around the room. "Don't you see what this administration is doing? They are trying to dilute faculty influence under the guise of recalibrating the Grade Appeals—"

"Everyone be quiet," the Senate president bellowed, pounding his gavel. "I'm recognizing Senator Storey."

"This is an unproductive dialogue," Sonja spoke as she stood, glad that she didn't warble and signal her exhaustion-clouded thinking. "I had hoped the Faculty Senate's climate would improve this year, that we would become the orderly, august body that we must be to effect change at this"—*backwoods university*—"institution of learning. Yet, we are bickering like unattended children on a playground. This is not how we become a force worthy of the administration's respect.

"Last semester, one of our peer institutions had its faculty senate dissolved for, and I quoting here from the *Higher Education Chronicles*," she said, lifting her cell phone in front of her face and reading, "for 'creating an adversarial relationship between the administration and faculty.'"

She lowered her arm. "If our lack of productivity continues, the administration could dissolve this senate for impeding progress. Then what? Who will be left to demand the changes necessary to make us into a nationally recognized university?"

With that, Sonja sat and rested her phone in her lap. As she listened to the arguing around her, it suddenly occurred to her that she no longer cared. Day after day, week after week, her life had become the same temporal copy of a temporal copy. And she had had enough.

She stood again, collected her possessions, and slipped out, mentally drafting the long, expository email she intended to write. But by the time she sat in front of her computer, her message was much simpler.

To the Faculty Senate of Western Highlands State University:

I hereby resign as a member of the Faculty Senate.

—Dr. Sonja J. Storey, Professor

She hit Send, then stood at her window and congratulated herself for leaving behind something that no longer served her.

"Elevate your life, Dr. Storey," she uttered the pronouncement, suddenly recalling the writing she had done as a teen.

What she had written was a series of over-the-top journal entries that she had called *The Storey Story*. She still had those journals in her garage; the language was too flowery for present-day Sonja to relate to. But she recognized that, at the time, keeping a journal had helped her imagine a bigger, bolder, brighter life. As she had aged, Sonja had transformed her fantasies into plans, wisely keeping them secret from her mother, a woman who was willing to sabotage a child's life to avoid being alone.

Now, fully grown, Sonja stood strong at her window. "It is time," she announced as if to convince herself, "for a new chapter of the Storey story."

Sonja spent the remainder of her workday compiling a reference list to outline her book proposal. It took over an hour of researching toxic relationships in the workplace before she found her rhythm. She identified two dozen journal articles and sent the list to the departmental printer. She flung open her door, intent on dashing to the main office to claim her pages before they got tossed out, and nearly ran into Ronnie Staller.

Caught off guard, she snarled, raising herself to her full height of five foot four. "What are you doing here? Office hours are not until tomorrow. You would know that if you read your syllabus."

"I was...wondering if... I was wondering if you was busy. I'm real stressed. Just needing a friend..." Staller trailed off, clearly miserable.

"I am your professor, not your friend. As I stated in my email to you, if you have questions based on readings and lectures, you may see me tomorrow during office hours."

Staller's face fell as Sonja went to close her door, but she opened it again. "Ms. Staller," she said, and watched the student's face light up at the sudden attention. "Your current approach to me is unacceptable."

Tears welled up in Staller's eyes as Sonja clicked the door shut. She really needed to grab her printout and review it, but she would wait in case Staller still lingered.

When she finally left at four in the afternoon, Sonja found a piece of notebook paper taped to her door. She unfolded it and read.

Im not sure why your begin mean too me. I have nobody to talk to. Like I say I need a freind. Please stop begin mean. Your making me loose it bad.

With the note still clutched in her hand, Sonja hurried to the main office and shoved it in Harmony's face. After reading it, the secretary handed it back to Sonja.

"I'm not sure what you're wanting from me, Dr. Storey."

"I will give you a physical description of this student. Circulate it to the staff. If you see her lurking around my office, call campus police."

Harmony looked at her. "Has this student threatened you?"

"I know crazy when I see it."

"I'm not a fan of that word, Dr. Storey. Calling someone crazy's plain mean."

Sonja leaned in. "The word applies in this case, whether you like it or not. Ronnie Staller is cracking under pressure, and we are not even at the midpoint of the semester. Who's to say she isn't the one responsible for what's been happening to me. The notes. The torn flier. Must I fetch my evidence folder?"

"No need for that, Dr. Storey," Harmony said calmly. "You showed me first thing this morning. Perhaps this is a matter for Jay."

"Perhaps you are right. The chair of the department and I have *much* to discuss." Sonja stalked out of the office, her heels punctuating her comment.

She added Staller's letter to her GAME? folder and tried to get back to work. Which is when she realized she had never retrieved her printout. Just as she was about to slink back to the department printer, her computer dinged. It was an email from Senator Christopher.

Sonja, I will swing by your office after I have a word with my subcommittee. I need to defend myself from your accusations. What you said today in Senate offended me. You must realize that I am a dedicated citizen of this university and a champion of—

Sonja looked at the time stamp on the email. Douglas had sent it from his smartphone ten minutes ago.

Jumping up, she grabbed her tote, slung it over her shoulder, the cool chains nipping at her bare skin, and snatched her blazer, barely remembering to lock her door. She hurried toward the closest exit, her heels clicking like a cranked-up metronome. Behind her, she heard Harmony call out to her.

"Dr. Storey, you have a call from a—"

"I am late for a meeting," she called out without looking back, the lie sounding convincing to her own ears.

"Well, okay. I'll—"

Sonja flew down the steps, a kaleidoscope of butterflies winging wildly through her insides. Outside, she immediately noticed about fifteen feet away that junior professor who had accosted her yesterday morning.

Was that only yesterday? She felt battered and exhausted, like she had been through months of chaos, not thirty or so hours.

"That's all I need. More Chatty Crystal," Sonja muttered.

Hanging back to let Byrd get farther ahead, Sonja watched as the woman talked on a cell phone and walked, shoulders back, posture strong but not rigid. Byrd even waved at passersby, once even stopping to throw her head back in laughter.

Byrd reminded Sonja of someone, but before she could figure out who, she watched as Byrd resumed walking, right toward where Sonja had parked.

"Shit," she mumbled. "Keep walking. Keep walking." Sonja followed slowly, head down, and watched Byrd pass by Bimmer, cross the parking area, and go into a building entrance.

As soon as the junior professor disappeared, Sonja picked up her pace and jumped into her car, driving out of the lot with an urgency that seemed to come out of nowhere. She sped off, briefly wondering which professor she would loathe encountering the most, Douglas Christopher or Crystal Byrd?

Oh, girlie, you know.

"Be quiet," she said, turning on the radio full blast. If she couldn't escape her thoughts, she could at least drown them out.

When she turned onto Summit Street, she caught sight of the father-daughter sales team. The father waved at her with a sweeping gesture.

Sonja sped up, determined to get into her garage before they could catch her. She grabbed her mail and pealed into her driveway, the garage door closing behind her.

She went upstairs into her bedroom, kicked off her Calvins, tossed her tote on the bed, and peeled off her clothes, tossing the body shaper into the hamper, her expensive hose into the bathroom sink to be handwashed later, and her suit into the growing pile of dry cleaning. She slipped into a navy belted wrap and matching lounge pants, went into the kitchen for a glass of pinot, and only after that, opened her laptop. Logging into her university account, she downloaded the references for her book project. Then she opened her inbox, intending to delete Douglas Christopher's email, but a newer message caught her attention.

Hi there! Remember me? I was the one crying in the restroom yesterday. LOL. I wanted to say thanks. Listen, it'd be nice to have a friend here. Let me know if you want to get together.

Warmly, Crystal.

Without a second thought, Sonja deleted Crystal's email. She refused to encourage a woman who apparently needed no encouragement, even after Sonja had been so brusque. She didn't understand people like that. They seemed to lack dignity, inviting repeated rejection.

Before closing out her email, she decided to respond to Douglas Christopher after all, but instead of rebuking him as she originally intended, she crafted a reply to head off future interactions.

Douglas:

There is no need for a discussion. Your dedication has never been in question.

—Dr. Sonja J. Storey, Professor

Sonja knew Douglas well enough to know that he would interpret her statement as a compliment rather than an indictment about his dedication to wanting to hear himself talk. He would soon forget about her, and Sonja would be left to her work.

Sonja hit Send just as the doorbell rang, but she ignored it, and eventually the intruders gave up. She would peek outside later to make sure it wasn't another package, but until she was certain that the father-daughter duo had cleared out, she nursed her pinot in peace and reviewed the next item on her agenda.

She could return to laying the groundwork for her book project or maybe even start developing her presentation for the upcoming seminar. She also needed to update her lectures before tomorrow. Sonja couldn't seem to motivate herself to work, though. She was filled with a sudden longing that carved its way into her psyche and pooled in her belly. But she couldn't name the source of the longing. Though, strangely, an image of Crystal Byrd popped into her head.

Don't fool yourself, little girl. It's like high school when you'd go chasing after girls wanting nothing to do with you. You're no good at friendship, no good at any kind of relationship.

Sonja silenced her self-pity and went out to retrieve Star Dancer, gingerly returning the telescope to its corner in the dining room.

"We'll star dance soon," she whispered to it, briefly troubled that the few pleasurable activities she had were constantly being pushed aside to make space for work, as if she were punishing herself for some reason.

Nonsense. You must work. There is no time for frivolities.

She rested a hand on Star Dancer's glossy surface, noticing how her nail polish and the telescope's glaze were a near-perfect match.

"I don't even remember buying you," she muttered a confession.

When the package first appeared on her doorstep—last year? the year before?—and she opened it to discover the telescope inside, Sonja had worried that she was developing memory gaps.

Was it another midnight drunken spending spree?

What was done was done, though, and Star Dancer became hers, connecting her to one of her rare happy childhood memories:

She had fled her mother's stinking, suffocating apartment one night and had been summoned by an old man on the other side of the complex's crumbling parking lot, where he had set up a telescope. That night, Sonja had learned how to leave behind earthly miseries by floating in the heavens.

With Star Dancer secure in its corner, Sonja prepared dinner, sprinkling cracked pepper on a half breast of chicken, placing it in the oven, and pouring herself a second glass of pinot. Then she went to her office to update attendance records in the university's course management system. Row by row, she entered the data until, near the end, she saw a name buried in the thirty-five lines of forgettable students. Her eyes widened, and she felt her lips fossilize into a hard shrunken smile.

Randalls, Corey.

Enrolled in her organizational communication course, the morning class.

"Could you be related to Jacob, Corey Randalls? Could you be leaving me notes? Toying with me because of what happened to him?"

She pulled the red sticky notes out of her GAME? folder and scrutinized each one again.

Let's Play a Game!

In that instant, her thinking cleared, and her spine stiffened. She drove her nail like a knife into the center of one of the red paper squares.

"Does this little boy want to play? Does he want revenge for your fuckup, Jacob?" The utterance of that name ruptured her fledgling zeal.

Even if Corey Randalls were pestering her with vaguely threatening sticky notes and a torn flier, she couldn't ignore her heartbreak over Jacob having flunked out of WHSU. Yet, her sorrow over Jacob did nothing to diminish her sudden hunger to know more about Corey Randalls.

She tapped out a steady beat on the side of her wineglass, glowering at the name on her monitor, watching the blinking cursor that seemed to be waiting for her to decide whether to delete *Randalls, Corey* from existence.

Instead, she reopened her university email and searched through the trash folder to recover Crystal Byrd's message. *Do that woman and I share Corey Randalls as a student? Could he have left the red sticky notes and the threatening voicemail for Crystal?*

"Data," she told herself. "I need data to investigate."

Your reasoning is overly convenient.

"Shush," she told the voice and typed an email.

Dr. Byrd:

I teach tomorrow, but I want to meet on campus to discuss a pressing matter. Meet me at the Bistro, 3:30 p.m.

—Dr. Sonja J. Storey, Professor

She logged off, then headed for the kitchen to finish preparing her meal of baked chicken salad. She set her plate on the French daffodil-yellow tray, folded a linen napkin, topping it with eating utensils, refilled her pinot, and took her meal out to the deck. While she sipped her wine, she surveyed the spotless railing, congratulating herself for escaping the scuff marks and dents that had sullied her childhood bedroom, each scar a remnant of the storm system that had been her mother.

"Give her credit, though. Her rage was...motivating," she slurred. Sonja glanced at her full plate before taking another sip of wine. "I haven't tried the old phone number in a while. Perhaps I should leave her another voice message. Apprise her about how well I am doing."

If poor Mommy's still alive, girlie.

She chuckled. But she shivered when she heard the manufactured glee, so she finished her meal in silence before ordering herself inside to clean up the kitchen, to shower, and to check her hair for gray, thankful to find only glossy, black strands.

"Should've checked Corey Randalls's student records before emailing Professor Byrd. I'm not thinking clearly," she said as she popped a muscle relaxer and climbed into bed, dozing off quickly.

Sonja jerked awake as the man took her in his arms and buried his face, then his teeth, into her breasts.

"No dreams," she mumbled and rolled over.

But her dreams didn't obey her command. She found herself in a cramped room, the floor covered in black soil full of decaying vegetables and writhing worms. On the far side of the room, the white door bulged and shook as someone outside pounded on it.

Sonja woke up on her deck, her arm wrapped around Star Dancer. She stumbled back, startled, and sat heavily on the foot of her lounger, trying to gather her bearings, trying to reassure herself that her night terrors had not returned. As she waited for her breathing to slow down and her heart to stop racing, she stared up at the night sky.

She wished she knew the name of the old man who had introduced her to the stars' silent symphony. He had said very little as he waved her over and showed her the equipment that looked like an ancient metal pipe screwed to a three-legged stand. Young Sonja had pressed her eye against the cool eyepiece as if drawn there by gravity.

And as she did that night long ago, Sonja stepped up to Star Dancer and surrendered to the universe.

Chapter 7

Withered to the Root

THE YELLOW LIGHT ON SONJA'S porch barely penetrated the early morning darkness, compounded as it was with a dense, swirling mist. The dampness made her briefly reconsider her choice of the Louboutin heels, but the shoes' flame-red soles ignited her sense of purpose, helping her walk bolder on days when she sagged.

She hitched up her black pencil skirt enough to allow her to bend and retrieve the weekly community newspaper, and as she did, teetering on the spiked heels, she swore under her breath at the SOB who littered her property every Thursday. She loved the pencil skirt, but it was impractical, and she was sure it would eventually trip her up.

Turning back to her doorway, she heard her pumps scrape on the concrete and congratulated herself for adding clear stickers to the lacquered soles. She glanced up to find a piece of paper stuck with duct tape to her storm door and peeled it off, leaving a gummy residue on her spotless glass. Back inside, she unfurled the paper flier and stared at the photo of a scruffy-looking calico cat. The caption read, *Missing! Mister Snuggles. Any information, please call...*

"Thought calicos were female." She tossed the newspaper and flier in the trash and hurried downstairs to her garage.

Sonja pulled into her regular parking spot with a yawn. She was sluggish from not sleeping well, but she was determined that her midnight encounter with Star Dancer would not interfere with the day's productivity.

To her left, the light shifted, and a shadow fell beside her. Sonja looked up, screeching at the silhouette near her window.

The figure lowered the jacket hood. "Sorry, sorry, sorry, Professor Storey. Scared you, huh?"

"Goddamn it, Ms. Staller. Do I need to call campus police?"

"No, no, no. Ple-e-e-e-ease," Staller begged. "Got to campus early. Library's still closed. Just need a place to go. It's cold out here. Wet too."

Sonja cracked her window. "Keep your voice down. That's a residence hall right there. People are sleeping."

"Sorry, sorry, sorry. You come in early. I was hoping you'd let me in your building, maybe let me hang out in your office. I don't have nowhere to go."

"Go home," Sonja ordered. *And go fuck yourself.*

"It's too far. I'd be late for your class. The traffic gets—"

"Figure it out. You are an adult. There are coffee shops, fast food restaurants." Then it occurred to her that the parking lot was empty and she was alone with this increasingly unstable student.

Sonja softened her tone. "Ms. Staller, I am not permitted to let you into my building before it officially opens. In about an hour," she added, hoping the long wait would discourage Staller from sticking around. "You will have to find another shelter from the damp morning."

Staller straightened, her frizzy hair backlit by the bright security light, and she raised her hood again, looking like a wraith in the predawn world. Finally, she bowed her head and turned away.

Sonja rolled up her window and climbed out of Bimmer, retreating to the safety of her building as fast as her spikey heels could carry her.

Sonja locked herself inside her office and debated filing another care report but decided instead to call Student Affairs between classes and demand to speak with Dean Lu about Staller's peculiar behavior. Until then, though, Sonja had a more pressing matter. If she could find the information she needed about Corey Randalls, she would cancel her meeting with Professor Perky Byrd.

She logged into the WHSU student records system and pulled up Corey Randalls's information. There was nothing to see except his permanent address, inoculation records, and fees owed, and examining his class records revealed no obvious connection to Professor Byrd. Closing her eyes, she tried imagining Randalls's face but, not surprisingly, she drew a blank. When she took roll or lectured, she didn't really *see* her students. She could identify smirks, inattention, and blank gazes, but she couldn't describe her students' features. They were simply nondescript.

Office visits were another matter. That's when she watched visitors carefully, having learned vigilance the hard way. As an assistant professor, she had once failed to register a student's mounting rage until he flung her out of her chair and slammed her face into the rough carpet, leaving a rug burn down one side. The rug burn had healed; the internal burn had not.

But she had learned from that incident to monitor microexpressions. Study the expression in their eyes. Observe the jawline for tightening. Consider how they hold their shoulders. Watch if their hands become fists.

She had learned other lessons as well. Keep the door open with all students and male faculty. Keep defenses up. Keep vulnerabilities hidden.

A lifelong student of people's mistreatment of her, Sonja had learned from each of her teachers.

Having found nothing illuminating in Corey Randalls's records, Sonja opened her inbox and deleted several emails without reading them, including another one from Douglas Christopher.

The only one she read was the one from Professor Byrd.

Hi there!

Coffee's out for me. Sorry. Meeting with my undergrad thesis advisee. Yikes!!! My first semester and I already have one. Guess I better buckle up. ☺ So that's a no-go on the coffee invite, but how about drinks? There's a bar called Ridges down the street. 5:30, say? Great hearing from you, Sonja. It's nice to have a friend here. TY, Crystal. P.S. Let me know about drinks.

Cringing at Crystal's informality, Sonja replied.

Dr. Byrd:

I will see you 5:30 p.m. at Ridges. I will be unable to stay long, however, as I have other pressing obligations.

—Dr. Sonja J. Storey, Professor

The mere thought of meeting up with Professor Perky made Sonja's skin crawl. Or maybe it rippled. She couldn't quite tell, but she resolved to go to Ridges to discover if Byrd and Randalls were connected in some way.
Convenient reasoning.
"Shut up."
Silence folded around her.

Students drifted into the classroom, a few sweet and sparkly, most sour and laconic. Sonja studied their faces as they arrived, occasionally nodding in response when greeted.

When Staller entered, Sonja intercepted her. "Ms. Staller, I would like to speak with you before class."

"Yes, ma'am—sorry, ma'am—Dr. Storey." Staller slapped her forehead.

"That's enough, Ms. Staller. Do we need to revisit the events of this morning?"

Eyes downcast, the student shook her head.

"Good. Take your seat. And do not strike yourself again. A professional woman always treats herself with respect. Am I clear?"

"Yeah, sure, uh…Dr. Storey."

Sonja marked her seating chart, going row by row, and she discovered the seat assigned to Corey Randalls unoccupied.

"Mr. Randalls, are you present?" she asked. No one answered. "Does anyone know Corey Randalls?"

"He's sick," someone finally answered.

Sonja surveyed the classroom. "Who is speaking?"

A student with the baseball cap pulled down over his face tossed up his hand.

Ah, you're one of those assholes.

Dr. Storey smiled stiffly. "Your name?"

"Trey."

"Last name?"

"Paulson."

"Very good, Mr. Paulson. Now, remove your cap so I can see your face. When you are in my class, you agree to the terms outlined in the course syllabus. Absolutely no hats. They obstruct my view of your undoubtedly pleasant visage."

Sonja stared at him until he pulled off the cap and revealed matted hair. "Better," she said and launched into her lecture.

For the remainder of class, she concentrated on chaos theory. Corey Randalls never left her mind, though. She wished she had memorized his face early on because he could follow her across campus, or even home, and she wouldn't recognize him.

"Dr. Sonja Storey for Dean Lu," she demanded of the person answering the phone for Student Affairs.

"He's...uh...not in."

"Take a message, then. Tell Dean Lu—"

"I'll transfer you to his voicemail."

"You are a student worker, are you not?"

"Yes, ma'am."

Then work! Sonja longed to thunder at the faceless student. Instead, she said, "Listen carefully. I want you to take a message. *You.* Tell Dean Lu that Dr. Sonja Storey—"

"Dr. Dorney—"

"No, Dr. Sonja, S-O-N-J-A, Storey, S-T-O-R-E-Y. Tell him I expect a return call today. I am available between three and five."

"Okay, between two and—"

"Three and five. Three and five. Make sure he calls." She slammed down the receiver, her eye twitching.

She was frothing with impatience, and her brain was boiling with thoughts about Ronnie Staller, Corey Randalls, and Jacob Randalls.

It had been at least a decade since she had seen Jacob, and while he had meant a lot to her during a horrific time, she never wanted to see him again.

Jacob had been older than her other students, and he showed great intelligence and maturity in her classroom. Together, they had explored tensions between scientific thought and his Southern Baptist upbringing, though he had never given up on either one. But what had sealed her admiration for him had been the time in class when someone had started shouting at her right after she returned the graded midterms. She forgot the exact words of the verbal attack against her, but she would never forget the aggressive tone. The speaker had said something like, "This exam of yours is bullshit. You tried crushing our nuts with trick questions."

That's all it took. Others jumped into the fray, shouting their objections to the midterm, to the class, and to her especially. She even heard them call her "cunt" and "bitch" until she felt less like a professor and more like a solitary sparrow heading into savage headwinds.

Unexpectedly, Jacob stood up, his tall, broad body giving her a semblance of shelter in the unexpected storm. He shoved his hands into the front pockets of his worn jeans and planted his scuffed, muddy boots in a solid stance. He looked and sounded like a stereotypical mountain man, but he spoke like a blend of poetic preacher and stately scholar.

"You're making fools of yourselves," he said. "Rather than complaining, y'all should be praising this woman. For anyone fully trained by a teacher will become like the teacher. Or don't you read your Bibles?"

He paused. "Here's what we're going to do. We're going to settle down and let the professor teach us. Maybe she'll even tell you why y'all did so poorly on the test. And if you don't keep quiet, I'll call campus police and tell 'em that you're harassing Professor Storey. I'll name every one of you too, especially those with your mouths clamped shut, too cowardly to defend her. And I don't give a damn if you folks get mad at me. You want to argue or fight with me, that's up to you. I've lived through worse, and my skin's a lot tougher than yours."

Whatever Jacob's classmates had seen in his face, it was enough. They settled down and didn't question Sonja again the entire semester. They even started taking notes during lectures, and it showed in their improved grades. It was the only semester that the department's phones weren't flooded with complaints about her.

Initially, she had been conflicted after the incident, resentful that the class had listened to a male classmate better than to her. Then again, it was the only time someone had ever stood up for her.

She sat in her office, coming out of the trance, then covered her eyes with her palms, desperate to dam up the memories. Withered to the root, she feared she would be whisked away in a floodwater of grief and regret.

Sonja shook her head to clear it, smoothed her clothes, and picked up her tote. It was time to leave for her afternoon class, and she was determined to stay upright.

Sonja's morning class usually limped along. Organizational Communication tended to be taken by sleep-deprived underachievers who needed the credits. But her afternoon class, Communication and Conflict Management, rarely disappointed her, and the course material seemed to intrigue the students. So she was flabbergasted when her lecture about conflict styles flopped, the students responding with as much vigor as room-temperature yogurt.

By the time she returned to her office, she had to pop three aspirins to take the edge off her back pain. As she settled into her chair, commanding her muscles to relax, Dr. Lewis Waters showed up. Every ounce of tension returned when the remaining member of the Gray Hairs stood in her doorway, grinning like a goofy garden gnome.

He mumbled something, bits of food flying out of his mouth.

"I didn't understand a word you said. What are you eating?"

He held up a finger and dramatically swallowed, then threw his arms wide in a ta-da gesture. "Wasa crackers. Terrible things. Dry, like students' bones." The professor ran his tongue around his mouth and teeth, then laughed. "Only kidding. My Ruthie has me eating the most awful foods since the ole heart attack."

Sonja had no idea who this Ruthie person was and she didn't care. "What can I do for you, Lewis? I'm in the middle of something."

"Wanted to say hi to my neighbor. Hi!" He chuckled.

"Well, I have work to do before an afternoon commitment," she said, dismissing him, and returned her attention back to her computer. She began writing an email.

Dean Lu:

You did not return my call. We must speak ASAP. Recently, I filed a report about Ms. Ronnie Staller. She is increasingly displaying concerning behaviors, some of which could be described as stalking. Your office must handle this matter. Call me for important details.

—Dr. Sonja J. Storey, Professor.

"Okey dokey, you're busy."

Sonja looked up, surprised to find Lewis still standing there, apparently chattering away about something or other.

"So, again, sorry for the mess. My best was far from good enough. Ruthie tells me that all the time." He chuckled. "Anyway, catch up soon? I would like your input on a matter."

"Goodbye, Lewis."

He waved and left.

Sonja got up and closed her door. She wanted to draft a table of contents and rough outline for her fourth book before she met Dr. Byrd. That way she could at least end her workday on a productive note.

Chapter 8

A Certain Shape

"SURE ARE A LOT OF naked women here." Dr. Byrd drank her whiskey, craning her neck to look at the various bronze nude sculptures decorating the bar.

"Does that bother you?" Sonja asked.

The younger professor laughed, a honeycomb sound, intricate golden sweetness winding throughout. "No, I don't have a problem with nudity."

"Why raise the issue, then?"

"You asked for it. Here's my rant. Bars and restaurants try to class up a place with painted or sculpted tits and ass. But display the real thing? Unacceptable! By the way, I should warn you. I have a potty mouth. Hope I didn't offend you, Sonja."

Sonja debated correcting Dr. Byrd on the use of her first name, but she didn't want to extend this interaction any longer than necessary.

"Back to your point. I like nudes. I just wish that I could live in a world where men didn't profit from stripping down women. But when women do it to themselves? The horror!"

"Interesting, Dr. Byrd." Sonja pushed her way into the woman's monologue, intending to pivot the conversation, but her companion blocked her.

"Call me Crystal, please. People who have seen me sob are instantly promoted to first-name basis. Unless they're the ones who made me cry. Then fuck 'em, am I right?"

Sonja knew better than to answer a question that could lead her into a trap. She had written an entire section on that topic in *Emotional Ninja*. On the surface, questions seem like friendly inquiries, but they had a sinister purpose when employed by con artists and narcissists. Instead of answering, Sonja steered the conversation toward her meeting agenda.

"About that voice message. What have you uncovered?"

"Damn! You don't waste time. Straight to the point. Kind of strange for a southern woman, especially a white one, but I like it," Crystal replied, putting down her glass and running her hand along her thigh to smooth the crease in her storm-gray herringbone pant leg.

Sonja toyed with the idea of correcting Byrd about her assumption that Sonja was a southerner, but she didn't want to provide personal information if she didn't have to. After all, Byrd didn't need to know that Sonja had been born in Maryland, making her a nearly lifelong outsider in the South.

"The IT help desk has been zero help," Crystal continued, apparently oblivious to Sonja's half-hearted listening. "Guess that makes them the no-help desk." She laughed at her joke. "All they've told me is that the bastard called from a campus phone. He sounded cis male and white to me, but that's auditory profiling, so I'm uncomfortable…"

Sonja's attention faded, and when she tuned back in, she had no idea what the assistant professor had been rambling about.

"…misogyny's been normalized, racism casually expressed—"

"Do you have Corey Randalls in any of your classes?"

"What? Who?"

"Corey Randalls. Do you have him in any of your classes? Or do you know him in any other regard?" Sonja didn't mention that she had already reviewed Randalls's current classes and hadn't found any obvious association to Professor Byrd.

"You give zero fucks for social niceties," Crystal said, but her eyes sparkled. She leaned forward to retrieve her whiskey, gently swirling the amber liquor that matched the color of her eyes. "I'm glad I ended up in that bathroom for my meltdown."

"Look, I don't mean to be rude—"

"Yes, you do. But you should know, you don't intimidate me. You remind me of some of my family." Crystal drained the rest of her drink and raised the empty glass in the direction of the server. "Fine, Sonja. Seeing as how you have an agenda, here's my offer. Drink your wine. Relax, if you're able. And I'll answer your questions."

"Will you be having a second round, ma'am?" the server asked when he appeared.

Crystal looked up at the waiter. "Call me Crystal. And your name? I'm planning on making this my regular spot, so I need to know."

"Elliot, Ms. Crystal."

"Nope, just Crystal. Another round, please, Elliot. My tab. And I'll need a menu. I'm famished. You folks serve good burgers?"

Sonja sipped her pinot and assessed Professor Byrd: figure-hugging pants softened with a mustard chiffon blouse and capped off with a pair of ankle boots. Hair shy of shoulder-length, warm chestnut in the low-lighting, natural, not straightened. Minimal eyeliner and mascara, no lipstick or blush. No jewelry other than a steel unisex watch.

Sonja drew two conclusions. First, Dr. Crystal Byrd added a certain flair to their hick town. Second, the woman wasn't to be trusted. The newbie professor was overly amiable. And something else tickled at Sonja's brain, but whatever hazy realization it was, it refused to reveal itself. She would figure it out later. Or maybe not, since this would be her last meeting with the woman.

"Randalls, first name, Corey," Sonja pressed after the server left.

Crystal chuckled. "Deal's a deal. You drink, I check."

"Are you an alcoholic?" Sonja asked out of the blue.

"No. Are you?"

"No." As soon as Sonja heard the bite in her tone, she knew she had lost the round.

"I should've asked before suggesting that we meet at a bar. Several of my friends and family are in recovery. I'm usually more sensitive than that. Now, let me check my courses. Randalls, Corey. Name doesn't sound familiar." Crystal laid her smartphone on the table and scrolled through digital rows of names.

Sonja's silent assessment resumed as she took in the woman's firm, smooth skin and bag-free eyes.

You don't need to cover your flaws right now, Dr. Byrd. But wait. Youth is unfaithful. It will leave you soon.

Sonja drank deeply from her glass, as if she could wash away the sour taste of envy in her mouth. "Corey Randalls," she prompted.

"You're impatient." Crystal looked up and flashed a smile even more beguiling than before.

Sonja returned it with a wilting stare, but Crystal didn't react, not even a flinch. That unsettled Sonja, who had long depended on her ability to get a rise out of someone, to knock them off-balance and give herself the upper hand. Now, she wanted to get the hell away from the woman even more.

Before it's too late. The warning floated into her consciousness unbidden, and she wondered where it had come from. And why.

"This will take a while. I have hundreds in my online classes. Besides, I like hanging out with you. You remind me of someone. She's combative too. And I suspect the moment I answer your question, you'll bolt."

"I have important work I must finish tonight," Sonja protested, losing another round to the novice academic.

"On it."

The waiter returned with a second round of drinks and two menus, and Crystal beamed up at him, "Thanks, Elliot."

You don't fool me, Byrd. I see you how you hook people. You make everyone feel special, wanted. But for what end goal?

Sonja had literally written the book on interacting with narcissists, warning readers to maintain boundaries, especially in the workplace—a lesson branded into her soul by her ex.

"Okay, done. That's a no-go on Corey Randalls. Sorry, babe."

"Do not be overly familiar with me."

"You know, Sonja, you're right. You're not my babe. But who knows? Cheers!" Crystal raised her glass and held it up until it became obvious that Sonja wasn't going to toast. "So, this Corey Randalls. Who is he?" she asked before sipping the whiskey.

"A current student."

"That's all I'm getting? And after I spent Tuesday morning crying on your shoulder."

"You exaggerate." *More manipulation.*

"You're right. I would have cried on your shoulder, but you ran away."

Sonja stared at the woman, noting the hooded eyes, faint smile, and the loosely crossed legs angled toward her, and she reached a conclusion. "Are you flirting with me, Dr. Byrd?"

Crystal choked on her whiskey, then coughed and cleared her throat. "You're blunt. Great dominance strategy. I respect that. Let me reciprocate, Sonja. Only a few days ago, an anonymous man reached into my office with his voice, into me, and tried crushing my ovaries. The fucker terrorized me, and in that moment, nothing else mattered. Not a goddamn thing. I felt stripped down, like these sculptures." She gestured at the nearest bronze nude. "It didn't matter that I busted my ass and worked my way out of my small hometown. It didn't matter that I was the first in my family to graduate college. It didn't matter that I'm a woman of color who has survived in the world of white academia. And I'm of a certain shape and shade, not your dainty, skinny blonde that southern culture loves to protect. No one gives women like me anything without a fight. And I've had to fight. For everything."

"I get your p—"

"Excuse me. You don't want people playing games with you. You don't want people wasting your time. I understand and accept that. But *you* asked me out, and I'm answering the question *you* asked."

Sonja reached for her bag. "This is an unproductive—"

"Please. Stay." Crystal's words were a command, but her tone was relaxed. "I won't beg, and I don't chase. I'll tell you something, though. I'm a great friend, colleague, date…whatever works out between us. But my department's small, and so is yours. I'm alone a lot, and you appear to be too. You've probably noticed that there aren't many BIPOCs in the academic boys' club. I'm not needy or clingy. What I am is human. And truthfully, I'm hoping to find some okay people here. You know, to help me weather things like that voice message."

After considering what Crystal said, Sonja replied matter-of-factly, "It is possible to survive at WHSU. You will have to grow thick skin, though."

"The women I grew up with, they didn't take shit from anyone. Momma…she faced so much prejudice, but she's a fierce bitch." Crystal snorted. "That's a joke she and I have. Hope I didn't offend you."

Sonja waved her hand, not wanting to acknowledge that she'd been called a bitch so often she had pretty much stopped hearing it.

"At home, I draw on my family for strength. Here, I have no one." Crystal leaned in and dropped her voice. "You're a southern white woman, or so it appears. Though with your hair, you could be light-skinned. Don't we teach that race is socially constructed?"

"How does any of that matter?" asked Sonja.

"You know it does. If not, I made a huge mistake coming here."

"I do know that," Sonja conceded, her face heating from embarrassment. Her strategy to gain the upper hand had been poorly executed. Worse, offensive.

"You also know what it's like for female-identifying folks. The interruptions. The condescension. The challenges to everything. So many ways to shut us up and shut us down. And those are faculty I'm describing. I didn't know I'd have to fight students too. I mean, damn. Teaching was a challenge in grad school, but this is different. There seems to be all kinds of rage directed at women who dare to hold positions of authority here. Throw in that I'm mixed race and I catch the attention of all sorts of bigots."

The woman's intensity was palpable. Sonja leaned back in her chair. "It's not your imagination. You will get used to it. It's like microdosing venom. You take a little bit every day, and when the big bite comes, it won't incapacitate you. And the big bite will come."

"Pardon me, but hell no!" Crystal sat up straighter. "You know what Angela Davis said about changing the things she couldn't accept instead of accepting the things she couldn't change. I'm changing some shit, and I'm starting by surrounding myself with the right people. You seem to be one of those people. Okay, you're not the friendliest, but I'm not looking for that. I'm looking for people who don't take shit from anyone. Is that you?"

Sonja nodded, then drained her glass, the wine flowing through her chest, easing tensions from her body.

"Corey Randalls," Crystal continued. "Is he your ovary crusher?"

Lulled by the pinot and seduced by the other woman's persistence, Sonja answered. "I'm unsure. He may be related to a student I taught years ago. That is another story."

"And I haven't earned that story." Crystal shot the rest of her whiskey and stood up. "Two's my limit. Any more and you'd get me in bed, you sweet talker."

"I'm not—" Sonja stammered.

"To answer your question. Yes, I am flirting with you. I'm a natural flirt, like Daddy. It's how he eventually won over Momma." Crystal dug into her bag and pulled out her wallet—a man's wallet, from the looks of it—and placed some bills on the table. "You, Dr. Storey, interest me. I have theories about you. When Elliot comes, that's enough cash for our drinks, plus a generous tip. Tip servers and bartenders early. They remember you that way."

"I will pay for my own."

"Next time I'll let you buy. But don't wait too long." Dr. Byrd pulled out a pen from her bag. "I don't have business cards yet, and I doubt you'd let me program my number into your phone, so here." She scratched numbers onto a cocktail napkin, put it on the table, and strode out of the bar.

As if on cue, the server appeared. "I thought you ladies were having a bite to eat."

Sonja pushed her empty wineglass toward him. "We are done."

"Was everything to your satisfaction?"

"Everything was fine." She picked up her tote and got up to walk away. She made it a few steps before returning to snatch the napkin off the table.

Throw it away. If you keep it, you'll call her one night after too much wine. Did Avery teach you nothing?

Sonja scrunched the napkin in her hand, suddenly not wanting to let it go. It had just dawned on her that her eye hadn't twitched the entire time she was at the bar with Crystal. Her back had relaxed too. And these revelations terrified her.

Chapter 9
Drinking All

As soon as Sonja drove into her neighborhood, she saw the father-daughter duo walking in the distance. The pair seemed to be relentless. Her own father hadn't stuck around long enough to see her grow up, yet this dad walked the streets every evening with his daughter.

She yanked Bimmer's steering wheel and cut a sharp U-turn, returning to the main road. She could reach Summit Street another way.

She pulled into her driveway, punched the remote, and pulled into the garage, then remembered that she had not retrieved her mail. She had a firm policy about never leaving her mailbox full; she had fought tooth and nail for her name and credit rating, and she didn't want to risk identity theft.

She dashed upstairs, unlocked the door, and brought in the package from the porch. Then she rushed out to grab her mail.

"Excuse me, ma'am." The man and girl hurried toward her.

"Not interested in cookies, magazines, or whatever you're selling," she threw out and began walking toward her house without looking at them. She couldn't outrun them in her spiky heels and pencil skirt, but she could ignore them.

"Not selling anything. It's Ms. Storey, right?" he asked, catching up to her. "Ms. Storey, it's about my girl's missing cat—"

"I know nothing about that," she said and headed for her front steps. Of course, she had come to suspect that the pancaked creature found on her driveway and the missing calico on the flier were one and the same. Still, she didn't want to get sucked into the family drama between a doting father and his daughter.

"Please," the father said, stepping closer. "I'm Bill Foster. This is April. We're new here. Just moved into the townhouses down the road. My daughter's cat got out. We've been looking for days, even put out a flier. Mrs. Patel—you know the Patels?"

"No. Now, I must go."

"Mrs. Patel said you might have information. I tried asking your next-door neighbor, but no one answers the door. I understand you're a busy woman. A minute's all I'm asking."

"Very well," she sighed, giving in. The wine was wearing off, and she was growing impatient with this man. "Tuesday, I discovered something in my driveway. "It appeared to have been run over. I have no idea how it got there. I don't even know for certain that it was a cat." Her explanation complete, she turned to leave.

"What did you do with it?" he asked, his refusal to let her off the hook perturbing her more.

"I tossed it over there." Sonja flung her hand toward the vacant lot across the street.

"You threw it away? Are you a—"

She turned to face him again. "Am I a what?" she asked. "A bitch? Cunt? Is that what you were getting ready to call me?"

He fell back as if she had slapped him. "God, no. I was about to ask if you were absolutely sure it wasn't a calico?"

"I thought it was a rabbit. I must go." She walked away, but not before she heard his last comment.

"What made you like this?"

Sonja clicked the door shut. *You'll understand when you crush your daughter's spirit.*

Inside, she brushed off the loathsome interaction as if it were a stink bug clinging to her silk blouse. Then she picked up and opened her latest package, a cashmere dress that she had rush ordered to console herself after the week's chaos.

She slept restlessly that night, her sleep punctuated by the reappearance of people she had previously vanquished. Even Mitch Grant, the leader of the Gray Hairs, showed up, and he hadn't haunted her dreams since he got locked away in a nursing home after a series of strokes scrambled his rotten egg of a brain.

Sonja threw her legs over the side of the bed and sat up, struggling to recall what Mitch had done in her dream.

Nothing worse than he did in real life. The memory of Mitch smearing her cheek with his sticky, wet fingers, marking her, flashed through her mind. *A solid day's work will set me straight.*

Following a breakfast of green tea and dry toast, she jotted down her weekend to-do list, resolving to cross off every item before Sunday evening. At the top was her review of Mary Ann's supposedly final edits of the inquiry report. Sonja assumed it would be easier to read Professor Chaos's social media posts this time, but she ended up skipping them altogether, enabling her to quickly finish the edits. She promptly emailed the report to Mary Ann.

Next, she turned to her upcoming presentation for the Women's Resource Office noontime seminar, still rankled at how Lynne Harrison, the office's director, had coerced Sonja into being a speaker.

"Come on, kid." In her mid-seventies and getting ready to retire, Harrison peppered conversations with endearments like "kid" to remind WHSU's elite that they weren't above her, no matter their titles or salaries. "Don't make me remind you about that letter of support I wrote to those men on your tenure committee. I hope those guys rot in hell for the way they treated women on this campus. All of them except Lewis. He's a good seed. Anyway, kid, you owe me, and I'm cashing in before I escape this shithole."

"Fine." Sonja seethed more over the comment about Lewis Waters than the coercion, but she accepted that those outside the department would never understand how the Gray Hairs had harassed her. "Mark me down for September. I will prepare something on handling toxic people in the workplace."

Harrison laughed, her voice sounding like cigarettes, whiskey, and not giving a fuck.

Afterward, Sonja had drafted several emails to the WRO director, intent on withdrawing from her seminar commitment, but Sonja deleted them because she knew Harrison would badger her until she relented.

Pulling her home copy of *Emotional Ninjas* from her barrister bookcase, she flipped through the pages and considered possible quotes. She typed several key words into the document but quickly deleted them. Thirty minutes later, desperate to make headway, she pasted in an image of a sickly and malformed tree and labeled it, *Get the Fuck Down from the Toxic Tree.* Then she dragged a text box onto each branch with subheads.

Traps with compliments
Overgrows boundaries
Casts shadows of doubt
Roots in negativity
Bruises and breaks

When she picked up her book again, a photo slipped out, bringing her work to a halt. She knew the picture only too well, although she had forgotten stashing it inside this book.

She stood up, sending the photo onto the floor. It landed faceup, and she gazed at her ex's face, mesmerized by the iron jaw, pewter eyes, and silvering hair, as if she could suckle warmth from beautifully sculptured, cold metal. She stumbled out of her office into the living room and lay gasping on the floor. The images from that day played across the ceiling.

Avery lifting her out of the chair as the university photographer cut across the nearly empty bookstore. Arm snugging her waist, Avery dragging her into his orbit. The sound of the telephoto lens, whirling, zooming in. Avery leaning toward the camera, his head covering hers like an eclipsing moon. Sonja unable to look anywhere besides at him, pulled by his gravitational force.

In the one photo of her book signing, Sonja was obscured.

"That was the old you, the weaker you. Get up this minute."

Staggering to her feet, she lumbered back to her office and picked up the photo with her nails, not wanting it to touch her skin. She glanced at it long enough to see Lewis Waters hovering behind her like a ghost. He looked at her with a forlorn expression.

"You're sad, Lewis, because I bested you."

Are you sure?

"Don't be revisionist now that he's an affable old man," she chided herself. "Lewis, you, Mitch, and Cole made my life miserable. But I defeated you, and that's why you looked sad at my book signing. You realized your campaign against me had failed."

She stashed the photo facedown on the bottom shelf of the bookcase and snapped the shelf door shut, trapping the picture behind glass like a small but dangerous beast.

Picking up her laptop, she went to the kitchen and poured a glass of pinot. It was only early afternoon, but she had earned some respite.

She went outside, sank onto her lounger, and entered *Dr. Crystal Byrd* into the search engine on her laptop. After sorting through various social media profiles, obituaries, and pageant photos, she finally found a sprinkling of inconsequential tidbits buried on a scholarly research website. Other than Byrd's assistant professor rank, WHSU affiliation, and university email address, there were no publications, no media buzz, nothing.

In academic terms, Dr. Byrd simply did not exist. Sonja cleared the search field, reminding herself what Avery had taught her: to reach the pinnacle of academia, she must surround herself only with successful people and high achievers.

You should search your half-sis, then. She's fabulously successful. Like Father.

Ignoring that voice, Sonja plugged in *Jacob D. Randalls* and hit Enter. Maybe she could find some association between Corey and Jacob. The results were more social media profiles, references to court cases, and wedding announcements.

"This is unproductive," she said as she scrolled. Sonja was just about to clear the search again when she saw a link to the obituary section of a newspaper.

She gasped, her hands covering her mouth, her fingers and lips trembling slightly.

Tears slid down her face. She smacked them away and kept reading the obituary.

Jacob was dead. But how had he died?

The same obituary appeared on multiple websites.

Jacob Darrow Randalls, 39, went home to the Lord on Saturday, June 1. He is survived by his parents, August and Darrow J. Randalls, and brother, Brian C. Randalls, along with numerous aunts, uncles, and cousins. He was a graduate of Pickens High School. At Western Highlands State University, he had been an honors student and a recipient of many awards.

Funeral services for Jacob Darrow Randalls will be held at the Pickens Baptist Church on June....

There was no clue as to what had happened to her former student after he left WHSU.

Got kicked out, you mean.

Sonja drained her wine and rubbed her eyes, digging her knuckles into them as if to punish them for what they had seen and for what she had done.

Returning to her search, she found herself on an overdose awareness website. Sonja clicked on the Tributes tab and scrolled down the page until she reached the posts from June and July, but only two had been posted around the time of Jacob's death.

JR, I was shitty to you. But come on, you deserved it lots of times. I love you, you bastard. Your my best friend. There are no words. Fly, my brother. I'll catch up to you one day.

And another

Jake—I can't stop crying, wondering Why? Your brother's bad off, lots of anger. Don't you worry, tho. I'll stick close, make sure the demon doesn't get him like she got you. Angel Hugs, Crysse.

The tributes shook Sonja, even though it was unclear that they were for Jacob. Sonja put aside her laptop and, loosened up by wine, picked up her phone, terrified to be alone with her thoughts.

The sun drooped and fattened by the time the doorbell rang. Sonja considered not answering it; her flailing emotions were under control now. Or she could simply send Byrd away and return to her to-do list. She would sort the whole Jacob matter out in the morning when she was fresh.

"This is why you drink wine alone rather than with other people. You make yourself vulnerable. You learned nothing from Avery." Her barbed tone raked at her soft parts.

She ran fingers through her hair to smooth the flyaways, and she adjusted her loungewear, quickly adding a matching sweater wrap.

Be quick. Be decisive.

Sonja cracked opened the front door, then opened the metal and glass security door just enough to be heard.

"Dr. Byrd, thank you for coming. Unfortunately, there has been a change of plans—"

"Nope. Back up. I'm coming in." She was wearing a garish purple track jacket and black activewear leggings, and she was holding a bottle of wine like a victorious Amazon displaying a prize from war. "I know nothing about wine, so I asked the clerk. She said wine snobs like this one well enough." Crystal squeezed through the door and herded Sonja into the living room. "Shoes on or off?"

"What?" Sonja clenched her jaw, annoyed that the woman had effortlessly invaded her home.

"My sneakers. On or off?"

"The floors are hardwood."

"Not an answer."

"Keep them on. While I appreciate you coming, you must leave. An obligation has cropped up."

"Uncrop it, then. Let's twist the top off this bottle, and you tell me what lit your fuse, as Daddy says." Crystal handed the bottle to Sonja, then stopped. "Are those sweatpants? Are you wearing sweatpants?"

"They are cashmere," Sonja replied.

"Cashmere sweatpants. With a shawl? I didn't know that was a thing."

"It is a sweater wrap, not a shawl."

Crystal snickered. "Sorry, babe. I didn't dress up." The woman plucked at her spandex leggings. "I was finishing yoga when you called. The classes at campus rec aren't half bad. Come with me sometime. You could even wear your fancy sweatpants." This time she laughed out loud. "I have a group. You know who I got to join me tonight?" She plopped onto the couch.

"That will not happen," Sonja said.

"Why are you making that pouty face? I come over, and bring you alcohol too. You're acting like I'm offering you piss in a bottle. Listen, about the wine. The clerk swore by it, so if it's shit, I'm blameless. Where are those glasses?" Crystal asked, one hand around the neck of the bottle, the other on the seat cushion. "Damn! This is nice. The material's really soft."

"It's a Bernhardt."

"Guess that means something. How the hell do you afford this stuff? Your clothes, your shoes, your furniture. What the hell is WHSU paying you that they're not paying me?"

"I do *not* discuss finances," Sonja replied, annoyed. Grudgingly, she fetched glasses. When she returned from the kitchen, her guest was snooping around the room.

"You caught me being nosy. Terrible habit. In my defense, you have fine taste. These wall decorations"—she pointed at the one with silver spokes arranged in a starburst, each spoke tipped with pear-shaped blue glass—"did you get them at T.J. Maxx? I think I saw this one there."

"Certainly not. That is an original piece by a New York artist." Sonja considered telling Crystal what that single piece of art had cost, but she thought better of it. "Come outside. The weather is nice enough."

"Sure. Hey, where are your photos? Momma and Daddy would have a fit if I didn't display my sprawling family," Crystal said, following Sonja onto the deck. Then she gasped. "This is gorgeous. Look at all this privacy. Right in the middle of the city—"

"Foxboro is hardly a city."

"It is compared to where I grew up. Look at what you have. You're two seconds from campus. No one's across the street out front. Plus, this wooded area out back! You could sit out here naked— Hey, wait!" Crystal protested when Sonja stopped pouring the wine. "Don't be stingy. I gave up my Friday night for you." Fresh-faced and wearing a ponytail, Crystal lifted her glass. "More."

Sonja grudgingly complied.

"So do you?"

"What?"

"Sit out here naked?"

"I will not answer that," Sonja stated unequivocally, pouring herself half a glass.

One glass. Let your guard down with Professor Perky, and you'll regret it.

"Got it," Crystal said, sitting on the edge of the lounger. "Momma says I get too personal too fast, that people want to keep their own counsel. I'm more like Daddy. He's never met a stranger."

While Crystal babbled on, Sonja leaned back against the cool metal railing and scanned the surface of her house, looking for the slightest sign of decay or deterioration. Just last fall, she'd had the trim painted, and its crisp, clean appearance pleased her—unlike that filthy place her mother had dragged her to after her father left.

"Earth to Sonja."

Sonja looked at Crystal as if she had forgotten she was there.

"You sounded a wreck on the phone. What gives?"

"I reject that characterization. I did not, as you contend, 'sound a wreck.'"

Crystal laughed. "Do you talk like a professor at home too? That must be exhausting." She took a swig from her glass and deliberately wiped her mouth with her purple sleeve.

Sonja cracked a small smile.

"Did I see Professor Storey smile? I'm putting that on my CV and listing it in my tenure application." Crystal grew serious. "Really, though, you sounded spooked when you called."

And just like that, the cheap wine and the woman's affability mixed and drained Sonja's restraint. "Give me a moment," she said, setting her glass on the table beside the lounger.

"Where are you off to?" Crystal asked.

"Wait."

Sonja retrieved the evidence folder from her study, all the while chanting *Putitbackputitback.* She returned to the deck slightly dazed, but she smiled when she saw Crystal. The woman was reclining on the lounger, wineglass on her pillowy belly, her eyes closed, her lips relaxed in a crescent smile. She was the picture of contentment and ease.

"I thought for sure that you got in your car and fled the scene," Crystal said, eyes still shut.

"I am going to detail some strange events." Sonja retrieved her wine and took a drink. "First, how old are you?"

"Non sequitur much?"

"How old?" Sonja asked again.

"Breached the big three-zero last February."

Sonja winced, wondering why she kept confiding in this woman. But the night and the wine conspired, enticing her to take some respite, perhaps even find pleasure in Crystal's company.

"And you, Sonja? Seeing as how age is important to you."

"Older."

"Unfair."

"Forties," Sonja responded. "That is all you are getting from me."

"Please tell me that you're not one of those women who's afraid of the age she's earned. You're a badass with a fierce wardrobe, and you're sexy as—"

"Enough of that." Sonja wanted Crystal to stop talking, yet she also wanted more, wanted to immerse herself in the woman's alto voice and soothe her internal injuries.

Crystal seemed to have an unrestrained exuberance intertwined with fierce intelligence, two qualities that Sonja found incompatible. But she was perplexed as to how someone so young had achieved that.

Crystal sat up and leaned toward Sonja. "Let's talk about why you called me. Is this about that Corey Randalls student?"

Gotobedgotobed. Stop this.

Sonja lowered herself onto the other lounger, folder in her lap, her knees almost touching Crystal's. Drinking all her wine, Sonja relaxed more, and the story poured out of her, ignoring the voice in her head that demanded her silence.

Chapter 10

Burning Face

"A COUPLE OF NOTES, A torn flier, spilled fish oil, and a dead animal," Crystal summarized, the skepticism evident to Sonja.

"You are oversimplifying the situation. I hear it in your voice." And in that moment, Sonja's agitation replaced the delicious blend of wine and companionship.

"I'm not following, Sonja. How is a rape threat against me somehow about you?"

"Shush. Let me finish."

Crystal bolted upright, her long legs swinging off the lounger. "I'm going to do you a favor and set something straight," Crystal said, her voice crackling with anger. "I spent a lifetime being told to be quiet. That was before I got my hands on the writings of bell hooks and Audre Lorde. When I read their words, my blinders came off. I started seeing how my story keeps getting colonized for the benefit of the colonizers. I promised myself I'd never let that happen again. Now, I'm sitting here listening to my story being co-opted, and by a woman who shushes me on top of it."

"How is you telling me this a favor?" Sonja tried to match Crystal's authority, but her icy tone melted under the other woman's heat.

"It's a favor, believe me. Most people, I'd walk out on them. You, I'm giving the benefit of doubt. This time."

"You didn't let me finish." Sonja dared to look at the woman's burning face.

"This is where you apologize."

"Fine. I am sorry," Sonja said frostily, determined to get the conversation back on track.

"Your apology is pitiful. I'll accept it. For now. But you need to know that no one tells me to be quiet and stays in my life. You've obviously been traumatized, and I'm trying to be patient, but I'm not seeing you reciprocate. That voice message hit me hard. I wonder if you understand that because, from my end, it sounds like you're appropriating my experience."

"Yes, I heard you."

Crystal stared at Sonja.

"Fine. I hear you," Sonja said. "That man, the one who left the voice message, sought to strip you of your accomplishments. Then I took your story and made it about me, and I asked you to be quiet while I—"

"Asked?" Crystal crossed her arms.

"I shushed you," Sonja admitted, her chest tight.

Crystal relaxed her shoulders a bit. "I'm beginning to wonder if I made a mistake coming here. To this university, this town. I've never lived in a place where I'm the only one. I wonder if I've put a target on my back. First that fucking voicemail, then... The other day I got asked *the* dreaded question, right there in the produce section of the grocery store. There I am, thumping honeydew, and this woman walks up to me and asks, 'What are you?'" Crystal stared toward the darkened woods. "I wished Momma had been there with me. She's thunder, lightning, and gale in woman form. I'm more like Daddy, too damn friendly, too damn forgiving. But I'm so *over* that fucking question. *What* am I? I've gotten that all my life. So there I am, holding a honeydew. Somehow, instead of punching her windpipe, I say, 'A professor with a PhD.' Then this bigoted bitch yaps at me about Mexicans and terrorists. And—I'm not fooling you—she says, 'As long as you're not one of those towelheads coming up over our southern border.' I wanted to bust out laughing while busting a melon over her racist, xenophobic head."

Sonja cracked a smile.

"Another smile? Good for me. Anyway, I needed to square away the whole shushing me thing. I won't give up my voice anymore, especially to another woman. I'm used to being silenced by men, but I have no patience when women do it to other women."

Sonja nodded stiffly. This woman kept getting around her defenses somehow.

"Back to your sticky notes, then."

"I'm being unclear. It's not about the stickies. It's about the words. 'Let's Play a Game!' Your caller said something similar."

"You didn't get threatened with rape," Crystal stated.

"Not this time," Sonja conceded. "Look, what I meant to tell you about is Jacob Randalls." She whispered the name almost reverently. "I suspect there's a connection between Jacob and everything else that's been happening."

"Is that why you asked me about Corey Randalls? Is he related to this Jacob guy?"

"I have no idea." Sonja was having a problem forming coherent sentences. Crystal seemed to have drawn the saltiness out of her, and she didn't know quite how to handle that. "I found out..." Her eyes filling with tears, Sonja paused, jerking her hand away when Crystal reached for it. "I think I killed Jacob."

Sonja rose from the lounger and stood by the railing, peering out into the shadows as if they could reveal something. Crystal got up and stood next to her.

"When I first started at WHSU, everyone hated me. My student evaluations were terrible. Students commented on my clothes, my body, my hair. They called me the Shrill Harpy of WHSU. This one senior faculty member, Mitch Grant, he thought it was hilarious. He'd call me Miss Shrill Harpy in meetings. He couldn't even call me Dr. Shrill Harpy."

"No one corrected him?" Crystal asked.

Sonja shook her head. "I was completely alone, surrounded by the Gray Hairs, this group of old, powerful men bent on destroying me." Sonja scoffed. "There I was, a trained social scientist, and I couldn't figure out how to manipulate the variables to control my circumstances. I prepared lectures, taught classes, attended meetings, served on committees. I didn't yell at my students. I didn't sleep with them."

"We're not born women. We become women."

"What?"

"Paraphrasing Simone de Beauvoir." The other woman studied her. "One isn't born a fully formed woman. She's shaped into one. You reject fundamental belief about what a woman should be. And you're punished for it."

"Eventually I became exactly what they loathed: Shrill Harpy, Dr. Freeze, Professor Cunt. As if I had a choice. I could be either hated but feared, or soft, loved, and compliant."

"You're talking the language of one of my favorite poets, Nikita Gill. She writes that it's easier being hated than to accept not being loved, easier being angry than to accept being sad. I'm not doing her words justice."

Sonja grimaced. "You are one of *those*. A quote for everything."

Crystal chuckled, an airy sound of falling star dust. "Guilty. Momma had books stacked everywhere. All kinds too. History, philosophy, poetry, fiction, classics from around the world. Nothing was off-limits, including erotica. Whenever I got my heart broken, Momma would point to a stack of books, pat my back, and say, 'The answer's in there. You have to search it out, though. No one's giving a girl like you anything.' Books, writing—they saved me. Momma too."

"Mother taught me too," Sonja said. "She taught me that I am detestable and to use that to my advantage. At least she prepared me for the Gray Hairs."

"Sonja, that's awful."

"What it is…is enough." She shivered, realizing that she had almost exposed the worst of her childhood to a stranger and member of the WHSU faculty. She rubbed her arms vigorously, exaggerating the movement to surreptitiously wipe the tear from her cheek with her cashmere-covered shoulder. "Time to go inside. It's getting nippy."

"Nipply, you mean." Crystal grinned and crossed her arms over her chest.

"You are quite immature, Dr. Byrd." Sonja dipped her head to hide her smile behind a curtain of hair. "Grab the bottle."

"It's empty, Dr. Storey. Where do you want it?" Crystal asked, stepping inside behind Sonja.

"The counter. I will take care of it later."

"Hey, that's a telescope," Crystal said, setting the empty bottle on the nearby dining table.

"Obviously."

"What a beauty. I used to keep a log. I detailed every star, comet, and constellation I could identify. That was back when I was a kid in Georgia. May I touch it?"

Sonja hesitated, overcome by a whirlwind of feelings. Part of her wanted to share Star Dancer with Crystal, just as the old man had shared his telescope with her ages ago. But another part of her shrank into a hard nut of possessiveness. Star Dancer had never known another's touch.

"I shouldn't have asked," Crystal said. "I violated a basic tenet of telescope etiquette. My sixth-grade teacher told us to never touch someone else's telescope without being invited. I'll wait for you to invite me to touch your beauty."

Crystal carried her half-full wineglass into the living room and plopped onto the couch, kicking off her shoes and drawing her legs up under her. Sonja, suddenly nervous, straightened the already orderly room, fluffing throw pillows and refolding a blanket draped decoratively over the corner chair.

"Come sit with me," Crystal said. "Let's get back to our conversation. I got derailed by your beauty—and I'm not just talking about your telescope." She laughed, a throaty ode to joy.

Sonja continued fussing about the room. Crystal's casualness left Sonja confused and riddled with impulses that clashed like fighting songbirds.

"Please." Crystal patted the couch. "I need a chaperone."

"I don't like being cajoled." Sonja protested weakly as she settled at the opposite end of the couch. She refused to make eye contact with her guest, worried that Crystal would pick up memories churning in her head about being forced to stay home from school and snuggle with her mother on the couch.

"So, this Jacob person," Crystal said, picking up where they had left off.

"He happened about a decade ago."

"I'm listening."

Sonja swaddled herself so tightly in the cashmere wrap around her that she suspected she resembled a burrito. "Jacob enrolled in my Crisis Communication course. He was an honors sociology major. Older than most of the other students. He was different from anyone I'd ever taught. He soaked up everything, like he was preparing for something big."

"Sounds refreshing."

"Back then, I was always in trouble, in Jay's office constantly."

"Who's Jay?"

"Jay King, department chair. I was constantly being summoned to Jay's office or I was on the phone with Student Affairs. It was exhausting. Students complained about everything: my exams, the way I looked at them, the way I didn't look at them, the way I spoke, my tone. Then there were the SETs. Mitch—the leader of the Gray Hairs—insisted that my student evaluations were going to cost me tenure."

He said other things. Did other things. Tell her, Pillows. Confess the horrible things you've let men do to you because Daddy didn't love you enough.

Sonja stared at Crystal's glass, wanting to drink the remaining wine, sedate the loud judge in her brain. By the time she refocused, she realized that Crystal was speaking.

"...students evals. I've had comments telling me to go back to Africa. Others, back to Mexico." She chuckled. "I have to laugh, or I'd cry—or start killing some fuckers. One time on a written eval—and this is word-for-word—someone wrote, 'You're proof that monkeys can speak but they sure as fuck can't speak good.'"

"Students attack my gender," Sonja said.

"You've got that bone-china skin. I bet they assume you're white. But your eyebrows are dark and gorgeous. Like black caterpillars. With your hair and those brows, you could pass for light-skinned in my family. We have all shades and shapes. You should see our family gatherings. We confuse the hell out of racists. They don't know how to hate us. They just know they do."

"My mother and I are estranged—no." Sonja held up her hand. "That's another story. My point is, I know almost nothing about my heritage. But that hardly matters on this campus. Everyone assumes I'm white; you're right about that. But they see my gender. To my students, I am a snooty bitch who needs to be taken down a notch. Jacob, though, sat in the front row, raised his hand, asked smart questions. He even wrote a letter for my tenure and promotion dossier. I needed that letter too, with the Gray Hairs gunning for me."

"What turned it bad? With Jacob, I mean."

"I reported him for plagiarism."

"In your class?"

"I was a reader for his undergraduate honors thesis. All I had to do was review it and sign off."

"But?"

"He had copied and pasted from papers he had previously written for me. Papers from class. He had not changed a word. He didn't even try to hide it." Sonja looked down at her nails, red as if she had ripped apart something, a small, defenseless creature. She tucked them between her thighs.

"Sounds like he got caught. His self-plagiarism wasn't your fault."

Sonja shook her head. "Something was not right. In class, he was great, but during his thesis work, he missed deadlines, meetings." She sighed. "After I reported him, he left school. I never saw him again." She stared at the thin layer of dust on her coffee table and squeezed her hands tighter between her legs to keep from jumping up and dusting. "He died in June. Overdose, I think, but I just learned about his death today, so I am not sure."

"You said you killed him," Crystal said softly and scooted closer to Sonja, "but the timeline doesn't add up. Jacob OD'd in June. At least according to the obit you showed me. And you reported him—what? A decade back."

"All correct. However, you're overlooking the real question: when I turned him in, did he..." Sonja stopped midsentence, the words lodging in her throat.

"Sink into depression? Turn to drugs? Or maybe he self-plagiarized because he was fighting a private battle. I have family living with bipolar, depression, addiction—you name it. Momma says those demons stick close and wait for an in."

"I punished him, I think," Sonja admitted, knowing she would later regret it.

"Okay."

"After he completed my class, we met for coffee. On campus," she added, as if the location provided context. "My professional commitment to him was over, but I didn't want our association to end. In some ways, I viewed him as an intellectual equal. I valued our conversations. They were stimulating." Sonja rubbed her forehead as if that would clear up the confusion she had felt back then.

"Professors get attracted to their students."

"Absolutely not." Sonja straightened her back. "I saw him as an emerging scholar, a mentee."

Crystal shrugged. "To clarify, I'm not saying you were sexually attracted to him. Attraction takes many forms. Intellectual, emotional, spiritual. To serve our students, we form bonds, and that means seeing them—*really* seeing them. And sometimes it's hard to let some of them go, especially after watching their metamorphosis."

"Maybe that's why I wanted to meet him for coffee. Maybe that's why I agreed to be his thesis reader." Sonja ran her fingers through her hair. "All I know is I was not ready to give up our scholarly debates, especially in my department."

"You found a spot of beauty in the middle of a cesspool. The lotus blooming in mud."

"He pulled away," Sonja shook her head, still unable to assemble the puzzle pieces after all the years. "He missed meetings, ignored emails. I took it as another rejection in a lifetime of rejections."

Girlie's drunk. Go on. Open up wide. Let her see your deep-down rot.

"I could have handled Jacob's self-plagiarism differently," Sonja confessed.

"You think you wanted revenge? For him ghosting you?"

"One minute he seemed to value my role in his life. The next, he vanished. No calls. No emails. Then one day, I received his thesis from his honors advisor. She asked me to read it. But I was angry. He hadn't responded to *my* emails. He hadn't acknowledged the missed meetings. When I read it, I thought I was going to vomit. He had lifted his previous papers word-for-word. He didn't even bother disguising it. When I contacted the committee head, she called it an oversight, assured me it would be corrected. But I didn't wait until she had finished investigating. I filed a report with the dean of the honors college."

"Would you have reported another student in similar circumstances?"

"The real question is, would I have reported him if he had not abandoned me?"

"And?"

"I don't know."

They sat quietly for a few minutes. Then Crystal got up. "We're not done. Just need to use your restroom."

Sonja led Crystal to the bathroom off the living room. Flameless candles flickered inside, transmuting sections of the wall into gold and the violet hand towels into slabs of granite.

"Fancy," Crystal said. She shut the door but continued talking. "It's like I'm peeing in a Monet exhibit."

Sonja stopped listening. She turned inward, curious over the unfamiliar feeling of relief. But when she heard the toilet flush, she was instantly transported to the last time Avery Bruce had used that bathroom. Right before he apologized for mistreating her. Right before he kissed her and she gave in to him again, a man she knew to be a sadistic lover, something he proved to be one final time. Sometimes in the middle of the night, she traced the bite mark he had left on the underside of her breast.

The water running in the bathroom sink brought her back, breaking the spell that Crystal had cast over her. Sonja ran around, collecting the dirty glasses. She poured the remainder of Crystal's wine into the kitchen sink, then loaded the glasses into the dishwasher. Behind her, Crystal spoke.

"This Corey Randalls. I'm guessing your working theory is that he blames you for Jacob's death. That he's playing some game of revenge."

"Listen, this evening must end." Sonja closed the dishwasher and hung her head over the sink. The evening had exposed too many of her vulnerabilities. "It is time for you to leave. If you had too much to drink, I will order a car for you."

"Wait! What happened? I go pee. When I come out, I'm in some sort of parallel dimension."

Sonja turned, and peered over Crystal's head, a technique to give the illusion of eye contact.

"I am tired, and we finished a bottle of wine."

"I had less than two glasses. And look," Crystal brushed past Sonja and pointed into the sink. "You poured mine out, it seems. I'm fine to drive. Fine to stay too."

"Reminiscing is an indulgence that keeps a person stuck, and I cannot afford to be stuck. I have plans." She went to stand by the front door. "I must get some sleep. I have a heavy workload this weekend."

Crystal seemed to glide like a form of pure luminescence crossing the room, and she stared down, her molten-bronze eyes heating Sonja's face. Crystal leaned forward.

Sonja jerked back, putting her hand on Crystal's chest. "What are you doing?"

"Saying goodnight." Crystal gently peeled away Sonja's hand and moved closer. "I don't know what happened. Guess you'll tell me when you're ready," she said, then kissing Sonja's cheek. "Goodbye."

As soon as the door closed, Sonja locked up, barricading herself against some unnamed danger. She carried her telescope onto the deck and gazed into the darkness. The stars above appeared like holes in a satiny universe, and she wondered if Jacob was staring down on her.

Chapter 11

Her Lips Red

SONJA TORE THROUGH HER WEEKEND to-do list, surprising herself with her productivity. She drafted a book proposal and introductory chapter, then got an idea that she couldn't shake.

She would confront Jay King.

After all, if she planned to write a book advising readers about how to take back their power in a toxic workplace, she needed to be credible.

On Sunday, as a reward for her productivity, she ordered an expensive kimono-style sweater that would add a touch of luxury to the dreary winter months ahead.

On Monday, while it was still dark, she showered and slipped into a Diane von Furstenberg sheath, a fitted navy crêpe that gave her a regal look. She put on her patent Choos, then painted her lips red with Christian Louboutin Diva—a near perfect match for her heels. By the time she reached her office on campus, Sonja regained the swagger that had deserted her on Friday.

Let's collect some heads. The mantra roared in her like the battle cry of an advancing warrior, and she smiled.

Then she saw the paper, neatly folded and taped to her office door.

Throw it away immediately.

But her fingers mutinied, opening the paper to reveal a message in at least a 100-point font.

CUNT

With that, her swagger fled, and the cage of her chest slammed shut again.

"How many times have I come to you over the years? You have never taken my grievances seriously."

Dr. Jay King sat behind his desk, smiling at her. "Sonja, please sit. My neck can't take this angle." He looked up at her and gestured for her to sit as if she were there for a friendly chat.

"Your affable guy routine is not going to work. I'm done with it. You have *never* supported me."

"That again, Sonja?" he chortled. "I thought that unpleasantness was behind us. Mitch and Cole are long gone."

"I would rather put it in front of us. All of it."

"Unfortunately, I don't have time today. Talk with Harmony on your way out. She'll find us a suitable meeting time."

"Cancel whatever obligations you have, or I promise you, Jay, I will leave here and go to Jodi Jenkins's office. I will name names. I will give her emails and dates."

"Let's calm—"

"If you tell me to calm down, we are done." Sonja moved toward the open office door and called out to the secretary, "Harmony, no calls. We will be awhile," then shut the door.

Jay sighed. "I'll need to make a call first." He picked up the phone, and Sonja took the opportunity to prepare herself for what she had been fantasizing about nearly her entire time at WHSU.

Sonja had mastered the art of sitting across from a man in authority who didn't want to hear what she had to say.

She squared her shoulders, expanded the space she occupied, and stretched out her forearms on the arms of the chair. She sat with her legs crossed but didn't bounce them. She kept her face blank. She trained her eyes, the color of wet gunmetal when in battle mode, on her opponent's face, occasionally scanning their clothing to make her judgment of their wardrobe evident. Sonja had chosen the tan chair with a jagged rip in the seat. The rip nipped at her expensive outfit, but the placement allowed her to fully display her polished aggression.

Jay, on the other hand, had mastered his common folk style. He kept his tie loose, his top button undone just enough to show his gray chest hair that emerged like the crooked, stiff legs of a dead cockroach. With his sallow skin and wiry beard, he looked like a good ol' boy, incapable of treachery. This style enabled him to be an effective dictator.

"I'll be a bit late." Pause. "Hold my spot." Pause. "If need be, push back my agenda item." Pause. "Yeah." Then he laughed hard. "Yeah. Mm-hmm. The meeting'll be a doozy." More laughter.

She cleared her throat and tapped her Gucci watch with her fingernail.

"Got to run. Okay, then." Jay hung up the phone, still chuckling. "That was—"

"Whatever you are preparing to share with me, don't. You are stalling."

"Sonja, there's no need—"

"Yes, Jay, there is. You try to avoid direct confrontation. That is *exactly* how you stayed in that chair for twenty years." Anger flashed in her like a grenade, but she forced her jaw to relax. Jay would exploit her rage, dismissing her as an out-of-control woman. He had done it before, as had the Gray Hairs. "Today I am going to speak, and I will make sure that my position is understood. Afterward, I expect you to call campus security and initiate an investigation."

"An investigation? Of what?"

Point scored. Remain aloof. He wants you emotional, pliable.

She opened the folder on her lap, slowly and deliberately flipping through each item until she got to the last piece of paper. She held it up and pointed with a frosted fingertip at the single word on the center of the page.

Jay flinched. "That's awful."

"Agreed. To be called a cunt is awful. And this is only one of several aggressions I have received. Aggressions that are rooted in a climate of hostility that you perpetuate through inaction."

"Sonja, please put that obscenity away." He gestured to the paper.

"And yet I've been called this word for years. You didn't seem upset those other times. Not when Mitch called me that word in front of you and

Cole. Not when students called me that in class. I can document the exact dates."

She watched his face, noting the changes of coloring as his skin shifted, his cheeks flushing slightly.

"My argument is simple, Jay. This latest incident is directly connected to a toxic department culture. You abdicated your authority during your early years." She stopped as he braced his hands on the arms of his chair as if to rise. "We are having this discussion. If you leave or refuse to listen, I will call Jodi."

"There's no need for that." Jay sat back in his chair and folded his hands over his protruding belly. "Say your piece."

His reaction nearly derailed her, but she quickly found her voice again by mentally replaying the scene of Mitch and his grotesque performance in her basement office, the office she'd had briefly while an assistant professor.

"I have three points to make. After that, one of us will make a call. First, my colleagues. They repeatedly violated harassment policies. And before you say I never notified you, I have emails documenting when I protested my treatment in meetings. For instance, the times Mitch shouted me down. Or when Cole Behringer told me, and I quote, 'When men speak, girls learn by opening their ears and closing their lovely lips.' You were present at both of those meetings, and you said not one word. Your silence amounted to tacit permission."

Jay's eyes flashed with outrage, then dulled as if doused.

"Then there was the touching. For years, whenever I went to collect my mail, Mitch would lie in wait for me, pushing up against me while he pretended to check his mail. Worse, he did it in front of everyone: Harmony, *you*, student workers. And you said not a single word to him. Did you ever ask yourself: if he behaved like that in front of people, how did he behave when there were no witnesses?"

"Sonja, you know I talked to Mitch. He denied everything. I'm not saying you made it up, but Mitch and Cole were from a different time. We did what we could. Lewis—"

Sonja laughed, a serrated, metallic sound. "You stayed chair because you refused to make waves. The department's climate has improved"— she paused for emphasis—"slightly. Not because of you or Lewis. Mitch and Cole retired, and due to budget cuts, you filled their positions with overworked lecturers and adjuncts. Now, I have two more points."

He nodded stiffly.

"Second, the staff. You have watched Harmony openly disrespect me. In front of student workers too. She refuses to make eye contact when I speak to her. She huffs when I ask for something. On the other hand, she makes photocopies for others, especially Lewis. She runs errands for them. For years, I watched her pick up lunches for Cole and Mitch, hand-deliver their mail, even pick up their dry cleaning."

"Sonja, be fair. Harm ran to the dry cleaners—what? Three times? And that was for regalia that—"

"Yes, Jay, let us be fair." She smiled coldly. "No one has fetched my regalia. And I retrieve my printouts from the main office right away or they are discarded. Additionally, on days when I need copies right away, Harmony sits behind her desk and points to the copier. When I need something delivered across campus, she tells me—and these are her exact words—'Student workers aren't delivery mules.' Meanwhile, Lewis leaves his materials everywhere, and Harmony picks up after him."

"If you would be nicer to her."

"That. That right there." She narrowed her eyes at him. "How many times did you tell Mitch to be nice? Or Cole? Did you ask any of the male faculty to bake cupcakes for her birthday?" *Because you sure as fuck asked me.* In danger of losing her temper, Sonja smoothed her dress and redirected her comments.

"Cole screamed at student workers. You remember, Jay. He spoke like a grand orator, until he lost his...cool." *Lost his shit, more accurately.* "Not to mention that monster couldn't keep his hands to himself. How many times did he *accidentally* brush up against young women? Do you think I failed to notice that Harmony only hired male student workers for a time? Jodi would find our student hiring data compelling."

Sonja picked invisible lint off her sheath.

"Mitch and Cole both exhibited predatory behavior, behaviors you overlooked. Lewis too. Presumably, the university overlooked their behavior as well. But I am done assuming you will handle it. And I'm done with your advice to 'be nicer.' That's always your recommendation for me—never for the male faculty members." She stopped to catch her breath and control the rising tide of emotions that threatened to overwhelm her.

"Is that it?" Jay asked, his laced hands tightening across his creased shirt, his anxiety betrayed by his white knuckles.

"No," she said. "I have a third and final point. Students in my classrooms have screamed at me, sworn at me, called me 'bitch' and 'cunt.' I documented these incidents with you and Student Affairs. No action was taken. None. 'Try being like a mom to them.' 'Praise them.' 'Make them feel seen and supported.' That was the advice I got. But I was hired to be an expert in my field, not to be a substitute mother."

"Fine, Sonja. You've made your points. What do you want?"

"I should have followed through on my threat to our dean." Sonja's voice had lost much of its fire. Her weariness surprised her. "During my tenure and promotion review, I should have reported every incident of harassment, hostility, and misogyny in this department."

"About that. You should know that Lewis...." Jay trailed off as Sonja inflated herself, holding her shoulders and back erect once more. Her gaze hardened.

"This department is going to change," she stated. "By the time I am through, the university will too." She raised the paper and flashed "cunt" at him. "Call campus security. Report this incident. One of your faculty has been repeatedly harassed. *Pretend* you care."

"We likely won't find the person who did this. Is it really worth it?"

"Yes."

Jay stood up from behind his desk and opened the door. "Harmony, call campus police. We need Officer Sounder, if she's available. It's important." He held out his hand. "The note, please, Sonja."

She had already taken a photo of the paper earlier, so she gave it to him.

"Harmony, please make copies and scan this page, then email it to my account and Dr. Storey's account. Knock as soon as you're done. We'll need that note back."

Jay closed the door again and said, "If you're up to it, I want to continue talking until campus police arrive."

"I have more to say." She forged ahead, describing the sticky notes, the fish oil, Ronnie Staller's concerning behavior, and the torn flier. But she omitted mention of Corey Randalls and the carcass in the driveway.

Those details might have adversely affected her credibility. By the time she finished, there was a knock on the door.

Sonja gave a statement to Officer Sounder, who made vague assurances about keeping the campus safe and more inclusive. Not to be outdone, Jay vowed in front of Officer Sounder to address the importance of professionalism within the department. But no one took the "cunt" note from Harmony, and Sonja was left to retrieve it, then retreat to her office.

She dialed Crystal's number the moment she closed the door and sank into her chair.

"You ignored my texts," Crystal said in place of a greeting. "Ready to take me off the shelf?"

"Let's meet."

"You mean, 'Let's meet, please.'"

"Please," Sonja replied.

"Office hours end in a half hour. I have a curriculum meeting on campus later. But we could walk and talk."

"I'll meet you outside the main entrance of the library in thirty minutes."

"Works for me."

"Thanks."

Crystal laughed. "I got a thanks. Amazing. Okay. See you in thirty."

The minute Sonja hung up, she started shaking, anger, fatigue, and frustration converging like separate weather systems pressing down on her until she could hardly breathe. She glanced at the clock on her computer with a mixture of relief, trepidation, and excitement.

Ain't that sweet. Girlie has a friend. Dummy, you've forgotten so much.

Sonja squeezed her eyes shut until the voice dissipated.

Chapter 12

Thick, Cold Blood

"I should be finalizing my presentation for Wednesday's seminar," Sonja huffed out, doing her best to keep up with Crystal's stride.

"I'm looking forward to it."

"You're coming? Why?"

"I want to. Besides, it's the Women's Resource Office. How would it look if the new assistant professor of Gender Studies missed a WRO seminar? And we have that program audit coming up. I'm being extra nicey-nice since I'll be—"

Sonja stopped walking. "I don't want you there."

Crystal, several steps ahead, whipped around and threw her hands up. "Why'd you stop?"

As if for the first time, Sonja saw the tall, curvy form wearing a smart taupe pantsuit, black camisole, and black boots, and a face easily cast in sunny moods and quick thunderstorms—but always compelling. Sonja knew she had made a mistake. Fortunately, it wasn't too late to fix it.

Crystal walked back to where Sonja stood and repeated, "Why'd you stop?" then added, "And why don't you want me there?"

"You will distract me."

"I'm distracting, huh?" Crystal smirked.

"I said that you will distract me. You don't listen very well." Without preamble, Sonja changed direction and headed to Terrell Center, determined to reestablish her boundaries with this woman.

"I listen to what's actually being said."

"I regret calling you."

"You do not. What's up, anyway?"

"I'm heading back to my office."

Crystal grabbed Sonja's wrist and gently pressed her thumb into her pulse point. Sonja flashed on Avery pinning her hands over her head, his thumbnail digging into the same spot.

"Please remove your hand," Sonja instructed, but there was a lurking need to be touched by Crystal where the old wound ached at times as if brand-new.

Crystal released Sonja's wrist. "Sorry. Was I hurting you?"

"I don't like being held." The statement was neither entirely true nor entirely false.

Crystal smoothed her chestnut eyebrows. "This push-pull thing you do, Sonja, isn't for me. It's making me think that I've returned to an old destructive pattern. I promised myself a while back: no more one-sided relationships."

Sonja pulled out her phone, brought up the image of the latest note, and showed it to Crystal. "I found this note on my office door this morning."

"Fucking fuckers!"

Crystal stepped over to a nearby bench, the cell still in her hand. Sonja followed, trying not to sink the heels of her Choos into the ground.

"One of Mary Ann's posters got tagged too. But that was months ago," Sonja explained as she sat next to Crystal, taking care not to snag her dress.

"Do I know Mary Ann?"

"Mary Ann Russel, co-chair of the informal inquiry committee."

"Inquiry?" Crystal turned to face Sonja, her eyebrows drawn together.

"It is part of the faculty disciplinary process," Sonja answered with a little more impatience than the situation warranted. "I also serve on that committee. I can't say more than that."

"Look, I don't want to piss you off, but"—Crystal handed the phone back to Sonja—"if this Mary Ann person had her poster vandalized too, shouldn't we be talking about a larger problem on campus? Like systemic sexism."

"I'm being targeted," Sonja insisted. "And I have something else to tell you." Sonja briefly recounted her conversation with Jay and Officer Sounder. When Crystal merely stared at her, Sonja snapped, "What now?"

Crystal shook her head, auburn curls reflecting the September sun. "I don't get you. You gave that officer Ronnie's name, but you didn't say a word about Corey Randalls."

"Staller is unraveling— You're too inexperienced to understand."

"That's condescending. Please don't speak to me that way, Sonja."

Sonja bit back, defensive. "What was I supposed to say? If I brought up Corey Randalls to the officer, that would bring Jacob into it." *And I'm not ready for that.*

"But if Corey is related to Jacob, and *if* he's after you—"

"I shouldn't have called." Sonja arched her back, trying to ease the ache. "This is unproductive. I have too much work."

Without warning, Crystal leaped up and raised her arm, blocking a Frisbee that was headed toward Sonja's face. "YES!"

Sonja looked down at where the red Frisbee had landed a foot away.

"You guys okay?" A young man ran over, his long blond hair tied back, his face drenched with sweat.

"Did you nearly hit me?" Sonja demanded.

"It was an accident. I'm sorry. We're sorry." He motioned toward a cluster of students trying to stifle their laughter.

Crystal spoke up before Sonja could. "I'm glad you folks are getting some exercise."

"That was an awesome block." The student laughed.

"Don't distract me with your flattery," Crystal said with a chuckle. "Seriously now, there's better green space on the other side of the library. You almost clocked my friend. Then she would've clocked you. Understand?" Her voice was a perfect blend of honey and bourbon.

"Thank you, ma'am. You're right, ma'am." He looked at Sonja, then immediately dropped his gaze as if it slid off a marble surface. "Sorry, ma'am."

"It is not ma'am. It is—"

"Okay, we're done here," Crystal said, intervening. "Go on. And don't hurt anyone."

The student picked up the disc and raced off. Sonja was speechless. It had been her face, not Crystal's, that was almost smacked by the Frisbee, yet Crystal had handled the entire encounter, leaving Sonja as a bystander in her own life, something she detested.

Sonja stood up and hurried toward Terrell Center.

Crystal easily caught up with her. "Did you see that? I slapped that thing right out of the air. Daddy would be proud. I've never been athletic. When it comes to sports, I'm a momma's girl. No skill. No interest. But damn, that felt awesome. Glad you didn't get hurt."

"This campus is trash," Sonja spat. There was a private war going on inside her between wanting someone like Crystal to watch out for her and wanting to be in charge of her own fate. She felt safer when she didn't rely on someone else.

"You make it hard," Crystal said softly. "I thought I'd found a badass woman here who could laugh with me at the paradox of being both powerful and powerless. Instead, I swear I'm beginning to think that all you want is a sidekick. White woman with her own personal Black mixed-raced marvel. What do you even want from me? You call me, then you're antagonistic, like I've harmed you somehow. Damn, Sonja, are you hell-bent on being miserable?"

More than the words, it was Crystal's tone that thickened Sonja's blood with cold, making her arms and legs feel encased in ice, so she went on the attack.

"What I am *hell-bent* on is not being interrogated." Sonja kept walking, not wanting to meet Crystal's eyes.

"I'm not interrogating you, and you know it. You hate how you're feeling right now, so you turn into an emotional ninja to regain a sense of agency."

Sonja stopped abruptly and turned to face Crystal.

"Told you. I'm a voracious reader," Crystal said with a crooked smile, "And yes, I'm reading your books. So should you. Then maybe you would stop these power plays with me."

Sonja swayed, knocked off balance by Crystal's assessment. Crystal clasped her hand and squeezed it gently, but Sonja yanked it away and continued to Terrell Center. Then she climbed up two steps and turned around again, placing her almost at eye level with Crystal. She wanted to reestablish her power. Or maybe she wanted something else, something besides winning and losing, something besides besting her latest opponent.

"Sonja," Crystal said, "this is the second time I've dropped everything to answer your call. Plus, I kind of saved your gorgeous face back there. Yet all you see is what I'm doing wrong. Look, I'm sorry about that foul note. Clearly, you've been mistreated and harassed. I bet we have some common experiences. Maybe ask me sometime. Until then, I'm going to my meeting, and I'll see you at your seminar. No"—Crystal raised her hand—"not every decision I make is about you. I have a job to do too. And part of that job is partnering with programs like the WRO. So, until then, goodbye."

And with that, Crystal walked away, leaving Sonja to escape to her office and lick her wounds.

Sonja booted up her computer and opened her presentation, determined to highlight her abilities at the upcoming seminar and humble a certain junior professor. But the endless loop of imagined retorts and rebuttals to Crystal's assessment made it impossible to concentrate.

Girlie's showing off for her new friend. What happens when she realizes you're nothing but white trash?

Sonja brought up a new blank slide and stared at it stupidly. That was when the knocking saved her. She got up and cracked the door open.

"Dr. Storey, if you have a bit," said Harmony. With her skinny arms crossed over nonexistent breasts and a gray floral cardigan buttoned up to a creased neck, with her gray roots and crow's-feet, Harmony looked like a starving pigeon.

"I do not have *a bit*." Sonja moved to shut the door, but Harmony blocked it with a scuffed loafer.

"I must insist on talking with you, Dr. Storey."

"Well, come in, if you *insist*."

Harmony slipped through the narrow opening, then pulled the door out of Sonja's grip and shut it. "I'm going to sit. I wish you'd sit too, instead of hovering over me."

"Aren't you bold. In my office too," Sonja said but moved to her desk and sat down.

"Jay says I owe you an apology."

"Yes," Sonja replied.

"I don't quite agree."

"Interesting." Sonja crossed her legs and leaned back.

"What I *am* willing to admit to is that I'm not always polite to you."

"And?"

"And that I do favors for other faculty but not for you."

"And?"

"Well, Dr. Storey, you're a smart woman."

"Woman? Interesting that you feel a need to qualify that compliment."

"Won't be picking a fight with you. I'm here admitting that you're not imagining the bad blood between us."

"I know."

"The thing is, Dr. Storey, I'm not your secretary, but you act like I am. I'm Jay's. I've been known to do kindnesses here and there, especially for Dr. Waters."

"Your point?" Sonja felt her body tightening.

"Dr. Waters is kind. He asks me for an occasional favor. But you bark orders and expect folks to jump."

"What a curious apology." Sonja grinned slightly in an attempt to disguise the twitching in her eye.

"Maybe I've treated you differently because you're a woman. I don't know. I'll be giving that some thought. I've been asked to. I'd like to ask something of you, though. I'd like you to think on how you've treated me. Dr. Waters remembers my birthday, asks about my family. He and Ruthie even came to the hospital when Dev was bad off."

Sonja had no idea who Dev was, or Ruthie, for that matter, but she refused to ask. "I didn't realize that you required special rewards for doing your job."

"That right there. You're always going on about the way people treat you because you're a woman. How about the way you treat the women you work with?"

"With whom you work. You dangled the preposition."

Harmony's eyes hardened, but she smiled. "Bless your heart for correcting me, Dr. Storey." She stood up and moved to the door. "I'll be doing some thinking about how I treat you. I hope you'll do the same. But you should know: I don't tolerate being treated poorly. That applies to my student workers too."

"Anything else?" Sonja asked calmly, though underneath, she simmered.

Harmony continued. "I'll ask the staff to keep eyes open for anyone acting strange. If you have any other requests, come directly to me. I'll hand out assignments, make sure they get done right." She turned and walked out, shutting the door behind her.

Sonja spun around and stared out the window at the cloudless sky. Her internal grousing was interrupted by the familiar ping of an email notification. It was from the university counsel's secretary.

Dr. Storey:

Jodi Jenkins needs to speak with you immediately. Please call me and I will put you through.

Sincerely,
Rose Herrin, Executive Aide

Office of University Counsel

It was official: Sonja's day had been hijacked.

"Dr. Storey. Thanks for calling. I need to apprise you of a situation."

"Go ahead, Jodi."

"Before I do, though, I want to assure you that we're on it. It seems your name has surfaced on at least one social media site. There are posts. About you. And they're unflattering."

Sonja took a deep breath before announcing, "I will examine them myself."

"Dr. Storey, if I were in your shoes, I'd want—"

"Stop managing me."

The university attorney continued. "Here's what I will do. I'll copy and paste them into an email." The attorney paused, then added, "Before I do, though, I need assurances that you will not respond."

"I want the link too."

"I won't send the link. And your assurance...I need it."

"Fine. I will not reply to the posts."

Sonja could hear typing on the other end, and a minute later, she received an email notification.

The assistant counsel continued. "Dr. Storey, we're looking into the matter. If these posts are related to the inquiry committee—"

"Let me read."

WSHU hires cuunts. Like Dr. Sonya Storry.

Dr. Sonya Story neds a good fuck Cheek her out on WSU.eud. But whod put a dick in her. Mabe me. If here face got smash in she coldnt talk.

"The bastard fails to spell my name correctly even once."

"The bastard has trouble spelling, period," Jodi replied.

"Are there more?"

"We don't know yet. But rest assured, the university will not stand for this."

"This university has stood for much worse."

"I understand your anger."

"I have asked you not to manage me. I'm no idiot. You and your office are concerned because this is bad PR for WHSU. Have other inquiry members been mentioned in these posts?"

"We're looking into that."

"I will take that as a no. I must go." Sonja hung up and left the office.

When she got home, she found that a waiting package did little to ease her agitation.

Sonja sat in the corner chair of her living room with her second glass of wine and watched day fade into night. When she looked down, she saw her phone in her hand. *Call Crystal, girlie.*

"Idiot," she scolded herself. "You have forgotten how charming Avery was in the beginning."

She turned off her phone and put it on the coffee table, but something tugged at her gut, as if she had tried and failed to cut the invisible cord connecting her to the other woman.

"Do you even like her? Or is she a sidekick, like she said?"

She finished her wine and set the empty glass beside the phone. She gazed at Star Dancer across the room, feeling the glittering galaxies waiting for her.

Go to bed so you are productive tomorrow.

She washed up, brushed her teeth, and took a muscle relaxer, then stared at her image in the mirror, looking for comfort in the scarlet Julianna Rae silk gown. She traced the black lace feathering at the top of the bodice and recalled the slumber party where she had worn a pair of cheap red PJs that she had to beg her mother to buy. The girls had mocked her.

"Those bitches would not make fun of you now."

She had begun the day painting her lips in red in anticipation of her victory over Jay. She would end the day wearing proof of her victory over her tormentors, even though the gown was too warm. She went to bed, but even fantasizing about the now pathetic lives of the popular girls back in high school brought her no joy.

Chapter 13

A Naked Hulk

SONJA MARKED ATTENDANCE ON THE seating chart. When she arrived at Corey Randalls, she noted him slumped in his back-row seat. She scanned his face, looking for any resemblance to Jacob, but he was too far away.

She launched into her lecture.

"Review your reading on chaos theory, including the four interacting elements: bifurcation, fractals, attractors, and self-organization. Recall that bifurcation involves a disruption of order, producing seismic changes, such as when a crisis compels organizational leaders to construct a recovery plan when they do not yet fully understand the broader catastrophe, including causal factors."

Sonja abandoned her distant lecture style in favor of stalking back and forth close to the front row. Several times, she stared at Randalls slumped in his seat like a pile of rumpled clothes. He leaned his head on his left hand and occasionally jotted something in his notepad. He never looked at her. Sonja suspected he had not listened to the lecture at all.

"Thursday, we will look at how chaos theory helps us analyze, even rethink organizational responses to crisis. Consider the authors' core argument in the reading: effective communication is essential to mitigating the damage done by catastrophes, both human-made and natural.

"Two reminders. First, the midterm exam is coming up. Second, your paper on organizational analysis is due in November. Historically, students who procrastinate on that assignment do not fare well in this class.

"Class dismissed. Mr. Randalls, I will speak with you before you leave."

Sonja watched for his reaction, but Ronnie Staller rushed up and blocked her view.

"Dr. Storey. I'm freakin' out—"

"Office hours." Sonja tried to keep her voice even, despite feeling as if the barometric pressure in the room had shifted, compressing her skull. "Another matter requires my attention. Goodbye," she said tersely as she shifted to one side of Staller.

She glued her eyes on Randalls, studying him as he stuffed his notebook into a battered black and blue backpack, his expression hidden behind a curtain of unwashed hair. When he finally stood up, he dragged toward the exit. "Mr. Randalls," Sonja called out, "I need to see you."

Randalls turned around and approached without enthusiasm, backpack slung over one shoulder. At last Sonja stood facing him, a student who looked like he could strangle her and walk away without a care.

Black hair. Black eyes. Bone skin. Sonja's story begins again.

The mantra that she had written in her journal after her father had traded up for another family popped into her head as Randalls stood before her, disdain wafting off him like steam from sewage.

She studied the unkempt young man before her, noting his wrinkled shirt and torn jeans. She recalled herself as a teen dressed in mismatched sweatpants and sweatshirt, hunkered over her notebook, authoring a new tale for herself.

The Storey Story, Sonja had called it, and with it, she'd remade herself.

By all appearances, Corey Randalls had made nothing of himself.

"Mr. Randalls, you were not in class last Thursday." Sonja examined his face but saw no resemblance to Jacob.

"Yeah." He looked around the room, and when he finally looked at her, he stared at her like she was a naked hulk, something wrecked, useless.

She bristled, struggling to keep control. "Students are expected to attend class." *This must be the bastard playing a sick game with me.* His body language emitted antipathy. Antipathy for her.

Are you sure he's the one? Or are you cherry-picking evidence to support your paranoia?

"I get two absences," he said, hitching up his backpack.

"Correction. You are permitted two unexcused absences. You are expected to show up, as you would at your place of employment."

"You're my teacher, not my boss," he sneered. "You don't pay me. But I pay you by coming here. That pretty much makes me your boss," he said, then muttered, "Cut me some fucking slack."

Sonja felt the blood rush to her face.

"Mr. Randalls, once again, you are mistaken. You don't pay my salary. That is a statement uttered by the ignorant. However," she said, taking a deep breath, "that is not the issue at hand. If you do not attend class, you risk consequences."

"You can't do shit." He reached up to pluck dead skin off his flaking lips.

Sonja felt her nostrils flare and her brain pump out neurotransmitters, releasing a wave of white-hot energy through her body. She wanted to level him.

"Look up the WHSU student code of conduct," she said. She felt her eye twitch. "And be aware that I am more than capable of dumping...a load...of shit on you, Randalls."

A sense of power surged through her—until she saw his response.

She froze.

Randalls's face turned bright red, and his pupils dilated. "Are you threatening me?" he hissed like a young man on the verge of transforming into a monster.

She walked over to her tote to distance herself from him and give herself time to cool down. Then she spoke from behind her authoritative exterior. "Certainly not, Mr. Randalls." She held her tote in the crook of her arm, resisting the desire to clutch it to her chest like a shield. "I am reminding you of our course contract, the one you signed. Now, on to another matter. Jacob Darrow Randalls—are you related?"

Corey straightened to his full height, towering above her, his chest puffed up and his hands clenched. And that's when Sonja realized that she had put herself into a dangerous situation.

To her surprise, he turned and stomped away, mumbling under his breath.

She crushed her tote against her chest, digging her fingernails into the leather. Furious, she called after him. "We're not done here. If you have something to add to this conversation, come back and face me."

He turned around. "'They're right,' is what I said. You're a nasty cunt."

The words slammed into her as if he had struck her, and she stumbled back. Recovering herself quickly, she yelled, "Don't come back to my class. You are done."

"No, you're done, bitch." And he slammed out of the classroom.

Chapter 14

Stars Rush Out

SONJA SHUFFLED BACK TO HER office and slumped in her chair, her dark hair covering her face, a mourning veil. Closing her eyes, she lost herself in the blackness.

Stars rush out.

The words sprang to mind, though she couldn't recall where she had heard them. They sounded familiar, like the remnants of a recurring dream or something she read long ago. It was how she felt: as if all the stars had fallen from the sky, leaving her in a bleak, lifeless universe.

She needed to pull herself out of this funk long enough to report the incident to Student Affairs. She couldn't move, though. She gave over to catatonia—like the first time that Avery had bitten her. Like when her student had knocked her to the floor and stood over her. Like the time with Mitch in her basement office.

Stop this nonsense. This is how Mother would act. Do something. File an incident report. Timestamp the verbal assault.

"Corey Randalls is scum," she said out loud. "I have survived worse enemies. Move forward."

That's what your half-sister would do. Of course, Dr. Ashley Storey would never have provoked such antipathy. Search for her right now. See why she got loved while you got left.

Sonja locked her gaze numbly onto the digital hand hovering over the *Report a Concern* button on the Student Affairs webpage.

A knock on her door summoned her back to reality.

"Dr. Storey? Are you in there? It's Harmony." More knocking. "I heard a strange noise. I'm coming in." Harmony opened the door without waiting for permission. "Are you all right? I thought I heard lowing."

Sonja rolled her head and stared blankly at the secretary standing in the doorway.

"Sounded like one of my parents' distressed cows in here. You're not looking so good, Dr. Storey."

"A student called me a cunt. To my face." Sonja laughed, then hiccupped, then laughed again, and she realized she couldn't stop.

The next thing she knew, Jay and Harmony were both hovering over her.

"Sonja, tell me what happened," Jay said.

Sonja pulled herself together and relayed the conversation, again omitting any reference to Jacob. Despite the previous hysterics, she managed not to cry. A lifetime spent detaching during crises had its benefits: her emotions drained into an internal reservoir, leaving her dazed and dry-eyed.

"Harmony, get Student Affairs on the line. If Dean Lu isn't available, then the associate dean, whoever. I don't care. I want to talk to someone now."

"Yes, sir," Harmony said and hustled out, closing the door behind her.

"We won't stand for this, Sonja."

Sonja bent over in her chair and pressed her chest against her thighs. She stared at her metallic-studded gray suede Prada pumps, but all she saw were glittering stars trying to shine in a sooty sky. Her designer armor had failed to intimidate her opponent today, and she felt dethroned. "I've been fighting so long," she whispered, as much to her heels as to Jay. "I don't know how to stop." She sat up abruptly. "Why support me now, Jay?"

He paused, then said, "I'm seeing the old days in new ways. The guys, for instance. They were pretty rough on you."

"Were the guys *pretty* rough?" Sonja snorted.

"I didn't go up against them. You're right on that account."

"You were a coward. Lewis too. He dodders around now, a sweet old man, but he was so treacherous back then."

"I behaved cowardly. I accept that. But Lewis, he's another matter. That's a discussion for later. Right now, I'm here. This department won't stand for you being treated like this. That student will—"

"What? Corey Randalls will be suspended? Expelled? This university needs students with pulses and payments. You've said that yourself in department meetings. 'More than ever, we need butts in seats. Do what it takes to keep them there.' Those are your words, Jay."

"Sounds like something I said." He shrugged and smiled feebly. "At least Corey Randalls's butt won't be in a seat in your class."

Someone knocked softly on the door. "Jay, I have Dean Lu holding for you."

"Sonja, I know you're capable of fighting your own fights," Jay said, "but let me do this. I want to do this."

"Whatever. I have to prepare for my afternoon class."

Jay and Harmony left. Sonja closed the door behind them and sat in the quiet of her office, lost in a void that reminded her that she was nothing and had never been anything. Like her mother had told her.

Sonja made it through her second lecture of the day as if she hadn't been traumatized, mainly because she had all her lectures memorized. She kept her voice steady, her posture erect. She only stumbled once. "Next class, we will discuss, uh, strategies"—she paused awkwardly—"uh, best practices for de-escalating conflicts." She almost choked on the words.

Tell 'em, little girl. Tell 'em how to stop a conflict from getting big and messy.

She told herself: only someone highly trained in behavioral cues would have noticed how often she glanced at the closed door or how she contorted her body to see who might come in to bash her *ugly bitch* face in, like had been promised to her many times.

After class, a few students approached to ask about the upcoming exam. She barely heard what they said and simply referred them to the syllabus, alert for any sudden movement.

Maybe it will be today. Will it be a gun? A knife? Maybe I'll be bludgeoned to death while everyone looks on.

She walked back to her building, barely noticing the buckling sidewalks. The conversation she had planned to have with President Knowles had receded into the back of her mind, and she wondered if she would ever care about WHSU's backwater appearance again.

As she entered Terrell Center, she no longer cared about the AC, and the lesions, blemishes, and scars seemed to have disappeared. She walked by the main office, stopping when Harmony stepped out to meet her.

"Dr. Storey, may I walk with you?"

"I have office hours soon," Sonja replied, her voice flat.

"I won't keep you." Harmony followed Sonja into her office. "May I?" she asked, gesturing to the door before shutting it. "Jay had to step out. He's wanting you to know that Student Affairs is handling Corey Randalls."

"That's it?" Sonja asked, her hands clasped in front of her to control their trembling.

"For now, Dr. Storey."

"None of it matters. Not a goddamn bit of it. If a student even hints at a lawsuit, Dean Lu will cave. Randalls's hand will get slapped. Asses in seats. Asses in seats."

"Jay pulled this kid's records."

"Corey Randalls is a man, not a kid. An angry one too. That's part of the problem. We talk about these students as if they were children. We coddle them, even when they do unspeakable things." She shook her head, and a clump of hair fell over her twitching eye. "What Randalls did is far from the worst assault against me." Through her fog, Sonja couldn't be sure if she spoke the words aloud.

Mortified, she waited for the fallout, the interrogation, the accusations, as she had gotten time and again. What had she done to bring on his behavior? While the poorly behaved men at the university got awards and accolades, she had gotten much different.

Instead, Harmony said, "It's probably cold comfort, but Jay talked to Officer Sounder. They're looking into if Randalls messed up in other classes."

"Fine."

"I'll be going unless you need something else. Do you?"

"Actually, Harmony, there is something," Sonja looked at the secretary's face and found deeply entrenched worry. She straightened, trying to regain some semblance of her authority. "Ronnie Staller is coming to see me this afternoon. Our meetings have become...unproductive."

"I'd be glad to come fetch you, if that would help."

"It would."

"Email me when you're ready. I'll be keeping an eye out."

"Thank you." She could barely squeeze the words out of her tight throat.

Harmony smiled faintly, but her eyes blinked nervously. "You're welcome."

"Dr. Storey, I'm sorry to interrupt your meeting."

"Yes, Harmony?" Sonja looked up at the secretary standing in her doorway.

"There's an urgent matter needing your attention."

"Thank you, Harmony." Sonja turned to her visitor. "Ms. Staller, no further discussion is warranted. We have reviewed your resources. You will contact Support Services and request tutoring to prepare for the upcoming exam. You will finalize your organizational analysis paper at least a week prior to the due date and have it assessed by Support Services staff. Finally, you will make an appointment with Student Health Services and look for ways to manage your test anxiety."

"But what about our misunderstanding?" Staller whined. "You reported me to the Student Affairs people. They said you told them I scared you. People don't get me right. You're not getting me right. It's like that fractals stuff and patterns. You're—"

Harmony broke in. "Dr. Storey, sorry to press. We must get going."

"Ms. Staller, after you." Sonja stood by her office door and waited for the student to leave.

Staller slammed a shoulder into Harmony as she stomped out.

"Excuse me, young lady," Harmony rebuked, but Staller did not reply.

Harmony looked at Sonja. "I'm starting to see what you mean about that student."

Sonja shook her head. "I will speak with her about running into you."

"Maybe let it drop. Your plate's full," Harmony said as Sonja closed her door. "By the way, I wasn't pretending. Jay's really asking for you."

As soon as Sonja entered the chair's office, Jay stood up and announced, "Good news. It looks like Corey Randalls will be withdrawing. Apparently, he's had a rocky start this semester."

"Thank you," Sonja responded, her voice flat.

"I thought you'd be relieved." Jay looked at her with a puzzled expression.

Sonja longed to tell him about her secret terror. With Corey Randalls banished from campus, she couldn't monitor him. And she wanted to tell Jay other things too. Like how certain men were capable of horrific things when no one was watching. About how nights were getting harder, that inner storms kept building up and whipping at her, and she no longer had shelter.

Maybe she had never had shelter.

Maybe she had only deluded herself with designer clothes, a luxury car, expensive furnishings, academic degrees, and a stout security door.

Maybe the carcass in her driveway was a signal she had never pulled herself out of the storm and never would.

Instead, she repeated, "Thank you."

"Happy to have helped." Jay smiled, and to Sonja it looked like a bright sunbeam on cold, dark waters.

But as soon as Sonja left his office, the chill set back in.

Chapter 15

Comes the Dark

A HEAVY THUD STARTLED SONJA awake in the middle of the night, and she bolted upright in bed. Loopy from the muscle relaxer and still half-asleep, she strained to listen, her inner rabbit kicking at the walls of a warren made of flesh, muscle, and bone.

Not hearing anything else, she stumbled out of bed and bumped into the nightstand, knocking over the empty wineglass she had left there. She reached out her hand to stop it rolling off the table.

She crept into the living room and walked smack into the coffee table. She grabbed her leg, biting down on the swear words before they shot from her mouth, and she scanned the dim space. Everywhere she looked, she saw sinister shadows pulsating, shifting.

She looked at her deck door, the drapes carelessly left open. Outside, blackness snaked across the yellow streams cast by the streetlight. Spellbound, she watched a dark shape press against the glass, the serpentine arms coiling and uncoiling. When it turned its head toward her, she screamed and fled into her bedroom, locking her door. She fumbled for her cell phone on the nightstand and when she found it, punched in 9-1-1, then waited to hear the shatter of glass from her living room.

"Ma'am, have you been drinking?" the heavyset, balding officer asked, his eyes on the empty bottle of wine on her coffee table.

"I'm not some drunk." She ran a hand through her hair to smooth it, hoping it wasn't as untidy as it felt.

"How about medications? Some prescriptions can't be mixed with—"

"I am neither drunk nor high, officer," Sonja said tersely, refusing to disclose the muscle relaxer she had taken before she went to sleep.

I am not Mothernotmothernot.

A second officer entered from the deck. His face was smooth, hairless. He looked to be about the same age as her students.

"Ma'am," he said, vexing her with his high-pitched voice, "I'm not sure how someone could access your deck. They'd need an extension ladder, and that'd be tricky, the way the backyard slopes. I don't see anything that suggests an intruder climbed up here."

"You don't believe me," Sonja stated.

She watched the older officer glance again at the empty wine bottle. "We're not saying that, ma'am."

"I am Dr. Storey, not ma'am." She immediately regretted having corrected him. Now he would view her as an argumentative lush. Or worse, a snotty bitch. Experience had taught her that angry men got shit done, but angry women got shit on.

"Officer Richards searched the premises, Dr. Storey."

"I didn't find anything outside," Boy-Cop said. "I'd be glad to take another look around your house, though. You have a lot of trees down the hill. Could've been a barn owl. My mamaw got attacked by one once when she was on her back porch at dusk. Beat her up pretty good. Frightened her awful. Or maybe the streetlight threw a strange shadow. I could see how you would be startled if you were deep asleep—"

"No." She no longer cared if they believed her. She wanted them gone. They weren't going to do a damn thing for her.

By the time they left, it was after two. She had planned to get up at four and go into the office to review and revise her presentation one last time before the noon seminar. She knew she would be unable to go back to sleep, so she showered and pulled on her cherry-hued Tory Birch shift, hoping that the bold floral patterns would distract from the bags under her eyes. She slipped into black Louis Vuitton heels with gold tone buttons on the ankle straps. Maybe they would work their magic and make her feel majestic.

"Let's collect some heads," she said, but her voice shrank in the empty house.

———————

Sonja blinked in the small room and looked around, trying to get her bearings. She wasn't sure how she had come to be standing in front of the four women in the windowless conference room. Her eyes felt as swollen as engorged ticks, and she blinked again, trying to vanquish her bone-deep fatigue.

She wanted to ask what she had been saying, but the whispering ash-blonde woman distracted her.

"Stop that whispering," Sonja barked, then wondered if she had spoken aloud.

The women's stunned reaction told her she had.

"It's... You're distracting me." Sonja heard the edge in her voice, though she had meant to soften it.

"Sorry for distracting you, ma'am," Ashy Blonde said. "I was saying to Rita here that I think I was in a relationship with a narcissist. He was my boss at my previous job." She giggled nervously. "It's just like what you were describing. You know, they're real sweet at first, like that love bombing you mentioned. Maybe I was stupid for trusting him."

Sonja tried to focus on Ashy Blonde through the bluish light, but she faded in and out, occasionally flashing back to her late-night encounter with the police. When she was able to refocus, she saw the woman crumpling.

"It crushed me." Ashy Blonde sniffled. "That's why I had to leave. I couldn't stay after that."

"Your whining does not help. It only puts a target on you."

"Sonja," Crystal growled a warning.

Sonja tried to explain away her harsh tone. "Narcissists do not respond to whining. They lack the capacity for empathy. That is all I meant. Their prefrontal lobes are...are..." Stumbling over her words, Sonja tried to figure out how to save her presentation and how to get Crystal to stop looking at her like that. "Come from a position of strength," she continued. "That is how you win."

"I'm not sure we're looking to win in loving relationships, Sonja," Crystal argued. "I think we're looking for authentic connection. Love isn't a battlefield." She chuckled. "Hey, wasn't that a song? You're making me leave, wanting me to stay, something, something, something," Crystal warbled, eliciting uneasy laughter from the tiny audience.

Sonja flitted her attention between Crystal and Ashy Blonde, finally focusing on the latter. Again, Ashy Blonde whispered to Rita-Regina-Ryleigh-Whatever. "If you're going to whimper," she heard herself say, but the rest of the words seeped out of her memory.

The women looked at her in stunned silence as someone flipped on the fluorescent lights. Sonja snatched her bag and raced out of the conference room into the corridor.

"Sonja, wait!"

Winged with fury, fatigue, and embarrassment, Sonja flew down the corridor, but Crystal easily caught up and latched onto her elbow.

"Let's walk and talk," Crystal said, escorting Sonja to the stairwell. "What the hell went on in there?"

Sonja watched the scene as if she floated above. "This place sucks you dry. You will learn that. You're too young, naïve—" She gulped air, trying to catch her breath.

"More condescending shit. If you're going to belittle me, Sonja, get new material," Crystal said. "I have survived a lot of viciousness. You would know that—*if* you ever got outside yourself. But you're so wrapped up in your own pain—"

"Enough," Sonja said in a weak voice, like calling for help through a winter wind. She wanted to pull her arm from Crystal's grasp, but something inside warned that she must never allow this woman to let go.

Crystal pulled in closer, dropping her voice. "You insulted those women in there."

"All four of them. Even Lynne Harrison skipped her own seminar series."

"I'm sure Lynne had a good reason. She's insanely busy laying the groundwork for my department's program audit before she retires. And who cares if there were only four attendees? We all took time out of our schedules to learn about workplace toxicity. And oh boy, did we learn. Damn, Sonja, I've never seen anything like what you did in there. It's like you were gunning for them, especially that young woman in the back."

I don't remember what I said to them. Everything's a blur! Sonja wanted to scream, but in her gut, she knew the seminar had bombed. No, it had exploded.

"You were brutal."

"I stand by what I said," Sonja lied, having no actual memory of what she had said.

"Really? And I quote, 'If you are going to be a bunch of whiners, then you deserve to be mistreated. Maybe being knocked around will wake you up.' Are you fucking serious? You wouldn't tolerate that from a male colleague."

"You're exaggerating." Sonja locked eyes with Crystal, trying to visually dominate this woman who was nearly sixteen years her junior. But she quickly looked away. "No wonder women get preyed on. They make the rest of us look weak."

"You said that too." Crystal released Sonja's arm and stepped away. "Fine, you've convinced me, Sonja. From the start, you tried to make me believe you weren't worth my time. You've been arrogant, self-absorbed... and you can be plain mean. I kept thinking if I dug deep enough, I'd find something amazing. Whew, I made a mistake...thinking you're anything like the women in my family. They know when and who to cut and slice. And they know when to stop. You don't." Crystal turned away and marched down the stairs.

Sonja slung her bag over her shoulder and followed. Once outside, she watched Crystal walk across campus, and she debated whether to try to catch up and explain.

Explain what? That you're becoming your mother? That your father left you, blocked you from exposing his new family to your taint?

Instead, Sonja headed in the direction of the parking lot. When she reached her car, she had no clue how she had gotten there.

After pulling into her garage, she climbed out of Bimmer and dragged herself upstairs without bothering to eat or even pour a glass of wine. She checked the deck door and reclosed the curtains, then went to her bedroom, closing the door, shades, and drapes, casting the room in the hue of cold, dead ash. She stripped off her clothes, pulled on her PJs, the satin dulled to phantom gray in the low light, and she fell into bed, burrowing under the covers.

At one stride comes the dark...one stride comes the dark...one stride...

The bubbling went on for a bit, but she couldn't figure out its origin or meaning. So she decided upon the words' insignificance, leaving them to be reabsorbed by her unconscious.

———————

She took roll in class the next morning, relieved to mark Corey Randalls absent. By the time she started her lecture, her confidence began trickling back. By the midpoint, she had recovered her stride and grew more certain that she was finally getting ahead of the chaos in her life.

"During Tuesday's class, we discussed chaos theory and strange attractors, the values and assumptions that draw people together to pursue shared goals. Attractors are *strange* because they may function in seemingly illogical ways during a crisis. You will need to master bifurcation, fractals, and attractors for the exam. Today, we will cover the fourth element—"

She heard the classroom door rattle, and she jumped, turning her head to watch the entrance, staring at the doorknob and waiting for Corey Randalls to burst in.

The murmuring of her students brought her back to the moment. She faked her way through the rest of the lecture, reading her slides verbatim, but inside, her stomach heaved. During her afternoon class, she caught herself glancing at the door and trailing off midsentence.

"Professor, you okay?" someone asked from the middle of the classroom.

"Raise your hand if you wish to speak," Sonja reprimanded.

After that, there were no further inquiries about her well-being, and by the end of class, she got her lecture back on track.

Back in her office, though, she relapsed into a fog. So when Harmony appeared in the doorway, she barely noticed.

"May I come in, Dr. Storey?" Harmony asked.

"Why?" Sonja shook her head subtly to shake off her stupor.

"I'm checking on you. Something, well, caught my eye when you passed by."

"What?"

"Your shoes," the secretary said, pointing. "You're wearing two different shoes."

Sonja looked down. One pump silver and the other navy, both Chanel.

"I dressed before dawn," Sonja protested. "Some of us arrive early to campus."

Harmony took in a breath. "It's only that, Dr. Storey—"

"Stop that. It's maddening."

"Stop what, Dr. Storey?"

"Saying 'Dr. Storey' after every utterance."

"But you've insisted that I address you that way."

"Well, I'm—it's infuriating. You may go."

"I don't think so, Dr. Storey." Harmony stepped into the office and closed the door. "We got a call. It seems that yesterday's seminar had a hiccup. Or fifty."

"What? Oh, that. Yes, my topic was too ambitious for the audience."

"I don't mean to embarrass you—"

"Then don't."

"May I sit?" Harmony asked.

"No."

Harmony sat anyway. "*Meltdown*'s what I heard. I won't say from who."

"'I won't say from whom.'"

"Whatever you say, Dr. Storey. It's just that people are concerned. You seem to be going through some sort of turmoil. We'd like to help."

"I do not need help. What I need is for people to do their jobs. Figure out who is terrorizing me. I mean attempting to terrorize me. It is rather an inconvenience. Nothing I cannot handle, of course. But I have important work to do."

"We turned the matter over to campus police, Dr. Storey. What I'm talking about is... Well, the way I heard it is you started, um, hollering, name-calling."

"I did no such thing. I am simply an emphatic speaker. Lay audiences tend to misinterpret."

Harmony squeezed her lips shut.

"What?" Sonja demanded. When Harmony didn't respond, Sonja picked up her keys. "I must go."

"Dr. Storey, please talk to someone. Our Employee Assistance Program is wonderful. We all go through hard times, and, well, being middle-aged can be tough on women. Things start surfacing."

"I am out of time."

Harmony rose and stood in front of the door, blocking Sonja's escape.

"Dev and me, we face a fair amount of poor treatment," the secretary said. "People don't always take kindly to those from different backgrounds marrying. Midlife, menopause...it made everything feel bigger too. All I'm saying, Dr. Storey, is I understand how painful life can get. That pain can drive a woman mad. Talking to someone pretty much saved my life. My marriage too."

Sonja cleared her throat. "You are in my way."

The secretary stepped aside, and Sonja pushed past, calling back, "Lock up behind you, Harmony."

She hurried to her car, intent on casting off her mismatched shoes before anyone else noticed. She stopped short. Sprawled on Bimmer's hood was a squirrel that appeared to be sunning itself. But its glassy eyes bulged out of its limp body, and a trickle of blood leaked from its mouth. It seemed to stare at her accusingly, as if she were the cause of its demise.

She feared that she may have been.

Chapter 16

Stars Dim

"MAYBE IT'S NOT—"

Jay and Harmony stood with Sonja at her car to view the evidence.

"Don't you fucking dare." Sonja set her jaw to keep back the molten rage that threatened to erupt.

Jay rubbed his forehead. "Sonja," he said, "I'm simply asking you to consider alternatives. Look overhead. There's a power line above your car. The squirrel could've fallen. It happens all the time."

"I wondered when he would show up," Sonja snapped, "and there he is, same old Jay. Tell me everything is in my head. Or perhaps advise me not to be so quick to react, to smile in the face of adversity. Your tyrannical positivity has always been about silencing me and upholding your authority."

Sonja opened the back door of her car and hurled her bag inside. The contents spilled out. She turned to glare at the secretary.

"How about you, Harmony? Do you think this is all in my head?"

"Dr. Storey, I hear you. Really, I do. It's just—"

"Stop." Suddenly, her fury hissed out of her like air from a balloon. "I know what you're doing. Both of you. You are trying to de-escalate conflict. I teach those techniques, remember?"

"Sonja, come inside. We'll call Officer Sounder."

Instead, Sonja got into her car and drove away. The squirrel stared glassily at her through the windshield, the blood that had oozed from its mouth gluing its fur to the hood. She imagined other motorists on the road watching the strange carpool, judging her as insane.

At home, she retrieved her mail and parked in the driveway. Then, pinching the bushy tail with her fingernails, she peeled off the carcass. She could almost hear the percussive removal of desiccated tissue from its metal base over the idling engine.

She hurled the dead creature across Summit Street and watched it disappear into the brush of the vacant lot. She envisioned the squirrel piled up next to the previous driveway creature, and it gave her a weird comfort that the two bodies were no longer alone.

Then she wailed, a low, primeval call that pierced her quiet neighborhood. Her fury expelled for the moment, she looked around for witnesses, relieved to find none.

———————————————

After another glass of pinot, Sonja dialed Crystal, but deleted the numbers before she could connect.

Isn't that cute? Girlie's memorized her phone number.

To avoid any future wine-related mishaps, Sonja tucked her phone into the drawer of the nightstand and closed the bedroom door. She went into her office and booted up her laptop, keeping her fingers glued to the keyboard as if they might act on their own.

Go ahead. Type Ashley's name into the search bar, a sadistic voice encouraged her. *Maybe you'll find another photo. Lovable sis beside Dr. Claude Storey, proud papa beaming over his daughter's accomplishments as if she's his one and only child.*

"No more searching Ashley," she chastised herself. "You know what you will find. Additional research would not be productive."

Instead, Sonja searched for social media posts about herself, overriding Jodi Jenkins's counsel. Creating a handle that reflected her mood, she registered as *DrBitch_Prof* and entered the internet rabbit hole. But after she figured out how to search the various platforms, she encountered another problem: the person posting about her had spelled her name inconsistently. Using variations of her first and last names, she finally uncovered two posts from *KalmeeJusteec27068*.

WSHU's "Dr" Sonya Story blames men for her failurez. Shed ate us if she culd

And:

Menhatter Sanya Storrys has it cumming to ehr.

It took her over an hour to uncover those two posts, sending her deeper into her funk. Even turning on her sculpted lamp that glowed like an art installation did nothing to dispel the grayness of her mood.

"Did you have the posts removed, Jodi?" she asked aloud. She resolved to call the assistant counsel the next morning to demand an answer.

Abandoning her search for social media posts, she began searching for a new winter coat and soon found herself in the world of Fleurette jackets, all expensive, all deliciously tantalizing.

Her browsing was interrupted by muffled thumping that sounded like a bass drum. It stopped, then restarted, getting gradually louder until Sonja had to face the fact that someone was knocking on her door.

She stood up, caught between hope and anxiety, and hurried into the living room. Peeking through a corner of the window covering, she saw a pink spandex jacket resting on a round and familiar bottom. Her heart somersaulted, yet she opened the door as if she had been expecting company all along.

In her right hand, Crystal held a bottle of wine. She raised her left hand and held up her index finger. "One. That's the number of chances I'm giving you tonight. You are rude, I go. I can't speak for her," she said, nodding toward the road.

Sonja's heart dropped when she saw two cars in front of her home and the pixie blonde trotting up the sidewalk.

"Me and Dr. Byrd are getting on friendly terms," Harmony confessed on arrival.

Sonja addressed Crystal as if Harmony had not spoken. "You were the one who ratted me out about that seminar."

"Be careful with how you talk to me," Crystal cautioned. "Yes, I am the rat. But Harm's the reason I'm here. She twisted my arm."

"We both care," Harmony said.

"Darling, it's intervention time." Crystal's gaze was relentless. "Let us in and hear us out, or we leave you to your solitude. Your choice."

"Fine." Sonja opened the door to let the women in, realizing that it was the greatest number of guests she had ever had in her home, if she didn't count the police officers the other night. And she did not.

———————————

Sonja stood in the center of the living room, trying to explain herself as the two women sitting at opposite ends of the couch scrutinized her. She pulled her cashmere kimono sweater tighter around herself.

"You're borderline ranting," Crystal said when Sonja finally took a breath.

Sonja couldn't quite recollect what she had been saying. She had intended to give a compelling defense of her seminar performance, but apparently, she had vomited up words like an ugly hairball.

"I think I'm getting the picture about what happened at the seminar," Harmony said, fiddling nervously with the top button of her cardigan. "'A yellow jacket stung her pooper.' That's what Mamaw use to say. And I venture that's what Mamaw'd say right now, Dr. Storey."

They look at you the way you looked at Mother when she bulldozed over you with her words.

"I frighten you," Sonja told the secretary.

Harmony licked her lips and rubbed her palms against her slacks. "You've got me real worried. That's why I wanted us to check on you."

Sonja pounced. "You have never liked me."

Harmony looked genuinely surprised. "Were you wanting me to? You never acted like it, Dr. Storey."

"Jesus, Harm," Crystal said. "Here you are, giving up your night for this woman, and you've known her how long? At least call her Sonja."

Sonja glared at Crystal. "That is my PhD you are erasing, Dr. Byrd."

Crystal leaned back and threw her arm over the back of the couch. "You're something else, Sonja. I worked my ass off for my doctorate too, and you don't see me acting like that. Do you have any idea how hard Harmony works? Hell, do you know anything about her? Like how she survived at WHSU without a fancy title or big salary?"

"I know exactly how she survived. By pandering to men."

"Apologize," Crystal ordered. "This woman has been nothing but caring since I first called her trying to track you down after I met you in the bathroom. And she's turning into a pretty good friend. So, yes, I called her after your seminar."

"But I was the one who called Crystal today," Harm added.

"You two gossip about me behind my back."

Just like high school, girlie.

Crystal stood up. "Okay, Harm, this isn't going to work. She's more interested in control than support. We're out of here."

The secretary scooched across the couch and reached up to touch Crystal's arm. "A bit longer, Dr. Byrd." Harmony nodded toward Sonja. "We've got lots of history. That history's not getting undone overnight."

Crystal looked down at Harmony. "It's Crystal. You keep calling me 'Dr. Byrd.' I want you to call me by my first name. I want friends here. Genuine friends. Not sidekicks," Crystal said, glancing at Sonja to emphasize her last comment.

"Okay, fine," Harmony replied. "I'm just saying Dr. Storey isn't wrong. I survived in that department by wearing a groove in my tongue from biting it—hard. Had to blind myself too. Back then, standing up to faculty—male faculty—that would've gotten me fired." She looked at Sonja. "You're right, Dr. Storey. Those men ganged up on you. They bullied you. They talked down to you. They ignored you."

"If only they had ignored me more." Sonja shuddered, surprised by her admission.

Harmony dropped her head. "I overheard a lot in our department. I sat right there listening to how they talked about you, convinced myself you were to blame."

"Because I'm a nasty bitch?" Sonja ventured. "You were the one who taught the student workers to treat me like some entitled cunt."

"Not on purpose." Harmony said softly, looking at Sonja.

"How about the touching? Did you know I was groped? Or did you know about the time Cole lifted me off the ground? He spun me around like I was a goddamn child, exposing my backside to everyone."

"Drs. Grant and Behringer never groped you in front of me...that I recall. And Jay just told me what Dr. Grant did to you when you fetched your mail. I swear I had no idea." Harmony shrank back against the couch. "But the day that Dr. Behringer lifted you, I do remember that. I told myself he was doing a bit of teasing. I...I truly don't know anymore. Looking back is like trying to make sense of the wreckage after a tornado. I don't know what's what or where anything goes."

"Still protecting them," Sonja accused, but she sounded angrier than she felt. Between the wine, the insomnia, and the stress, she was worn down, but she struggled to remain in control in front of the secretary. In front of Crystal too. Especially in front of Crystal.

"You're right. I overlooked a lot. Until that time I walked in and found the student worker crying right after Dr. Behringer left the office. Never did get the truth out of her."

"Is that when you started hiring only male office workers?" Sonja asked, not waiting for an answer. "Yet you didn't do a goddamn thing to help me."

"Did you ever think to check on me, Dr. Storey? There were so few women in the department."

"Haven't you ever been curious how Harm navigated the institutionalized misogyny?" Crystal asked. "You had a PhD and your own office. She had to share her space. And by the sounds of it, those men freely wielded their power."

Sonja spun on Crystal, ready to spew about everything Mitch had done to her in private, but Harmony cut her off.

"It's okay. Let it be." Harmony brushed Crystal's hand, and Crystal smiled at her.

Theirs were gestures of easy familiarity, like a foreign language that Sonja could translate without truly understanding, and she was suddenly overcome with a fierce desire to deeply know that language.

Girlie's jealous. Weird. You used to like 'em blonde and freckled. This one looks a bit—

Sonja exhaled, the fight leaving her. "Everyone, drink your wine."

"You'll sit with us," Crystal stated rather than asked and sat back on the couch, reaching for her glass.

"As soon as I return." Sonja turned away and retreated to the master bathroom, intent on loosening the heavy armor that had weighed her down for so long. She stared at herself in the mirror.

She had once considered herself handsome with her sculpted cheekbones and bright eyes. These days, though, she looked haggard. Even her ebony trouser set and mink-colored kimono-sweater did nothing to raise her self-worth. She lifted her hair and found silver strands, each one a sign of her losing control over her own life.

She blotted her face with a damp washcloth, then rested it against her neck. As the coolness seeped into her, so did the truth: under the ice floe inside her was bottomless darkness.

Crystal and Harmony fell quiet as she reemerged into the living room.

"I have something to say," Sonja announced. "Listen. Please."

The wine is causing you to lose control. Did I teach you nothing about vulnerability, Pillows?

"I see what you are trying to do for me," Sonja admitted, "even when you have your own difficulties. Crystal, I doubt I will ever get to where you think I should be, and I don't know if I want to. I've been through too much. And I've seen cruelty inflicted on those around me. I am uninterested in making myself vulnerable to anyone." *Particularly you.*

"Sonja, your behavior…it's like some kind of PTSD," Crystal said. "Like you've survived trauma that you haven't faced yet."

"If you are looking for some *big* assault," Sonja replied, "you'll be disappointed. It's the everyday assaults that have lacerated me over time."

"The tiny, vicious cuts of misogyny," Crystal acknowledged.

"Perhaps." Sonja shrugged and sat in the corner chair. "There is one thing I haven't told anyone else yet. It's about the other night. I would like to start from the beginning to ensure that everyone has the same information. It may give you both perspective about my quote, unquote meltdown."

She began her tale about sinister sticky notes and a sloppy seminar, weaving in a thread about the intruder on her deck and the do-nothing police. Silently, though, she blamed exhaustion and the wine for her overwhelming need for witnesses to the recent chaos. By the time she was finished, the stars had dimmed in the overcast sky. But her mood had lightened, slightly.

Chapter 17

Fled to Bliss or Woe

HARMONY STOOD UP. "GOT TO get home to Dev. He'll have dinner on. But I'll be keeping my eyes open"—she paused—"Sonja. And next week, I'm going to have a sit-down with our student workers. There're going to be some changes in that office."

"Very well," Sonja replied offhandedly without getting up, then glanced at Crystal, who mouthed something. "Oh. My appreciation, Harmony." She got up to see her guest to the door.

"You have a beautiful home...Sonja. Very good taste."

"Thank you, again." Sonja pulled the door open. "Good night. See you Monday."

Harmony giggled. "Got it, got it. Third wheel." And with that, she walked to her car.

"That was a weak-ass thank you," Crystal said when Sonja returned to the living room.

Sonja shrugged, poured herself another glass of wine, and stood awkwardly.

Crystal's voice broke the silence. "Ask me to stay."

"You are welcome to stay," Sonja said, trying to sound casual, but to her own ears, she sounded anything but.

"Ask."

"Stay."

Crystal stood up and picked up her car keys. "I'll be on my way. I don't stay where I'm not wanted."

"My preference is that you stay," Sonja said. "Please."

"There's that poetic charm. Sappho reborn." Crystal sat back down on the couch. "Come sit with me." She patted the cushion next to her. "I want to tell you about my day, and I won't shout across the great expanse."

"No foolishness," Sonja cautioned, but inside, waves were radiating through her chest and down her arms, making her fingers and toes tingle. It had been years since her body had vibrated this way.

"I had a good meeting today." Crystal launched into detailing her day. "I wasn't looking to lead our program audit—sure as hell not with my teaching load. But how could I pass on the opportunity? Especially since I want to run the program one day. Oh, this rumor may interest you: supposedly, Lynne's retiring sooner than expected. From what I've seen, that's so like her." Crystal laughed. "Give the university the finger, leave the WRO directorship unoccupied and the audit team in the lurch. Can't be mad, though. Sometimes the most powerful thing a woman can do is quit on her terms. Don't let the bastards keep using you, even if it creates a leadership vacuum…"

Sonja sipped her wine, intent on following Crystal's monologue, but her mind kept floating away.

"Are you even listening to me?"

"What?" Sonja asked, realizing that Crystal was staring at her. "Of course," she said indignantly.

"You were not," Crystal countered. "You were back in Sonja's world."

"I *was listening*. Go on. The program. The audit," Sonja urged and gulped her wine, trying to be at ease.

At some point, Crystal started playing with Sonja's hair while continuing to talk, her fingers rolling up and unrolling in the locks, like aerial silk artists. Sonja usually did not tolerate anyone except her stylist touching her hair, but she didn't pull away. Clearly this woman had too much influence over her.

"You're gay." The slurred words seemed to pop out of Sonja's mouth on their own.

"Mm-hmm. Queer. Poly, more precisely, as if there's anything precise about us polys." She laughed, and it sounded like music that rippled across Sonja.

"And I'm a mean bitch," Sonja whined. "I don't mean to be a mean bitch."

"You? A mean bitch? No way," Crystal replied, her voice oozing sarcasm while her fingers played with a strand of hair near Sonja's cheek. "Your hair's interesting. The texture, color. I'm thinking you have some Persian, Italian, or Indigenous—"

"My mom could be one. Dewy sweet in public, a wrathful bitch when I was trapped in our shitty apartment with her. Loud, angry. That's how she covered her inadequacy. And I'm becoming her."

Shut up! You're drunk. Send this woman home.

Crystal rested her head on Sonja's shoulder. "I'm curious about your struggle. My last counselor said I'm addicted to people who struggle. Auntie Laura and I, we're both drawn to them the way some people are drawn to explore the Mariana Trench or observe the Helix Nebula." She moved her mouth closer to Sonja's, her breath like a summer breeze spiced with ripe plum and tart cherry.

"I think..." But Sonja lost her thought in the frothy sensations.

"By the way, it's okay."

"What is?"

"We all fear genetic determinism." Crystal cupped the back of Sonja's head, then paused, a swollen pause that heated Sonja like a sun.

"I'm not gay," Sonja whispered.

"No problem. I'm not looking for the Marina Trench or the Helix Nebula. Just an exploration of joy."

"You speak nonsense," Sonja muttered, then stopped, her mouth pulled along an invisible line to Crystal's lips. She followed it until she arrived, soft flesh opening, yielding. The feral animal in Sonja stirred, poised to claw, but then it lapsed into purring.

Languid kisses blended with languid caresses. Crystal sighed and whispered into Sonja's ear, "Have I fled to bliss or woe?"

"Those words, I know them," Sonja murmured.

"I'm sure you do. Weren't we all force-fed works by dead white males in high school?"

Sonja extricated her mouth from Crystal's and rolled her head against the back of the couch. "Source?"

"*Rime of the Ancient Mariner,* Samuel Taylor Coleridge."

"How could I forget? Was obsessed..." Sonja breathed out as her mind drifted into an iridescent abyss, like a ship under an endless glittering sky.

Crystal reached around Sonja's waist with one arm and sank lengthwise onto the couch, pulling Sonja down with her.

Lips brushed against Sonja's cheeks, followed by the soft tip of the nose traveling down her neck, sniffing, inhaling. Then it all stopped.

"Coleridge warned us," Crystal whispered. "One thoughtless cruelty... yields...so much...suffering."

Sonja found Crystal's lips again, no longer caring about the poem or anything else. She sank into the alien sensation of bliss. Behind her eyes swam luminescence, shimmering swarms that swooped from her crown to her toes then back up, exiting through her parted lips and disappearing into the balminess of Crystal's kiss.

You're drunk. But the warning was muffled as if submerged.

Pulling her mouth away, Sonja led Crystal into the bedroom's eddy of charcoal, indigo, and heather light and into a pool of satiny bedding.

Her mind wine-besotted, her body pleasure-drunk, Sonja sank into a softness she had never known. All that bound her was being peeled away, her nakedness buffeted by waves, some small and tender, some large and consuming. But Sonja came to with a jolt when Crystal cupped the breast that Avery had marked. Sonja wiggled out from under Crystal.

"What is it?" Crystal asked, moving to rest beside Sonja.

Moments ago, Sonja's muscle were sponges, swaying and twitching, moved by the waves of passion. But now they hardened, exposed to her scorching anger: Avery had left the bed long ago, but Sonja had never let him go.

"Talk to me. What do you need?"

"Control."

Sonja couldn't tell if she had said the word aloud. But she found that she was reaching for Crystal's wrist, pressing her thumbnail into the satin skin. Images from Avery's savagery flashed in her mind, and Sonja froze.

"I don't know. I'm drunk, lost. Tired," Sonja confessed.

"Let's sleep, then."

"No. He took everything, even my ability to rest." *My ability to feel pleasure.*

"Who?"

But instead of answering, Sonja moved toward Crystal, intent on taking back what had been taken from her. She kissed Crystal hard, a kiss that turned into a bite of a lip, of a neck. Then she dove downward to nip the cushion of Crystal's inner thighs, re-energized by the heady mix of salty moisture and freshly popped oysters in her nostrils.

"Stop," Crystal said, gently but firmly pushing Sonja's head away. "This aggression isn't working for me, darling."

Anger rose abruptly in Sonja, but it drifted away as Crystal stroked between her shoulder blades and down her spine. Sonja sat back on her haunches, still sandwiched between Crystal's legs. She hid her face. "I'm sorry," she choked out, her face heated by shame. "I don't want to hurt you, but I don't know what else to do."

Crystal reached out and hugged Sonja close. "Do you want me to guide you?"

Sonja buried her face into Crystal's neck and breathed in the scent of warm coconut and sea salt. "Yes."

"Lay back," Crystal said.

Sonja squeezed her eyes shut and let the powerful arms encircle her, then reach down to her thighs, gently spreading her, each kiss, each flicker of the tongue, pulling her deeper into silvery ecstasy, a place she had never gone before, a place she never wanted to leave.

Sonja was parted further, and she felt Crystal enter her darkness until she was carried away on a current, a smile like limp seaweed spreading across her face.

A finger of light coming through the window woke Sonja. She had neglected to draw the blinds and release the curtains. An image from last night's dreams flashed through her mind, making her wonder if she had dreamed about *Girl Diver and Octopi,* a woodblock print by Hokusai she had once seen. A voice punched through the image.

"I know that look." Crystal rolled onto one side to face her. "Just remember, gorgeous, we had a lovely time."

Sonja fought the urge to tunnel under the covers.

What did I say, Pillows? Cold bitch outside, tame bitch inside.

"Relax," Crystal said, throwing off the covers and exposing their nakedness.

Sonja grabbed the sheet and pulled it up tight around her neck. Her head was pounding, her stomach was doing flips, and her back was stiff.

"I run my mouth to my tribe, but I'm discreet." Crystal stretched and got out of bed, rubbing her bare arms and legs without embarrassment.

Sonja looked away, then pulled the covers over her head and tried to straighten out the hitch in her back without the younger woman seeing what happened when youth eroded.

"Babe, up. It's time for breakfast. I need something greasy. I'm thinking maple bacon, cheesy grits—"

"What time is it?" Sonja asked, poking her head out. They couldn't have slept more than four or five hours.

"After seven. Up and at 'em, as Daddy says. I'm famished."

"You go." Sonja sat up, bringing the sheet with her to cover her breasts. "I must work." She flirted with the idea of taking a muscle relaxer after Crystal left to ease her back pain—and shame. But even one pill would knock her out, preventing her from accomplishing anything, and tackling her to-do list was the only thing that would keep her mind off this fiasco.

"Damn, you're sexy as fuck. Those sheets look like purple frosting on a moist vanilla treat." Laughing, Crystal dove back onto the bed, landing on her belly next to Sonja. "Wait! No comparing women to food, right?" Crystal laughed, picked up a corner of the Egyptian cotton sheet, and said, "Yum, yum, yum. Breakfast is served."

"Stop that." Sonja slapped Crystal's hand. "These sheets cost a fortune. I'm not in the mood for foolishness. My head's screaming, my back's—" She cut herself off, not wanting to sound like a decrepit old woman.

"Whatever you say, babe." Crystal flipped onto her back, stretching out to her full length, offering Sonja an unobstructed view of the undulating female terrain of golden-brown swells and valleys. Unexpected longing coursed through her.

Thankfully, as Sonja's body started humming again, Crystal hopped back up. "Come on. Ridges has a surprisingly good breakfast. Throw on some clothes and run a brush through your hair. I'll drive."

Sonja didn't move.

"That's the only way you'll get rid of me," Crystal added with a wink. "Besides, there's something I want to talk about."

"The last time you wanted to talk, you ended up seducing me."

Crystal chuckled. "Fear has narrowed your world and limited those you've known intimately." She walked around the room, collecting her clothes. Piece by piece, the delicious folds, rolls, and curves disappeared under yoga pants and a sports bra. Crystal's act of dressing wasn't a graceful performance, making it even more riveting to watch.

"I never understand your nonsensical talk."

"That's Anaïs Nin you are insulting. Or rather my paraphrasing of her masterful words. And I didn't seduce you. I helped you widen your world."

Climbing out of bed and trying to hold up the sheet around herself, Sonja asked, "You're not wearing the same undergarments you wore yesterday, are you?"

"Who gives a damn? No one else is getting near my walleye today." Crystal hooted. "That's a bad joke Momma and I used to make. Walleye is a type of fish she and Daddy used to catch, and I took to calling my vulva that. Don't look at me that way."

"I'm not looking at you any way."

"You're giving me the queerest look. Queer joke. Funny ha-ha. Too soon?" Crystal wiggled her eyebrows and put her hands on her round hips. "If it bothers you that much, let me wear a pair of your undies. Assuming you have something that can accommodate my gorgeous figure. I'll wear you all day." Stripping off her clothes again, she stood as naked as the Venus of Willendorf.

Heat swept across Sonja's skin. She shuffled to her dresser, the sheet catching underfoot and nearly tripping her. "My panties cost a fortune," she said as she fished through the layers of neatly folded satin and lace. "Most are Prima Donna."

"And you accuse me of talking nonsense. Prima who?"

"Go freshen up first," Sonja directed, still not making eye contact.

"Come make me."

Sonja looked up to see Crystal standing in the bathroom doorway.

"I told you I'm not in the mood for foolishness. My head's throbbing."

"You're throbbing, huh?" Crystal smiled.

"How immature," Sonja retorted, but panties in hand, she stepped toward Venus in the bathroom doorway, abruptly and overwhelmingly, yearning for divinity in her life.

Sonja huddled in the corner like a shy schoolgirl, just out of reach of the shower spray.

Crystal pulled her under the water. "You need to get a shower cap for me for next time. I can't get my hair wet. I'd have a head of fizz if I used your white lady shampoo. I'll wash your hair instead."

"Absolutely not." Sonja pulled away from Crystal's reach. She had never taken a shower with another person before. It was all too intimate, making her queasy and excited at the same time.

"Come here. Besides, you white women are constantly touching Black women's hair. Your turn," Crystal said, gently pulling Sonja under the spray with her.

"I do not touch other people's hair," Sonja snarled, not that it mattered. Crystal was already babbling about family.

"...used to take care of Daddy's hair when I was younger. I loved washing, combing it. It was so silky." She squeezed out a handful of Sonja's expensive shampoo. "Momma and I have different textures..."

Sonja braced herself.

"Loosen up," Crystal lightly slapped Sonja's hip. "I'm not torturing you."

Yes, you are.

Sonja clenched her jaw and tried to listen to Crystal ramble on about porosity and coil type, but the more her head got tilted and her body repositioned, the more out of control she felt. "That's enough," she finally gasped.

Instead of releasing her, Crystal pulled her in closer, rinsing the shampoo off and leaning down to kiss her forehead. When her kisses trailed down the side of her face, Sonja pulled away and climbed out of the shower.

"Where are you going?" Crystal shut the water off and poked her head out. "That was anticlimactic. You must be hungry. For food." She held out a hand. Droplets of water fell from those beautiful fingertips, stirring

Sonja's insides. "Towel, please. And I should've asked before if you have an old cotton T-shirt I could use for my hair."

"I do not own T-shirts," Sonja snapped, hiding behind her enormous towel.

"Maybe I'll bring one next time." Crystal smiled slyly and reached out. "Towel, please. Underwear too. Hand them over."

Sonja reluctantly handed Crystal a pair of full briefs, the only pair she owned, having purchased them when she was a little heavier. Crystal shimmied into the panties, more than filling out the luxurious satin and lace.

"Damn things barely fit."

"Those are the only ones I have close to your size," Sonja said.

Crystal's face fell. "You're saying I'm fat?"

"I said no such thing. Don't put words in my mouth."

Crystal smiled. "I'm screwing with you. You can't help it if your ancestors passed a skinny ass down to you. Kidding, babe. You're beautiful. No thin-shaming. Only body positivity here. Now, let me drive you to breakfast."

"I do *not* simply rush out of my house after showering. I have a routine. I need to—"

Crystal sighed dramatically, then walked over and kissed Sonja, who jerked away. But Crystal held on tight. "You like me," she purred, kissing Sonja again. "Your pupils give you away. Plus"—another kiss—"your mouth trembles"—another kiss—"ever so slightly." And another kiss, even longer this time.

When the kissing stopped, it dawned on Sonja that her backache had vanished. Inside, she was quaking, brought on by a tsunami named Crystal. Sonja was aware that soon the vibrations would lower her resistance and muddle her logic. And that terrified her as she never had been before.

Chapter 18

One Glittering Eye

"Told you. Hardly anyone comes here on Friday mornings," Crystal said, plopping down beside Sonja and gesturing to the empty room. "Ridges is the best-kept secret in Foxboro. A good southern breakfast in an upscale bar."

"Too close." Sonja shifted her seat away until she could no longer catch Crystal's heady scent of ripe citrus, freshly overturned soil, and sea salt. She scanned the menu. "You really eat this garbage? Biscuits and gravy. Sweet potato waffles. Red eye gravy. Country ham. No wonder this region suffers from an epidemic of obesity, heart—" Sonja looked up to find Crystal staring at her. "What?"

"Do you ever allow yourself to be happy?"

"If it can't be measured, it doesn't exist." Sonja looked back at her menu, refusing to meet Crystal's eyes.

"What does that even mean?" Crystal squealed before Sonja could answer. "Elliot! You're working mornings now?"

Sonja glanced up. The server stood at their table, bowtie and suspenders perturbing her.

"Dr. Byrd," Elliot said, breaking into a grin, lessening his hipster Lucifer persona. "Someone didn't show for their shift, so here I am. How are you today? You're off work?"

Crystal shook her head. "It's Crystal to you, El. We've been over this a billion times. And you know professors are never off work."

The two laughed as if sharing a private joke.

Sonja pushed her menu toward the server's rail-thin midsection. "I'll have the berry parfait with steel-cut oats."

"Yes ma'am," he replied without missing a beat. "Would you like toast with that? We have white, wheat—"

"Wheat, dry. Hot tea, green. That will do."

Crystal studied Sonja, then shifted her attention back to the server, her eyes sparkling with mirth.

"I'm hungry, El. I want a bowl of your cheesy grits"—Crystal cupped her hands together—"not that skimpy cup y'all tried serving me last time."

"I understand, Dr. Crystal."

"Wrong again. Just Crystal."

The server laughed. "And what else? I see that look…Crystal. You have an adventurous palette this morning."

A peppery taste coated Sonja's mouth and tongue, a sure sign of spicy emotions rising from her depths.

There's that jealousy, girlie.

"What do you think about the biscuits and gravy?" Crystal asked, seemingly ignoring Sonja's glare.

"Everything is made in-house, fresh," he replied. "Our regulars love that dish. I find it indulgent." He stroked his oiled beard, making Sonja want to hold him down and pluck out every one of his facial hairs.

"Sounds perfect," Crystal said. "I feel like indulging today. Let's do it, El!"

After he left, Sonja asked Crystal, "How often do you come here? You and that server have a distinct rhythm."

"Pretty frequently." Crystal picked up the white linen napkin and draped it across her lap. "You've got to remember, I'm new to town. I'm trying to find my place, my people. That means going out to meet folks. Didn't you do the same?"

"Certainly not." Sonja's terse response was immediately drowned out by Crystal's continuing chatter. As Crystal talked, her hand floated like a butterfly on invisible currents.

Sonja watched Crystal's hand, flashing to the previous night—the luscious circles drawn on Sonja's body, the playful poking, the insistent stroking, followed by a deep drink of nectar.

Crystal suddenly began moving around utensils and condiments to make room, and Sonja realized the server had returned with their drinks.

"You have your hands full, El. Here you go. There's space now."

"Thanks, Dr. Crystal—Crystal." He tucked the empty tray under his arm but lingered.

"That will do." Sonja dismissed him, then turned to Crystal. "You said you wanted to discuss a matter with me." The intoxicating buzz she had felt moments ago faded.

"What?" Crystal gave Sonja a puzzled look. "Oh, there's time for that. Right now, I just want to sit with you, talk about stuff."

"You want to talk about stuff? An interesting word choice from a scholar."

"Code switching." Crystal smiled, swiveling that beautiful head, offering Sonja a view of one glittering eye. "Women of color get damn good at talking all sorts of ways. It's fucking exhausting, but I don't want to discuss that right now. It'd ruin my morning glow." Crystal flashed a sultry smile that made Sonja shift and cross her legs. "Tell me something you haven't told me before. About *you*, babe."

"You first," Sonja countered, struggling to resist Crystal's effect on her.

"Okie dokes. According to Momma, the first thing to know about me, I'm a Daddy's girl. The second, I'm a Georgia girl, a country one at that. Yeehaw, bitches." Crystal hooted. "Should have told you. I get goofy after sex. It's the oxytocin. Anyway, where was I? Yeah, my hometown's about an hour or so outside of Hotlanta. I'd offer to take you there, but if you think Foxboro is Hicksville...oh boy. There's nothing to do but fish, eat, and go to one of a million churches. I love it, though. Mainly because of my family. We're close, ridiculously close."

"So why come here? Why WHSU?"

Crystal shrugged. "You remember how it was to juggle a dissertation, teaching, *and* job hunting. I saw an opening. Auntie Laura had been in this part of the country, said it was pretty. I jumped when I got an offer."

"Do you regret it?"

"At times. But"—Crystal wiggled her thick eyebrows—"not this morning." She stopped talking abruptly and looked over Sonja's shoulder. "Goody. Our food. Can't believe you ordered a parfait after the night we had." She smacked her lips loudly.

"Do not be a spectacle."

Crystal stared at Sonja without speaking while the food was dropped off, adding, "Thanks, El." After he left, Crystal said, "Please don't tell me you're one of those self-loathing queers. Because I thought I was with a woman who gave zero fucks about what others thought."

"I told you. I'm not gay."

"I said queer. Fluid, if you prefer. You were out of practice, but I could tell. You've been with a woman or two." Crystal picked up her fork and cut into the gravy-smothered biscuit.

"Keep your voice down," Sonja whispered.

"Elliot is *family*."

"You're making no sense. Again," Sonja accused while gazing at Crystal's plate, appalled by the brown bits of carcass swimming in oily gray goo.

"Sonja, seriously." Crystal dropped her fork, the metal clinking on the plate. "Stop playing dumb. You've been with women."

"Fine. Yes. However, since coming here, I haven't been with many people at all. Period."

"Details, please." Crystal smiled coyly.

"No."

Crystal's smile faded. "You shared your pussy with me. Your stories, though…those are off-limits."

Shut up! Sonja wanted to shout, but instead, she scooted closer. "Keep your voice down. Please," she added. "There was a situation. Years ago. My ex was deliberately indiscreet. People on campus found out about my private affairs. My enemies got ammunition." Sonja ate a spoonful of parfait, stalling so she wouldn't cry.

"That sounds horrible. Bastards. Something similar happened to me in grad school."

"Except we got to leave grad school. I couldn't leave WHSU without giving up everything I had fought to win."

"Darling, you're spectacular. Really, you are. But you're also one of the most disconfirming people I've ever met. Whenever I try to connect with you, you have these shitty ways to tell me that my experiences aren't as important as yours."

"If you recall, I asked you about your recent incident. You declined to speak on the matter."

"Maybe I want to talk about something other than a prick who left an anonymous threat. Maybe I want to have an actual conversation with you, share secrets like lovers do. Maybe I want to tell you about the time I slept with a guy in my PhD program, one of those progressive fucks who constantly announces their allyship because talking about it is all they have. He got drunk at a party, bragged in front of everyone—me included—that he'd bagged the hot dyke. There were some professors there too." Crystal scoffed. "The whole thing erupted, igniting a philosophical debate. I went from the resident LOC—"

"What is that?"

"Lesbian of color. I went from resident LOC to fake lesbian overnight. The rest of the semester was a nightmare. Every goddamn professor and grad student weighed in on how I select to please my pussy. All 'cause I fucked a cishet male who couldn't use his mouth properly, so he ran it about me instead."

"How did it resolve?" Sonja asked.

"He finished the program. Next semester, everyone pretended nothing had happened, including those who'd accused me of betraying *the family*. Except they were the ones who betrayed me, expecting me to live up to *their* narrow definitions of *my* life." Crystal took a bite of her food, chewed, and swallowed. "That's one of my sad stories. Your turn."

Sonja scanned the restaurant for eavesdroppers before she spoke. "I will be brief. He was a highly regarded full professor. I was an assistant professor. I thought he would be my mentor and later a boyfriend and that we would become a powerhouse academic couple. Instead, he was baiting me."

"Baiting?" Crystal asked.

"He had specific tastes, and not the consensual kind." Sonja dabbed at her mouth with her napkin, hoping her hands wouldn't tremble. "Sadistic narcissist," she summarized with the detachment of a clinician.

"That explains a lot. Like in the seminar when that woman talked about her narcissistic boss. And last night. Must've been triggering."

"Thank you for the therapy session, Dr. Byrd."

Crystal waved her fork and shook her head, the ponytail catching a stream of morning light. "No fighting." She squeezed the words out of a stuffed mouth.

"I am fine. I pulled myself out of a bad experience, got tenure, got promoted. He left. I have outlasted most of my enemies."

"But, honey, have you given yourself a chance to feel and heal?" Crystal's eyes shone like candles in a foggy night.

"Everything is good now," Sonja whispered weakly. She straightened her back and said, "I selected the wrong mentor. I paid for my mistake. Now, that is enough of that. There's no point in revisiting one's past."

Sonja checked her Holzkern wristwatch. She liked how the real peacock feather inside the dial made her feel lighter, even whimsical. Right now, though, it reminded her that she had work to do.

"I must be going soon. Fridays are my most productive days. Now, shall we get to that issue you wanted to discuss?"

"Hold on. Hold on." Crystal dug her cell out of the interior pocket of her jacket and glanced at the screen. "Daddy's calling. Sorry, honey, have to take this. Right back." She pressed the phone to her ear and stepped over to the hallway outside the bathrooms.

Suddenly famished, Sonja dipped her long spoon into the yogurt-and-berry-parfait. The raw oats stuck to the back of her throat, and she washed them down with lukewarm tea. She looked longingly at Crystal's plate, ravenous for the greasy mess, but instead, she threw her napkin on the table, grabbed her bag, and slipped off to wash her hands—and to distance herself from temptation. Crystal, with one shoulder against the hallway wall and her back to the women's entrance, didn't notice her.

Sonja pumped foaming soap into her palm, then stared at her reflection in the mirror. Her skin sagged around her mouth and lines spiderwebbed beneath her eyes, but what was even more disturbing was the faint blush of her cheeks.

Idiot. Remember how good it felt with Avery at first. How many times do you have to make the same mistake? You are not meant for love. No, she corrected herself, *you are beyond love.*

She leaned closer to the mirror. "Go home. Write books. Get lucrative keynotes. Publish."

Earn happiness. Maybe become chair, then associate dean. Or establish a center for crisis communication. That last idea was new and pleasantly burned in her chest. She smiled at her reflection.

Still smiling, she opened the door in time to hear Crystal say, "Yes, I will, Daddy," her voice cracking slightly.

Sonja heard a man's voice booming through the phone's speaker. "You keep in mind your responsibility to family. Us down here, those up your way."

"Yes, Daddy."

"Don't forget what I told you, Crissie. Family above everything."

"Love you, Daddy," Crystal said and ended the call, her head down, her shoulders slumped.

Sonja cleared her throat.

"Oh, hey there," Crystal said and turned to Sonja as she wiped away a tear. "When did you sneak up?"

"I did not want to interrupt." Sonja studied Crystal's features, sensing something beneath the surface, something faintly disturbing. "Your father. He calls you Crissie?"

"He's called me that since I was a kid," Crystal replied. She rubbed the cell's screen against her pullover. "This thing gets so greasy." She looked up, her eyes still moist, her skin flushed. "I'm all yours, babe. Let's go sit."

Sonja pulled a bill from her bag and held it out. "I must go. This should cover my expenses, including the gratuity."

"It hasn't even been an hour. Come on, stay a bit longer," Crystal said.

"I cannot." *That would be unwise.*

"Why? What did I do *now*?" Crystal's alto voice climbed an octave. "Was it because I answered Daddy's call? Was it because I lured you here, saying I wanted to talk to you about something? Okay, I'll 'fess up. I wanted to spend the morning with you, share breakfast. Sorry I took Daddy's call. I could've waited, but as I said, I'm Daddy's girl."

"It is strange. I am a full professor. Yet I'm more worried about getting work done than a tenure-track faculty member."

"No sparring, Sonja. I'll pay the bill. We'll walk out together."

Sonja waved the cash. "Take it. My debt to you is paid in full."

"Don't be silly. I got breakfast. I'll be right back." Crystal called out to the server. "Elliot, the check. We need to leave, stat."

Instead of waiting, Sonja slipped out of the restaurant and hurried to Bimmer, relieved that she had insisted on driving separately. As she pulled out of the parking lot, she tried to slow her thumping heart that seemed to beat the two syllables of one word: *Crissie.*

Or was it Crysse?

Chapter 19

A Soul in Agony

SONJA STARED AT HER LAPTOP, struggling to concentrate. When her cell vibrated a second time, she took it into the living room and threw it on the couch. It bounced off the back cushion and landed face up.

"Call all you want, Dr. Byrd," she spat. She stepped back into her office, at last ready to do what she had been avoiding since arriving home. Opening the OD website and clicking on the tribute page, she located the same post she had stumbled on a week back and zeroed in on one vexing line.

I'll stick close, make sure the demon doesn't get him like she got you.
Angel Hugs, Crysse.

"No, Crysse, you won't get me. Never again," Sonja vowed, dismissing the voice in her head that warned she had reached a conclusion without sufficient data.

Now you're remembering, girlie. No one hurts you worse than the bitch you willingly let inside.

She had known from the start that something was off about Crystal. Only months after Jacob's death, an affable professor mysteriously appears in the restroom and keeps showing up. But the most important detail was that Crystal had seemed interested in Sonja, and no one feigned interest in her unless they had a hidden agenda.

Her mental advisor tried again. *Your behavior is symptomatic. Addiction to anger. You've read the studies about the grievance-revenge cycle. You cherry-pick evidence to justify your rage.* Sonja cut off the voice.

"I never should have let that woman into my life. A danger at worst. An unnecessary distraction at best. End of debate."

She X'd out of the website and opened her draft of the midterm exam for her morning class, intent on checking off something on her to-do list, but her brain continued vomiting up half-digested messages.

What had Crystal's father said? Something about having local family.

Sonja couldn't remember his exact words, but she remembered what he had called her.

CrysseCrysseCrysse.

Sonja bolted out of her chair to escape her chattering brain and went to her bedroom. The unmade bed was like an altar to the recent chaos that had plagued her.

Angrily, she ripped off the expensive sheets, ignoring the musky aroma woven like fine threads into the Egyptian cotton, and carried them to the laundry room.

Each motion summoned a memory.

As she stuffed the linen into the washer, she saw Crystal crying in the campus restroom.

As she poured in the detergent, she saw Crystal standing on her doorstep in a jacket the color of grape juice.

As she started the wash, she saw Crystal in her bed, eyes hooded, breasts heavy, pubic hair full and aromatic.

As the water filled the basin, Sonja concluded that she had been dragged into a game that she didn't yet understand, maybe never would, but she could at least eliminate one variable: Dr. Crystal Byrd.

She returned to the living room, picked up her phone, and saw that Crystal had called again. Sonja set the phone face down on the coffee table and retreated to her office. Gathering her concentration, she checked her email.

Im sorry whats happenin to you. Its goin to get worst. Cant you see whats comin

Her gut roiling, Sonja studied the email.

The sender: Storms Comin.

The email address: StormsComin@mailbox.com

The subject line: Storm Comin

Reclaiming her phone from the other room, she called the WHSU help desk, drumming her fingers on the desk until a tech finally picked up.

"Happens all the time to professors," the tech replied after she detailed the mysterious email. "Forward it to me. Probably nothing I can do. Probably from a dummy account."

"Fine." She ended the call, wishing the cell had a receiver she could slam down.

Though not expecting anything to be done, she forwarded the email with a copy to Jay and added Harmony as a cc address. But just as she was about to hit Send, she remembered something.

On the day of the fish oil incident, Harmony had been eating canned tuna.

Then something else struck her. The secretary and Crystal had become chummy out of the blue. Harmony had started being nice right around the time Crystal had catfished her in the restroom. Why was Crystal even in that restroom when her office was on the opposite side of campus?

She probably explained. You fail to listen unless the content serves your interests.

Backspacing over Harmony's email address, she muttered, "How could I have missed key evidence? I cannot believe I almost trusted you, *Harm.* Or you, *Crysse.*"

Exhaling loudly, Sonja released her connection to the other women like a heavy cord retracting. It left her unattached, unencumbered, and completely alone—her preferred state of being—or so she told herself.

By midday, Sonja was backpedaling. Even the Sergio Rossi heels she had discovered on a reseller website couldn't quell her unease.

She prepared lunch, sprinkling turmeric and a dash of cayenne pepper into boiling bone broth. As she stirred, she jerked her shoulder away as if Crystal had walked into the kitchen and reached for her, beckoning her. The unwanted mental visits continued. By afternoon, Sonja decided she would engage in the light aversion therapy that she had developed shortly after her time with Avery.

Sonja sat at her dining table and stared at the antique porcelain teacup delicately painted with intricate violets. It was a gift she had given herself after breaking up with her college boyfriend. The teacup had survived unmarked over the years, a pristine reminder of her inferior origins and boundless ambitions.

"You've spent years studying toxic communication in the workplace," she observed while tracing the fragile rim of the cup with the tip of her finger. "You still failed to see Avery for who he was. Very likely, you're failing to see her too."

Yet she couldn't deny the difference between Avery and Crystal.

If Crystal was like an autumn field, warm and inviting under a harvest sun, Avery was a frigid lake at midnight, growing colder the deeper she plunged.

Sonja had met him at a college event where the dean had bestowed some blah-de-da prestigious award from some blah-de-da prestigious association on Avery.

Granted, Avery was attractive, but it was what he represented that had drawn Sonja to him. Dr. Avery Bruce dressed impeccably in a heather-gray blazer and pants pressed into sharp creases. His cologne was a blend of citrus and sun-warmed teak. But it was the white button-down that captured her attention.

Sonja didn't often wear white, and she had a fascination with those who did. Her childhood had taught her that white clothing revealed a person's grooming, their access to professional cleaners, and the pristine environment in which they lived and worked. Avery wore the white button-down with a self-assuredness that impressed her far more than it should have. Later, she would realize that she had mistaken his unconscious privilege for conscious refinement.

When she introduced herself to him at the post-meeting reception, he shook her hand with a firm but not too firm grip and pumped it exactly twice, revealing his understanding about how to greet a professional woman. Typically, men at WHSU either avoided shaking her hand altogether or overcompensated by squeezing it until her rings dug into the sides of her fingers. Avery had looked directly into her eyes, his full lips parting in a smile that revealed brilliant white teeth.

Later, she would come to understand: Avery displayed an elegant style to ensnare prey.

When Sonja suggested that they meet midweek at an upscale tapas bar, she told herself that she was only searching for a suitable mentor, someone who could advise her as she built her program of research and navigated the treacherous tenure trenches.

Avery wore a button-down the color of fresh snowfall, the starched collar crisp under a V-neck pewter sweater. As she wiggled her toes in her cheap heels, she wondered how much he invested in his wardrobe. Time and again, she glanced at the silvery chest hairs peeking out from under his shirt right where he had loosened his tie. The hint of informality further lowered her guard.

To her amazement, Avery asked her probing questions about her work instead of talking about himself. Alarms should have blasted inside her skull each time he nodded and validated her embryonic professional vision. What started as an hour-long meeting almost doubled, and he nursed his glass of scotch the entire time. That single glass that had cost him around fifty dollars, and inside it, surrounded by golden liquid, sat a piece of ice shaped like Earth that had promised Sonja the world.

Soon, fantasies ran in her head like a movie marathon as she envisioned them as the powerhouse couple who would reshape the backward campus into a more reputable one. They would jointly deliver keynote addresses at international conferences. They would travel to Charlotte and meet her estranged father atop a swanky rooftop restaurant. Effortlessly, Avery would best Dr. Claude Storey intellectually, eventually winning him over. And Ashley Storey would not be invited.

The first time she went to bed with Avery, her fantasies burned to cinders.

"I thought you enjoyed yourself, Pillows. You did not say no, did you? I saw you as a sophisticated woman, hardly someone with conventional mores. I see now how you fooled me."

That time he had *only* left fingerprints on her breasts—his "pillows," as he had named them.

In retrospect, Sonja realized how her ex had turned her into his prey. His tactics were subtle, a microdosing of reward-and-withholding mixing and muzzling her mental advisor.

You cannot compare Crystal to that monster. She has only been kind, caring, pleasing. The gentle voice fluttered in her mind, carrying with it images from last night that left her tingling.

"That woman has not hurt me—yet," Sonja chastised herself aloud. It was an absurd habit she had developed over decades of solitary living, and one that seemed to be growing stronger. "When I lower my defenses, I behave recklessly."

To be fair, the period between her *dates* with Avery had been protracted enough that she could rewrite his sexual appetites in her memories. Each subsequent incident, she promised herself, would be the last, and she persuaded herself that the two of them had clarified their misunderstandings and now shared expectations. What in fact happened was that Sonja had deceived herself into believing a convenient falsehood: bruises from rough sex disappear, but professional and personal successes do not.

By the time Sonja picked up her cup, the tea had turned cold and tasted like liquid mold. But she finished the expensive imported blend, grimacing at the disturbing flavor.

"Your decision to end the dalliance with *her* is wise," she reassured herself. "After all, you did not have the strength to leave Avery. Never forget that." *Never forgive.* She hadn't even had enough sense to stop seeing him. Instead, his attentions wandered, leaving her in uneasy peace until the day he showed up at her office door, smiling like a jackal. Afterward, as she sat frozen, he had gone down the hall into Mitch's office, speaking loud enough for her to hear:

Mitch: *"Good seeing you, old friend. Was I right?"*
Avery: *"Cold bitch outside. Tamed bitch inside."*
Mitch: *"Craves a firm hand."*
Avery: *"I offered her one or two."*

Sonja faded into a gray netherworld, blocking out the remainder of the further mastication of her reputation, her career. That was months before Jay abruptly informed her that her office would be relocated to the basement. The move was brief, and while she naïvely believed that the remote, windowless office would provide her with sanctuary, Mitch found her anyway. Mitch always found her.

Now, in the safety of her home, years removed from Avery and Mitch, her skin still blazed and itched, rage sweeping through her like an arid desert wind, lifting and flinging old things that should have settled long ago. They banged around in her gut, her breast cavity, and her skull. Her arm jerked involuntarily, sending her teacup smashing into a wall. The shattered pieces looked like bits of bone.

Sonja stood on quaking legs. As she kneeled to pick up the scattered remains of her cup, she nicked her finger on a sharp edge, drawing blood. A single tear slid down her cheek. She shook off her self-flagellation and disposed of the evidence of her emotional storm. Then she blew her nose, freshened her face—refusing to look like a pitiful soul in agony—and went to pour some pinot. She held up the glass to toast her ex.

"Thank you for teaching me, Avery. My success will be my liberation."

She returned to her office, eager to lose herself in work. Two hours later, she beamed at the exam she had devised for her morning class.

"You think I'm a bitch now," she said to her invisible students, "wait until you see this test."

She tossed back the last of her wine, her lips twisting into a crooked smile. She had passed her own test. She would not grant Dr. Crystal Byrd entry into her life.

Satisfied, she took a muscle relaxer and crawled into bed, breathing in the scent of lavender from the newly washed sheets instead of the aroma of last night's foolhardy indulgence.

Chapter 20

Howled and Roared

"FIVE, FOUR, THREE, TWO, ONE. Up!"

And with that, Sonja hauled herself out of bed, yanked on her yoga pants, and pulled on her too-tight high-end sports bra. Dragging herself into the living room, she began a punishing workout.

Fifteen minutes later, Sonja's back howled and roared, but drenched in sweat and gasping, she ignored her pain and discomfort and reached for her cell to finally play Crystal's last message.

"I'm not sure what happened this time around, Sonja. What I am sure of is that I don't need this drama. I wish you well. I may wave if I see you on campus, but I won't stop and chat. Please don't call. If you do, I won't pick up. And maybe, just maybe, read one of your own books or listen to one of your lectures. That Dr. Sonja Storey is pretty amazing. And...well...consider seeing someone, a professional. Compounding traumas by—shit! Doing it again. Never mind. You're a smart woman. You'll figure it out. Or you won't. Okay, that's it."

Sonja wiped her sweaty face and deleted the message.

You're making a mistake with Byrd.

She shoved aside the thought, determined to not further complicate her life.

"Hi there, Sonja!" Harmony called out to her from the main lobby as she entered. "Restful weekend, I hope. Mine was good. Good fellowship, good food, you know."

Sonja squinted at the approaching secretary. "Question for you, Harmony."

"Sure."

"Do you eat tuna?"

"Strange question. But yeah, I do."

"I have started a new health plan, a plan to detoxify my life," Sonja said without offering her insights into the fresh suspicion that had arisen over the weekend.

"That's great! You and Lewis on your health kicks. Maybe we should do some department thing," Harmony said good-naturedly, oblivious to Sonja's icy tone. "We could take on a wellness challenge. There are those daily yoga classes at the activity center."

"Mm-hmm." Sonja unlocked her office, then turned to face the secretary again. "Harmony."

"Yes."

"Call me Dr. Storey."

She felt her comment land, a verbal pebble that would leave a hairline crack and expand throughout the day.

Sonja had barely settled at her desk when her office phone rang. The digital display announced it was the university counsel. She swallowed hard and hit the speaker button. "Dr. Storey."

"Good morning, Dr. Storey. Please hold for Jodi Jenkins." The secretary's voice was like a poorly tuned banjo.

"This is not a good time," Sonja protested. But it was too late.

"Dr. Storey," Jodi said. "Sorry to jump on you first thing, but I need to know if you have time to meet today."

"Not unless you plan to read this article on chaos theory applications and update my lecture for me."

Jodi snorted. "That's a hard pass. But listen, there are developments. We really need to meet with you over here."

"Is this about those posts?"

"Another matter. Dr. Russel's coming in"—Jodi's voice became muffled "Rosie, when's Mary Ann coming over? Okay, thanks"—then cleared. "Dr. Storey, are you still there?"

"Where else would I be?"

"Can you be here in forty-five minutes?"

"So your convenience supersedes mine."

"I promise you, I wouldn't be doing this if I didn't have to."

"I will see you, then."

She hung up and opened her slides for the next day's class, managing to add one new one before it was time to go. She typed a paraphrased quote from the assigned reading.

Chaos isn't undesirable. Savvy leaders harness chaotic forces to bring about necessary change for the good of the organization.

The instant she saved the document, she imagined Crystal advising: *Listen to one of your lectures. Read one of your books.*

Without taking time to think on it further, she grabbed her tote and hurried across campus, keeping her eyes open for a certain assistant professor.

———————————

Dressed in jeans (*of course!*), the Health Sciences professor had already arrived and was sitting on the assistant counsel's couch chatting with Jodi, who leaned against her desk. The two women looked like they were brunching rather than having an urgent meeting.

"Oh good. Thanks for coming, Dr. Storey. Take a seat. Do you want something? Water? Coffee? Wait! You drink tea, if I recall."

"I am fine. Make this quick." Sonja sat in the cheap leather chair rather than beside Mary Ann on the couch.

"Right. Here's the deal. When the inquiry committee submitted their report, your recommendations were accepted. Dr. Watson's suspension was upheld, and his case advanced to the formal hearing committee."

"You did not summon us here, Jodi, to provide information we already know," Sonja said impatiently.

"Go ahead and say it," Mary Ann said. "Sonja and I are being targeted for legal action."

"Your names have been mentioned in subsequent discussions with Dr. Watson's attorney," Jodi explained. "More than likely, this is simply legal wrangling."

"Where are the men?" Sonja's eye spasmed like a 7.0-magnitude earthquake.

"Right now, all they're doing is tossing your names around. They don't have a legal leg to stand on unless we give them one, and we are not going to do that."

"Was it because we authored the report?" Mary Ann asked.

"Because we are the only women on the committee," Sonja suggested.

"I won't speculate," Jodi responded. "But when the hearing committee convenes, I anticipate the heat will come off you both. You simply upheld the initial decision by the dean, vice president, and university counsel."

"Is Horace allowed to approach us?" Mary Ann's voice was filled with urgency. "I have a wife, children. The Horace I used to know wouldn't dare, but this Horace—he's deteriorated. Something's wrong with him. I mean, his tremors, and the rambling during our meeting with him. Not to mention his vile posts about those poor young girls. They're nearly incomprehensible. I suspect he has some sort of progressive cognitive impairment. His symptoms remind me of frontal—"

"I'm going on repeat here, just a friendly reminder, though. It's best not to speculate, Mary Ann. Don't get into the practice. Look, if there's trouble, don't respond to him. In person, through email, on social media. No engagement whatsoever." Jodi glanced at Sonja, then looked back at Mary Ann. "Call me immediately. You have my cell. If it's an emergency, call 9-1-1. I know this is scary. We're behind you, though."

"He is *not* going to intimidate me," Sonja announced, "and that includes his online distortion campaign against me. What have you done about those posts, Jodi?"

"There are more posts?" Mary Ann looked at Sonja.

Without taking her eyes off Jodi, Sonja said, "I received an anonymous email. I am unconvinced it's related to the Horace matter, though."

"Forward me the email." Jodi said. "Regarding the posts, I'm handling the matter, personally."

"What posts?" Mary Ann swiveled toward Sonja, then Jodi. "Shit, are there posts about me too? What if my kids get ahold of them? And my wife's a teacher—public schools too. You know what trouble that kind of publicity could bring."

"I am also interested in your answer, Jodi." Sonja crossed her legs to take pressure off her throbbing back. "Have you found posts about Mary Ann? Because I found several more targeting me. These are under a different username, though."

"Mary Ann, let's address your concerns separately." Jodi then looked back at Sonja, her expression hardening. "Dr. Storey, send me those links, then stop searching. If you respond to them, an already volatile situation could escalate, personally and legally."

"I am not a fool."

"Agreed. You're no fool. Here's the thing, though. It's easy to get provoked when out of sorts. Small slights snowball into big messes." Jodi looked at both women. "Remember, I'm on your side."

Sonja stood up and announced, "I must go," then stalked out.

Jodi called out after her. "We're taking care of everything, Dr. Storey. I'll be in contact. And please! Forward that email and those links to me ASAP."

"I am sure you'll take care of everything," Sonja mumbled as she punched the button to summon the elevator. She would have liked to yell back that she knew the administration would sacrifice her in an instant to save itself.

As Sonja stepped into the elevator, she was overcome by waves of nausea. She closed her eyes and tried to slow her breathing. Behind her eyelids, something flashed. But whether it was a fragment of a memory or a nightmare, she couldn't say.

A yank into darkness. Her mouth flooded with salty water. Nostrils too. A voice said, "Get yourself out, girlie."

She thought she saw her mother in the watery images, face buried in something. A magazine perhaps. She did not see her father. That made sense. His academic advancement—and student lovers—had always been more important than his family. His first family, at least.

When Sonja stepped out onto her floor, she still tasted briny water, and it felt like she was moving against an invisible current.

She staggered across campus, and when she reached her office, she collapsed in her chair, still sensing the tug of the current. In a daze but determined to work, she pulled up her morning lecture.

A persistent knocking finally lifted her out of the riptide.

"Wait!" she called out, prying herself out of her chair.

She opened her door to find Lewis Waters wearing a stupid hey-buddy grin.

"Sonja."

"I am in the middle of pressing work."

"I came to tell you something before tomorrow's faculty meeting. I would've told you sooner, but we keep missing one another."

"What is it, Lewis?"

"You folks are finally getting rid of me. I'm retiring at the end of the year. Well, you won't be completely free of me. There are things in the works." He cackled.

"Good for you," Sonja said and started to close the door.

"My boss at home insists on me slowing down. After the old..." He drummed his knuckles on his chest.

"Excuse me?" She pulled the door open again.

"The wife twisted my arm." Lewis turned around, putting his arm behind his back as though someone were in fact twisting it. "She's been after me ever since that heart episode. You'll get some young hotshot to replace me. You know universities. Shove out the old, make way for the new."

"And underpaid," Sonja interjected.

Lewis chuckled. "You aren't wrong, friend, but you *are* busy. I'll let you get back to it. But I really want to catch up. I'd value your input on an initiative."

"Very well," she said, and closed the door, mumbling, "Good riddance. And I am not your friend."

People saw Lewis as a sweet old man, a gentle Gray Hair who smiled easily and patted students on the back. Sonja still saw him huddled with Cole Behringer and Mitch Grant, and she could replay their discussions like a focus group transcript.

"Legs, easily an A-plus. Breasts, maybe a C-minus. C-plus, if I'm being generous, but curving her grade would require research."

"Observational and experimental. The testimonials about her have been intriguing."

Laughter.

"That face, though. The constant scowling. The highest I'm giving for that face is a C."

"Imagine having to look down on it. I'd have to flip her over on her hands and knees. A perfect position for a bitch."

Crude laughter.

She never heard Lewis join in, but neither had she heard him object. Now, at the tail end of his career, he acted as if the harassment had never taken place.

"Crawl away and die somewhere, Lewis."

With that, Sonja shifted her attention back to her work. Soon, though, she got another idea. That idea beckoned to her until she stopped working on her lecture, gathered her things, and returned home to gestate a plan pregnant with promise.

For several hours, she fleshed out her plan, typing notes in preparation. At one point, she almost picked up the phone to call Crystal but caught herself before she pressed the green button.

She shut off her phone and stashed it at the bottom of her Coach duffle, debating whether to take the bag tomorrow. It was too casual for her tastes, but it had cost several hundred dollars, requiring that she use it occasionally to justify its purchase.

She drew her cashmere wrap around herself and took her glass of wine out onto the deck. She stalked along the railing like a vixen pacing her territory. Whenever she heard a rustle or a snap below, she swung around to look, certain she would discover the source of her misery, but she saw only twisted shadows and gnarled forms.

As soon as darkness fell, she brought out Star Dancer, but she ended up scanning the terrain more than the sky. Finally, tired and cold, Sonja gave up her search of the landscape and lost herself in the stars overhead until clouds moved in, obscuring her sight. By then she realized that the strange attraction that pulled her toward Crystal had diminished, and she returned indoors.

After a hot shower, she slipped on her Julianna Rae robe, caressing the silky material, stroking her belly and breasts, imagining Crystal's hands on her skin, sensuously kissing her body like it was beautiful and worthy.

See? You were mistaken. About so much.

Sonja reached for her bottle of muscle relaxers and shook it. It was over half-empty. She had another bottle from the original prescription stashed away. Maybe she didn't need one tonight, though; her muscles felt loose enough. Nevertheless, wanting to be fully rested and recharged for the faculty meeting, she popped a pill. She couldn't be distracted as she had been years ago, back when her nights were filled with aches and spasms and her days cluttered with medical appointments, diagnostic scans, uncomfortable injections, and therapeutic sessions. Treatments had helped—in the short run. What was really the cure, though, was when Avery, Cole, and Mitch exited the university. The aches and spasms had eventually ceased, and she'd tossed the prescription bottles into a drawer, ignoring the follow-up calls from medical providers. She had reclaimed her life.

"And I will do it again."

She slid the pill bottle into the nightstand drawer, lay back on the bed, and fell asleep, only waking long enough to beg her mother to stop banging on the door and leave her in peace.

Chapter 21

Fog

SONJA GLANCED AT THE CLOCK on her PC, barely seeing it through her mental fog. Twenty-eight minutes before the afternoon faculty meeting. She shouldn't have tried doing the online sexual harassment training between her second class and the end-of-day meeting, but the email instructing her to complete the modules immediately made it clear she couldn't put it off any longer.

Sonja ran her hand down the front of her satin crimson blouse and returned her attention to the annual training.

Disparate Treatment Discrimination: action that treats similarly situated persons differently.

"Fuck you, Jay," she said, startling herself. These days, it was as if she had sprung a leak. Her emotions kept seeping out unchecked, leaving her to constantly tidy up.

She advanced to the next slide, then the next, finding it difficult to process the text. Instead, she saw the younger version of herself in a department meeting and heard Jay's voice.

"Harmony's birthday is coming up. How about a sweet assignment, Sonja? Whip up some cupcakes or a cake. Your choice."

That was how it had begun: Jay smiling at her, freezing her in place as her male colleagues snickered. She had insisted that she didn't bake. But he simply said, "I trust what you'll do in the kitchen is more than these guys can do." And he pointed at Mitch, Cole, and Lewis, twirling his finger like a conductor and summoning baritone laughter from the all-male chorus.

Sonja made Harmony's birthday cupcakes for years, but at least she derived some enjoyment from watching the members of her tenure and promotion committee devour her special mucus treats.

The standoff came in the first meeting after she was promoted to associate professor and her tenure was made official. Sonja refused Jay's *request* in front of the entire department. It was Harmony who ended the standoff, claiming that her doctor had ordered her off sweets. And with that, the era of Sonja's special cupcakes had drawn to a close.

CONGRATULATIONS!

The message jumped onto the monitor, jarring Sonja out of her reflection. The module was completed for another year, but she didn't remember much of what she had read, her attention elsewhere.

She exited the program and applied another coat of lipstick. She was Jezebel going to meet her enemies.

But this painted Jezebel would be victorious.

Sonja, intentionally late, noisily maneuvered between rows of lecturers and adjuncts, disrupting Jay's announcement.

"Folks, give me some good news," Jay said. "Who's done what?"

A lecturer spoke up. "Our gal made the travel team."

Sonja dropped her tote on the desk with a thud and dug inside for the agenda printout and a pen.

"Once Dr. Storey gets settled, we'll continue," Jay said, sounding cheerful, but she heard the admonishment.

Sonja flicked a hand at him. "Go ahead," she said without stopping her disruptive search.

"We'll wait."

Finally extracting the agenda, she smoothed it on the table and slapped a pen down on it. She sat, crossed her arms, and stared at Jay.

The chair proceeded. "We have a special announcement. For thirty years, Dr. Lewis Waters has served this university. He has received multiple teaching and service awards. He has published numerous articles—over a hundred, Lewis?"

"Don't look at me, Jay. I can't count above ten," Lewis said, drawing laughter.

Sonja watched the retiring professor wave away Jay's accolades. The old man's gesture of modesty infuriated her, and she reminded herself that he was leaving.

"Don't listen to him," Jay directed at everyone. "Lewis is a giant in his field, and we're sorry to see him go. No tears now." He shook his finger at two female adjuncts sitting at the front of the room. "We'll see him around, right, Lewis? I have it on good authority that he'll be heading some retirement-relations initiative. A personal request by President Knowles."

Lewis stood and saluted the room as everyone applauded. When he locked eyes with Sonja, his smile wilted, and he sat back down.

"I will chair the search committee." Sonja's voice rose above the chatter. Jay turned to look at her. "We're not there yet, Dr. Storey."

"Why not?" Sonja asked, relishing the rising tension in the room. "The best candidates get hired early. We need a job description placed by early October, midmonth at the latest. That gives us two weeks at most. Thankfully, I have already begun the initial planning."

"Okay, okay." Jay smiled through gritted teeth. "Let's not be so quick to replace Lewis."

"We must move on the search. I will lead it," she insisted, knowing that if she didn't win here, Jay would initiate a behind-the-scenes effort to control the search—if he hadn't already.

"Chairing a search takes a ton of work," Jay said, barely suppressing his condescension. "And frankly, Sonja, you have a lot on your plate right now."

"I do not recall you being so paternalistic with other faculty members."

Jay looked down at the stack of papers on the podium. "We'll address that issue in a more private setting."

"Address it here. You repeatedly call for transparency in our department." She looked around the room. "Are there any objections to me leading the search?" No one spoke; no one met her eyes. Then fixing her eyes on Lewis, she asked, "Lewis, do *you* have any objections?"

Lewis beamed at her. "I think it's a wonderful idea. The first female-led search in our department. Far overdue. Wouldn't you agree, Jay?"

"There. You see, Jay? The matter is settled." Sonja smiled like a victorious queen, but she was quietly stunned by Lewis's public support.

Jay winced in return, adding smoothly, "Thanks, Dr. Storey, for your service."

"Watch for my emails, people," Sonja said. "Respond quickly if I select you for the search committee. We are already behind schedule."

And with that, Sonja stepped closer to remolding the department into *her* department.

————————————————

Sonja nestled cross-legged into the corner chair of her living room as the storm raged outside, and she opened her laptop to WHSU.edu. She clicked on the Highlanders Retirement page and searched until she found the announcement. Then she snuggled deeper into her chair, sipping her pinot and rubbing her bare feet on the luxurious fabric.

She looked at Dr. Mitch Grant's retirement announcement. This was only the second time she'd seen the photo. The first was back when his retirement had been announced in the university newsletter. Now she looked at the photo and wondered how she had ever been so afraid of him.

Last semester, after a ghastly nightmare about him, she had called the nursing facility, telling them that she was an old friend from the university, and inquired about visiting hours. In truth, she wanted to be sure he hadn't escaped to come for her. The facility employee had urged Sonja to visit.

"Mr. Mitch don't get many visitors. Seeing you would do his heart good. Don't expect much, though. Those strokes did a number on him. He don't talk much, least not so's anyone can understand him. You being here will be good enough. Just pat his hand to let him know you're there."

Pat his hand.

After nearly retching, Sonja had disconnected the call abruptly. Otherwise, she might have explained to the kindly employee how much damage *Mr. Mitch* had done with his hand. Still, the call had been worth it. Sonja had relegated Mitch to the back of her mind and hadn't dreamed about him since. Tonight, though, she longed to tell the son of a bitch about her ultimate victory over the Gray Hairs.

In the safety of her home, she studied his retirement photo, critically examining his cheap blazer the color of pencil lead, the powder-blue shirt underneath, and the bland navy tie. He was bald on top with a ring of gray hair around his head. His neck sagged like melting putty. On the whole, he appeared ordinary. But the twinkle in his cobalt eyes belied his maliciousness.

"Has your memory of *that* time been eaten away?" she asked the digitized version of the man who had terrorized her. "Am I the only one left to remember? Or did you do *that* to other women too? Other students?" It was difficult to believe that his first time had been with her.

He had sat in a chair, blocking her office door. As soon as she'd realized he was masturbating, she froze. She didn't call campus security. She didn't lunge at him or smack the gleeful expression from his face. She didn't scream. Hell, she didn't even whimper. Dr. Sonja J. Storey had sat in her office like a naughty girl on a time-out rather than an ice queen in training.

She barely flinched when he finished and wiped a line of his filthy residue on her cheek.

If it happened today, though, she would rise to the occasion.

"You could not withstand me now, Mitch." But her queenly voice was lost to the gale outside.

These masochistic ruminations must stop. These aversion treatments of yours are harmful. You know why you froze. He was a pathetic, disturbed man, but he had power. He could have destroyed everything you had worked for.

The kinder inner voice darted in like a gentle songbird, and her focus on Dr. Mitch Grant took flight.

"Goodbye, Mitch."

Sonja exited the website and signed into her university email, planning to proofread her message to the search committee one last time. She had hand-picked two lecturers along with Mary Ann Russel and Samson Matovu from the informal inquiry committee.

Before she could open the email, though, she saw a familiar sender name, waiting like a hyena at a watering hole. StormsComin@mailbox.com

I fell sorry for whats happen to you. you should be scarred whats comin

The grayness moved in, darkening her previous victory. Sonja forwarded the email to IT and promised herself that one day, she would have more control over her world and would squash people who tried dragging her into darkness.

She logged off for the night, then immediately realized that she had neglected to send the email to the search committee. She promised herself to send it first thing in the morning.

In an effort to recapture her previous celebratory mood, she topped off her glass of pinot. If it weren't a stormy mess outside, she would have taken out Star Dancer. She craved the whirling cosmos, a reminder of something beyond her home, beyond her life. Instead, she took her wine into the bedroom, nesting under the covers and flipping through an issue of *InStyle*, considering another makeover of her office or maybe her dining room. Then an advertisement for a pair of leaf-green dress pants caught her eye, and she argued with herself about whether the color was right for her and what blouse would complement them.

Chapter 22

Slimy Things Crawling

She woke, her head feeling fat and floaty. Wisps of her dream drifted in her memory like a light February snow.

A sapling with pink blossoms. Snow pouring from a dark sky. A flock of songbirds descending, covering the ground.

In her dreamscape, Sonja saw herself seeking shelter in a cinderblock garage with a gray floor. She closed the white door to shut out the raging storm and watched it bulge as if something were forcing its way inside.

"I'm running out of time," she heard herself say.

She was shaking from head to toe. "I'm running out of time," she repeated.

Slipping out of bed, she threw on her robe, put her ear to the bedroom door, and listened. Nothing. She cracked the door open.

She crept into the living room and, holding her breath, peeked out at the sooty blackness from the front window. A single faint streetlight glowed dimly a few houses away, casting swirls of graphite and onyx onto her section of the neighborhood. She detected no movement, though.

She returned to the bedroom. Had the dream awakened her, or was it something else that had disturbed her sleep? Reaching for her phone on the nightstand, she checked the time: 11:02.

Keeping her finger on the call button, she went back into her living room. As she turned to face the curtained deck door, she heard something slam into it. She screamed, but then her rage took over, shoving aside her terror. "Who the fuck's there?" Through the gap at the foot of the curtains, she glimpsed slimy things crawling outside on her deck.

She retreated quickly into her bedroom and locked the door, then frantically dialed and hissed into the phone: "Someone's here. Someone's come for me."

Inside, she screamed, *I'm out of time.*

Over the sound of the wind and the rain, Sonja heard the knock at the front door.

"Is that you?" Sonja whispered. She clutched her cell in one hand and a triple-cut steel nail file in the other. She hurried out to the living room, dropping her cell and nail file on the couch as she passed, and looked out the window. Seeing Crystal, she opened the door and pulled her inside.

"The hell? You scared the shit out of me!"

Sonja caught a flash of metal in the younger woman's hand. "Did you bring a gun? Christ!"

"No. This is a stun gun. I carry it everywhere after..." Crystal trailed off as she looked around the living room. "What the hell's happening anyway? You said someone tried to break in. I kept my high beams on as I drove up Summit, and I didn't see anybody. The hill gives me a pretty good view of your property, one side, at least."

Sonja shook her head, trying to emerge from her groggy state.

You're losing it. The taunt sounded like it came from inside a padded cell. Sonja closed her eyes, and when she reopened them, she locked onto Crystal.

"Sonja, answer me."

"What?"

"I asked if you're drunk. You're acting intoxicated."

Standing straighter and smoothing her robe and hair, Sonja tried to reassert her authority. "Of course I'm not drunk. I took the medicine my doctor prescribed for an old back injury. Drowsiness is a side effect," Sonja added defensively.

"What are the other side effects?" Crystal asked, looking down at Sonja, doubt etched onto the beautiful face.

Sonja staggered into the kitchen to dab her forehead with a wet napkin and hopefully clear her thinking. With her back to Crystal, she said, "You're treating me like those police officers did." She turned and pointed to the deck door. "Out there. Something knocked. It woke me up."

"Someone knocked on your deck door? Your deck's a gazillion feet off the ground."

"I'm telling you what happened," Sonja stated firmly. "This is the second time too. The first time was the night before my seminar. I called the police, but they thought I hallucinated everything. I thought when I called the resident campus feminist, I'd be met with more support." Sonja leveled an accusing gaze at Crystal.

But the truth was, Sonja didn't remember dialing Crystal's number.

"Don't start. I rush over here, and I'll be damned, you're picking a fight." Crystal walked over to the deck door and pulled back the heavy navy cloth and cream sheers. "Let's have a look."

"Wait! Don't wrinkle them."

"This turns on the outside light?" Crystal flipped the switch without waiting for an answer.

The light punched a small hole into the darkness. Outside, fog and shadows swarmed and fluttered like bats in the yellow glow.

Crystal leaned against the glass, cupping a hand over her eyes to see. "Seeing lots of limbs. Are those—?" She peered out into the night. "Yep. Tulip poplar limbs. They drop easily in storms. It prevents the tree from toppling."

Sonja stepped away from the doors, retying the sash around her robe. It snugged her breasts and hips suggestively, and she was suddenly self-conscious. "Thank you for the horticulture lecture, Dr. Byrd."

"Have you gone outside?" Crystal stared down at Sonja. "By the way, it's an arborist, not a horticulturist."

"Look who's picking a fight now." Sonja looked away, pretending to look outside, but all she saw was her insubstantial reflection next to Crystal's. "I haven't gone outside. Not after everything that's happened. Not after those emails."

"What emails?" Crystal asked, still fiddling with the lock on the door.

"Don't do that." Sonja slapped Crystal's hand away.

"*You* don't do *that*!" Crystal spun around. "I've been smacked before, and I'll be damned if I'm going to take it from you."

"Well, you're being stupid. Going outside—"

"That's it. I'm gone." Crystal headed for the front door.

"Don't go," Sonja pleaded. "You're the only one I knew to call."

Crystal spun around, her sneakers squeaking on the hardwood floor. "You have no one to call, Sonja, because you shove everyone away, then act like you didn't have a hand in your fate. Next time, call the police."

"Fine. I'm sorry. See? I apologized," Sonja said, her voice raised almost to a shout. She pulled her robe tighter around her as if to shield herself from her emotions.

"For a smart woman, you can act dumb. Look at you. You're terrified. Your life's in the shitter—"

"It is not! My life is great! It's fantastic! Other than some psycho playing a sadistic game with me." Sonja stopped talking when she realized it was her mother's voice bellowing.

Only days ago, you thought Crysse-Crystal was part of the conspiracy. But as soon as you hear a little noise, you run to her. How many times did you slink back to Avery like a beaten bitch?

"Get help. For your sake." Crystal's eyes filled with tears, turning them a burnished gold. "Seriously, babe, get some fucking help. I don't know what happened to you. Maybe someone *is* after you. There are a lot of mean fuckers eager to punish a powerful woman. Yet, here you are, shoving away allies. Fuck, you've pretty much kicked me in the teeth whenever I've tried to help you." Crystal shook her head and crossed her arms over her chest as if to barricade her heart, a harsh laugh coming through soft lips. "Look at me. Once again, CDAF. Codependent as fuck!"

Sonja sucked in her breath. "Are you saying I deserve what is happening to me?"

"Stop. Whatever you're getting ready to do, just stop."

"Whatever you say, Crysse."

"Don't!" Crystal growled, but the blood rushing to Sonja's head made her itch for a fight. Anything to stop feeling so insignificant.

"Say no more, *Crysse*. I get it. I am to blame. Would you say that to a victim of abuse? Rape?"

"Don't you fucking dare," Crystal roared. "I was raped. You put filth in my mouth to manipulate me. That's evil shit. Evil, evil shit. I didn't...say... you deserved it...and you know that." Crystal gasped out the words, then folded over, groaning.

Sonja froze. She had gone too far. She guided Crystal to the couch. "Come. Sit. I'll make tea."

With Crystal settled on the couch. Sonja slipped into the kitchen and put on the teakettle, hearing the ragged weeping in the background. By the time the water boiled, Sonja had identified the heaviness in her chest.

Shame.

Sonja set the tray on the coffee table and joined Crystal on the couch, leaving a gap between them.

"Do you want to talk about it?" Sonja asked softly.

"Not with you," Crystal said with a shiver. "I raced over here because you sounded terrified. It's a gut twist for me when something scares a fierce bitch like you." Then she laid Sonja's discarded cell phone and nail file on the coffee table. "I found these on the couch." Then she picked up a cup and swallowed a mouthful of the hot tea. "Shit, that hurt." She stuck out her tongue with a grunt.

Sonja grinned. The woman's authentic charm was disarming.

Crystal is always Crystal, something you routinely disregard. Sonja brushed away a strand of hair from her face as if she could brush away the thought.

"When I see a badass woman crumpling," Crystal continued, "I can't stop myself from trying to help, no matter how long I've worked on it in counseling. It goes back to the only time I saw Momma really lose it. There she was, crawling across her bedroom floor, brought to her knees by the death of her brother. What a dumbass I am." Crystal wiped her runny nose with the back of her bare hand. "I could use some tissues."

"Of course." Sonja rushed off to the bathroom to get a respite from Crystal's emotional onslaught, from her own shame...and before Crystal's runny nose dripped on her couch. Grabbing a handful of tissues, Sonja hurried back as if she could clean up the mess she had made.

Crystal snatched the wad of tissues and blotted her eyes and nose. "Besides, I don't trust you."

"What?" Sonja asked.

"I. Don't. Trust. You!" Crystal enunciated.

"That is fair," Sonja said and sipped from her teacup. "I did hear something at my door. I am not crazy."

"Labeling women as crazy is a way of silencing them. I wouldn't use that word."

The two remained silent for a bit, sipping their tea and listening to the howling wind.

Crystal spoke first. "Small acts of abuse get layered. Eventually, a person winds up buried alive," she said. "I wasn't believed when it counted, except by Momma and Daddy." Then she muttered, "You better not use my empathy against me."

"You commented earlier about how I shove people away, even allies. I can't tell the difference between good people and bad people. My parents taught me that a woman who trusts others is a fool."

Crystal nodded, then switched gears. "Let's go outside and check things out. After that, I've got to get some sleep."

"Sleep here," Sonja suggested sheepishly, though she was embarrassed by her need for Crystal's company.

"Hell no."

"It's too late to drive."

"I wish you could be honest with me, with yourself. But honesty requires bravery. And bravery requires vulnerability. And you hate vulnerability more than you love control."

"I want you to stay." *It would please me very much. And I want to please you. Or learn how to.*

Crystal closed her eyes and shook her head.

Sonja tried again. "I am asking you to stay. Please."

"Fine." Crystal opened her eyes to focus on some point on the wall. "I'll sleep on the couch."

"Unacceptable. The bed is more comfortable. Besides, this couch cost a fortune."

"You are rude, Dr. Storey." Crystal smiled faintly. "Okay, but nothing's happening tonight. I've had plenty of casual sex, but I won't with you."

"I was not asking for that."

"Mm-hmm." Crystal stood, grabbing the stun gun off the coffee table. "Let's go check the deck."

They went out into the night but found not a single sign of the slimy, crawly things that Sonja thought she had seen.

Crystal took Sonja's hand and led her back inside.

Sonja felt her panic resurfacing. Twisting out of Crystal's grasp, she flipped the lock, tugging the handle repeatedly to be sure it had latched properly, then closed the curtains.

"Bedtime," Crystal said from behind her. "Two conditions to me staying. Nonnegotiable."

"What are your terms?" Sonja had regained her voice of authority, but nervous about Crystal's conditions, she continued to fiddle with the drapes.

"One... Are you listening, Sonja, or is your head up your ass?"

"There is no need for crassness." Sonja turned to face Crystal, crossing her arms over her chest and meeting the eyes that seemed to see right through her.

"One, you call a counselor, make an appointment. First thing in the morning. I know someone. She's smart, no-nonsense. She won't waste your time. Deal?"

"I will think on it."

"In that case, I'm outta here. And I'll block your number the moment I step out that door. I mean it. It hurts to be around you."

"Fine."

"What does that mean?"

"You give me the number. I will call."

"In the morning. In front of me. You make an appointment. You cancel or fail to show, I block you from my phone, block you from my life."

"Agreed," Sonja said. "Second condition?"

"Your toothbrush. I need to borrow it."

"Absolutely not."

Crystal headed to the front door.

"Wait. I have an unopened pack. You may have one."

"Okay. Maybe I'll even keep it here. If you're a good girl."

"Ick," Sonja said, but to her dismay, her body hummed.

"Oh, one last condition. A silk scarf. I need to wrap my hair. Our last night together did a number on it."

Sonja fetched one of her Burberry scarves, biting her tongue to keep from commenting on the hundreds of dollars being tied around Crystal's head.

Chapter 23

Killed the Bird

When Sonja awoke, she opened her eyes to see Crystal, her head adorned with the red and black mermaid scarf, a scarf that Sonja treasured but didn't wear often to preserve it. She leaned in, watching the woman breathe, watching those heavy breasts rising and falling and thinking that her bedmate vaguely reminded her of someone.

She whispered into Crystal's ear, "Did you know Jacob Randalls, Crysse?"

Crystal's lids fluttered open, revealing the tiger's eye gemstones underneath. "What? I was sound asleep."

"I asked if you have family nearby. I remember your father saying—"

"No, I don't. And stop waking me up with loony questions. What time is it anyway? I'm exhausted," she said, rolling over and immediately falling back sleep.

Sonja slipped out of bed and went to make her morning tea. As she munched on dry toast, she considered Crystal's response to her question, comparing it to what she remembered *Daddy* Byrd having said during that phone call. Something about Crystal's family up here, up this way. Sonja searched her memory, trying to recall the exact quote, but she couldn't. Still, to be on the safe side, she required more data.

And just like a capricious house cat, her suspicions returned, clawing her insides, reopening old scars.

Determined to not lose her morning to rumination, Sonja took her tea into her study. Soon, though, she found herself reading a document she hadn't opened in a long time. The words both chilled and warmed her heart.

Engrossed in her reading, she suddenly felt a weight on top of her head. With a screech, she spun around.

Crystal fell back. "Damn, you're loud. I thought you heard me calling you." She moved back to the doorway. "You remind me of those house wrens that used to nest in Momma's ferns. Tiny, cacophonous little beauties."

Sonja touched her crown, still feeling the weight of Crystal's incursion. "Why the hell are you sneaking up on me?"

"Kissing you good morning, Dr. Grump."

Sonja turned around to close her laptop. "Student records," she said, snapping the lid shut and turning to face Crystal again. "I am busy working while you're skulking about."

Crystal grunted and leaned against the doorjamb. "I can't deal with this version of you before coffee. Speaking of coffee, where is it?"

"At the grocery store. I never drink liquid dirt. The teakettle should still be warm. I have tea. Green, black, lavender, and herbal."

"All that but no coffee. You definitely have to call my counselor friend. Anyone who doesn't drink coffee has deep troubles."

"And there she is—Dr. Nag, come to harass me. And it's not even eight."

"Nope, I am *not* doing this," Crystal said, rolling off the doorjamb and out of the office.

Sonja reopened her laptop, sitting at an angle so she could monitor the doorway. She reread the words on the screen, Jacob's indictment of his peers.

I sit here, downright offended by these comments about Dr. Sonja Storey. We should give her thanks, not call her filthy names. As a Christian man, I am disgusted at how you treat her. She could be teaching at one of those big schools where rich kids go. But she came here to teach us. I thank God Almighty that He called her to us. She deserves better than this! Dr. Storey is a great professor and a woman of honor. And lest we forget Luke 6:40, "The disciple is not above his master."

Reproachfully, Jacob Darrow Randalls.

Sonja struggled to remember what he had said during one of their meetings, something like: "Dr. Storey, I hope I don't offend you, but I couldn't hold my tongue. I said my piece on that professor-rating site."

His confession had motivated her to wade into the treacherous swamp filled with biting, stinging creatures that was RateMyTeacherKissMyAss. com in search of his comment.

But now she felt nothing, her insides a smudge of something that had once been. At least if she had a handwritten note, she would have more substantial proof of her impact on Jacob. All she had remaining was the text she had copied and pasted to preserve it.

She closed out the document.

If the teacher rating website was a swamp, Jacob was the rare, gentle bird that had lured her into that place. And she had killed the bird. Maybe not directly, but somehow she had played a part in Jacob's demise.

"I'm leaving," came a voice from the doorway.

Sonja looked up to find Crystal leaning against the doorjamb, holding the stun gun, and wearing yesterday's clothes—and yesterday's judgmental expression. "So?"

"So?" Sonja hit the word back like a tennis ball.

"I'm not playing. The therapist."

"Fine. Text me her number."

Crystal fished her cell phone out of her jacket and typed a message. "Okay, there. You better not renege on our deal."

"I will call. But there is another matter," Sonja said, intending to raise again the question she had asked that morning.

"No, Sonja. There's no other matter until you call the therapist and make an appointment. Call her today. Otherwise, no late-night calls or rescues. No late nights, period."

Sonja turned away from Crystal. "You are being offensive. I wonder if you know when to stop your nonsense."

"I do," Crystal said and walked away.

"Wait!" Sonja called out. She wanted to say more, maybe something about how much she appreciated last night, but when Crystal reappeared in the doorway, she lost her nerve. "The scarf you borrowed for your hair. It—"

"Let me guess. It cost a fortune," Crystal said dryly. "I left it on the bed, thinking I could use it next time. But next time depends on what you do. Decide wisely, gorgeous." And she left.

As soon as Sonja heard the security door slam shut, her anxiety returned like a prickly briar that she kept pruning back. To reassure herself—or perhaps prove the veracity of her suspicions, thinking she must have missed something—she performed another online search of Crystal.

On the fifth page of search results, she located a story in *The Messenger*, a newspaper from Podunk Town, Georgia. Under the Community section, wedged between stories about a turkey shoot and the fishing forecast, appeared a brief article.

PCHS welcomes back Dr. Crystal Byrd

Friday, PCHS graduate Crystal Byrd spoke with Mrs. Ruby Carter's AP English class. Byrd credits Mrs. Carter for her success in graduate school. Now she wants to help her fellow Eagles.

"You may think your teachers are too tough. But they're preparing you. Do your homework, read the books, attend class. Embrace change too. It's coming whether you like it or not. Change isn't always bad, even if it shakes you up," Byrd told the 25 students.

Daughter of Eva Hargrove Byrd and Cleo Byrd, she wanted to ...

Seeing nothing of consequence, Sonja closed the website. It seemed Crystal really had but a small footprint in the world. And yet Sonja repeatedly traipsed after the other woman.

A few hours later, Sonja closed the door to her office, thankful that she had at least sent an email to the search committee, despite getting sidetracked by Jacob and then Crystal. It was too late for her workout, so she checked her cell for notifications.

I mean it.

Crystal's terse text got Sonja moving. She showered, fixed her hair and face, pulled on her black LNDR leggings and a matching long-sleeved running top that she had never actually run in. Then she picked up her cell phone and retrieved Crystal's text with the counselor's details.

Abby Wake, LCSW

"Not even a PhD," Sonja complained, setting down her phone and aggressively stripping the linen from the bed that Crystal had sloppily made. "That does not surprise me, coming from you, Crystal. To recommend that I give my limited time and money to an underqualified professional." She remade the bed, smoothing the covers and plumping the pillows to perfection.

Her phone buzzed again.

You have until 11:59 a.m.! NOT 12. After that, BLOCKED

"Fine, Crystal." She bit out the name, shaking her head as she dialed Ms. Wake. Her voicemail picked up.

"This is Dr. Sonja Storey," she said after the beep. "I am a colleague of Dr. Crystal Byrd's. I am interested in consulting with you on a matter." She left her number and ended the call without a thank-you or goodbye. Afterward, she texted Crystal.

Done.

She wanted to add *Now, get off my back*, but she decided against it. Just like Sonja's bed, Crystal had a steel frame underneath the smooth, fluffy layers.

Feeling angry at Crystal's victory over her, Sonja steadied herself with work, just as she had as a child. When her mother had become crazed, wailing and thrashing in their tiny apartment, Sonja studied harder, aced exams, and wrote stellar papers. When her mother smacked her for the first time when she was in high school, Sonja got straight As and maintained that streak of perfection until she graduated. The worse life got with her mother, the better Sonja performed, and not just academically. Bit by bit, she liberated herself.

Over time, young Sonja learned to minimize her reliance on her mother. By dressing in clothes donated to the school for needy students, she put a target on her back, attracting the wrath of privileged girls. But at the same time, she freed herself from depending on her mother, and she ultimately realized that she didn't need anyone else to survive.

Fired up now, she worked through the items on her to-do list. Even Jay's late-afternoon email didn't derail her.

Sonja, it's my understanding that you have already convened a search committee and provided them with a working job description. I recognize that you're itching to get the ball rolling, but there is protocol to follow. Route me the job description, then let's meet this week and get those procedures hammered out. Jay.

She replied.

Once the committee has finalized the job description, I will be in touch.

—SJS.

"I dare you to micromanage my search, Jay."

When her phone rang, it yanked her out of her fantasy argument with the department chair. She looked at the screen and let Abby Wake's call go to voicemail.

———

By Thursday morning, Sonja's mood had improved, aided by her red Anne Klein wrap blouse. She even enjoyed her predawn walk on campus, imagining the university as it would become rather than seeing it as the shithole it was. As she unlocked the door to her building and slipped inside, she applauded herself for having secured the search committee's email approval yesterday. And no one requested changes to the job description.

Even Jay had relented last night, allowing Sonja to direct Harmony to enter the faculty position into the online jobs system.

Teaching proved uneventful, and by office hours, she remained confident, even when Ronnie Staller entered.

"You seem to be having a rough time, so I made you something," Staller said, holding out a plastic bag.

Sonja remained seated and looked at the bag, a sense of foreboding settling in her chest. "I do not accept gifts from students."

Undeterred, Staller dug into the bag and removed a stunningly painted butterfly on a small rectangle of heavy paper. "Based it on a red admiral butterfly. Went with red and black 'cause you wear those colors lots." Staller presented the bookmark as if it were a gift to royalty. "Plus, you read. I thought...bookmark!"

"I appreciate the gesture." Sonja had rarely been put in the position of refusing a gift from a student. What further complicated the current situation was that the painted butterfly was extraordinarily rendered. Sonja would have loved to hold it, study it. "You painted that?" Sonja asked. Her voice conveyed an admiration she did not intend.

"Sure did. One-forty weight gives the paper heft. And oil paint makes it pop."

Sonja appraised the fine lines, observing the feathering of colors in some spots and the stark delineation in others.

"You are skilled at this," Sonja admitted. "But I am unable to accept this gift. It would be an ethics violation."

"But I made it special for you," Staller whimpered. "It's based on what you've been sayin' in class. The butterflies and such. I thought it'd make you happy, me learnin' somethin'." The more nervous Staller got, the more the Gs disappeared from the ends of her words.

"You mean the butterfly effect."

"Yeah, butterflies bringin' storms." Staller held out the bookmark again. "When small stuff makes big messes."

Sonja squared her shoulders.

"Ms. Staller, I have already explained to you that I am unable to accept a gift." Technically, she *could* accept a gift below a certain value, but she had personally adopted a rigid no-gift policy. "Yet you keep pressing this bookmark on me. What is your exact goal?"

"I told ya. You've been lookin' like you're havin' a rough time. I swear, the bookmark didn't cost me nothing but time to draw and paint it. It helps me remember what I read."

The student looked at the bookmark still held in her extended hand, then slowly lifted it until it looked as if the butterfly were rising of its own accord in the air and landing on Staller's chest.

"Good, Ms. Staller. You are finding methods for retaining information. And you are preparing for the exam and not simply painting?"

Staller stuffed the bookmark back into the plastic bag and sniffled. "I was tryin' to be nice."

Sonja took in Staller's splotchy skin and shallow breathing. "Do you understand that this behavior is inappropriate? You have an exam in my class, a class in which, by your own admission, you have struggled. A gift could be viewed as an attempt to sway my assessment of your performance."

Staller plunged her fingers into the mass of tangled hair atop her head and repeated, "I was tryin' to be nice."

Sonja's concern mounted. She glanced at the open door, briefly reliving her former student's attack and his spit on her face.

"This discussion is concluded. Now, the midterm approaches, and I cannot stress enough the importance of earning a passing grade. If you have specific questions about the material, I am here to help."

"Yes, ma'am. I mean, yes, doctor ma'am." With that, the student jumped up and, turning quickly, collided with the visitor chair, knocking it over. Without picking it up, she ran out of the room.

Weary from the exchange, Sonja shut the door and straightened her office. Then she remembered the voice message that Abby Wake left yesterday and decided that a professional consultation might be exactly what she needed. She checked the message and was pleasantly surprised that the therapist spoke in low tones instead of high-pitched squeaks.

"This is Abby Wake returning your call, Dr. Storey. I have a cancellation for tomorrow at four thirty. If that day and time don't work, we're looking at the end of October. I'm booked solid."

Sonja looked at the time, and before she could convince herself otherwise, she returned the phone call, telling herself she was simply consulting a mental health specialist about the insanity that swirled around her these days. She left a message saying she would be there shortly, confident that Wake would hold the spot for a university professor and fellow social scientist.

As Sonja closed her office door, she found Staller's bag containing the bookmark hanging on the doorknob. Exasperated, Sonja snatched it up and dropped the bag in her tote. "I'm only preserving evidence," she lied to herself. She wanted that damn butterfly. Its beauty gave her...the butterflies.

She walked away quickly in case Staller was lurking and watching her accept the gift before it flew away.

Chapter 24

Sad as Sad Can Be

As SHE DROVE AWAY FROM campus, Sonja promised herself that there would be no dredging up childhood nonsense. This was a meeting with a criminal profiler. Nothing more.

Images of her mother thrashed in her head, amplified by the memory of a slamming door, the sound of brutal pounding.

I am running out of time. The words slithered from a dark hole inside her and into her consciousness. Sonja bit down on her bottom lip until the anxious feeling passed. "This counselor will smell weakness on you. Keep your emotions in check. Otherwise, she will think you're a whack job."

Glancing at the route on the GPS, she saw that she was headed to an upper middle-class part of town. The line of spacious, handsome homes credentialed—barely—the therapist as a professional worthy of her time. The more attractive the neighborhoods that she passed through, the more Sonja considered that this meeting could be an opportunity. Perhaps the counselor would have a private home office off a courtyard and surrounded by a high brick wall, maybe even a water feature and a Zen garden where two social scientists could stroll and consult with one another.

But the next turn took Sonja into an industrial sector, away from the pristine neighborhoods and her fantasies. Warehouses lined both sides of the road, their parking lots empty. The asphalt cracked and buckled as if underground dwellers had clawed their way up.

There must be some mistake. But the GPS confirmed her route. Now she was driving by grimy storefronts: a convenience food market, a discount tobacco store, a dark café. She gripped the steering wheel, terror gurgling inside her as if she were time traveling back into her old neighborhood toward her mother's prison-like apartment.

"Damn you, Crystal. Have you sent me to some quack?" Her terror morphed into a simmering rage at the person who had sent her to this horrible part of town.

As she turned into the deserted office park, she wondered how a professional woman like Abby Wake had ended up in such a lowly space.

It is downgrading and degrading.

She chuckled. "Downgrading and degrading. I must remember that as a chapter title for my next book."

Sonja parked and climbed out of her BMW, gingerly placing her designer heels on the pavement. Weeds poked through sidewalk cracks. As she passed the dark windows, the glassy eyes of dead businesses, she decided she *needed* to see the therapist, to gather evidence, to inform Crystal that the woman was a fraud or, at minimum, an incompetent fool.

Finally, she spotted a carved forest-green sign, a bit of color in a gray hellhole. It was almost pretty.

Abby A. Wake, LCSW

Sonja stepped into the waiting room. The décor looked like a berry-filled blender had exploded. Fat pillows the colors of blackberry and raspberry were tossed everywhere, covering the rattan loveseat and matching chairs. Tapestries in various shades of ripened fruit hung on the walls, tiny mirrors sewn into the material.

Sonja stood just inside the door, shifting her weight from one foot to the other, her Valentino tote pulled close. Just as she considered slipping back out, a woman stumbled from the hallway into the waiting room.

"I do that every single time," she announced, drying her hands with a crumpled paper towel before smoothing her black hair, an unflattering asymmetrical-bob style. "I love my runners. They brighten the place, but I keep catching my feet on them. Dr. Sonja Storey, I presume. I'm Abby. I'd shake hands, but they're still damp. We're back here." She turned and led the way down the hall.

Sonja followed the woman, abandoning her illusions of an invigorating debate between colleagues while they strolled through a Zen garden.

The berry-hued theme continued in her office. One wall was painted a shade somewhere between blackberry and blueberry, and the remaining three walls were the color of not quite ripe strawberries.

Wake sat in an overstuffed chair and picked up a notebook from the rattan table beside it. "Have a seat. Wherever you're comfortable."

"I am comfortable in my home. Perhaps I should go sit there," Sonja said.

The counselor snickered. "That's funny. I'll have to remember that one."

Sonja picked her way across the area rug that had bunched in the middle. "These are tripping hazards," she noted, "as is the hall runner."

"You're right," Wake replied matter-of-factly. "I keep meaning to do something about them. Though I'm guessing you're not here to help me with interior design."

Sonja sat on the couch, as far from the counselor as she could get, and she appraised the woman, zeroing in on the clunky pleather shoes. She wished she hadn't worn her understated black pointed-toe Calvin pumps. She should have worn something more upscale to compensate for feeling downsized by the surroundings.

"You're welcome to set your purse down." Wake pointed to a wooden rocking chair off to one side. "Today we'll mostly get a sense of one another, so I want you to be as comfortable as possible."

"I am fine." Sonja clutched her Valentino on her lap.

The woman appeared to be anywhere between late forties and early sixties. Her dark hair had clumps of silver in it, but her face was smooth. She wore a fleece jacket the color of faded oranges and taupe pants. It looked like Abby Wake had picked out her wardrobe from an L.L. Bean catalog.

Sonja detested that catalog.

"Today I want to learn about your goals and expectations, and you'll get a sense of my approach," Wake said. "Let's begin by you telling me what brought you here."

"I am in need of a consultant, a mental health professional. Not for me. I am uninterested in that inner child drivel."

The counselor's expression didn't change. "And what's going on that you feel you need a consultant?"

"Someone is playing a sick game with me." Sonja's voice sizzled, and she thought Wake flinched slightly. She brought her tone down to a more measured tenor, speaking as a scholar would. "I brought my evidence folder. Emails, notes, various documents. I assume you would like to assess them for yourself."

"Perhaps later. Right now, I'm more interested in hearing you describe in your own words what's happening."

As Sonja summarized the events, she impressed herself with concise details about the suspicious incidents and potential suspects. When she mentioned Jacob Randalls, her voice cracked, and she pivoted away.

Stay focused or this woman will dine on your past like a vulture.

"There is—was— a student whom I consider a primary suspect. Corey Randalls. I have not quite figured out how he could have deposited the animal corpse in my driveway, but I believe it is part of a revenge plot for Jacob's death."

"Let's pause here," Wake said. "You've already given me quite a bit of information about your circumstances. Before you continue, I want to make sure we get to the reason for you being here today. I would like to help you explore your reactions and decisions in the face of the challenges you've described."

"I am uninterested in exploring *my* reactions to these incidents," Sonja clarified. "I am here today for your input. Who would do something like this? Leave notes, rip through my photo. Not to mention the dead animals and midnight visits. I require a personality profile for starters. After that, I will reassess my needs."

"You have reported these incidents, correct?"

"Yes. Most of them, at least. Not that anyone takes me seriously."

"I'd like to hear more about your sense that others don't take you seriously, Sonja."

"I prefer that you address me as Dr. Storey."

Wake laid her pen on the notebook in her lap. "Why is that important to you? For me to use your title?"

"I earned that title."

"Certainly. I'm not questioning your professional credentials. I'm asking you to reflect on why you put yourself in a power position." Wake studied Sonja intently. "Counseling tends to make us feel vulnerable. You seem to be feeling something. Would you share those feelings with me?"

Sonja recrossed her legs, pulled her wrap blouse tighter around her, and clutched her Valentino closer. "I find your approach fascinating. A bit cliché, but fascinating."

"What prompted you to call now?" Wake asked, obviously ignoring Sonja's dig. "It sounds like these incidents have been taking place over the past few weeks."

"Dr. Crystal Byrd urged me to come," Sonja said. "To consult with you."

"And Crystal's opinion is important to you?"

"She is *not* why I am here."

"Let's put a pin in that. I suggest we set an agenda for our time together. What would you like to prioritize?"

"The sick game," Sonja said. "The sick game," she repeated, as if to bludgeon her opponent. "That is the only reason I am here. I may have prematurely decided on Corey Randalls's culpability. I need a profiler to review my list of suspects, perhaps even broaden that list in case I have overlooked someone."

"You have mentioned Corey Randalls several times. Why him?"

"I explained that. Revenge."

"For the death of"—Wake glanced down at her notebook—"Jacob."

Sonja scoffed, exasperated. "Correct. I also mentioned Ms. Ronnie Staller. And Dr. Horace Watson, who may be targeting me on social media. Then there are the storm-is-coming emails. I have two prime suspects, both taking my chaos theory class. Except Corey Randalls has been removed." Sonja uncrossed her legs and sat up, her back screaming for relief. "I have been perfectly clear in detailing my persecution. That leaves me to question whether you have been listening."

Wake set aside her notebook and pen. "Let's do a check-in. How are you feeling right now?"

"Interrogated."

"Tell me more about that."

"I have been interrogated my entire life, and I have no interest in paying someone to do that now."

"You look uncomfortable, Dr. Storey. Would you be receptive to a body scan? I find—"

Sonja snorted.

Wake leaned back in her chair, a smile spreading across her face. "You're right," she said. "It sounds ridiculous, but there's a great deal of research about how survivors of childhood trauma detach from their bodies as a coping mechanism."

"You people cannot resist exposing every past bump or bruise," Sonja scoffed. "I did not come here to discuss my freak show parents. I am here to better understand whoever is after me. If you want to analyze someone's childhood, analyze *my stalker*. I must get the upper hand on this situation."

Wake leaned forward, rested her elbows on her thighs, and clasped her hands. "That sounds hard. Growing up with parents you characterize as a freak show. If you're willing to share, I'd like to listen."

Sonja slumped and hugged her Valentino closer. "'Sad as sad can be.'"

"You are?"

"No, not me. I do not entertain sadness in my life. My mother." Sonja rubbed her eye to hide the spasm from Wake. "'Twas sad as sad can be.' I am quoting a poem I studied in high school. I hadn't thought about it in years. Now, it seems, I cannot stop thinking about it."

I can't stop thinking about all manner of foul things.

"What poem is that?"

"Samuel Taylor Coleridge's *Rime of the Ancient Mariner*. When I read that one line back in high school, I thought—" Sonja looked at the counselor, who gazed at her without blinking. "None of that matters. What matters is that you think I have concocted everything because of an erratic mother and an absentee father. How trite."

"Then tell me more about this evidence folder," Wake suggested.

"That would be pointless. Certainly you are familiar with confirmation bias. You have already decided that I'm just a freak who never escaped my freak show family. You will doubtlessly conclude that my misery is nothing but a cry for help. So, no, I do not think it would be productive for you to review the documents in my folder."

"You've used that word several times."

"What word?"

"Freak. Could we touch on that?"

Sonja stared at the counselor, then angled her head and looked at the diploma on the wall.

Abby A. Wake

Master's in Education in Counseling with Emphasis in Marriage and Family

Western Highlands State University

"Abby A. Wake. A bit on the nose, is it not?" Sonja said, trying to provoke a response.

But Wake didn't bite. "Someone of your background will be familiar with the research, Dr. Storey, about how our names influence the paths we take."

"You are out of education." Sonja knew her disdain was evident in her voice. "I read you were out of social work."

"A master's in social work, a master's in education."

"You have a diploma missing." Sonja studied the counselor suspiciously.

"It fell. I'm having it reframed."

"You collect degrees," Sonja said, sensing she had found traction at last.

Wake tapped her index finger on her clasped hand twice. Sonja picked up on the counselor's frustration that any other client would have missed.

"I earned my MSW when I worked as a program director in a large behavioral health system. Later, I realized family and marriage counseling was a better fit for the next phase of my life. That led to my master's in counseling. I'm pursuing my EdD presently. While I will hold a doctorate, it won't be a PhD. Is that important to you?"

"No offense intended, *Ms.* Wake," Sonja said. "Professionals with an advanced degree in education are fine. They simply lack the required social science training." Sonja smiled coldly.

Wake sat back in her chair. "We seem to be at an impasse, then. I trained at WHSU, the same university that employs you, and I specialize in ACEs and CPTSD. That's—"

"I am familiar with the acronyms. No need for a lecture." It was a lie, but Sonja would look it up later.

"Great. Then I don't have to explain to you why I chose *not* to pursue a PhD in psychology. If that's important to you, I can refer you to someone else."

"Unnecessary. I simply wanted to consult a mental health professional. This discussion has been illuminating. What do I owe you?"

Wake stood up and led Sonja to the door. She was little more than five feet tall, even shorter than Sonja.

"You owe me nothing," Wake said. "Consider this meeting a professional courtesy, but *Dr.* Storey, I recommend that you make an appointment with another therapist. Unaddressed trauma has a way of creating waves and retraumatizing. I can give you names and numbers of—"

"Unnecessary," Sonja repeated more firmly this time. She hoisted her tote, flashed an inauthentic smile, and stepped into the waiting area.

From behind her, Wake said, "Fighting those waves gets exhausting. We can lose sight of shore."

Once in Bimmer and on her way home, Sonja called Crystal. "I went to my appointment."

"Wait! What? You got in that quickly?"

"Yes."

"With Abby?"

"With whom I consult is private."

"It's just...she's in huge demand."

"Well, I went, and *Ms.* Wake and I agreed that I do not meet the criteria for someone in need of counseling."

There was a moment of silence, then Crystal said, "That doesn't sound right."

"Are you accusing me of lying?"

"Here's the deal, lover. I've been in therapy since my teens. You've survived some ugliness, and that was before all these alleged break-ins. Did you even tell her how scared you've been?"

Alleged break-ins.

Sonja's vision narrowed. She could barely see through her windshield. *AllegedAllegedAlleged.*

From her left side, a truck cut in front of Bimmer, nearly clipping her car. She jerked the wheel, veered off the road, and screeched to a stop on the shoulder. By the time she looked up, the truck was speeding away.

"Sonja? Sonja?" Crystal's frantic voice emerged from the cell phone.

Sonja unclasped her seat belt, and she reached for her cell that now rested on the passenger side floorboard. She picked it up, her hands shaking. "Someone drove me off the road."

"What?"

"Someone tried to kill me."

"Oh, Sonja. Do you have a description of the car?"

"Red truck. WHSU parking sticker. A student sticker."

"Call 9-1-1. Report it."

"It won't do any good." *No one believes me. Even you think I'm a crazy freak.*

Sonja hung up. She was alone in an increasingly hostile world.

Chapter 25

Evil Looks

THE NEXT MORNING, SONJA'S BRAIN crackled like an electrical cord plugged into an overloading socket. She hadn't slept well, even after taking an extra dose of medicine, but she didn't really feel bad either. Rather, she felt—

Ready.

Ready for what? asked the trained researcher occupying her frontal lobe.

Battle! responded a voice from the primitive part of her brain.

She decided to go to campus to work, even though she usually worked at home on Fridays. She needed to put herself on display, to warn her enemies.

She reached for her Lafayette 148 blouse that reminded her of a Union officer's uniform. It was a silk with long sleeves, a high collar, and bell-shaped ruffled cuffs. The neckline encircled her throat like a smooth garrote. Then she pulled on matching slacks and red Choos. Checking herself in the bathroom mirror, she smoothed her hair one last time and ran a finger around the outline of her mouth, making certain that her MAC Ruby Woo lipstick did not bleed outside the fleshy borders.

So severe, Dr. Shrill Harpy. She snickered.

For a brief time during her undergraduate days, she had softened her appearance, highlighting her hair and adding wispy bangs as if these changes could overwrite her fundamental programming. Then, one night, her boyfriend said something inane, words so inconsequential that she couldn't recall them. And poof! She reverted to her original genetic operating system.

After that, she ignored the boyfriend's calls. When she ran into him at the campus dining hall a few days later, he asked "Why?" Tears welled in his eyes, and his mouth puckered in an unflattering pout.

Without a word, she stepped out of line, slid her empty tray onto a nearby table, and left. She didn't answer him because then she would have had to explain about dart frogs. Dart frogs aren't toxic at first. They become toxic. It's in their environments. What they feed on alters their essence.

Dart frogs are not lethal. They are made lethal.

That is what she had wanted to say to him, but she knew he wouldn't understand.

Afterward, she let her bangs grow out, let the caramel highlights fade away, draping her head in darkness once more. She had worn the shroud ever since. By the time she was hired at WHSU, she had completely transformed. Her eyes, her voice, her words—her entire body brimmed with toxins.

And Jacob Randalls had succumbed to her.

Crystal had confessed how much it hurt to be around her.

Only Avery Bruce had been able to withstand her. Because he, too, was a dart frog.

Most people failed to recognize the truth about her until too late. Sonja secreted poison, and there would be no changing that.

As she drove through campus, Sonja looked for a red truck with a WHSU student parking permit. But other than a few vehicles around residential halls, the parking lots and roads were deserted.

She parked Bimmer and was instantly met by the buzzing of leaf blowers. The noise merged with her own internal buzzing.

She mounted the steps into Terrell Center, unlocked the door, and fumbled for the light switch, her fingers spidering along the wall. "I swear someone moves you around simply to antagonize me."

Suddenly, she sensed someone watching her, making her skin crawl. She peered into the dark hallway. A shadow shifted ever so slightly, but the movement was just enough for her to notice.

"Who's there?" Hearing nothing, she jangled her keys. "Who the hell is there?"

Someone moaned.

"You want to play a game?" she challenged. "I'll play. Let's start with me bashing in your goddamn face. Then I'll tear open your chest and eat your fucking heart. Answer me, you sick fuck!"

She heard a muffled noise and advanced, keys clutched in her hand.

The fluorescent lights flickered on. Lewis Waters stood by the light switch at the far end of the hall, his pallid face looking ghostly against his camel hair blazer. One hand remained on the light switch, and the other held a mug with a utensil sticking out of it. He was shaking so hard she could hear it clacking.

"Lewis, what are you doing skulking about? I almost—" Sonja took a breath. "You should have answered me."

He removed his hand from the light switch and pointed at the mug. "Oatmeal with peanut butter," he said apologetically, still trembling. "Mouth...full...couldn't... Sorry, Sonja. So sorry. I tried."

"Next time, turn on some lights." *Instead of haunting the hallways like an ancient ghoul.*

Without another word, Lewis turned and shuffled away.

When Sonja reached her office, the incident was driven from her mind by the folded paper that had been slid underneath the door.

She opened the paper, instantly wishing she hadn't.

Sonja knocked on the office door. "Lewis, are you in there?" No reply. "Lewis? I require a moment of your time." She tried the handle, but it was locked.

Sonja refolded the note, slipped it into her pants pocket, and returned to her office to consider the possibilities.

Could Lewis be the culprit? Could he be paying her back? After all, she had gone to the college dean back when Mitch had taunted her with threats that her tenure would be denied.

"There is a culture of intimidation and harassment in my department. My persecutors are Mitch Grant, Cole Behringer, Lewis Waters. The chair of the department appeases them."

The somewhat melodramatic statement to the dean during her tenure consideration had been a warning to him and to the administration about the stink she could make concerning WHSU's treatment of female faculty. As a result of that complaint, her tenure and promotion were approved by unanimous vote.

Sonja tried to remember how Lewis had reacted after her conversation with the dean. What evil looks had he given her? She couldn't remember Lewis's reaction, but she did remember Mitch and Cole's intensified harassment.

Retribution right before retirement. That is exactly what I would do. Lie in wait, then attack when my opponent is complacent.

With the note still in her pocket, she went to the main office. Harmony had not yet arrived. She shoved aside the thick textbook left on the copier, scanned the note, and emailed it to herself. When she returned to her office, she opened the attachment:

UGLY FUCKING BITCH, I WOULDN'T PISS ON YOU IF YOU WERE ON FIRE!

The typed message screamed at her above the image of her faculty headshot. A black slash cut across her face.

"F for originality. Get new material," she advised the anonymous author.

After sticking the note in her GAME? folder, she checked her other email messages, looking up only briefly to notice the brooding, red-streaked sky outside the window. Sometime later, she looked up again, disturbed by a commotion from the department office. She heard Harmony shout "Sarah," then say something else.

Sonja ignored the disruption until the shouting got to be too much. She stood up, straightened her uniform, and marched into chaos.

While the secretary hollered, the student worker wept.

"This noise is unprofessional, Harmony," Sonja scolded.

Harmony shoved past her into the hallway without a glance or word.

Sonja followed her. "What happened?"

Harmony slumped against the wall across from Lewis Waters's office and pointed. "I was returning his book."

Sonja glanced at the scene inside where three people in navy uniforms squatted in a circle. A camel hair blazer rested on the back of a chair.

"Is he dead?" Sonja asked.

The secretary sobbed.

Sonja swallowed the bile coming up in her throat, looked away from the scene in Lewis's office, and lowered her gaze to her red pumps and inky pants. That's when she realized that she wasn't dressed for battle. Instead, she had dressed in the colors of the *Ranitomeya reticulata,* the dart frog that had most intrigued her.

For a second, she wished she could cry. But dart frogs didn't shed tears. Dart frogs oozed toxin.

Chapter 26

She Steadies

WHEN SONJA COULDN'T ERASE HER thoughts that weekend, she set them ablaze. Carrying Star Dancer into Summit Street in the middle of the night, she got away from the trees, allowing her to view a larger slice of sky.

After the telescope had first been delivered to her house, it had remained in pieces, each component boxed separately and stacked neatly, like smaller coffins atop larger ones. Sonja had flipped through the assembly instructions, trying to sort out the eyepieces, mounts, knobs, and rods, but within thirty minutes, her brain had rebelled. The telescope had gone in the back of the closet where she cast the other possessions that confounded her.

One day, however, Sonja gathered her courage, fueled by two glasses of pinot, and figured out how to assemble the red beauty. Aligning the finderscope required setting the tripod on a flat, stable surface during daylight hours—a task that exposed Sonja to the scrutiny of her neighbors.

For more than an hour, she stood in the middle of Summit Street, focusing the finderscope on a distant neighbor's house until the chimney appeared crisp and clean in the crosshairs—upside down. No matter what she tightened or tilted, the images refused to flip. So back into the closet Star Dancer went until finally she got curious enough to research and learn that the system of mirrors and lenses inverted the images. Later, after several nights of seeing the universe upside down, she turned the world right side up.

Over time, she learned how to twist the knobs and adjust the slender rods, and she silently thanked that old sky watcher from her youth for introducing her to the stars. Evenings spent in Star Dancer's company were blissful, interrupted only occasionally by the suspicion that eyes watched her as she watched the sky. When that happened, she would retreat behind locked doors, telescope in tow.

But such was not the case the weekend after Lewis Waters died. Nothing interrupted her. Not her phone. Not work. Not sleep. Friday through Sunday night, Sonja took her bottle of pinot, and she and Star Dancer became a fixture in the middle of the street.

As soon as Sonja returned to work on Monday morning, the heaviness returned along with unwanted childhood memories. Sonja blamed her mood on people's drab outfits in colors of decomposition, with their bodies sunken in by grief and their eyes rusted.

Ducking inside her office and shutting the door, Sonja escaped the silence that covered the department like rank mold, but she seemed to catch whiffs of her mother's decaying garden throughout the day, and soon, decades-old memories plagued her.

During one manic episode, Sonja's mother had ordered a bunch of indoor gardening supplies. "Time for a fresh start." Her mother had frantically torn into the cardboard as if salvation had been shipped inside the flimsy boxes. "Fresh start, fresh start," she repeated obsessively as she pulled out seedling starter kits, bags of soil, planting cups, and an assortment of trowels. Piece by piece, the wooden slats and shelves got stacked haphazardly into a tiered garden stand, but as her mother's mood darkened, the unassembled pieces got scattered. The stand could have cheered up their dreary apartment—had her mother assembled it correctly. Instead, it ended up in a dark corner. Shrunken vegetables lined the shelves like rotting internal organs from a diseased body. Fuzz grew in the potting soil like white furry caterpillars. Even worse, the smell of decay mingled with the mildew in the apartment, and the perfume of despair burrowed into Sonja's nostrils, festering into hatred.

Each time Sonja laid eyes on that neglected garden stand, she boiled. For what it had cost, she could have replaced her outgrown clothes—her mother always claimed that they didn't have money to "fill up the closet of a snooty bitch." That was before Sonja got smart about securing her own clothes.

With the scent memory burning into Sonja's brain, she retrieved the custom-blended spray of clean linen from her tote and showered her office with it.

Once she could breathe without smelling mildew and rot, she resumed the work she had neglected over the weekend. Certain that her book proposal would be accepted for publication, she poured energy into the literature review section. So intent was she on researching terms like "dysfunction" and "toxic coworker" that she barely registered the ping of a new email notification.

With a glance, she saw that Jay was calling for an emergency meeting that afternoon.

She responded decisively.

Jay:

I have prior commitments. I am unable to attend your meeting.

—SJS.

Less than five minutes after she sent her response, someone knocked at her door. She got up and yanked it open, knowing exactly who was on the other side.

"Jay, I am in the middle of something. You should have received my email."

"A word, please," he said.

"Be quick. I'm on a deadline." Never mind that it was a deadline she had established for herself.

He sank listlessly into the spare chair.

Sonja swiveled her own chair to face him. "You look terrible," she said, noting his bloodshot eyes.

"I need you at that meeting. You're our senior faculty member now."

"That is not possible." Sonja hardened her heart against his emotional manipulation.

"The department is looking to us. We must show that we can hold this family together."

"We are hardly a family."

"I'm extending a hand of reconciliation."

Sonja scanned the deep trenches of worry in Jay's face. He had caught her off guard, and her grief struggled to get out, but she shoved it down hard.

"It's true that I didn't stand by you when you were—"

"Harassed," she finished for him. *Assaulted.*

"I'd like to give you my side of things."

"No."

"Let's at least find a new path forward. I will accept the blame for everything. Put everything on me. Lewis"—he swallowed—"doesn't deserve this. He protected you."

"Ha!" The laugh escaped, startling her.

"He tried to protect you from the start," Jay said. "Lewis was a quiet man. It's easy to overlook how hard he fought for this department—and for you."

"Spare me your quiet-man drivel. Those men harassed me. Repeatedly. And Lewis laughed right alongside them."

Are you sure?

Jay held up his hands. "He did his best."

"You are determined to defend Lewis. Why didn't either of you defend me from Mitch? Strange how no one noticed those damp stains on the crotch of Mitch's pants after his encounters with me. And you want me to be grateful for Lewis's *protection*?"

Jay opened his mouth but closed it again and lowered his head.

He's feigning shame, manipulating you.

"None of it matters now anyway," she concluded, getting control of her emotions. "But you're correct. Lewis was a quiet man. He didn't say a word in my defense."

Jay jerked his head up. "He threatened to quit," he snapped, then said, "That came out harsher than I intended. I'm sorry, Sonja."

His genuine apology set Sonja off balance, and that made her even angrier.

"What you went through with Mitch," Jay continued, "was horrible. I had hoped it would make you feel better to know what Lewis did for you. Behind the scenes, granted. Like when your tenure committee intended to deny you. Mitch wanted you gone, especially after your stunt with the dean."

"Stunt?"

"That's how Mitch saw it. Cole too. A powerplay. And by a woman. Lewis came to me. I was green then. This was my first chair job—"

"Irrelevant."

Jay wiped the sweat off his forehead with a handkerchief. "I'll concede that point. This is about Lewis and you. He approached me early on. That must have been your second year with us, maybe the beginning of your third year. Mitch and Cole were relentless."

"I know." The words sizzled.

"Lewis insisted on being your tenure chair. He helped me understand what you faced, how Mitch was gunning for you. But Mitch had seniority and he held a strange sway over everyone. Except Lewis."

"Yet, how many times did you leave me alone with that monster?"

"We tried to insulate you. That's why we moved your office to the basement. It was Lewis's idea. He thought it best to keep you out of Mitch's way—"

"When in reality," Sonja interjected, "it gave him privacy. And Mitch valued his privacy."

"Somehow, Lewis suspected that too," Jay said. "That's why we moved you up here again, but this time to Lewis's old office. He vacated it, moved to a more remote office." He sighed. "Sonja, despite how it appeared to you, we tried. Lewis especially. It was a different time. Mitch wasn't going anywhere. There had been numerous previous accusations. The former dean, the provost—hell, the entire administration, did whatever they could to cover them up."

"I don't want to hear this. I have no interest in assuaging your guilt."

"I never told you, but back then, I met with the special assistant to the president. She's retired now. She assured me that an investigation would be launched. But nothing happened. Nothing ever happened."

When his voice quavered, Sonja felt a flash of pity, and she knew it was time to end the meeting.

"That's it." She rose. "You need to leave. Immediately. I refuse to comfort you for the poor handling of my harassment."

Abuse! Assaults! A hunger for revenge drowned out any sense of pity.

But Jay wasn't finished pleading. "Lewis was strong in ways I wasn't. He understood the tenure process. He understood how to maneuver the committee. How to write the report. And believe it or not, while he couldn't control Mitch and Cole, he knew how to twist their arms."

"I don't care," Sonja said loudly. "Leave."

"Lewis brought a letter of resignation to your tenure vote and put it in front of Mitch. He would have done it. He would have gone to the media too. And for some reason I'll never understand, Mitch capitulated."

"Do not make Lewis the hero of *my* story," Sonja said with ice in her voice. "I deserved tenure. I deserved promotion. And I deserved a safe place. You and Lewis failed to give me that."

Jay nodded. "Okay, I'm done. I've asked you to stand by my side at this meeting. Or I'll stand by yours. Whatever you want. Together we can make this department better."

"You will do fine on your own today. I will be in touch when I am ready to update you about our search for a new hire."

Jay opened the door and turned around, his shoulders drooping, reminding Sonja of her mother's neglected garden stand. "I hope this works for you," he said. "This need to defeat everyone." He turned and walked out, closing the door behind him.

Sonja turned back to her computer, entered her password. and continued working on her literature review. When the phone rang, she answered on speaker. "Dr. Sonja Storey."

"I've been calling and texting for days. I didn't hear from you the entire weekend."

"Hello, Crystal. I have been busy."

"I heard one of your faculty members died."

Crystal's voice soothed her, but Sonja threw it off and hardened her feelings to keep herself vigilant. "University Relations sent out an announcement. Check your email." *Or check with Harmony, your new best friend.*

"You don't sound upset."

"Lewis was old." Sonja said, still studying a research abstract. "Shoot, I thought this article would help with my book, but it's not what I need. It's about narcissism in romantic relationships. I need workplace research."

"You're working."

"Of course. Professional commitments don't die." *When people do.*

"Well, then…" Crystal said, and paused. "Sonja, are you still there?"

"I am." *Unfortunately.*

Crystal's breathing filled her ears. The memory of her warm breath spread down the back of Sonja's rigid neck and across her taut shoulders.

"There's a memorial," Crystal continued. "You probably have the details. Want to go together? It sounds like it will be more a celebration of life—"

"I will not be in attendance."

"Sonja, I know you're hurting. I know you're at war. But there's got to be a better way." Crystal paused again, then said, "You know, your life is up to you. I'll be at the memorial. In case you change your mind."

The phone clicked off, and Sonja remembered another line of the Coleridge poem. *"She steadies with upright keel."* It was the same line that had given her comfort when she was barricaded in her bedroom, listening to her mother's emotional torrent on the other side of the door.

"I steady," she promised aloud, looking at the blue sky through her window. Maybe it would be clear enough for stargazing later. But until then, she had work to do.

Chapter 27

An Awful Red

By the time Sonja reached campus Tuesday morning, her mood was bleaker, exacerbated by a sleep full of nightmares. She leaned her head against the steering wheel and dozed off, only to be awakened by knocking on her window. But when she looked up, no one was there. Alarmed, she climbed out of Bimmer and headed for the safety of her office.

In the hall outside her closed door, the hushed whispers of grieving faculty and staff clanged in her brain. At one point, as she tried to prepare for her morning class, she looked down at her forearm and saw trails of red flesh. She couldn't remember scratching her skin.

At her morning lecture, Sonja watched as a male student repeatedly leaned in, tilting his tablet toward the blonde who sat in front of him. He seemed to be pressing his lips close to her hair each time, his windbreaker rustling. After what seemed a dozen times, Sonja exploded.

"You, whatever your name is. If you pick up that goddamn tablet one more time, I will call Public Safety and have you dragged out of my class. Afterward, I will call Dean Lu and lodge a formal complaint against you for creating a negative learning environment. You may express your foul opinions about me on one of those professor-rating websites, but when you enter my classroom, you will give me. Your. Full. Attention."

Insane rant. Like Mommy. Just like Mommy, little girl.

The classroom became as silent as the interior of a steel-lined coffin that had been buried deep in an abandoned cemetery. The offending student raised his hand.

"Dr. Storey, remember?" he said in a trembling voice. "I-I emailed you at the beginning of the semester. The readings are on my tablet. All I was doing was pointing out the case overview to Lauren Ashley here."

AshleyAshleyAshley.

Sonja stiffened, and her face burned at the mention of her half-sister's name, but she recovered quickly.

"Very well," she said. "You could have sent me a follow-up email. Everyone, take note. Review your syllabus. Follow the policies about electronics in my classroom."

She returned to the lecture and clicked the remote to bring up the next slide. "In crisis communication, our goal is to achieve predictive understanding. However, we must do so without relying on established causal patterns."

As Sonja read the slide, her heartrate slowed, her face cooled, and the certainty rose that she would pay dearly for her loss of control today.

Following the lecture, the students fled, giving her a wide berth. All except the young man with the tablet. He approached her with his device in hand. Sonja couldn't remember his name, but she recalled that he always arrived on time for class and had never missed one.

Such a respectful young man too.

"Dr. Storey, look here. Can I show you what I was looking at?"

"That will not be necessary. I recommend that we put your infraction behind us. In the future, minimize your disruptions."

"Yes, Dr. Storey," he said humbly, shrinking into himself.

After he left, she picked up her tote and wondered which anonymous student would be next to slide a note under her office door or send her an email.

This time, she thought, she had it coming.

"Hello, Dr. Storey," Harmony said, peering over the top of the cardboard box she held in her arms.

The secretary hurried to catch up as Sonja unlocked her office.

"If you are here to report a flood of complaints, save your breath." Sonja walked in and dropped her tote onto the visitor chair, cutting off any ideas Harmony might have had about sitting. "What do you want?"

"I won't bother you long. Whew! I have to put this down." Harmony lowered the box to the floor outside Sonja's office. "The memorial. I've been talking to Ruthie, and she wants something fun, something that will bring people together, warm their hearts and all." The words seemed to catch in Harmony's throat. "Anyways, I'm emailing details today."

"I will not be in attendance."

"I haven't even told you when it is," Harmony said.

"I assume the department will send a floral arrangement. I will donate. You may sign my name to the card."

Sonja brushed a strand of hair off her charcoal-colored cashmere dress. It had been easy to wrap around her body this morning, even with unsteady hands and rubbery muscles.

"It's just that he... Never mind. I'll be emailing about flowers, the memorial too, in case you change your mind."

As the secretary leaned down to pick up the box she had set down earlier, Sonja noticed something. "Wait! What's that bottle? The glass one on top."

"It's fish oil." Harmony put down the box again.

"Is it yours?" Sonja asked.

"No, it belongs, belonged to Dr. Waters. I'm packing up his things. Ruthie already has enough to do."

That has to be what was spilled outside my office.

The fish oil that had started the most recent chaos. Or maybe it was the notes. She had trouble recalling the timeline of events.

The chaos extends beyond a note or oil. You know that.

Harmony was still talking. "...but Dr. Waters told you about the accident."

"He most certainly did not tell me about the *accident*," Sonja scoffed.

"I believe he did tell you," Harmony replied. "Ruthie was making him drink fish oil every day after his last heart attack. One morning he dropped the bottle. It shattered, and the oil went everywhere. He cleaned it up as best he could, but he missed some. He felt awful when I told you you slipped on it."

"And why would he tell *you* this information?" Sonja asked, frowning.

"I saw him taking it one morning," Harmony said, her face turning white. "Was that last week? I don't..." She cleared her throat. "Dr. Waters said he'd already apologized to you about the accident, explained it." Harmony looked at Sonja. "You know what? It doesn't matter if you believe me. I'll tell you something, though. Dr. Waters felt real bad that you slipped. For some reason, that good man cared about you." As she reached to pull the door shut, she said, "Dr. Storey, I don't think you deserved it."

"Agreed. I do not think I deserved the fish oil either. Clearly, my theory was correct. He enjoyed a last taste of revenge before retirement."

"That isn't what I meant. I don't think you deserved his affections for you. You only care about you, and you think your pain is the only pain that matters. Dr. Waters likely told you about spilling that fish oil. You just weren't listening, had your head up your rear as usual." And she closed the door.

Harmony's words had drained the fight from Sonja, and when she looked down, she saw she had resumed scratching her arm, leaving lines that were an awful red.

The email announcing the memorial arrived and drew her attention.

From: harmonysingh@whsu.edu

Subject: Dr. Lewis Waters—Celebration of Life [Ridges]

Ruthie Waters asks us to join her at Ridges for an evening of music (featuring WHSU's own Highlanders Harmonizers) and drinks.

Wear your dancing shoes—

Sonja deleted the email and left for her second class. As she lectured, she caught a few pointed stares and decided that gossip about her dressing down her student that morning had already circulated. She dismissed the class early, telling them to use the time to study for their midterm, and she canceled her office hours. Then she headed for Bimmer and drove home before anything else could happen to her today.

Chapter 28

Beyond the Shadows

SHORTLY AFTER SUNSET, SONJA COLLAPSED into bed, her entire body vibrating. Instead of falling asleep, though, she stared at the ceiling, trying to recall when she had last had a good night's rest. With a sinking feeling in the pit of her stomach, she realized it was when Crystal had slept beside her.

Desperate, Sonja popped a second pill and waited. But nothing, including her medicine, seemed to be working.

Eventually, she faded into a fitful doze, stirring periodically, waiting to hear a blend of Crystal's percussive and lyrical nocturnal sounds.

At one point, she found herself standing and jabbing her finger at a leering shadow. "No, I must pull myself out." As she emerged from her stupor, the humanoid form morphed into her drapes.

After that, she gave up on sleep. Craving Crystal's warmth, she stumbled into the living room for a workout, but her movements were sluggish, and she hardly broke a sweat. Next, she tried taking a shower hot enough to scald her skin, hoping to satisfy her desire for heat. She cocooned herself afterward in cashmere loungewear as if she could shield her vibrating skin.

Unprepared to face her department's grief and the student complaints that were surely keeping the office phones ringing, Sonja stayed home to finalize the next day's exams. For a time, she was able to enjoy the thrill that came with crafting tricky questions. After she uploaded the midterms to the cloud, Sonja made a cup of tea and took it out on her deck to enjoy the October air. Below, the untamed wooded area appeared in her eyes like an unshaven mons pubis in need of a good trim.

As she was looking down, something caught her eye—a foreign shape, an element out of place, something hunched in the surrounding green. Tiptoeing inside, she grabbed her cell, then crept back out and snapped a photo. But when she scanned for the shape again, she couldn't find it. Whatever had been there was gone. But the sensation of being watched lingered.

"Look, Sonja," Crystal said, sounding exasperated, "I'm getting ready for a campus event. Call 9-1-1 if you're concerned. I'm hanging up."

"Someone was in the woods watching me," Sonja insisted. "I'm texting you the photo."

"There's no need— Okay, fine. Got it." After a momentary silence, Crystal said stiffly, "I don't see anything."

"It is right there. Look again. Beyond the shadows. See under the big tree that looks like a deformed spider."

"Oh, you mean the loblolly pine." Crystal was silent again, then said, "I don't see anything."

Are you blind?

"Anyway, Sonja, you know the terms of our deal. If you want our relationship to continue, get some counseling. If Abby didn't work out for you, find someone else. If you want to spend time together—without drama—join me tonight. You may be interested. It's at the university's planetarium. Join me. Or don't. Join me at the memorial tomorrow for *your* colleague. Or don't. I will be going to support Harm. I think getting out of the house would do you good. But you...you do you. I'm hanging up now."

Stunned, then furious, Sonja stormed into the kitchen to make another cup of tea, but instead she filled a wineglass, then went to check her email, hoping that her faculty search had moved forward. And to her surprise, it had.

"There's a win." She clapped her hands in solitary celebration.

Her job description for the tenure-track search had been quickly approved by the Office of Equity and Inclusion, also HR. Before anything or anyone could derail her, she submitted the faculty posting to several academic listservs and emailed her search committee, cc'ing Jay to document the process and to test whether he would interfere.

Search members:

We will meet Monday, 2:00 p.m., conference room, Terrell Center.

—SJS

She heard a ping almost immediately.

Sonja: I appreciate your diligence as search chair, but maybe the meeting should be postponed. People are still reeling from Lewis's death. I'm not sure this aggressive timeline is helpful.

—Jay

She fired back.

Jay:

The essential functioning of the university doesn't stop. We must press forward. Otherwise, we risk losing top candidates. The posting will be published next week on two listservs. I anticipate submitting it to at least one more. I will have a review procedure in place before applications arrive.

—SJS

She didn't hear back from Jay, so she emailed and directed Harmony to reserve the conference room for the search meeting. By the end of the day, she felt almost jubilant. Loosened up by wine, she opened the WHSU home page and searched the university calendar.

WHSU PLANETARIUM FALL OPEN HOUSE

STAR STORY 7:30 pm–10pm

Before she could change her mind, Sonja dressed in a pair of Ann Taylor high-waisted ebony trousers and a poppy-colored ruffled wrap sweater.

Then, after applying lipstick and checking her hair, she hurried down to Bimmer and raced out of the neighborhood.

Sonja walked into the planetarium, immediately regretting her decision. There was a dense but small crowd with pockets of people swirling about. Crystal stood at the center of one of the pockets like a sun in a solar system.

Crystal was chatting with Professor Samson Matovu when her eyes settled on Sonja, and the woman's smile gave over to shock and then a wave.

Sonja slipped between the bodies and made her way to Crystal's side.

"Dr. Storey, it is a pleasure," Matovu said, nodding tersely.

"You received my email regarding Monday's meeting?" Sonja asked him. He replied that he had.

Crystal laughed. "It's always work with you, Sonja."

Sonja glared at the junior professor for poking at her in front of another professor. Just as she was about to correct Crystal's overstep, an announcement was made that the show was beginning, and the crowd began moving through the double doors. Sonja again considered leaving, but Dr. Matovu stopped her.

"I valued serving with you on the inquiry committee," he said quietly. "It's an honor to be requested to serve on your department's search committee. I will be there Monday. Now, though, I must find my wife." He smiled at Sonja, nodded at Crystal, then turned away.

Before Sonja could consider escaping again, Crystal linked arms with her, and they walked together through the walnut doors.

Inside, the seats were filling quickly. Crystal tried to steer them to the front while Sonja tugged toward the back. They ended up sitting in a middle row.

As the lights dimmed, a digital night sky stretched overhead, clearer than anything Star Dancer had ever shown Sonja, transporting her into a radiant universe.

The narrator spoke in low tones, the seat cupped her body, and Crystal emitted a sunlike warmth that enveloped Sonja; these combined with Sonja's fatigue. She drifted in and out of consciousness, floating through constellations, barely listening to the narrative. Sonja surrendered to a dreamlike state as she soared among the glittering pinholes, glowing worms, and lustrous globs, and she faded in and out of corporeal existence.

Crystal's occasional whispering in her ear became a solar wind that entered her, heating and cooling, expanding and contracting, uniting and dividing. When Crystal took her hand and stroked her fingers, Sonja felt herself merge with the nebula, this one a red blend of apple, berry, and currant that appeared to her like a crimson butterfly on black satin. She closed her eyes as the space outside and the space within met.

"Sonja. Sonja." Crystal's voice pulled her out of the glittering cosmos behind Sonja's eyes. "Darling, you look gorgeous sleeping, but I assume you—"

Sonja bolted upright and looked around. She and Crystal were the only ones still in the planetarium. Voices drifted in from the lobby.

"I wasn't sleeping," Sonja protested groggily. "I closed my eyes. To listen."

Crystal cradled Sonja's chin with her fingers. "You need rest. You're exhausted. Let's go."

Sonja struggled to her feet, surrendering to Crystal's arm encircling her waist, and looked up, her head still inside the womb of the universe. As if responding to gravity itself, Sonja reached up to pull the tall woman's head down to her for a soft, brief kiss. Then they walked out into the lobby. Under the bright lights, Sonja's tension returned. Crystal was immediately drawn into a conversation about the program audit.

When Sonja caught sight of Faculty Senator Douglas Christopher making his way through the crowd toward her, she quickly exited.

Safely in Bimmer, Sonja texted Crystal.

I must go.

Part of Sonja still drifted inside the planetarium, and she longed to communicate something more, to explain that she had fallen asleep because Crystal was at her side, to thank the woman who illuminated her universe. But she simply dropped her phone into her bag.

When she arrived home, she went straight to bed, passing out seconds after her head hit the pillow.

The sound of pounding woke her. She latched her fingers onto the top of her sheets, trying to determine if the sound was a dream or reality. After a few minutes, she threw off the covers and crept toward her front door, but all she heard was the creaking of the house.

She tiptoed to her couch and crouched on it to peek through the window, scanning the road where shadows separated and collided.

Someone stood by the wild tangle, a hunched body of pitch black. Finally, Sonja could see her stalker with her own eyes. She wasn't insane.

She rushed to unlock, and fling open her doors. "I will destroy you and everything you love!" she shouted into the night.

When her eyes adjusted, the figure had disappeared, replaced by night-darkened shrubs and trees. *But it had been there.* She looked right, toward the Patels' house. Then she peered into the thicket. Then she looked left. Other than the eerie security light at her hermit neighbor's house, she saw and heard nothing.

Sonja raced back inside, locking the door behind her. She had seen someone. She had been right all along. She had imagined none of it.

Or maybe you're going crazy. Like Mommy, girlie. She drove everyone away too. Call her old number. Maybe she'll pick up this time. Maybe she's still alive, drunk on sweet wine, watching sappy movies about happily ever afters.

Sonja slunk back into her bedroom, locking the door as if she might try to escape. As if she had ever been able to escape. She cleared off her nightstand and, unconcerned for once about scarring the floor, scooted it across the bedroom and against the door. The nightstand wouldn't prevent someone from breaking in, but it would slow them down and wake her up.

From her bed, she watched the door and listened until she drifted into a restless sleep and dreamed something about the bulbous, tentacled Jellyfish Nebula.

Chapter 29

Within the Shadows

SONJA PACED AT THE HEAD of the classroom, her pewter Sergio Rossi heels clicking on the hard floor. She wore a black Norma Kamali sheath, a rectangular shape that concealed her swells and curves. She had transformed herself into a metronome, ticking back and forth in a monotonous rhythm.

She observed the students' hunched shoulders and scribbling hands. As they finished and began dropping off their exams, she half-hid behind the media console. From there, she could see their downcast faces and skittering eyes, and she watched as they stacked the papers.

For a brief moment, she wondered if she had been unnecessarily harsh with the exam. Then she wondered if she had been unnecessarily harsh most of her adult life.

When Ronnie Staller appeared at the front of the room and spoke to her, Sonja nodded but processed nothing.

After the last student had left the classroom, Sonja shoved the exams into her gray leather Gucci tote. The color didn't quite match her pumps, something that usually irked her. But not today.

She shuffled across campus to her office and collapsed into her chair, depleted. When it was time for her second class's exam, she again paced in front of the room, then hovered behind the media console. Students drifted by, not seeing her, as if she were invisible behind its shadow.

By the time her office hours began, she had resigned herself to the inevitable. When Jay knocked, she exhaled and told him to enter.

Jay let himself in and closed the door behind him. He drew the visitor chair closer. "Sonja, we're concerned." He took a deep breath. "There have been calls. Allegations about erratic behavior in your classroom."

She looked at him, trying to bring him into focus. She folded her arms against her stomach and took in his pallid skin and dull hair.

"They're claiming you screamed at a student," he continued. "An exaggeration, I assume."

"Unfortunately, no." Having no strength to choose her words carefully, she said, "I shouted at a student who did nothing wrong beyond being a minor distraction."

Jay nodded once and waited for her to continue.

"I'm not sleeping well," she confessed, briefly tempted to take him into her confidence, tell him about the pains that had returned and were making her rely too heavily on medication. She wanted to disclose every nasty detail about Avery, Mitch, Cole, and Horace to this man she despised. She wanted to tell him about the student who attacked her and spit on her, a secret she had carved into her heart in an invisible act of self-harm. About Douglas Christopher, too, and her suspicions that he wouldn't stop until he cornered her and punished her for publicly damaging his ego.

But she said nothing, fearing he would use it against her, blame her for every bruise and grope. After a time, Jay rose.

"We've all been hit hard by Lewis's death. Let me see what I can do to address these student complaints. In the meantime, consider the Employee Assistance Program. Times have been hard for you for a while, Sonja. And before you say anything, I don't mean that as a slight. You have faced far more than you should have, and you faced it alone."

And with that, he left.

She stared at the door until an email notification drew her attention.

StormsComin@mailbox.com

You look riley bad. Some one should take cair of you

Sonja leaned back in her chair, closing her eyes to keep from crying, but she fell asleep. A heavy pounding on her door woke her up. She stood up, swaying, groggy, and smoothed her sheath, wiping specks from the silky black material. The pounding started again, this time as she dragged her fingers through her hair, and she swore she felt coarse gray strands that nested beneath the dark upper layers.

She opened her office door and stood stunned. Corey Randalls had slicked his hair back, revealing a widow's peak. His pale skin was mottled and his eyes sunken, giving him a ghoulish appearance. He wore a wrinkled white button-down shirt with faded stains and a frayed collar.

"Mr. Corey Randalls." The name slithered out of her mouth. "What do you want?"

"Come to talk to you," he muttered.

She motioned him in and went to sit in her chair. "Leave the door open, Mr. Randalls. Then sit."

He sat, dropping his ratty backpack onto the floor next to him. "My advisor says I have to talk to you so I can graduate next year."

Adrenaline flooded through her, and she became hypervigilant. She wasn't about to have another student encounter that left her sprawled on the floor. She studied him closely, watching for his breathing to become shallow or his hands to clench. If they did, she would scream like a banshee. She looked at the metal stapler on her desk, prepared to grab it and bash him with it if he made a sudden move.

"You've got to let me back in your class."

"Do I?"

"I can't withdraw. I've got to graduate and get out of here."

Her fingernail tapped the desk. "Question, Mr. Randalls. Do you think you should have considered that before you *departed* my class?" She watched him shrug, then continued. "Sadly, Mr. Randalls, it is too late. My students have already taken the midterm and begun their written analysis. I suggest you talk further with your advisor. The matter is out of my hands."

"That's not true," he snarled, then adjusted his tone. "My advisor says you could sign a late add and take it to the dean."

"Why would I do that?"

Corey plucked at the armrests of the chair. "Because I got to graduate."

"You have said that. Let me ask you. Were you at my house last night?"

He looked at her, puzzled. "What?"

"That is not a denial. How about email? Are you StormsComin, by chance? Are you brave enough to confess?"

He shook his head. "I don't know what the hell you're even talking about. I mean, how would I even know where you live?"

Sonja waited for her opponent to give something away.

"Look, lady, I've done awful stuff. If—" He flinched, as if terrified by something he saw in Sonja's face.

"Is that a confession? Are you punishing me for Jacob? Well, Do. Your. Best. I'm through with you and your sick games."

Corey picked up his backpack and stood up. Turning around at the door, he said, "I don't know what the fuck's your problem, but you're crazy. Just so you know, I'm complaining to your boss."

"I look forward to it. After all, I am—what did you call me the other day? A 'nasty cunt.' You should know, Mr. Randalls," she said, pausing for effect, "nasty cunts make nasty enemies."

"Fucking crazy bitch." He stormed out.

Sonja picked up her tote with the completed exams inside and hitched it over her shoulder. She longed for the safety of her home—or a place that had once been safe.

That felt like ages ago.

Chapter 30

Coiled and Swam

SONJA HAD JUST TAKEN THE first bite of her salad when someone knocked on the front door. She stopped chewing as if the crunching of romaine would give away her presence while she waited for the visitor to leave, but they only knocked louder and faster, and Sonja could hear a muffled voice on the other side of the door.

Crystal.

Butterflies tickled her insides. Crystal hadn't responded to Sonja's text after the planetarium show and maybe wanted to reply in person.

Sonja slipped quietly out of the chair and peeked out the living room window. Her butterflies plummeted to the pit of her stomach, a lifeless clump of emotion.

It wasn't Crystal. It was Harmony, wearing a black dress with long, tapered sleeves.

Sonja opened the front door and spoke through the security glass. "You are disturbing my private time."

"I need a word."

"It will have to wait until I am back in the office next week."

Harmony rattled the security door insistently.

"Stop that." Sonja grabbed the inside handle and held it tight.

"Open up. Otherwise, I'll stand out here hollering...good...and... LOUD!"

That did it. Sonja unbolted the door and flung it wide, hoping to hit Harmony, but she missed. "Come in before you make a spectacle of yourself."

Harmony walked in and sat on the couch. "I'll take a glass of wine."

"You should have brought a bottle, then. I am out."

"I doubt that." Harmony smiled, almost coldly.

"Fine. One glass. Then leave."

Sonja went to the kitchen and poured three ounces of wine for her unwanted visitor and five ounces for herself. She handed the glass to Harmony with a glare.

"What a generous amount."

"Sarcasm does not suit you. Besides, you do not need more. It appears from your dress that you have somewhere to go. So drink up and say what you came here to say, then leave."

"I'm dressed for the memorial for Dr. Waters," the secretary said and drained her wineglass. "I'll have a refill. I have time."

"Find yourself a second glass elsewhere. Get to why you intruded on my solitude."

"Sounds like you're having a rough time these days. Rougher than usual. Students are complaining. You're running around blowing your stack. You're not going to like this…"

"Spit it out." *Before I kick you out.*

"I called Crystal."

"You called Dr. Byrd?"

Harmony smirked. "Get used to me and Crystal being on friendly terms."

"That is hardly what brought you to my home. Say what you must. Then leave."

"Like I was *trying* to say, Crystal says you're tormenting yourself about some wicked game being played with you. And you're not completely wrong. I told Crystal that too."

Sonja raised her eyebrows. Finally, someone believed her! But she never thought it would be the secretary.

"I've got something to say, but once I say it, it's over," Harmony continued.

"You are delaying."

"I'm fixing to tell you what I came here to tell you. After I do, reconsider going to the memorial. Crystal and me, we're meeting up. We think it'd be good for you to pay your respects and all."

Sonja gritted her teeth. "Harmony, out with it."

"I found out something. Those notes you've been lugging around in the folder. I know who did it. Some of it, at least."

The dart frog leaped up and down Sonja's throat. "Give me a name!"

"First, promise me. No revenge."

Sonja snorted and drained her glass.

"Seeing as how you need a refill now"—Harmony held up her empty one—"I'll take another."

"You must be kidding."

Harmony fixed those lapis eyes on Sonja.

Sonja shook her head, retrieved the bottle from the kitchen, and poured another three ounces of wine into the secretary's glass.

"A bit more."

Sonja reluctantly obliged, then said, "That is enough. You will need to drive soon. And don't you dare spill wine on my expensive couch."

Harmony continued. "This is difficult to admit. Usually, I'm a pro at work. No gossiping, no complaining, no backbiting."

"I disagree," Sonja interrupted.

"Sure, you're right. There've been times I grumbled about how you treated folks, especially Dr. Waters. You were downright nasty to him. He was a good man. He knew my birthday, my husband's health problems. He asked after my family, and when my mother took ill—"

"You're stalling."

"I'm explaining myself." Harmony held Sonja's gaze. "I complained about you now and again. I admit that. And my student workers, they're as protective of me as I am of them."

"Who is it?" Sonja demanded, hearing her mother's rage in her tone.

"All I'm saying is that Sarah—"

"Sarah? Which one is Sarah? Is she the one with a thrift store wardrobe? I'll have her job. I'll have her expelled. I'll have her dragged from campus—"

"I told you I handled it," Harmony insisted. "And I don't like the way you describe her. You sound—"

"Like a bitch."

"A snob."

Sonja looked around the living room for her phone. She would call Jay. She would call Dean Lu. She would track them down at home if she had to. She would unleash a storm in the department. Hell, on the entire campus.

"It's been taken care of. Sonja, listen to me. Your jaw tightens like a fist when you've grabbed hold of something that you're too bullheaded to let go of."

But Sonja's anger blazed, inflamed by her desire for justice.

Revenge, you mean.

"If you don't stop and listen to me," Harmony said, standing and raising her glass, "I'll dump my wine all over your precious couch."

"You wouldn't dare, Harmony," Sonja seethed, but she did stop in her tracks.

"I would dare, Sonja. Now, go sit your hinny down and open your ears."

They glared at each another until Sonja backed off and went to her chair. "There's no need to ruin my couch. I will listen." She sat.

"Sarah told me everything. She confessed, blubbering like a little girl."

"That *little girl's* been terrorizing me."

"I understand. Sarah knows what she did was wrong. She feels awful. But she hated how you talked down to everyone. And the cold way you've handled Dr. Waters's death sent that girl over the edge."

"It's time for you to leave."

In response, Harmony drank more wine. "I came here to help you out. I'm hoping you'll find some peace of mind. There's no grand conspiracy against you. Do you hear me? It was just an angry girl acting out. She did wrong, and she faced the consequences."

"What's her last name?"

"She's already gone. I fired her." Harmony teared up. "She's humiliated. She was the first one in her family to go to college, and if she can't get a work-study position somewhere else, she won't be able to continue her education. She'll have to drop out. Isn't that enough? We're talking about a couple of typed-up notes."

But Sonja's wrath circled back around, the emotional stormfront strengthening. "I will obliterate her. I'll go to campus police and Student Affairs. This is not over—"

She stopped, her mind suddenly filled with rising suspicions. "How convenient, Harmony," Sonja said in a measured tone. "Dead Lewis was responsible for the oil. Now this. A student worker stalked me, and she's fired and gone." Sonja peered at Harmony accusingly. "It was you all along, wasn't it? Everything. The notes. The dead animals. The lurking outside my home."

Harmony's face fell, and in that moment, she appeared ten years older. "Crystal tried warning me," she said, her voice cracking. "But I had to stick my nose in. You really do see everyone as an enemy. I feel sorry for you. I mean, you dress pretty, your hair's real nice, and your paycheck's probably decent. You have everything"—she gestured around the living room—"but you're downright miserable, convinced you're surrounded by enemies."

"That's because I am surrounded by enemies."

Harmony scoffed. "That girl's gone. There will be no more torn posters or notes slipped under your door. At least from her. It's done. Be happy. For the love of God, be happy."

"And the emails?"

"I don't know about any emails. But face it. You've stirred up several hornet nests. I've been answering the calls from upset students. And before you start barking at me"—she held up her hand—"you're right. In some ways, it's unfair. Drs. Grant and Behringer were mean SOBs. To their students, to our workers. Students didn't dare complain. The rumors... awful stuff."

"Yet you left me alone with Mitch."

Do you know even what he did to me?

No, they don't, answered another voice. *You never told anyone. Your secrets have metastasized, turned malignant.*

The secretary shrugged. "I think we were hoping you being faculty would protect you. Then Lewis and Jay moved your office, hoping that would work. Things were different back then, complaints getting swept under the rug. I'm sorry, truly sorry that I didn't stand up to them. I'm trying to do better by you, but you don't make it easy."

"Being nice is not in my job description."

"Maybe not. But kindness is necessary for being human."

"How many times have you been called a bitch or a cunt for doing your job?"

"Never." Harmony put her half-empty wineglass on the coffee table. "But I've been called those names for no more than driving down the road. I can't imagine how it was for you in the department, having to face that."

"And were you ever locked in an office with a senior faculty member who masturba—" Sonja stopped abruptly.

Harmony gasped. "Oh, I…No wonder you've turned to stone. I had no idea it went that far."

"You had the clues."

Harmony nodded. "I've been pinched, my backside patted. Got talked down to by those two. They treated me like I only existed to serve them. I told myself it was normal to be treated that way. I had such hopes when you joined the faculty. I was excited to have another woman around. Reckon I got my feelings hurt when you didn't want to be friendly."

"I had to be a cold bitch. I wouldn't have survived otherwise." Sonja retreated back to her corner chair and stared at Harmony from across the room. "You spoke to Crystal."

"She's worried. So is Jay. Me too. You've got us all real worried."

Sonja said nothing, merely stared at the secretary.

Harmony picked up her glass. "I'll tell you one thing. It was kind of fun watching you go after those old boys. I'm just sorry you had to. And I'm sorry Dr. Grant—what that bastard did to you was gross. To think you've bottled that up inside all this time…"

"This is the first time I've heard you say anything about how I handled them," Sonja said stiffly.

"After you got tenure, they didn't know what hit them." Harmony chuckled. "I remember that first meeting. You being a new associate professor, coming in like an avenging angel, dressed in a fancy black suit and wearing blood-red lipstick—but those cupcakes. I hated you being put on the spot. I should've said something a long time ago. I just didn't know how."

"We were both surviving," Sonja said and wondered if she could forgive this woman.

Dart frogs don't forgive. Dart frogs poison.

"These days, though, you don't seem like your old tough self. You seem to be coming…undone."

Sonja stared into her glass, swirling the remaining wine around.

"You don't know how to stop, do you?" Harmony asked. "The fighting. The fretting about who might be out to get you."

Sonja drank the last of her wine and listened.

"I'm asking you to remember that *I* handled it. And things are going to change in that office. Student workers will act professional, or I'll let them go. You have my word." Harmony got up to leave. "I'll say this one last time. Come to Ridges. Say goodbye to Dr. Waters. He tried to help. Sounds like he was the only one. Anyway, it will be a celebration, not a somber evening. At least come and let Crystal know you're okay." And she left.

When Sonja heard the front door close, she was suddenly engulfed by the emptiness of her house.

She put away the wine and glasses, knowing that if she had even one more sip, she would rush off to the memorial. *Just to see her.* Was it only last night that Sonja had soared with Crystal across the universe? But as the house darkened, unpleasant emotions and thoughts coiled and swam in her mind.

Which is how she wound up driving Bimmer to the memorial, an ebony cashmere shawl wrapped around her black Jackie O dress, only to sit paralyzed as she watched someone roll Mitch Grant in his wheelchair into Ridges.

Chapter 31

Spring of Love

Sonja was roused from her fugue-like state by someone tapping on the driver's side window. She looked up. Crystal stood outside, a finger pressed to the glass. Then she went around to the passenger side and knocked again. "Sonja, let me in."

Sonja apparently unlocked the car because the next thing she knew, Crystal was beside her, passenger door closed again.

"Harm says you've been out here for a bit," Crystal said. "Guess you saw Mitch Grant go inside."

Sonja stared at the steering wheel, unable to speak.

"Okay, here's how this is going to go, babe. We'll sit here until you're ready. Ready to go in, ready to leave, ready to scream or cry. Whatever increases your sense of agency."

Sonja looked at Crystal. Somehow the woman glowed in the muted light. "Is this Dr. Byrd's female empowerment hotline?" Sonja asked.

Crystal smiled. "There she is. Welcome back, Your Royal Highness of Haughtiness."

"That is humorous," Sonja said without laughing, but she meant it. A small part of her enjoyed Crystal conferring a title on her. "Yes, to answer your question. I saw that hideous man. Admittedly, I am"—she paused—"conflicted."

Crystal remained quiet.

"I would be willing," Sonja said slowly to disguise her halting speech, "to consider your input on this matter."

"Well, gorgeous, I won't tell you what to do. Harm didn't say much. But from the little she said…sounds like that piece of shit forced too much on you already. If you want, I'll tell you how I handled my sexual assault."

"Continue," Sonja said, then added, "please."

"Okay. It's been a while since I've thought about these details." She mumbled something, as if dislodging the bitter memories from some dark, dank storage space.

"First things first. I shared a class with my piece-of-shit rapist. Early on, I skipped classes, trying to avoid him. At some point, though, I decided that fucker had taken enough away from me. I went back to class, my head held high. A month or so later, he tried to strike up a casual conversation with me, the piece of shit. I've used that term already, huh?"

"It bears repeating." Sonja gripped the steering wheel.

"But, Sonja, darling, I didn't call him out. I acted like being around him didn't bother me. The fact that I pretended to be unruffled by what he did has haunted me ever since." Crystal blew air out of her mouth. "Damn, still hurts. Telling someone about my survivor trauma…like opening up deep wounds. Even after all this time. It used to be I'd get pretty much laid out when I talked about him or even thought about how coolcalm"—she said it as a single word—"I'd been to my goddamn rapist. I had to work through some shit in counseling before I forgave myself for not nut punching that fucker."

"Forgive yourself," Sonja said, then chuckled. Her small laugh turned into braying that lasted for a while. When it finally tapered off, she clarified, "Crystal, I do *not* find it funny that you forgave yourself."

"You laughing doesn't bother me. I've laughed, cried, and screamed. Got piss drunk too. Fucked strangers. Fucked friends. Post-trauma reactions vary. Now, anger was the emotion I had the hardest time with—still do. It was easier to be enraged at myself than at him. That's fucked up, but it makes a kind of sense."

"Anger empowers. Anger at yourself—" Sonja fumbled for the right words, but she gave up.

"Anger gives you something you can do," Crystal said. "That's why we enculturate women and girls to be mad at themselves instead of those in authority and the system that keeps them powerless. There's this author I love—"

"Please forgo the lecture, Dr. Byrd. Send me a list of references later."

Crystal released peals of laughter that rang in Sonja's ears. "The closest I came to confronting him— Ugh. I hate this part." Crystal took a breath, then continued. "One day, he touched my back right at the end of class. I remember everything like it's burned into my brain. The clock on the wall, the paint on the cinderblocks. When he laid his hand right between my shoulder blades, he tainted everything about that classroom. And I liked it: the way the light hit the room in the morning, the way the instructor pulled us into discussions." Crystal shook her head. "I've worked years to reclaim what I wanted to reclaim, and I've let go of the rest."

"Fuck him." Sonja said.

"Yeah. He thought he had the right to touch my body. He transgressed once, so after that, I was just property to him. Fuck that fucker."

Sonja released the steering wheel and leaned her head back on the headrest. Somehow, she felt grounded and somewhat unburdened.

"Anyway," Crystal continued, "I said to him, 'Take your goddamn hand off me. Never touch me again.' And I ran out of the room." Crystal choked up. "Fuck. I started crying back then too, but I'd be damned if he was going to see me weep. And, Sonja, hear this: I never reported him." She moaned, a low, sensual sound. "The Lord saved me."

Sonja faced Crystal, surprised at the revelation.

"Let me be clear," Crystal said. "I mean Audre Lorde. She wrote how some women wait for change. But when nothing changes, some of us change ourselves. Lorde's poems are my prayers now. Anyway, since I couldn't forgive my rapist, I worked on forgiving myself. It's been a long, tedious process."

"How could you even blame yourself?" Sonja asked. "I was a professor, an adult with a PhD, and I failed to report Mitch. I didn't even tell him to stop. I looked away, but I could hear every squishy sound. When he finished, he wiped his, his fluid on me, marking me as his."

"Darling, I'm going to say something that gets me in trouble with some of my feminist fam. You cannot get this wrong. Whatever you decide to do tonight short of killing him—"

"Not opposed."

"Yep! But seriously, whatever you decide to do, minus killing or torture, do what's best for you."

Sonja turned her head to study Crystal's kind face in the mauve lighting. A warm spring of love unexpectedly erupted in Sonja's chest, startling her, terrifying her. She wouldn't speak about it, probably not ever. The sensation was too fleeting, too unreliable, and could not be trusted.

Love is an addiction. A biochemical trap. You've read the research.

"If you go inside," Crystal said softly, "I'll be right there with you. You can talk to him or not. You can cuss him out or not."

"Nut punch him, to use your vernacular?"

"Or not. It's not worth getting locked up for that fucker," she said, snickering.

"Well, let's go collect some heads."

"You mean metaphorically, right, babe?" Crystal reached for Sonja's hand and squeezed it.

"Of course," Sonja said, giving her a maniacal smile.

A space in Ridges had been cleared for a three-person band that played upbeat, jazzy music. A cluster of people were gathered around a tall, willowy woman with sleek, marble-white hair. She had a dazzling smile. Sonja surmised that this must be Lewis Waters's widow, and for a split second, she wondered how someone in mourning could be so joyful.

It's possible to be both happy and hurt, whispered the optimistic voice that had recently taken up residence in Sonja's head.

It is a sham, purely performative, said the sour voice that had been her loyal companion since childhood.

Sonja blocked out the widow and surrounding mourners and trained her sights on Mitch Grant.

He hovered at the outskirts, beaming and tapping his foot. Sonja approached her target, determined to find the sadistic glee through his façade. Crystal squeezed her left elbow once. Sonja barely registered the reassuring gesture or the arrival of Harmony at her other elbow.

As Sonja got closer, she saw that Mitch had shrunk. Once he had loomed over her, or maybe his power had made him seem larger. This Mitch was shriveled, a shrunken body slumped in an oversized wheelchair. His useless arms rested in his lap.

Professor Mitch Grant, her tormentor, grinned when he saw her.

Sonja's mouth went dry, but the rage inside her still burned. She glowered at him.

"Mitch," she said simply.

He looked up at her, still smiling.

"Hello, friend." His words were slurred, and he looked at her without recognition. Then he looked back at the musicians.

"Ma'am?" She turned to face the voice that came from her right. A man approached the back of Mitch's wheelchair. He smiled at her. "Dr. Grant won't remember you or your time together," the man urged gently. "Those strokes did a number on him. He won't understand anything you say or do."

Sonja stepped back, a little off-balance, but hands on either side of her kept her upright. She looked to her left at Crystal, then right at Harmony, each gently holding one of her arms.

"I'm ready for a glass of wine," Sonja said.

"I'll get drinks," Harmony volunteered. "I've got a table in the back. Go on."

Crystal guided Sonja away from the chattering and swaying bodies.

"He doesn't remember me." Sonja said when they were seated. "He's forgotten everything. Meanwhile, I remember it all. In detail. If I painted, I could frame and hang my memories in the Fitzwilliam. Right beside *The Rape of Lucretia*. At least I would have something to show for it. Maybe I could finally get the recognition that men seem to get when..." She trailed off, the words abandoning her.

"I'm so sorry, Sonja. I have nothing better to say except you're right. He gets happy oblivion. You get harsh aftermath. It sucks." Crystal drew circles on the back of Sonja's hand with a long index finger.

"You said I couldn't do this wrong," Sonja whispered. "It feels worse now."

"It'll feel bad for a while." Crystal took Sonja's hand in hers. "These encounters have a way of morphing over time, especially if the original trauma is healed as much as it can be."

Harmony walked up with their drinks. "I'm going to rescue Ruthie from the talkers," she said, placing them on the table and leaving.

Sonja stared at the glass of purplish-red liquid in front of her. It was the color of a deep and painful bruise. Her mouth soured, and she knew she would vomit if she took a sip.

"I must leave," Sonja said, getting abruptly to her feet.

Someone clinked a glass and started speaking. "Folks, listen up. Everyone..."

"You want me to come with you?" Crystal stood up, her arm sliding around Sonja's waist.

Sonja gazed up at Crystal and was overcome with loathing at the concern—no, pity—she saw encased in those amber eyes. "You are kind. Too kind for me. Please don't call me. I can't do this with you. You deserve... *more*."

She staggered out the door, away from the music, away from the celebration of life. She stepped into the night, fearing the darkness would never end, that she would live in it forever like her mother had. In a short time, Sonja had felt a gurgling spring of love in her chest, then, just as quickly, felt its dormancy. But what frightened her most was that her anger had vanished too, leaving her frozen and exposed, like the bronze statues of naked women inside.

.

Chapter 32

A Short and Uneasy Motion

JACOB SAT AT THE FOOT of her bed in a white button-down, his back to her. She studied him, gazing at the ripples of his russet hair until he blended into her window dressing.

"Forgive me," Sonja said, a morning prayer to a dead man.

She lay curled on her side, the specters of dying dreams whirling in shades of gray and purple. She blinked, each one a short and uneasy motion that brought a muddled world into focus.

Even if he were still alive, he wouldn't forgive you, little girl. You as good as killed that poor boy.

Sonja dragged herself out of bed and threw on a silk robe over her leaden limbs. Grime coated her teeth, and her hair was in disarray, but Sonja skipped her morning routine. She rubbed her aching back, yearning to pop a pill, then another and another, longing to drown in oblivion.

In the dining room sat the untouched exams where she had left them yesterday. She ignored them and headed for the stove to fill her tea ball with dried lavender leaves. Loose tea sprinkled the counter, but she couldn't be bothered to brush it away.

Picking up the unwashed cup that she had used yesterday, she dropped in the mesh ball, the metal clinking against the fragile porcelain. Without waiting for the kettle to whistle, she poured the lukewarm water over the tea ball.

Sonja took the tepid tea and sank down in front of the exams, two collapsing columns that reminded her how unstable everything had become. She pushed them aside.

"Did you notice my hair that day?" The question escaped her lips without her consent.

She thought back to her meeting with Jacob at the campus café. She had softened and smoothed her features and styled her hair until it flowed in shiny locks down to her shoulders. Smudging her eyes with kajal, she had turned them into ringed reptilian orbs, a portent that she'd overlooked about dart frogs.

She had once read that a dart frog could lose its toxicity, and she wondered if that was true.

Only in captivity, a cold, clinical voice answered. *Dart frogs aren't poisonous if fed a special diet by their captors. Is that what you want? Do you want Crystal to handfeed you, make you a pretty pet? Or do you want to be the lethal creature you were meant to be?*

As she had in college, Sonja briefly resisted her toxic nature after Jacob left her classroom. She ordered a dress of blended silk wool from Neiman Marcus in pearl violet, the color of an evening cloud just before a coming storm. This time, the dress wasn't intended as armor. Instead, its V-neck, bell sleeves, and belted waist revealed her as the woman beneath the ice queen.

After Jacob proved himself to be her defender, he had earned entrance into her domain. But then he had pulled away from her, a rejection that had pierced more than other rejections. So she covered the pearl-violet dress in a plastic cover and banished it to the depths of her closet.

Sonja sipped the cool tea and set the cup atop the exams, knowing it would create a ring on the top paper. Normally she detested stains, but not today. Today she had a tea ball of apathy at her core, and its contents seeped to all parts of her.

At last, she got up from the table and opened the drapes. Then she showered, twisting her wet hair into a messy bun, mimicking the style her mother had worn on bad days. *Tiptoeing up to the line. See how close you can get without turning into her.*

As if tempting an unsavory past to return, she dug out the pearl-violet dress, hung it on the closet door, and considered its fate as she painted her nails indigo, the color of a sulking sky. Maybe she would donate it. She imagined stuffing it into a plywood box outside a local thrift store and driving away, but in the end, she returned it to the closet. Only this time, she moved it closer to the front, closer to a fate yet to be determined.

She ignored the teacup's sepia stain on the top exam and plowed into grading. After a few hours of work, she found a rhythm, and when she felt the sun warming one side of her face, she took a break and checked her email. She deleted all new messages except one.

Sonja:

Please call ASAP.

—Jay

She looked at the time stamp: *11:27 a.m.*, nearly three hours ago.

And just like that, her prickly annoyance shoved aside her sticky apathy.

She picked up her cell and switched off airplane mode, releasing an onslaught of notifications that made her phone buzz like a bumblebee trapped in a jar.

No message from Crystal, though.

Jay picked up on the first ring. "Sonja, thanks for getting back to me. I know you're busy."

"Grading midterms," she explained before she could restrain herself.

"Do you have a—"

"Corey Randalls."

"How did you know?"

"He filed a complaint, I presume. It must be a serious allegation, or this conversation could have waited until next week."

"Actually, it's his father, Jerry Randalls. He would like to meet on Monday, lunchtime."

"When did we become high school teachers and you our principal?"

"I'm aware of your opinion about parental involvement in the education of college students. But this man, he sounds like a worried dad. I'd be happy to meet with him. Or—"

"Here it comes." Sonja felt more tired than defensive.

"You could call him. I'm not asking you to meet with him face-to-face. A quick call. That's all."

Sonja paused to consider. "I see," she said finally. "You are concerned about a lawsuit. If something happens to Corey Randalls, the family sues us, and your legacy gets a black mark."

"In my defense, it's my job to worry about such things. So, if it's important to you, Sonja, then, yes, you're correct. I'm acting like an administrator. But there's something else: I'm concerned about this young man. From what his dad says, he's struggling."

"Fine," she said flatly. "Text me the number. I will consider the matter and inform you of my decision." She paused, then continued. "You are doing it again."

"What?"

"Protecting fragile men at my expense. Have you even asked me about my recent experience with Corey Randalls?"

"I'm—"

"Do *not* apologize. Your words of contrition are insincere. As long as we have worked together, you have asked me to contort myself for the men in our department—faculty *and* students—under the guise of professionalism. Would you have asked Cole to call a parent? How about Mitch?"

"Tell me more about Corey Randalls."

Quickly, Sonja recounted for Jay every encounter she'd had with Corey, adding some details from the recent meeting in her office. As usual, she didn't mention Jacob Randalls.

"What else should I know?" Jay asked when she finished.

"That will do."

"Do me a favor. File another report, email me the details. That would be helpful. If you want me to meet with the father." Then he added, "It was good seeing you at the memorial last night. But Sonja."

"What?"

"We didn't know that Mitch would be there. It was something Ruthie and her son arranged at the last minute. Apparently, Lewis visited Mitch in the nursing home. He has no one else."

Mitch has no one because he deserves no one.

"I need to know none of this," Sonja said, sounding aloof.

"It's—You're right. But I wanted you to know that we would have warned you if we had known. Seeing him had to be...challenging."

"Your validation is not required. However," she said cautiously, "I do not hold you or Harmony to blame for Mitch being there. Now, I must go." She hung up quickly, fearing that if Jay said anything more about Mitch, she would lose the little control she had regained.

A few seconds later, Jay's text arrived with Jerry Randalls's phone number. She recalled her morning dream and saw Jacob sitting at the foot of her bed, his shoulders sturdy, his back strong.

"Fine," she agreed. She would meet with Jerry Randalls, mainly to satisfy her curiosity about a possible connection to Jacob. Besides, she reasoned, she had to be on campus Monday for a meeting with the search committee.

She called the number.

"Jerry here."

His twang instantly reminded her of Jacob, making her even more certain that there was a connection. Long ago, she had been embarrassed about that twang, and privately she had debated with herself about how to advise Jacob on replacing his dialect with something more refined. But as she listened to Jerry Randalls, she was drawn into the cadence. The twang didn't annoy as much as it comforted.

"Dr. Storey, Mr. Randalls. I only have a moment. I understand you requested a meeting."

"Yes, ma'am. I—"

"I have arranged to meet with you in my office on Monday at noon. I will text you the location and a link to the campus map. Mr. Randalls," she added, "this meeting is for you alone. Corey is not permitted to attend, and I will not share any private information with you."

Just as she was about to launch into a lecture about the Family Education Privacy Act, he said, "That's fine, Dr. Storey. I appreciate you doing this. See you Monday." And he hung up. No arm twisting, no fuss, no fury. Sonja was perplexed, but she didn't want her day further derailed, so she texted Jay to finalize this matter.

I have scheduled a meeting with him and will apprise you if necessary.

Then she got back to work, resolving to stay put until she accomplished at least one goal. By the time she finished grading both sets of exams, her neck and back felt as knobby as the ancient apple tree in the vacant lot across the street.

She took a muscle relaxer, vowing to wean herself off tomorrow, and crawled into her unmade bed, the latest issue of *House Beautiful* on her lap and a glass of wine in her hand.

Chapter 33

Wash Away

SONJA STARED DOWN AT THE moldering leaves and plunged her fingers into the decay. Her feet were bare, and she wore nothing but a translucent nightgown. She opened her mouth to speak.

That was how she woke up.

Looking around, she found herself in the middle of Summit Street. The front door of her house was wide open, as if aghast over her witchy antics. Without having to see them, she felt her hands coated with dirt, and, for a reason beyond her understanding, she tilted her head and stared at the dull stars in the hazy sky, demanding an answer from them:

"What the fuck am I doing?"

Then she ran her eyes across the vacant lot, the trees and shrubs nothing more than winged distortions. Her terror was slowly replaced by certainty that she was standing at the *gravesites* of Smushed Driveway Creature and Squashed Squirrel—or at least the general vicinity of where she had thrown them.

Sonja had no memory of leaving her bed—much less her home—no memory of crossing the road. What she had a vision of, though, was squatting and clawing at the damp soil and muttering like a madwoman.

She looked back down at the hole she had dug at the edge of the thicket. Both carcasses were gone.

"I was going to bury you," she delivered her statement like a poor eulogy.

Her peripheral vision picked up a whisper of movement in the center of the road, and she turned. A fox watched her.

"Did you dig up these carcasses for your dinner?" she asked, but the fox faded from her vision, going within the shadows, and leaving her to question if she had even seen it. For once, though, she didn't worry about her inability to distinguish reality from imagined events. Out in the midnight landscape, madness seemed a fitting state for an anguished soul.

She looked back down at the hole she had created. It was barely large enough for a mouse. Then she glanced back at her home as if it could give her guidance about whether to finish the job.

As she crossed Summit Street and stepped onto her sidewalk, she turned to look for the fox again, but she saw only darkness and shadows that vaguely resembled human shapes. One shape hunched, but when she blinked, it was gone, and it occurred to Sonja that she had simply imagined a shorter, more twisted version of Ruthie Waters.

Sonja returned indoors to wash her feet and hands, and she did so with the reverence of a new convert to an ancient order. She went to bed, sensing that the universe had applauded her private dance with the cosmos.

For once, she slept well.

The next day, Sonja couldn't shake the sense of foreboding. What eased the sensation somewhat was when she dwelled on her Monday meeting with Jerry Randalls.

You're hoping that man will wash away your shame, girlie.

She ignored her mother's ghostly jeering and made herself shower, style her hair, and fix her face, moving sluggishly through her routine. She even repainted her fingernails, covering up any remaining evidence of last night's digging.

Once ready, she quickly sent a text before her brain could catch up with her actions.

Can we talk?

Hours later, Crystal still hadn't replied.

"Surely, you didn't expect a response," Sonja chastised herself. "She's kind, but she's not an idiot." *You throw the best people out of your life and keep the ones who punish you.* Sonja didn't bother to protest with her mental advisor, not this time.

She passed the rest of the weekend rechecking and finalizing her exams, ordered new nail polish and lipstick, then returned to her book proposal.

By Sunday afternoon, she could think of little besides her cell phone's lack of notifications.

To keep from unleashing a storm of texts on Crystal, she pulled on a pair of navy trousers and a little-worn silver sweater that glittered like a disco ball, climbed into Bimmer, and backed out of the garage into the turnaround. But once she drove forward up her steep driveway, she was suddenly seized with a bolt of anger, and she slammed the gas pedal hard, peeling out for the first time in her life. It left her deliciously satisfied, and she drove out of her neighborhood, cackling as if deranged.

Less than ten minutes later, she arrived at Ridges and claimed the corner table that she and Crystal had previously shared. She looked at the spot where Mitch Grant had sat three nights earlier. Only an hour ago, she had convinced herself to come to this place so she could beat her memories of the memorial into submission.

The reality was, though, that she didn't know where else to go. Other than the campus and her home, Foxboro remained a foreign land to her.

She was on her second glass of pinot when her meal arrived. She poked at the sea bass and pushed around the wild rice that appeared as appetizing as a heap of broken twigs. The darkness was moving back in, sinking slowly around her, and obscuring the glee that she had felt when she burned rubber in her driveway.

The pinot tasted vinegary now, but she finished it as she watched the waitstaff knot and part, apparently unaware of the weather patterns enveloping her.

We're birds surviving a storm together. But she was alone, and she longed for the bird she had chased away. Which is why she remained at Ridges and ordered a third glass of pinot.

When Sonja finally drove herself home, she glanced at Star Dancer and walked toward it as if approaching a lover. Stroking its smooth surface, she said, "I should have let Crystal touch you. She brings me joy, like you do."

But, unlike Crystal, Star Dancer didn't overwhelm her when yielding to the depths of the universe.

Monday morning, she shot out of bed, systemically attacking her predawn rituals. Before leaving the house, she stood in front of her bathroom mirror, checking her hair and makeup, admiring the classic lines of her Ann Taylor midnight-blue pantsuit with the silver satin button-up blouse underneath.

Confident that she was on the verge of regaining her authority, she left for WHSU.

When she reached her office, the sun barely breaking over the horizon, she switched on her lamp and electric kettle. Then she looked at her chair. A large gash bisected the leather, exposing the padding.

Sonja wept as though she had stumbled upon the ravaged carcass of a beloved pet.

After a prolonged cry, she snapped a photo of the chair, then sat. The damaged leather parted beneath her.

The thought of revealing her assaulted chair nauseated her nearly as much as the idea of revealing what had happened with Avery, Mitch, and her student attacker. Sonja persuaded herself that the vandalism was a parting gesture by Sarah Fired Student Worker, and she closed her office door.

Conceal everything. Like Mommy taught you, girlie.

There was only one person she wanted to tell about this latest incident, but when she checked her phone, there was no message from Crystal.

She twisted in her chair, grinding herself into the seat hard and mercilessly. Feeling the tear widen, Sonja fantasized about disappearing through the hole into Wonderland and stealing the throne from the Queen of Hearts. "Collect some actual heads," she muttered, sounding like the insane woman she was rapidly becoming.

Outside, she heard the department coming to life. People's voices rang out and feet pounded the floor rhythmically. Everything seemed to call her into the human fray, but Sonja didn't know how to join, so she didn't try. She simply waited for Jerry Randalls and, possibly, salvation.

She struggled to make her fragmented brain work as she tried reading an article, but her eyes kept straying to the clock in the corner of her monitor. As noon approached, her heartrate sped up. As noon came and went, she grew queasy. By twenty minutes after, she finally acknowledged that she had been stood up.

"Serves you right," she admonished herself. There would be no convenient solution to the messiness of her life. *No absolution.*

She should have rescheduled the search committee meeting, left campus, and gone home, but instead, she slumped in her ruined chair and batted at her computer mouse like a bored house cat. She watched emails come in, including one from Douglas Christopher, but she left them all unopened.

When Sonja heard someone knock, she rose, her heartrate quickening again. She straightened her pantsuit, stared down at her chair briefly, wishing she could hide the gaping wound, then went to the door and opened it, resolved to face whatever was on the other side.

———————————

He could have been Jacob—had Jacob lived.

Fighting off waves of nausea, she looked at him.

His hair was faded, though it might have been red at one time. His freckles looked like dried tobacco sprinkled across sun-bleached leather. His hair fell in waves across his forehead, ending just above his eyebrows. Jerry Randalls wasn't handsome, but he was striking—a man who had spent decades under the mountain sun.

"Mr. Randalls," she said, her mouth suddenly dry, her eye twitching once.

"Dr. Storey." He smoothed the T-shirt under his worn jacket. The gesture reminded her of Jacob's nervous movements when he met with her during office hours. "Apologies for being late. Had a heck of a time parking. Even the visitor spots had been taken. Reckon it'd hurt these kids to walk ten feet."

"Come in," she said, stepping aside and resisting the urge to start grilling him.

As he entered, he glanced at her once magnificent chair. He opened his mouth, but he held back whatever it was he started to say.

Jerry Randalls remained standing, like a well-rooted tree, steady and solid.

She gestured to the spare chair. "Please sit, Mr. Randalls."

"Jerry, please." He lowered himself into the seat, keeping his boots planted wide.

"How may I help you?" she asked as she closed her office door and returned to her assaulted chair.

"My son, Corey. I won't ask how he's doing. You teachers have all sorts of privacy laws. I get that. Mainly, ma'am—"

"I prefer Dr. Storey."

"Certainly, Dr. Storey." He seemed unruffled by her directive.

Just like Jacob. She pinched the inside of her elbows to keep from crying.

"I wanted to talk to you in person. I'm not asking you to let Corey back in your class. That's not why I'm here."

"Then why are you here?"

"Frankly, ma'am, I'm ashamed. Corey won't say much, but what he did tell me…" Jerry shook his head. "I told him he needed to come back, take responsibility for his actions. Apologize. From the sound of it, he handled himself poorly."

"He did." *I did too.*

Jerry stared down at his hands as if the lines and cracks in his skin could help him find the words.

"Corey used to talk to his momma like that from time to time. She'd take it from him, insist that a good momma's supposed to be patient and loving. I didn't often disagree with her, but I did on that account. Sounds like you didn't tolerate bad behavior from my boy. Want you to know I appreciate that." He flashed a half-smile—another reminder of Jacob—then continued.

"Corey's struggled as far back as I can remember. I was hoping he'd gotten right with himself. He started back at church. School too. But instead of finding salvation, I think he might have found drugs again."

"I'm sorry to hear that." Sonja steeled herself, preparing for the man to begin hammering her with sad stories to manipulate her into doing his bidding.

"He's gotten treatment before," Jerry said. "Outpatient's all we can afford. And we can't much afford that. When his momma passed, well, sad to say his old ways cropped back up. He started missing class. I pressed him about why. That's when he told me some of what happened between you two. Sounds like he dumped his anger on you." He looked her in the eye.

I mishandled everything.

Jerry dropped his gaze. "I promise he didn't learn to treat women that way from me. The devil has taken hold of that boy, brought out the wicked in him."

As he continued the sad story about his son, Sonja concluded she needed to wrap up the meeting. She leaned forward, gripping the arms of her chair, ready to push herself up and escort Corey's father to the door.

"I know who you are, Dr. Storey."

She froze, her fingers digging into the armrests. She studied him for signs that he was about to transform into a raging beast.

"You may not remember him, but you also taught my oldest brother's boy."

"Jacob," she whispered. She leaned back into her chair.

"You remember him. How many years has it been?"

"Around a decade." She could have told him the exact number of days.

He smiled. "I appreciate that you haven't forgotten him."

"I have not."

"Jacob had his struggles too. Pretty much my whole family has been in the devil's grip. My own momma drank 'til the Lord called her home. It got real bad at the end."

"What about Jacob?" Sonja tried to steer him back without appearing like a hungry dog snatching at a morsel.

"My nephew did all sorts of knuckleheaded stuff in his youth. Nowadays, it's easier for a man to drink and pop pills than ask for help."

Some women too.

"But Jacob was different," Jerry said. "He got off our mountain, went to some meetings. Even met with some kind of therapist. The family didn't much like that. Most wanted the mountains to hold our secrets. They told him, 'Get good with the Lord and you'll be healed.' Me and his dad don't believe that. Jacob either. He used to say that the Lord works through doctors. Teachers too.

"It took a bit, but Jacob got better. We thought he'd beaten it, so we took our eyes off him. We'll be beating ourselves up over that 'til it's our time to go home."

"What happened?" she asked. "He did well in his classes, then—" Sonja stopped, afraid she was about to crack open wide.

"It's not one thing that ruins us." Jerry ran a hand through his hair. "The Randalls are strong people. But bit by bit, we have a way of whittling away the good and building up the bad."

Sonja felt an urge to pour out her insides to this stranger, to let him know that she understood about being the architect of one's own misery. She wanted to double over, weep with him over the losses suffered at one's own hand. But again she barricaded her pain inside.

"Is that why Jacob left, left the university?" *Left me?*

"He had a problem with one of his papers. Least that's how I understood it. They were going to let him fix it. But he up and dropped out. Some lady called him. His advisor, I think. She done a real good job of hounding him. I thought she was going to straighten him out, but he up and stopped taking her calls." Jerry shrugged. "After a time, she stopped calling. Jacob went into a bad slump for a couple of years after that. Then something happened, and he started putting himself back together. We'll never know what it was. That boy could keep his own counsel." He looked down at his hands again. "The night before he joined the Lord…"

That damn wild rabbit got loose in her chest again, scampering under her breastbone, giving her heart several good thumps the closer she got to knowing what she did—and did not—want to know.

"That night, Jacob said to me, 'I'm setting things right.' He said he was going to call you folks the next day."

"What went wrong?" Sonja asked.

Jerry shook his head. "The family's had more than a few arguments about that before we stopped talking about it altogether. Some say he OD'ed. I think they're more comfortable with that than suicide. Suicide doesn't sit right with most of us. But…we'll never know. Not while we're on Earth, anyway."

He stood up. "Didn't mean to lay our family burdens on you. Sure you get lots of troubled students, Dr. Storey. I'll bet these young people use their woes to get your heart in a twist." He turned toward the door, but she wasn't ready for him to leave. Not until she had the answer.

Did I kill him?

And as if reading her mind, Jerry answered. "Jacob and I got real close before he died. There were only a few years difference between us. We were more like brothers than uncle and nephew." He cleared his throat. "He liked to cite Proverbs. 'Many women do noble things, but you surpass them all.' I hope I don't overstep, Dr. Storey, but he said that about you."

She looked away, hoping he wouldn't see the tears escaping.

"I'm sorry if I made you uncomfortable. My wife used to say I had no sense when it came to running my mouth."

"You did not overstep."

"If I said too much— Well, Jacob's gone, and I don't want his respect for you to go to his grave with him. You saw a goodness in him, Dr. Storey, and he struggled to see goodness in himself. You helped him see what he could become. That meant the world to him. He thought he let you down. He talked about making things right with you. Said how important you'd been to him, and he was going to be the man worthy of the faith you placed in him."

Howimportanthowimportanthowimportant.

"He even talked about studying to become some kind of doctor. Your kind, not a real doctor." He chuckled, a low, gentle sound that cupped her heart. "Sorry, Dr. Storey. A family joke. That's how we teased Jacob when he got too full of himself." He opened the door and stepped out of the office but changed his mind and came back in.

"Dr. Storey," he said, putting his hands in the pockets of his workpants. "You did so much for Jacob, I got my hopes up when you turned out to be Corey's teacher. It just didn't end up the way I wanted. My son had something against you from the start. Not just because you're a woman teacher. He's messed up where Jacob's concerned, a jealousy that's gotten worse after…the death and all. You got hit with problems that aren't yours."

"Is he dangerous?" Sonja asked.

"Corey's a hothead, but he doesn't hit women. He tormented his momma, but he never raised a hand to her. Course if he had, I would've straightened him out real quick."

"You don't know for certain, though. About your son not ever assaulting a woman."

"Guess that's right, ma'am." He put his hand on the door handle. "If he comes around here bothering you, you give me a call. I'm going to wrestle my son out of the devil's hands if it's the last thing I do."

Sonja got up from her chair and took a step toward him. "Mr. Randalls, if Corey gets his life in order, tell him to make an appointment with me. I'll find a seat for him in my class, but only if he demonstrates commitment and self-control."

"Proverbs 31:29 sounds right. I see what Jacob meant. You're a good woman. Appreciate your time, Dr. Storey. And I'd be grateful if you accept my apologies for my son's behavior."

"Thank you," Sonja said.

He nodded over her shoulder. "Couldn't help but notice your chair. I've done some leather work. I'd be glad to see what I could do with it. She's a fine piece."

Sonja looked back, not seeing a queen's throne but instead recognizing it as an ordinary chair with metal, padding, and leather, a tangible object that no longer represented an intangible ideal.

"I may have to let it go." She looked back at him again and he nodded.

"Offer stands," he said. "Whether Corey's in your class or not." He stepped out and closed the door behind him.

Sonja crumpled in her chair, feeling like she had cut herself off from an umbilical cord that had been draining instead of nourishing her.

"Jacob, I'm so sorry for whatever you faced alone. I wouldn't report you now. We would've found another way." She stared up at a tea-colored stain on the ceiling tiles, and it occurred to her that maybe it was appropriate to have an office with such a blaring imperfection.

Something in that stain gave her the energy to make her way out into the corridor and down into the main office where Harmony sat.

"May I show you something?" Sonja whispered, leaning over the secretary's privacy barrier.

"Um, sure." Harmony followed Sonja out of the department office. "I feel awful about Mitch being at the memorial. It wasn't a setup."

"You are not to blame for him being there. There is another matter, however."

They arrived at Sonja's office and stood in the doorway, shoulders touching.

"What—?" Harmony sputtered.

"Did that student worker do this before you fired her?" Sonja asked.

"I don't know," Harmony said. "She could've gotten the keys out of my desk when I stepped away. Maybe that's why she came undone and confessed everything. Her breakdown came out of the blue."

Harmony stepped away and began pacing up and down the hall. "I'm angrier than a hornet. I want to track that girl down and give her a good paddling with a willow switch, the greenest I can find. Oh Jesus, I'm burned up. I'm going to call Officer Sounder myself."

"Let it go," Sonja replied, not ready for anyone else to see her chair. *Maybe I'll never be ready.*

"But this is too much," Harmony responded. She stopped pacing. "You don't deserve this, Dr. Storey."

"I should be furious. I should want her head. I'm just—"

"Worn out," Harmony suggested.

"I think I want to stop being so damn angry all the damn—"

She was interrupted by a text notification. She dashed over to her desk to pick up her cell phone, hoping, and having that hope fulfilled.

"Have to reply to this text, Harm. Let it go for now. Please."

"Whatever you want, Sonja," the secretary said before leaving.

The phone vibrated with more messages, and Sonja closed her door, wanting to read each one in private.

Been visiting parents. Crappy cell service.

Then: *Hitting the road. Back tonight.*

For the second time that day, Sonja stood in her office and sobbed, but now with relief. Pulling out a tissue, she dried the tears from her face, then sent a reply text.

Please come by tonight. Please.

She sent another text.

Safe travels.

And another.

I miss you.

And a fourth.

Sorry for everything.

For the first time in a long time, she felt washed clean, so much so that she decided she would call her mother. But not before concluding two other matters. She sent an email and rescheduled the upcoming search meeting she had called to establish procedures and review candidate criteria. All that could wait. The second matter could not. She opened the email she had been avoiding.

Sonja:

When I saw you the other night, it reminded me that we have unfinished business. You insulted me, and I insist on being heard. You continue avoiding me, but we will inevitably run into one another at graduation, convocation, the student research symposium. I will have that overdue conversation with you. It would be best for all involved if we met before the end of the semester.

—Douglas Christopher, PhD, Associate Professor

Sonja responded by typing more than thinking, tired of calculating the potential impact of each word.

Douglas:

Be advised. I will not speak with you about this issue. If we serve together on a committee in the future, we will keep our interactions professional and relevant to our assigned duties. Continue contacting me through any means regarding the alleged insult, I will file a claim of harassment with Assistant Counsel Jodi Jenkins.

In the meantime, I recommend that you review your past correspondence with me, a full professor and a woman. You routinely declare yourself to be a champion of marginalized voices on campus, yet there seems to be a claim–evidence disconnect.

It is neither my job to make you feel better about your actions nor is it my job to help convince you of your potentially problematic behavior. You are responsible for you. Do not contact me again regarding this matter.

—Dr. Sonja J. Storey, Professor.

She pressed Send without reviewing her reply, and it felt like she had taken another step into more fully occupying the space of her life.

Chapter 34

Laughing Loud and Long

By the time Sonja reached home, collected her mail, and changed into her cashmere tunic and pants, she had a better idea how to proceed with a call to her mother—a call that, unlike previous times, she would make without the full-bodied assistance of pinot noir.

She took a step stool into the walk-in closet and dug into the sweaters stacked in the corner of the top shelf. The photo was right where she had left it, wrapped in the vintage Louis Vuitton scarf she had lifted from her father's second wife during her final visit. She was determined to remain impartial while analyzing the photo, so, as she flipped off the light switch, she did the same to her emotions and went to sit at the kitchen table. She tightened her cashmere wrap before she pulled the neatly folded scarf toward her.

The few times she had visited her father's had been less than satisfying, but she had been rewarded with two parting gifts. The first was the silk scarf, snatched from her stepmother's extensive collection. The woman had been friendly, almost caring. But her father was as standoffish as ever, including when he had *requested* that Sonja depart after her spat with her half-sister—the little brat. Calmly, coldly, he directed her to gather her things, escorted her to the door, and shut it behind her while his young wife wept quietly in the background.

When Sonja returned to her campus residence hall, she discovered that she had swiped a Louis Vuitton scarf, pink and purple silk with tiny flowers. She detested it, but she also felt vindicated in taking it. After all, her stepmother—her father's former student—had robbed her of her father.

The second parting gift was the picture frame now wrapped inside the scarf, the lettering on the frame reading, "Daddy's little girl 4ever!"

Sonja had torn up and flushed the original picture without really studying it—unable to bear the image of a tiny, grinning Ashley perched on Father's lap—and replaced it with the only family photo she had. It was this photo that Sonja would use to assess her readiness to call her mother.

On the back was a blue stamp that indicated the photo was printed in June, but the year was faded and unreadable. A crease ran down the left side of the photo, her attempt as a teenager to crop out the image of her mother. She wasn't sure why she hadn't finished the job.

Sonja flipped over the photograph and leaned in.

In the lower left section, a young Sonja, perhaps nine or ten, sat on the bottom step of a two-stair concrete porch attached to a brick ranch house. That girl in the photo was looking down, which emphasized her uneven home haircut.

She looked next at her mother, who appeared to be younger than Sonja was currently. But Mrs. Claudette Brooks Storey was an unkempt woman sporting a messy bun, a wrinkled peach T-shirt, and a bitter expression.

Sonja took a breath, grounding herself, and looked at her father.

Dr. Claude Storey was a handsome man with thick salt-and-pepper hair even back then and tanned skin that glowed. He wore a white short-sleeved button-down shirt and had a dazzling smile. And, unlike her mother, Father looked directly at the photographer.

He wasn't hugging the girl in this photo, as he had hugged Sonja's half-sister—both in that original framed photo and in the one she'd found online. Instead, he leaned toward the photographer and away from the girl.

"Who was the photographer, Father? She must have been a young, attractive female, perhaps one of your student lovers. You appear enraptured."

With her hand shaking and her eye twitching, Sonja returned her only family photo to the stolen frame and rewrapped it in the stolen scarf. When she thought about hiding it again, she suddenly couldn't. She left it on the kitchen table, her childhood imprisoned in silk, and she deliberated whether to show it to Crystal, a means of explaining herself and her actions to a woman she had repeatedly mistreated. But she tabled that decision.

Sonja straightened her clothes, smoothed her hair, and dialed her mother's number.

A robotic voice delivered the outgoing message without giving a name, and Sonja's breathing eased. She considered hanging up, but instead, she placed her phone on the table, turned on the speaker, and waited for the beep, her hands fused together in her lap as if welded by the heat of anticipated confrontation.

"Mother," she said slowly in a voice as robotic as the one that had answered. "It is Sonja, your daughter. If you receive this message, do not return my call. I am simply informing you of a significant development." She picked up her pace, wanting to get to the point before she lost her nerve. "I succeeded, despite your failure as a mother. I put myself through school, both undergraduate and graduate. I am an author and a professor. Full professor. And I want you to know something." The dart frog that lived in her throat mutated into a bullfrog.

"You were wrong. Those times you told me—screamed at me—that I would end up like you, that I was destined to be alone and bitter...you were wrong. I met someone, and she is nothing like our family. *Nothing!*"

Sonja closed her eyes and pictured Crystal asleep beside her. She saw the morning light filtering through the sheers and turning a lilac hue that drenched Crystal's body, hair, and face, a face that had seemed familiar to her from day one.

"She's chestnut, honey, and whiskey, and she smells like sea salt and coconut. She's brilliant and kind. I like her, and—"

You more than like her, girlie. But it'll fall apart 'cause you've built everything on sand.

The late afternoon sun streamed through the deck door, and Sonja wiped her damp forehead, then rested one sharp fingernail there. She wished she had a way to carve out her mother's cruel voice, to keep it from haunting her as it had for most of her life.

"You held me hostage. But I am free of you." And she hung up.

It was over.

Leaving her phone on the dining table, Sonja stepped onto her floating perch, laughing loud and long until she cried. When the tears stopped, she went back indoors to see if Crystal had texted.

Instead, she found a message from her mother's number.

SWN. Hav2say ur moms a POS

Sonja typed the acronyms into her cell's search bar. *Sorry, wrong number. Have to say, your mom's a piece of shit.*

She laughed even harder.

When Crystal arrived, Sonja threw open her front door and fumbled to unlock the security door with trembling fingers. Finally succeeding, she rushed outside and into Crystal's arms.

"This is new," Crystal said, not returning Sonja's embrace. "Give me a minute. Sonja, give me a minute."

"Please let me stay here."

Crystal sighed and relented. "Only for a moment."

Sonja buried herself in the woman, breathing in the scent of salt and stability. "I will make it right."

"Let's go inside. I'm road-weary and starving."

But Sonja held on, and Crystal snaked an arm around her.

"I have a lot to say. And you have a lot of listening to do."

"I will make it right," Sonja repeated, then fell silent, simply enjoying the sound of Crystal's breathing.

"Oh fuck," the younger woman whispered, kissing the crown of Sonja's head. "CDAF. Codependent as fuck."

Chapter 35

Heart Within

CRYSTAL SAT ON THE COUCH and threw one arm over the back, amber eyes hard, impenetrable.

Toolatetoolatetoo—

Sonja ignored the voice looping in her head. Come what may, she would listen to what Crystal had to say. She kept her hands in her lap and the glass of pinot out of reach, and she waited for Crystal to speak.

"I know you've been having a hard time," Crystal started. "The other night with that Mitch fucker…that must have been excruciating. You know I have empathy for what you've been through. And if you don't know, well, that's your problem. Your healing, *that* is on you too. Which brings me to what I want to say."

"I'm listening," Sonja reassured Crystal—or that was her goal—but her tone retained a hammer-on-nail quality.

"To borrow from Spike Lee, I am not your Magical Negro."

Sonja's mind raced, trying to discern the meaning of Crystal's words.

"Certainly," she replied, feeling anything but certain.

"You have no idea what I'm talking about." Crystal held up her hand as if to block Sonja's denial. "Your eyes turn into black tar and your lips flatline when you're trying to retain control. Look at you. Even when we're on the brink, you're too arrogant to admit when you don't understand."

Sonja wanted to go on the offensive, but she recognized the determination in Crystal's eyes. "Tell me more," she said, the ice melting from her voice.

"It's not my responsibility to educate you." Crystal leaned back again, crossing her arms against her chest. "You're a researcher, so research. I'm not patiently waiting around to help you figure out your shit and solve your problems. Here's what you need to hear: if I have to be the villain in your story to be the hero in my own, then so be it."

"Okay." Sonja said with a nod, not trusting herself to say anything more.

"You are constant drama," Crystal said. "There we were at a memorial, and it *still* ended up being about you. Then you tell me we're done, for me to find someone else. Then you say you're sorry. I should have expected it. Push, pull, push, pull. Your standard dance."

Crystal gazed off into the distance, continuing after a pause. "My *raison d'etre* isn't to fix your life. *You* fix your life. I'm busy. Not that you notice or act like you care. I'm a professor, and a good one too. And I'm going to put WHSU on the map. Under my direction, our department is going to be overhauled. We're going to stretch beyond our outdated, white-centric, cishet focus and become a top-choice university for sexuality and inclusion studies.

"So, your drama-filled phone calls and demands for late-night visits will stop. Somehow, someway. I'm not some mystical character who appears to cure whatever ails you, then disappears once the white woman learns her touched-by-an-angel lesson. Got it?"

Toolatetoolatetoolate. You teach chaos theory, but you didn't see that you're the butterfly that flaps its wings and causes the storm.

Sonja nodded again, having no clue what else to do.

Crystal looked at her. "You keep bobbing your head like one of those bobblehead dolls. Say what that bobbing means."

"Yes," Sonja said without hesitation. "Yes to everything you said. I have treated you like my...my fixer. I would like to tell you that that is all over. However, recent events have illustrated that I have work to do."

Crystal threw her arm up on the back of the couch again. "Such as?"

"For one, I will return to that therapist," Sonja promised.

"I'll assume a wait-and-see position about that."

Sonja picked up her untouched glass of wine from the coffee table. She sipped it, then held it out to Crystal, who waved it away, so Sonja made another offering.

"I want to know about your trip, your family. Whatever you want to tell me."

"Right now, I'm raw. Some of it has to do with you. Some of it has *absolutely nothing* to do with you. Imagine that! Me existing outside of Dr. Storey's story." Crystal's tone was sharp, but then she leaned over and snatched the wineglass out of Sonja's hand.

"When I was home, I ran into my third-grade teacher—" Crystal stopped herself. "On second thought, maybe I'm not ready to tell you this."

Sonja looked down and waited.

Crystal drank the wine like a whiskey shot, coughing and sputtering. "Shouldn't have done that." After the coughing ended, she continued, "What I'm getting ready to tell you... I don't give this story to just anyone. And let's be clear: you haven't earned this story."

"Understood." Sonja uneasily met Crystal's piercing gaze.

"In third grade, I had Miss Hinnie." Crystal had apparently found whatever she had been looking for in Sonja's eyes. "I ran into her at the gas station when I was home. I hate that bitch," she hissed, then snickered lightly. "I don't usually give hate room in my heart."

Crystal shook her head, her ponytail swinging back and forth. "I see my former teacher pumping gas. I walk up to her and say, 'Hello there, Hinnie. You may not remember me, but I was in your class ages ago. My name is Crystal Byrd. It's Dr. Byrd, now. Not bad for a mongrel.' That's what she called kids like me. *Mongrels.* Can you imagine?"

"I cannot," Sonja murmured, suddenly and overwhelmingly embarrassed that she had contributed to the mistreatment Crystal had faced.

"Miss Hinnie turned so pink, her ears looked like fried bologna. Her hands started shaking. Hard. Some kind of palsy, maybe. She shouldn't have been driving. Damn! I'm pathetic...feeling compassion for someone who spread her hate like a deadly virus.

"Her eyes," Crystal grunted. "They were exactly how I remembered them. Chalky with crystal-like spots cobwebbing out. When I was a child, just a look from her made me break out in goosebumps. Damn if they hadn't gotten more terrifying with age."

Crystal held up Sonja's empty glass. "I finished your wine."

"I'll get more," Sonja offered.

"Not right now. I'm too mad-sad to drink. I keep seeing Miss Hinnie standing there, gas nozzle in her claw hands. Even when she was younger, she had fishhooks for hands. Boney, sharp things that hooked kids, reeled them into her snarling mouth.

"Back in third grade, I walked up on her and her teacher's aide. She didn't see me, too busy running her mouth. I think—" She stared at the ceiling, considering. "That must've been after Momma and Daddy came to a teacher conference— How old are third graders?"

Sonja shrugged. "Seven, eight?"

"Just a goddamn baby..." Crystal sighed. "Telling this story...it's like I'm back there, seeing her in a high-collar dress, hem way below her knees, hair tied up in an old-lady bun. Buttoned up, covered up. That was Miss Hinnie." She scoffed. "I can still hear her spewing poison. Only inches away from kids too." Crystal raised her pitch in an apparent imitation of Miss Hinnie. "'I pray to God every night, ask His forgiveness for standing in the presence of sin. It's not right, that white man marrying a colored girl. Mongrel offspring's what they sown. It's against God's law.' Something like that. I've probably filled in details based on hometown stories. But that's the gist of it."

"She sounds horrible. I'm...I'm sorry." Love unexpectedly gurgled up into Sonja's hard-packed heart, tearing it open, leaving her nearly gasping from the beautiful sensation, almost an exquisite violence done to her chest. She wanted to embrace Crystal, a woman who deserved to be treated better by the world, and by her too.

Crystal shifted to angle her body toward Sonja. "I'm trusting you with this. And I shouldn't, not after how you've acted. Hell, I haven't even told Momma or Daddy what I'm about to tell you. I didn't want them going to jail for murder. So, okay. I remember this exactly, though I didn't understand what it meant until much later." She took a deep breath. "That day I overheard Miss Hinnie calling me a mongrel, she...she stuck her finger down her throat and gagged. There I was, a child witnessing how my very existence nauseated her. She turned around and caught me watching her. Glared at me as if I had done something wrong for catching her without her Christian lady mask on."

"You amaze me," Sonja admitted. "You don't let things like that scar you." She reached out and put her hand on Crystal's knee.

"I have scars, but I don't become them." Crystal removed Sonja's hand. "Work the trauma, or the trauma works you. Can't remember if I heard that somewhere or if I made it up. Regardless, I hold tight to that philosophy."

"Of course." Sonja retreated, sitting back against the couch. "How did the interaction at the gas station end?"

"Our sloppy stories seldom have tidy endings. Sometimes the best we can do is to lift our heads high and smile at the nastiness. That's what I did. I gave her a huge fuck-you smile, and I left her behind at that gas pump. Truthfully, I feel a bit sorry for her. She looked like she'd spent a lifetime weathering storm after storm."

"Storms of her own making."

Crystal locked eyes with Sonja until Sonja looked away. "I'll take some more wine now," she said.

Sonja leaped up and went to the kitchen to pour two fresh glasses of pinot. She returned to the living room and handed one to her guest, then settled back onto the couch. "Earlier you said we have a lot to discuss. I am ready if you are."

"I'm not sure how ready I am. I'm still figuring things out. I talked to Momma when I was home, told her how I'm trying to keep my head above water, how I keep getting caught up in you. Like there's some strange attraction that keeps drawing us together."

Holding her wine on her lap, Sonja nestled into the crook of the couch. When her mother had forced her to skip school and snuggle, Sonja had found a measure of comfort in the space where the couch's arm and the back fused, as if she could escape into the crease.

"Momma knows my history," Crystal said. "She's been through the wringer with me. She said I really know how to pick 'em."

"Your mother told you to run." *You should run.*

"She trusts me to make my own decision. I'm not sure I trust myself. I've conspired against myself way too many times. Used to, I blamed Daddy for filling me up with romantic stories about how long and hard he chased Momma before she warmed up to him." Crystal drank some wine and closed her eyes for a moment. When she opened them, she said, "I can't keep blaming Daddy for my soft heart anymore. But I'm done wasting away on thin love. Toni Morrison's books helped me see how thin love isn't love at all. Never again. That's what I came to tell you."

Sonja conceded. "You stood by me longer than you should have."

"Correct." Crystal blew out her breath as if to rid herself of something unwanted. "I'm a sucker for beauty that's been overlooked. I'm drawn to the discarded, the disenfranchised, the detested truthtellers. All that has brought a fair amount of pain my way."

Crystal tapped the side of her glass, her nail producing a low ring. "This time, I won't settle. I'm going to be with someone who's strong enough to be with my strongest me. Otherwise, I'm going solo."

"I will work with the counselor," Sonja promised. "I will file down my sharp edges." *To stop cutting you and myself.*

Crystal gazed at her. "Wait and see, darling. Wait and see."

"I accept your terms," Sonja said quickly, as if they were forming a verbal contract that Crystal could withdraw from at any moment. "Now, please stay for dinner. I can prepare a salad—"

"Fuck salad. I swear you live on dry toast and plain romaine. I need real food. If we keep seeing one another, that shit's going to change."

If we keep seeing one another. Ifififif... Sonja savored the words as if they were the finest French pinot noir. "I suppose we could have something delivered," Sonja suggested. "I assume someone delivers in Hickville, North Carolina."

"Stop that. You're being a snob. This town's growing on me. So is the campus. It's white as hell, but I may make it home, give this area some much-needed color. I'm going to start an association on campus for BIPOC faculty and staff. I spoke with Samson Matovu about it at the planetarium and the memorial, and we're going to meet soon. Eventually, I may expand it off-campus, but forming a queers of color group comes before that, I think. I'm considering all options. But those options will keep me in Foxboro for a time, so I don't want to hear any more hillbilly this or hick that."

"That sounds"—Sonja tried to find the right words—"like important work."

Suddenly Crystal yelped. "I know a place. You will absolutely hate it! Thick-crust pizza, layers of gooey cheese. And they deliver." She pushed out her belly until it rounded under her stretchy black slacks.

"I do not do pi—" Sonja stopped herself. "Fine. You call in the order. I will make the salads." She stood up and walked into the kitchen. "Do you want yours with pine nuts?" she called back to Crystal.

248

"Pine nuts!" Crystal howled with laughter.

The next thing Sonja heard was the sound of Crystal's sneakers hitting the floor, and combined with the laughter, it was like the music of forgiveness and renewal.

As Sonja pulled romaine leaves from the fresh head, she sang a verse under her breath: *This heart within...*

In high school, she had recited Coleridge's line as her mother shrieked on the other side of the door, envisioning her heart rotting like the tomatoes in her mother's neglected indoor garden, praying that someone would rescue her from the inevitable decay.

Tonight, though, something else swelled in her chest. Her heart plumped up, made juicy and ripe, and while that terrified her, she welcomed the sensation, inviting it to stay for as long as it would.

Chapter 36

Walked Together

THE NEXT MORNING, SONJA FOUND that Crystal's legs and arms had draped over her like ropes as they'd slept. Instantly, she panicked, her body becoming rigid.

"What's wrong?" Crystal asked drowsily.

Sonja turned her head and looked at Crystal's face, head exquisitely crowned in the Burberry mermaid scarf. Though her first instinct was to dodge behind a shield of lies, Sonja realized something curious: she didn't want to hide from the woman beside her.

"Before you, it had been a while." Sonja turned her head and looked up at the ceiling. "I am not communicating clearly."

Crystal placed a hand on Sonja's chest. "Be naked with me, love. Emotionally naked, I mean."

But therein was the problem. Sonja felt more naked than she ever had, and she had never developed a vocabulary for describing that feeling. But she tried anyway. "The last time was in college. The last time I shared a bed, that is. Without sex." *Without being drunk.*

"Must be overwhelming, even a bit suffocating."

"Unsettling, but"—Sonja searched for the right word—"lovely in a way that's strange to me."

Crystal removed her hand from Sonja's chest and tucked it between her head and the pillow. "I'd like to suggest something."

"Continue."

"Let's take it slow, babe. Let me touch you. You touch me. No sex. Not this morning. Maybe not even for a while. Just adoration. A lover did this for me a long time ago. I had just gotten to college and thought I was ready to reclaim what my rapist had taken. But the moment I tried receiving pleasure, I came undone. My lover helped me understand something. Before I could surrender to pleasure, I had to excise the scar tissue that kept me numb."

Sonja nodded almost imperceptibly, and Crystal responded by stroking where Sonja's forehead disappeared into her hairline; then those velvety fingertips traced her face and the bridge of her nose, then the outline of her lips. As Crystal stroked down Sonja's neck and tickled her under her chin, Sonja giggled. But she lay flat, motionless, allowing herself to become an artist's canvas, a smooth, white surface brushed with colorful hues. And, before she could stop them, tears slid from the corner of one eye.

"You are divine," Crystal whispered into her ear. "You always have been, even when others failed to see your divinity, or mistreated it." The tender whispers were soon replaced by kisses on Sonja's lips. Their breathing mingled, exhalations fluttering against one another like mating swallowtails. Then the kisses migrated to the underside of Sonja's marked breast, and Sonja wept as Crystal's tongue bathed the scar that Avery had left.

After a time, Sonja turned on her side and faced Crystal, who lay back without a sound.

Sonja fingerpainted Crystal's cheeks, chin, neck, collarbones, and ribcage, down the belly to one rolling hip, then one thigh. She studied the ridgeline of muscles.

"You have no hair on your legs." Drunk from her journey across the human terrain, Sonja only vaguely recognized that she had spoken aloud.

"Arms either."

"Why?" Sonja instantly regretted her question, fearing she would break the spell.

"I got tired of being the hairy one at family reunions. We'll leave it at that right now. Everywhere else, I'm a natural woman."

Sonja resumed her exploration, tracing a line down one long calf, discovering more ridgelines and valleys. She angled herself across the bedsheets until she reached Crystal's feet and pushed inquisitive fingers into each pad. With one sharp crimson fingernail, she followed Crystal's steep arches before meandering up to the pillowy interior of Crystal's inner thighs, kneading them lightly and earning a sigh from her lover. *My lover.* Sonja inched forward and parted the wet wings of the butterfly and revealed the sublime bud within.

"You're breaking the rules," Crystal said huskily.

Sonja moved her body up and rested her head on Crystal's belly. "I break all sorts of rules in your presence," she murmured, desire and delight swollen in her throat, fattening her lips and plumping her tongue. She combed the silky black curls covering the pubis mons then parted the butterfly wings once more, yearning to make the bud swell until bliss cocooned them both.

Afterward, Sonja got up and dashed off an email to her students, canceling both her classes, something she had never done before. When she returned to bed, Crystal was sound asleep, so she pressed against her lover and fell into a heavenly rest.

Over the next few weeks, Crystal migrated her things into Sonja's house, and the two of them shared spaces until the borders disappeared. They huddled together over meals. At night, they met in the center of the bed. Sonja was increasingly comfortable with the closeness, but it also gave rise to a new fear: loss. She found herself wanting to tell Crystal about this fear, along with other secrets she had kept locked up for far too long in a dark, private vault inside her.

One evening, Sonja called Crystal into her office and pointed with a shaking finger at the *Crysse* post on the OD website tribute page.

"That's why you asked those questions. You wondered if I knew Jacob and was out to avenge him. Damn, Sonja, that was months back. You've been holding onto this suspicion for that long?"

Crystal spun Sonja around in her chair and crouched down, hugging Sonja's legs and looking up with a steady gaze. "Here's the deal, babe. Daddy is bolted down good and tight to his hometown. He's left only a handful of times. His sense of place is rather…limited. Auntie Laura lives an hour or so outside of D.C., but Daddy still thinks that her place and Foxboro are close by. He has no clue that she's about a six-hour drive north. In a sense—a geographically liberal sense—I do have local family. But no, darling, I am unrelated to Jacob Randalls. And I'm not out to punish you for your supposed wrongdoings."

Crystal stood up, bent over to kiss Sonja, then pulled back and stared. "Now, seriously, lover…"

"I know," Sonja mumbled. "No thin love."

"Thick, juicy love. Nothing thin. You have questions or concerns, raise them directly instead of playing some long game with me." She took Sonja's chin in her hand, kissed her lips, then licked the tip of Sonja's nose.

"Ick. I hate that."

Crystal chuckled. "Consider it your punishment, darling."

"You said you weren't out to punish me."

"Fair point, but we've talked about that beautiful brain of yours, how it wants to argue you out of every bit of happiness."

Sonja tried and failed to pull away from Crystal's grasp. "Okay," she said, relenting. "I was an idiot."

"A gorgeous, brilliant idiot who has faced layers of trauma. But you're responsible for your healing, and that means asking for what you need." She released Sonja's face and held out her hand. "Time for our walk. And the subject for tonight's walk-and-talk will be that closet of yours. I need more than an inch of space for my things. Besides, your closet is bigger than my shitty apartment."

Sonja detested that Crystal kept pushing her to behave in ways that she found distasteful, including sharing her closet. But at the top of Sonja's list of gripes was their evening walks through the neighborhood, their intertwined hands on display.

They walked together down and back up Summit Street, as had been their routine for weeks, and, annoying Sonja, Crystal waved at everyone. Before long, the neighborhood accepted Crystal, although Sonja remained the distant onlooker whenever Crystal stopped to chat with someone. Repeatedly, she and Crystal met up with the father-daughter team, the likely owners of Smushed Driveway Creature, the man and girl smiling easily at Crystal while casting wary looks at Sonja.

"Darling, please be friendlier," Crystal pleaded. "Our neighbors are good people. They aren't out to get you. And a gentle reminder…we stay informed by talking with them. Seems one of them found someone in their garage. Sounds like dementia…"

Crystal's latest neighborhood news report was lost on Sonja, who silently repeated:

Not out to get me, notouttogetmenotouttogetme.

Sonja often repeated those words to herself on their walks, wishing that she believed in the world's grace, as Crystal did. But Sonja didn't. Plus, no matter how hard she tried, she couldn't rid herself of the dread that remained in her core like a dark mineral deposit. Though, perhaps for the first time in her life, she tried digging down deeper in search of her own store of splendor.

And she did this, not during those evening walks, but by sharing the cosmos with Crystal.

Even as temperatures dropped, she and Crystal ventured into the night and took turns peering through Star Dancer's eyepiece. As she listened to her girlfriend's exclamations of awe for the stars and planets, Sonja watched the sky that stretched out like a wing of an iridescent starling, and she realized how small she was in the universe.

But beside Crystal, Sonja also felt mightier.

———————

"During our last visit, Dr. Storey," Abby Wake began, "you said your mother passed on."

"I called her old number. It is no longer hers. I assume she is dead. Hence, our discussion of her is dead as well."

"Circle back around. What can you tell me about the broader context of that phone call?"

"I have explained everything to you already. You scribble in your notebook, but you do not listen. Frankly, it is irritating."

"Are you game for trying something else?"

"No."

"Consider it first," Wake prodded. "Role-play your phone call, give yourself a safe space to say to your mother what you wanted—"

"No."

"All right, then. We'll change gears. You've spoken several times about your half-sister, Ashley. You say she stole your life."

"She did."

Wake looked down at her notebook, her short hair falling around her square face like silver-tipped bat wings. "According to what you previously told me, you felt driven away from visits with your father because your half-sister, and I quote, 'acted like a whiny brat.'"

"Correct," Sonja confirmed, and when Wake remained silent, she continued—reluctantly. "Fine." Sonja hugged her tote tighter. "Whenever I came up from the basement—that's where they kept me when I visited. Not in a guest room or even on a couch. They buried me alive in that gray basement," Sonja said, knowing she was being overly dramatic.

She loosened the grip on her tote and brushed off nonexistent lint from her suit jacket. "The basement steps creaked like an alarm, so whenever I started up them, my sister wailed loudly enough for everyone to hear. As soon as I stepped into the kitchen, she'd race down the hallway, yowling like an injured cat, and hide in her bedroom." Sonja snorted. "Of course, she didn't just go into her bedroom. She hid *under* her bed."

"That sounds devastating. To find the courage to reach out to the father who abandoned you only to be rejected by a child."

"I survived."

"I'd like you to consider, Dr. Storey, that your half-sister is a grown woman now. And a professor, like you. Perhaps—"

"Ah, reframing. You want me to think of earlier behaviors in new ways. No need. I am confident in my analysis of her. She's a little shit who, along with her mother, stole my father. That's my story. That's all there is," she said firmly to keep from saying more, maybe even mentioning the family photo stashed in her closet.

"It seems like you have more to say, Dr. Storey."

Sonja itched to spill everything, every injustice, every cruelty. She wanted to vomit up stories, present photographic evidence of her life of rejection. She could even disclose the digital picture she had located of her father and Ashley that depicted their radiant joy.

Dr. Ashley Storey dressed in doctoral regalia, her head covered with a velvet tam, a saffron tassel dangling. Strong jawline, pointy chin, skin the shade of sun-drenched golden sand. Behind her stood her proud papa wearing a wide smile. The caption read, "It's all in the family! Dr. Ashley Storey joins her father, Dr. Claude Storey..."

And with that image forever imprinted on her mind, Sonja had stopped looking for news about her half-sister until one day she happened upon a press release about Ashley's award-winning book, *Get At it! Transforming Followers into Leaders*. Foolishly thinking herself strong enough to face her past once more, she read about the standing-room-only turnout at the university's book launch event.

Now, as far as she was concerned, there was only one Dr. Storey.

When she returned her attention to the session, Sonja found Wake watching her.

"You seem to be mulling something over. Would you care to share?"

"These walls are in need of a fresh coat of paint," Sonja said, looking around the office.

When Sonja again faced the counselor, Wake resumed. "Something you said earlier. "'That's my story.'"

"What of it?"

"What if we use story analysis? We could use these sessions to transform your personal narrative."

"This should be interesting." Sonja checked her nail polish, pretending to be bored, though her body was screaming at her to flee before Wake could see the darkness within.

"The story you've told yourself is that you are unlovable," Wake prattled on. "And you are perpetually being punished for being unlovable. Your father left you because he saw you as an extension of your mother. Your half-sister, only a child at the time, rejected you because she also saw you as defective. Time and time again, you were judged and found deficient. Those early patterns get programmed into us. We use them to make sense out of events and make decisions, even if those patterns are incorrect or outdated.

"But what if the story you've told yourself has been wrong all this time? What if you had nothing to do with your father's abandonment? What if he left because of something having to do with him, not you, like, for example, a brain disorder—"

"Fascinating," Sonja said, looking at her Holzkern peacock feather watch. She was thirsty these days for colors that contradicted the starkness of her soul. "Unfortunately, I am out of time." She stood, instantly heading to the door.

"We have a bit longer, but you must decide how to use our time together."

"I will call to schedule our next session." Sonja purposely ignored Wake's previous statement. "I must insist, though, that next meeting, we *will* move beyond this family drivel. I am heading a search committee for a new faculty member. Additionally, I am working on my fourth book. And no, I am *not* cloaking my vulnerabilities by credentializing. I simply have no time for unproductive conversations."

Liar.

Sonja hurried out before Wake could call her on her bullshit. As she exited the office, she felt heavier, as if the excavating of her history had increased the weight of her load.

Once inside Bimmer, she pushed down the resurrected memories, intent on transforming herself back into an ice queen who reigned over a world of frozen emotions. At least until she got home. There, Crystal waited, the primary source of Sonja's warming trend.

When Sonja pulled onto Summit Street, she found Crystal's car blocking the driveway, and she slammed her hand down on the horn, as if Bimmer could scream for her.

Crystal flung open the security door. "What?"

Sonja rolled down her window. "An accident," she said to excuse the horn blaring. "You will need to move your car, however. Oh, and please grab that package off the porch."

For a moment, it looked as though Crystal would stand there forever, arms crossed, judgment palpable. Finally, Crystal bounded down the steps, passing by Sonja's newest package without touching it, and moved her car to the curb.

Sonja waved at her girlfriend, then steered Bimmer into the garage, cut the engine, and sat, feeling the weight of her new life pressing down on her. She wondered when everything would come crashing down.

With each new day, Sonja's life improved. There were no more fish oil spills outside her office, no threatening messages slipped under her door, no dead animals left for her to find, no spooky emails from anonymous senders, and no red stickies littering her classroom. The night terrors had also dissipated, largely because Crystal woke Sonja up as soon as she started thrashing, and before her dreams morphed into sinister specters that drove her from the bed.

Her sleep improved, and her waking hours did too. And this terrified Sonja in ways that the chaos had not. She waited, almost breathless, as if living in the eye of a storm, certain that her old life would reemerge.

The fall semester marched on with the changing season. From her office, Sonja watched the emerald trees catch fire and burn into citrine, topaz, and garnet before curling and dimming. The world was becoming drab and colorless, exactly how Sonja felt. Every day, her paranoia, hostility, and anger mimicked the falling leaves, dropping away from her, and she wondered who she was without all her flashing and blazing.

What if the story you've told yourself has been wrong all along?

Sonja's sessions with Wake had started to challenge her thinking, and new questions and insights pestered her even in the classroom. Soon her students had started warming toward her. They met her eyes when she lectured, raised their hands, offered relevant comments.

One day, a student called out to her on his way to the door. "Good class, ma'am," he said, and she realized the young man complimenting her was the one she had dismembered in front of the other students a month or so back.

"That's Dr. Storey," she retorted, disconcerted that he seemed to have forgiven her. *Tell him that you appreciate his engagement in class. Tell him he didn't deserve the way you spoke to him before.* But her original programming kicked in, and she said nothing else.

When the last student had filed out, Sonja listened to the laughter and chatter filling the corridor. She muttered, "What would you think of this development, Jacob? What Bible verse would you quote about me? Perhaps one about not looking back for fear of turning to salt?"

Even more disconcerting than the shifting classroom environment was the way students suddenly came to office hours, seeking information, asking questions. Some dropped by unannounced and without specific intent, making her worry that she was being duped in a new and unknown way.

Ronnie Staller also came by, and she flopped into the visitor chair without waiting for permission. "Everyone's talking. You're lots nicer, look better too. Some says you're in love."

"It is 'some say,' Ms. Staller." Sonja corrected the student without her usual harshness. "You must decide the story you wish to tell others about who you are. Your dialect is part of that story." She yearned to impart her wisdom to another, perhaps discover another Jacob.

Act and talk like an ice queen with a frozen heart and people will bow— out of fear, not love. At least they will bow.

"That's okay, Doc. I like the way I talk. I mean, you talk good too. But that's not me."

Sonja retreated to a familiar territory: defensiveness. "Inquiries into my personal life are unacceptable. Office hours are for discussions related to coursework."

Staller's eyes twinkled.

Don't you dare ask. Don't give her the satisfaction of knowing that her possible actions impacted you. But Sonja was annoyed enough to dismiss her mental advisor.

"Have you emailed me, Ms. Staller? About a coming storm."

"Sure. You know, I wrote you and all. Class stuff, like butterflies bringing storms." Staller said.

In a flash, the old Sonja reappeared, and she toyed with the idea of punishing Staller—not just for the anonymous emails that Staller had seemed to author—but for the entire semester's chaos. But that impulse was quickly extinguished, and Sonja realized that she no longer hungered for revenge as she once had. She steered the discussion back to class-related matters.

"Your classwork has shown a degree of progress, Ms. Staller. I recommend that you set ambitious goals. Push yourself to improve, and you will pass."

Staller stayed slouched in the chair, and she smiled impishly.

"You are staring at me like I am a curiosity on exhibit," Sonja snapped. "Why are you here?"

Staller shrugged. "Stopped by to say hi."

"Our discussion is concluded." Sonja needed solitude, something she didn't get enough of these days.

"Sure thing, Doc." Staller stood up, scooping her backpack off the floor. "You look lots better. Like someone's taking good care of you." She started to go but stopped. "By the way, that bookmark I made for you. What happened to it?"

Sonja blinked, caught off guard. "I explained to you, Ms. Staller. I am prohibited from receiving gifts from my students." The truth was, Sonja had put the bookmark into one of her *Storey Story* journals that she had dug out from the garage and stashed in her bedside drawer. Occasionally, Sonja removed the bookmark to admire the rendered butterfly, but she would never admit that to Staller.

The young woman watched Sonja, then gave a smile of secret knowing.

Sonja popped the collar of her glacier-white blouse outside her navy blazer. "We are done here."

After Staller left, Sonja chastised herself out loud. "This creature you are turning into is unacceptable. Write your book. Hire the new professor. Transform your department, your university. Become a woman of significance."

She repeated the words like a mantra until she convinced herself that she had indeed begun a new story, a story that would end in her triumph over chaos.

Chapter 37

A Father Bends

A FEW DAYS BEFORE THE Thanksgiving break, there was a knock on the door of her office. Sonja got up to find Corey Randalls outside.

"Dad says I need to apologize," Randalls grumbled without stepping inside. "He says to tell you I'm getting doctor help for my anger and such. And...I need your class next semester to graduate." He glared down at her.

Destroy him.

Sonja ignored the voice.

"Come in, Mr. Randalls. Leave the door open. Sit." Somehow, she managed to sound like her old self, even if she didn't feel it.

Sonja returned to her Manhattan chair; an expensive Burberry scarf, decorated with assorted butterflies and blooms, now hid the gashed leather seat.

"Regarding your *apology*, I will take a wait-and-see approach." Sonja winced at Crystal's words coming out of her mouth. "Perhaps I will permit you to take my class in the spring. However, your apology will have no influence on whether you pass or not. You will attend every lecture, complete every assignment, and meet every deadline. In other words, you will earn your grade. Am I clear?"

"Yeah. Sure...uh, ma'am," he said, teeth only slightly clenched this time.

"You will address me as Dr. Storey or Professor Storey." She repeated, "Am I clear, Mr. Randalls?"

"Yeah, Dr. Storey, ma'am. Got it."

Sonja studied his face, but no matter how hard she tried, she could not see Jacob in Corey's hard, pinched features, and yet she considered offering this young man another chance and letting him back into her classroom.

"So, you'll do it?" he pressed.

For you, Jacob, she thought. "Email me your request. I will consider it."

Randalls rose without a word of appreciation and slunk into the hallway, the fluorescence reflecting off his greasy hair.

Spent, Sonja sagged in her chair, rubbing its arms like they were worry stones. She immediately began questioning her decision. Two hours later, she took her doubts to her date with Crystal. Sitting at their usual table at Ridges, Sonja described her encounter with Corey Randalls and watched her girlfriend's eyes darken into puddles filled with autumn leaves.

"Does he scare you?" Crystal reached for Sonja's hand across the table.

"He terrifies me," she said, relaxing under Crystal's touch. "There's something about him. He balls his fists, then his fingers spring open like they've been overtightened and suddenly released. And his eyes smolder with something deeper than hatred. I swear I see..."

"What?" Crystal prodded.

"Chaos."

"Please don't let him into your class."

"He already emailed me a surprisingly articulate request. Reminded me of..." *Jacob.* "It is done," she finished. "I directed Harmony to issue the permit."

"You couldn't save Jacob, so... Damn it, Sonja. You cling to your pain like it will keep you safe."

"Thank you, Dr. Byrd, for the free counseling session. Anyway, this way I'll be able to monitor him."

"Monitor him for what?"

"I can watch him in class, direct him to appropriate campus resources if I notice anything amiss. But enough about work." Sonja overlooked how Crystal's eyes sparked. "A toast to the near end of the semester." She raised her wineglass.

Crystal raised her whiskey to join the toast, and she grinned, her innate optimism appearing to overshadow any lingering concerns about Corey Randalls. "The semester nears its end. While we're at our beginning."

They clinked.

Crystal drank, then said, "By the way, I have an idea about who may have left those red sticky notes back in September."

Sonja set down her glass and waited, unsure of the exact suggestion Crystal would advance this time but sure that the suggestion would be the same in one way: Sonja had conjured the chaos.

"I had a student in my office the other day. Education major. She was telling me about her pedagogical courses and recent best practices research about playing games in the classroom. That got me thinking."

"Of course it did."

"Bear with me, love. So I log onto the system, check the schedule, and find that, yes, there are education practicums. Right before your morning class and your afternoon one too. Now, I'm speculating here, but could it have been an education student who left those sticky notes? 'Let's Play a Game!' was a message not to you but was more a reminder about an application activity. That seems like something that might happen in pedagogy training."

"I will consider it," Sonja responded, having no such intention. She picked up her wine and enjoyed the metallic taste of resentment in her mouth.

It's not too late, girlie. Be who you really are.

Resentment was the key Sonja could use to unlock her old, formidable, cold self. But once again, Crystal—knowingly or unknowingly—melted down that key, and Sonja along with it.

"What do you want to do for Thanksgiving?" Crystal asked. "Admittedly, it's a problematic holiday, but— Anyway, I already told Momma and Daddy I won't be coming home, and they were *not* pleased. So…"

"I avoid all holidays." Sonja lowered her gaze, not wanting Crystal to see the longing there for a kind of childhood she'd been denied.

"Not this year. I want an excuse to cook and celebrate with you, darling. And we're going to do just that." Crystal laughed in that unrestrained way that Sonja both adored and envied. "I'll even eat your damn salad."

Sonja smiled despite her ambivalence. "If I have to celebrate a holiday, then you have to eat pine nuts."

Sonja raised Crystal's theory about the red sticky notes during her next meeting with Wake.

"As uncomfortable as this will be for you, Dr. Storey, let's stay with this possibility," Wake said. "Two weeks back, you diverted our session into a lecture about chaos theory."

Sonja stiffened. "Is that a criticism?"

"An observation, leading me to a question: could those sticky notes have been your butterfly wings?"

"I do not pay you to keep uttering nonsense," Sonja snapped.

Wake flipped through her notebook and put a finger on the page. "You talked about Loren—"

"Who? Oh!" Sonja snorted. "You mean Edward Lorenz. Not Loren. You are quite mistaken."

"That's it. The butterfly effect."

"Your point?"

"What if those two notes were the flapping wings of a butterfly? The wings caused a tsunami in your life, shaping how you perceived and reacted to everything that came after."

Sonja swallowed a memory like something sharp, but it came back up, and this time, she spit it out. "I think Ashley said those words to me during my last visit with my father and his wife." She rubbed her eyes. "It's fuzzy, her words. But I hear a squeaky voice saying, 'Let's play a game.' Or maybe it was, 'Do you want to play a game with me?'"

Sonja pressed her lips together, but they reopened, almost against her will. "I remember her hiding under the bed and hearing her wail." A laugh snuck out of Sonja, as if she were telling a funny tale about an old family drama, but soon pain replaced the hilarity.

Tell the whole story, girlie. Tell her what you said to sweet little Ashley. "Get the fuck away from me, you brat."

Sonja shuddered, trying to convince herself that the exchange wasn't that horrible, but the specter of her mother in her head disagreed.

Girlie, say what you can't stop seeing: a father bends to coax out the replacement daughter from underneath the bed and turns his back on the original. And keeps it turned.

"Ashley's mother couldn't get her to come out. Neither could Father. That was the end. Invitation retracted, to that visit and future ones." Sonja scoffed. "To clarify, my father never invited me in the first place. I invited myself. He only agreed because of his second wife."

"Your stepmother stood up for you?"

"That made me hate her even more."

"Sonja, that's big. You saw those words on the red stickies, and they unleashed a storm. A storm that had been building since your childhood."

Sonja squeezed her eyes shut, blocking out Wake and the berry-colored office. When she reopened them, Wake's obvious pity greeted her, reminding her of how her stepmother had looked at her. She picked up her tote and clutched it to her chest. "Just because my bratty half-sister said words similar to the notes doesn't negate the fact that I have a tormentor, maybe even more than one." Sonja glared at Wake. "I swear, you and Crystal want to convince me that I imagined everything."

Wake closed her notebook and clasped her hands. "You said yourself that the campus police found nothing."

"Officer Sounder *found* nothing. Not that *nothing happened.* That one student worker didn't perpetrate every torment I've been facing. There is someone else." *There is still a game being played against me.*

Wake put her notebook on the side table. Then she leaned forward and said, "You're at a crossroads. We could expend energy on these mysterious incidents, or we can work on changing the narrative."

"For someone who deals in complexity and nuance, Abby, you sure as fuck know how to present an oversimplified binary."

Wake raised an eyebrow.

Sonja continued. "Choice one: remain vigilant about my stalker, and in doing so, harm myself and everyone around me. Choice two: surrender to the unknown and unknowable. As if I am incapable of doing both."

"A happy, healthy human cannot live both hypervigilant and contented."

Sonja stood up. "I have another engagement."

"Same time next week?" Wake had stopped protesting Sonja's abrupt termination of her sessions.

Sonja didn't answer. She wasn't sure how much more of this mental-health crap she could take before going completely mad.

She drove through the industrial sector, absorbing the weathered concrete and neglected metal structures. This part of town seemed to free her to think unthinkable thoughts and call forth ugly truths:

Maybe these chaotic months *had* been a byproduct of deeply entrenched childhood patterns. Maybe she really did interpret each incident as a threat, magnifying disturbances until the world seemed to rage around her?

"Check the facts," she muttered. And when she did, she didn't like the results.

She had stopped hearing from Storms Comin. The mysterious emails had evaporated, and Ronnie Staller had strongly hinted at a confession. The posts that had taunted her on social media had vanished as well. That might have had something to do with the inquiry committee finishing its work.

Once the formal hearing committee had voted to strip Dr. Horace Watson of his tenure and dismiss him, the threatened lawsuit against Sonja and Mary Ann disappeared. Consequently, Jodi Jenkins had stopped contacting her. Even Douglas Christopher had backed off, likely spooked by her promise to file harassment charges against him. Once more, Dr. Sonja Storey became invisible, unworthy of even the attention of madmen.

By the time Sonja reached home, she concluded that, in fact, she might have conjured everything.

On bad nights, though, her suspicions reemerged, fertilized by back pain and insomnia. The muscle relaxers usually helped her fall asleep, but after her girlfriend started interrogating her about the pills and their side effects, Sonja began taking them secretly.

Those times when she lay awake, instead of reaching for and confiding in Crystal, she reengaged in old habits, tiptoeing into her home office to conduct internet searches. Sometimes she searched for designer clothes, hungry for vibrant colors, but more often, she plugged various spellings of her name into search bars, going from one site to another, convinced that her tormentor still played a game she hadn't figured out yet.

Her nocturnal research never bore fruit. Exhausted but not sleepy, she would rub her aching back and take another pill, seeking rest that still eluded her even when she was on the verge of having the life she wanted.

Chapter 38

All Things

Sonja opened emails from the search committee. As she did, she rejoiced:

Each member's rank order of the job applicants was amazingly consistent and matched her own rankings. Of course, she had harangued them all, underscoring her selection criteria for the ideal candidate. All this meant that they were ahead of schedule and their upcoming meeting would be shorter than planned.

She gathered her handwritten notes about the search and rushed to the main office to scan everything. In the middle of scanning, she received a text.

Have to talk @ home. Important but no 911. LuvU babe

"What now? A neighbor missing their guinea pig?" she muttered, rolling her eyes, putting down the phone, and resuming her work—until Jay interrupted.

"Sounds like you have promising applicants for the assistant professor position." He peered over her shoulder.

Sonja swept up the pages and clutched them to her chest like she had her diary whenever her mother had come snooping.

"We finalize rankings today, virtual interviews by the end of the semester. Campus interviews begin late January, completed early February," she outlined curtly.

"Ambitious timeline, but you have it under control, then. Thanks, Sonja." Jay walked away.

"Jay," Sonja called after him.

He turned back. The fluorescent lights emphasized the wrinkles crisscrossing his face, and she regretted some of her harshness toward him this semester. She might never trust or forgive him, but she also wanted to find a way forward.

"I do have it under control," Sonja said. "The person we hire will help build the department and transform WHSU into a respected university." Then she offered him an olive branch. "I would like you to host each candidate for breakfast and provide the committee with your feedback." She thought she actually meant her words to him.

"Sounds good. Update me as you see fit." He disappeared into his office, his shoulders slightly less slumped.

She sensed Harmony watching her. "Yes?" Sonja faced the secretary.

"I'll be seeing you Saturday." Harmony half smiled. "Crystal invited me for drinks on the deck. A chill's setting in, so I'll dress warm. It's not as cold as it used to be in the mountains. Winters were real bad once upon a time." Then she added, smile widening, "Hope you'll be joining us instead of hiding out in the bedroom."

With barely a nod in response, Sonja grabbed her cell and left, wanting to get away from the gloating woman. She briefly fantasized about going home, shoving the mortgage statement into Crystal's face, and yelling, "Who owns this house? I do. You don't. Stop inviting that woman into my home."

But to do such a thing would be to risk Byrd flying away from her, and for good this time. So she would hold her tongue as she did more and more, and she would try to enjoy life with her annoyingly well-adjusted girlfriend.

Hours later, exuberant after a successful search meeting, Sonja dashed out of Terrell Center, eager to celebrate her victory over a glass of pinot at home. She hustled to the campus parking lot as fast as her black pencil skirt and burgundy Calvins permitted, her new Fleuette coat flaring out like a cape.

After a bumpy start at WHSU, Dr. Sonja J. Storey was on the cusp of owning the department. As soon as she hired a newbie PhD, she would mold them into a colleague who would share her vision. She wouldn't overthrow Jay as chair, his administrative experience too useful. Soon, though, she would have enough influence to essentially run the place.

When she got to her car, she peeled off her coat and laid it neatly on the back seat, and for the entire drive home, she drummed Bimmer's steering wheel. As soon as she pulled up in front of her house, Sonja's excitement mounted: her girlfriend's car was gone. *Finally! I will have my home to myself.* She ended her percussive performance on the steering wheel with two toots of her horn and a third, more prolonged.

She pulled Bimmer to the curb and, leaving it running, hopped out to grab her mail.

That's when the screeching started.

She jerked her head right toward the unearthly noise, causing her to teeter on her heels. With her legs bound by the tight hem of her pencil skirt, she fell backward just as something pounded with a *rat-a-tat-tat* against the metal mailbox.

She thrashed about on her back like a helpless cockroach, struggling to roll onto her side. Her pump was still on her right foot. Her other foot was pinned underneath her, shoeless and wedged between her rump and the rough pavement. Nothing hurt. Yet.

"Yougame," someone yowled, sounding more like a wounded cat than human.

Sonja watched as a gnarled form began shuffling around the nose of Bimmer: a woman—Sonja now saw—with a head of white hair that stuck up like stalagmites and dressed in a ratty housecoat and dirty slippers.

For some reason, Sonja noticed these things before she noticed the pistol.

"Stop," Sonja ordered. She eyed the pistol aimed at her as she tried freeing her trapped foot. But her skirt was like a straitjacket binding her legs.

"Houseturn idiot. Red tower spy." The woman spoke in the rhythm of language but the content of gibberish.

"I don't know who the fuck you are. Or what you're saying," Sonja yelled, then realized her mistake.

Silence. You are the girl who saved herself from drowning, pulled herself out. Pull yourself out. Cool detachment wafted over her like winter fog.

"Your name, please?" Sonja asked.

"Act thief cunt." The woman laughed excitedly, twisted her face, and mouthed something that went unsaid, or unheard by Sonja.

As calmly as she could, Sonja placed one hand on the road, then wiggled her foot out from beneath her, ripping her skirt and hose in the process. The nail of her index finger bent back and tore off, shooting pain all the way to her bicep. Sonja gasped; her head spun.

"Grannie you," the woman shrieked and shook the gun at Sonja.

Sonja responded through the agony in a strangled voice, "I live here. I live in this house." She pointed at her home, glancing at her index finger, unexpectedly fixating on the blood around it.

You're going into shock. Manipulate your nervous system.

Sonja slowed her breathing and made herself study her opponent. The woman with wild, white hair and red-ringed eyes looked like a deranged albino racoon wearing a henna mask.

"I am Dr. Sonja J. Storey," she announced as if introducing herself at a professional mixer, her jaw nearly clamping shut from pain radiating through her body. "Your name, please?"

"Gramps nether." The stranger slapped Bimmer's hood with one hand, swallowed hard as if gulping for air, then laughed shrilly. "Beenfooling woods."

Jumbled words, slurred speech, grip loosening on the pistol. Signs of confusion, fatigue.

Sonja dug into her memory, trying to remember one of Crystal's boring reports about neighborhood news—something about dementia.

"I'm going to stand. To hear you better." She struggled to get her feet under her while monitoring her opponent. *Left knee buckling, right shoulder sagging.* Sonja thought the arm holding the gun lowered another inch, maybe two.

"Trucker pussy—" More laughter, more snarled gibberish.

"Hi there, Liz."

Sonja remained on her rump, thankfully, because she swayed, dizzy with the sound of Crystal's voice. She shifted to see her girlfriend holding open the security door. "You're home! Damn it, Crystal, inside! She has a gun," she cried out as she labored harder to stand, fighting agony, gravity, and her goddamn pencil skirt.

At last, Sonja contorted herself, planting her lopsided feet under her, one throbbing inside a burgundy pump, the other howling inside blood-saturated nylon, and she rose onto her haunches.

"Hi there, Liz!" Crystal repeated, ignoring Sonja's command to retreat indoors.

Frozen in place, Sonja glanced up long enough to see Crystal offering an absurd and neighborly wave. The woman slowly started angling toward Crystal.

"Ma'am!" Sonja screamed with such force that she wobbled in her uneven squat—one Calvin stubbornly clinging to her foot—and she nearly tipped back over. "Ma'am, look at me," she panted, furiously working to maintain her balance. "I'm the one working with Grannie, Gramps, Trucker. Your problem's with me. I'm the one who did the bad things. I'm the one trying to destroy you. And I *will* destroy you if you turn your back on me."

Crystal sang out over Sonja's loud antagonism. "My darlings, it's okay. We're okay." Gliding down the steps and along the sidewalk, she slowly moved toward the woman, waving pleasantly, and maintaining a sing-songy voice. "Liz is our lovely neighbor, Sonja. Liz and I met earlier today. Remember, Liz? I knocked on your door. You showed me your pellet gun, Liz, darling." Crystal pointed at the gun and smiled. "*That* pellet gun you're holding. Remember, Liz. Sorry. I didn't introduce myself before today."

Liz sloppily aimed the gun at Crystal, making Sonja's heart thud and her head roar, but the woman's gesture seemed weaker, less threatening. "Wakesteal," Liz said, imploringly.

Sonja's knee and back were screaming, but she disregarded them and stood, kicking off her remaining pump while fighting a weird compulsion to glance down and assess the damage to her outfit.

Crystal drew closer to the mailbox, eyes locked on Liz. "Your husband," she hummed more than spoke, "left you that pellet gun. Right, Liz? Left it for you to protect yourself."

"Nag." Liz turned back to glare at Sonja and blinked rapidly.

"Crystal—" Sonja started, but Crystal held up a finger for her—a *hold-on* gesture—then swapped it for a thumbs-up.

"Liz, Liz, darling, we're talking." Crystal held the thumbs up high and steady and smiled. "Poor, Liz. You patrol all night, guard your..." Crystal's rich alto was briefly lost to Sonja over the sound of Bimmer's idling engine. "...with your pellet gun. Right, Liz? Keep them away."

As Sonja listened, she realized that Crystal's lyrical cadence was directed at Liz. But the content: that was for Sonja, and pieces started clicking into place—finally, a puzzle Sonja could solve.

"That sounds horrible, Liz," Sonja said, her tone measured, her panic slightly subsiding, and she began limping toward the two women. "It's exhausting. To remain awake all night. To ensure your safety. You're the owner of the property at the end of the street, Liz. We are neighbors. Thanks for patrolling the street and down in the woods, Liz."

As Sonja closed in, she adjusted her stance, crouching subtly like she had when dodging her raging mother. Her injured knee screamed, but she regained sufficient footing and prepared to hurl herself at the armed albino racoon.

"Sonja, it's okay. No need, no need for that. All is well. Come greet Liz," Crystal cooed, gesturing at Sonja, then Liz. "Maybe Liz will show you her pellet gun. Her husband left it to her, I think. Did I get that right, Liz? We had a bit of a rushed chat today." Crystal closed in on Liz, pointing at her own chest and then at the pellet gun, and held out her hands, palms up, as if ready to receive precious treasure. "Liz, you've had to deal with so much nastiness. How about letting me carry your gun for a short while? It looks heavy."

"Roofpeel," Liz rasped. "Can't nightmoonblinds." The woman fumbled the gun into Crystal's hands.

Crystal tucked the weapon under one arm and wrapped the other around Liz who sagged against her.

Sonja staggered, coming to stand with the women, and she gingerly touched Crystal's sweat-drenched pullover, relief flooding her. With her battered hand, she cupped Liz's upper arm, keeping her bloody finger extended, but through her own pain, she still felt the loose skin and the shrunken muscle under the thin housecoat. The rancid scent of her neighbor's unwashed body assailed her nose.

"Faceswitch," Liz moaned, pressing into Crystal's body. "Toforget... no."

"Liz, I understand. I think," Sonja responded, teary-eyed.

And maybe for the first time in her life, she sensed that she truly did understand another. She leaned in and hugged both women with arms untrained in giving kindness.

The police took a report, and an ambulance took Liz away.

That night, Sonja remained restless, and she began to panic. It was the last week of classes, and she couldn't cancel on her students tomorrow, not this close to their finals. Even Crystal's warmth didn't stop the chaotic zigzagging of dark images in Sonja's mind, causing her skull to vibrate and buzz.

Liz loaded into the ambulance, sobbing, babbling. Crystal's arm tight around Sonja. Mailbox dented, nearly buckled in on itself. Boy Cop saying words that Sonja couldn't process. Crystal's sedan parked in her garage, taking Bimmer's spot.

Sonja wiggled closer to Crystal, seeking a sense of safety that would let her sleep. Instead, she heard Boy Cop's voice.

"It's a pellet gun all right, ma'am. Good thing she missed you. These things can do some bad damage."

His voice faded into other memories, ones that flashed in her mind like a broken warning signal.

Crazed hermit holding a gun. Pencil skirt in the trash under a bottle of pinot, wilted romaine leaves. Ravaged Calvins kicked deep into her closet. Liz's steel wool pubic hair peeking out, missing housecoat buttons. The stench of her neighbor's self-neglect, the neglect of others.

Unable to escape the mental barrage, Sonja left the warmth of her bed and went out into the chilly night. The late autumn breeze carried the promise of winter, and she discovered that she breathed more easily on her deck.

The door opened behind her, and an arm snaked around her upper body, pinning her arms in place.

"It's over, darling." Crystal's voice floated like applewood smoke in frigid air.

"See, I didn't manufacture my persecution." *I'm not crazy.*

"I know."

"She's my future."

"You're not going to wind up like Liz. I—*we* won't let that happen."

Sonja said nothing, not wanting to explain that she wasn't just thinking about their hermit neighbor. Her mother haunted her, likely always would.

"We can't predict every storm," Crystal said softly. "We can only figure out what to do when facing them…and who we face them with. Now, come back to bed. Rest."

"You go. I'll be there momentarily."

"Don't take another pill."

"It is not just some *pill*. It's medicine. I reinjured my back tonight when that lunatic attacked me." She growled, and Crystal surprised her by hugging her tighter.

"Those muscle relaxers can cause vivid dreams, hallucinations," Crystal claimed. "No more, please. I'll rub your back, and in the morning, we'll find a doctor, update your diagnosis, pursue treatment options."

"Where did you read that about my medicine?"

"On a medical website. Let's crawl into bed."

Sonja pulled away and faced Crystal. "Wait! I didn't hallucinate the pancaked creature in my driveway."

"That's partly why I sent you that text, babe, about us needing to talk. Seems Liz did that."

Sonja tried checking her girlfriend's expressions, but there were too many shadows. "How do you know?"

"I worked from home today. During a break, I went to move my car so it wouldn't block the driveway. That's when I saw something above the garage."

"What? I notice everything about my property."

"I grew up with pellet guns. Daddy and Mamma used them on rabbits in the garden. I shot trees, sometimes a neighbor's mailbox. I might have even shot my rapist's vintage Mustang." Crystal snickered. "Anyway, I found damage on the side of your house. Some of it looked pretty recent."

Sonja protested, "That isn't possible. I notice all problems here."

Except that side of your house rises too far above your driveway. You don't notice it if you can't check it.

"There was a dented gutter. Gashed white coating. Dinged soffits," Crystal detailed. "I actually stood on my car to get a better look—couldn't find a ladder. I suspected a pellet gun had caused that damage. So I went to talk with the only neighbor with a clear vantage point of that side of the property. At first, Liz wouldn't answer the door. When she finally did, she launched into a meandering rant. It was early enough in the day, so she spoke clearer. I've had experience with sundowning. My relatives—"

"Crystal," Sonja prodded, but managed not to growl, *Get to the point.*

"Yeah, sure. Anyway, I got the gist of her problem with you. You stole her car, tore the roof off her house. On top of that, you antagonize her with loud noises. Oh, you also drag race up and down the street at all hours and spy on her with your telescope. At some point, she mentioned a big, brown truck that delivers top-secret packages to you from her grandparents. Seems the driver ran over the cat as a warning. The longer she talked, the more jumbled her speech became. One moment she insists the cat was yours and she returned it to you. The next, she's telling me she dumped it in your driveway to let you know she was onto you. Poor thing. Dementia's a cruel bitch."

"This is too much." Sonja huffed.

"There's more, but it'll keep until you're rested."

"Tell me now. Please." *I must know.*

"She patrolled her property at night to keep tabs on you because of your role in the conspiracy against her. But then she started talking about having shootouts with intruders. Like I said, I have some experience with relatives. The confabulation, visual and auditory hallucinations. Apparently, you got into a gunfight with Liz. Is there something you're not telling me?"

"No gunfight. I might have enjoyed that. Not with her, though."

Crystal snorted, then her tone turned serious again. "I texted you. I wanted to confer with you before calling for a safety check...since it's your house. Should've gone ahead and done it. If I had..." She suddenly burst into tears.

"It's okay." Sonja hugged Crystal, offering comfort, though her arms felt insufficient for that task. "I can't believe that hermit opened the door for you. And you got her name."

"I think she mistook me for someone. Initially."

"I never saw her until today," Sonja said. "How did you manage to get so much information from her?"

"There's something about me. People let me in. Always have. Now, let's go back to bed. I'll remind you how friendly I am. Besides, we've got to get some sleep. There's still a semester to finish."

Crystal pulled Sonja back into the house, and they locked up, then returned to bed.

You've been lulled, said the primitive part of Sonja's brain. *You heard what she said about people letting her in.*

Crystal interrupted Sonja's hissing brain, whispering, "I love you, babe, and all things about you, great and small, weird and wonderful."

"I love you too, Crysse." Sonja breathed in the scent of the intoxicating woman, and the mental voices quieted.

Chapter 39

A Sadder, Wiser Woman

By Friday morning, Sonja's cuts and bruises had healed enough that she limped and winced slightly less. She was starting to relax now that she could see the semester's end. Too, Liz remained hospitalized, so the midnight disturbances had ceased. Sonja felt lighter, despite Harmony's impending visit that weekend.

She watched Crystal sleep, admiring the woman's swells and dips. She followed the lines up to the spray of hair that had darkened to the color of wet driftwood in the morning light. When her eyes wandered over the breasts, she was reminded of rolling sandy hills under the early morning sun, golden and divine.

Her eyes widened, and she finally saw what she should have seen from the beginning, what her reptilian brain had been trying to warn her about all along.

"Ashley," she whispered.

Her lover stirred, opened her eyes, and smiled a drowsy smile. "What did you say, darling?"

Sonja's vision darkened, and the currents pulled her once again toward the blackness.

Pull yourself out, girlie.

She struggled to break free, but her dark, churning thoughts refused to release her. Again, she struggled, this time latching onto Crystal's hand, squeezing an SOS. Crystal squeezed back, and Sonja was buoyed.

"I need to tell you...Ashley," she choked out, feeling as if her mouth were full of saltwater.

"Later. We'll make time later, darling." Crystal gave a kiss of resuscitation.

And Sonja yielded to that kiss, surrendering to the salty pleasures and the majestic terrors beneath waves of bliss.

Sonja put her hand in her lap and fidgeted with the sash of her LilySilk robe.

"There is something I must say." Sonja had no clue where this revelation would take her, take them. "I only became aware of it this morning. And I fail to understand why... Why now?"

Crystal leaned in across the kitchen table and clasped Sonja's uninjured hand. "Out with it, love."

"This is difficult, even disturbing." She paused, unsure how to begin.

"Would you like to run to your office and design presentation slides for this seminar, Dr. Storey?" Crystal smiled amiably.

"Very well. You...it seems, well, you resemble my half-sister. Somewhat." Once she started speaking, the words rushed out. "At least in the photos I saw from years ago. Your hair, your smile, the shape of your face, your skin. They all remind me of her."

"That explains it!" Crystal released Sonja's hand and smacked the top of the table. "I kept trying to figure it out. You excise people from your life with ruthless precision, yet you kept pulling me back in."

Sonja dropped her eyes and stared into her cup of tea, certain that Crystal would be out the door any minute. "Abby will orgasm over this," she muttered.

"Confession time, darling." Crystal unwrapped the mermaid scarf from around her head, releasing the ripples. "I've hinted pretty hard, but you remind me of—"

"Aunt Laura?"

"Momma, of course—minus the beautiful Black woman part. We can't mess up Abby's forthcoming Freudian analysis."

"No wonder you didn't have enough sense to stay away."

"Yep, babe. But you've got to know. I don't give a good goddamn why we fit together, as long as we do."

278

Space widened for Sonja, and she expanded into it. Ideas about the larger world that had once repelled her now intrigued her.

"I got an email yesterday. I deleted it immediately." Sonja babbled nervously.

Crystal sipped her coffee. "I'm listening."

"The Highlander Harmonizers, Harmonizing Highlanders…whatever those nerds—musicians—call themselves. They're performing tonight at Ridges. There'll be drinks, dancing." Sonja's face heated as she stumbled around this new expanded space. "Not that I can do the dancing part with my sore body."

Crystal recaptured Sonja's hand. "Never thought you'd be receptive to attending such a frivolous event. It has everything to do with having fun and absolutely nothing to do with your obsessive professional parkouring. I love the idea, babe. It will be our debut as a WHSU powerhouse couple." Crystal grinned. "On second thought, maybe you can get some parkour moves in."

"That's not what I was thinking, but you raise an interesting point. It could be the beginning of our joint campaign to raze WHSU to the ground."

"Or here's a crazy idea. We build up our university, our community. Together."

Sonja drank in Crystal's warm honey eyes. "One moment." She stood up and hurried to the bedroom closet, and when she returned, she watched Crystal slumping in the chair, eyes shut, humming, and looking perfectly at home.

"Would this be too much?" Sonja displayed the pearl-violet dress with bell sleeves. "For tonight."

Crystal's eyes opened and settled on the dress. "It's perfect. Reminds me of the sky right before a huge storm hits."

"Or maybe it's the color of the sky after the storm," Sonja countered, tossing the dress carelessly across the back of a chair where it landed askew.

Bridging the distance between them, Sonja pushed into Crystal's arms. In the rosy glow of a fresh morning, she embraced her lover in a way that only a sadder and wiser woman could, the kind of woman also better prepared for storms on the horizon.

Other Books from Ylva Publishing

www.ylva-publishing.com

Requiem for Immortals

Lee Winter

ISBN: 978-3-95533-710-0
Length: 263 pages (86,000 words)

Requiem is a brilliant cellist with a secret. The dispassionate assassin has made an art form out of killing Australia's underworld figures without a thought. One day she's hired to kill a sweet and unassuming innocent. Requiem can't work out why anyone would want her dead—and why she should even care.

Mine to Keep

Wendy Hudson

ISBN: 978-3-95533-882-4
Length: 391 pages (77,000 words)

Plagued by childhood nightmares since losing her mother, Erin embarks on a journey to rural Scotland, hoping to trace her father and put the darkness to rest. When she meets Abigail, they quickly become search partners and together pick apart fact from folklore. Erin takes sanctuary within Abigail's castle walls as her nightmares start to close in. Can she defeat them and learn to live again?

A Heist Story
Ellen Simpson

ISBN: 978-3-95533-958-6
Length: 315 pages (113,000 words)

Life gets weird for Marcey Daniels when an art thief dies and leaves her a curious and much sought-after book. Suddenly a determined Interpol agent named Wei is sniffing around, along with the mysterious, flirtatious criminal, Kat. Everyone has their own agenda in this intricate suspense thriller. As the double-crosses pile up, can Marcey unpick the trap within the puzzle?

A Curious Woman
Jess Lea

ISBN: 978-3-96324-160-4
Length: 283 pages (100,000 words)

Bess has moved to a coastal town where she has a job at a hip gallery, some territorial chickens, and a lot of self-help books. She's also at war with Margaret, who runs the local museum with an iron fist. When they're both implicated in a senseless murder, can they work together to expose the truth?

A funny, fabulous, cozy mystery filled with quirkiness and a sweet serve of lesbian romance.

About Ana

Ana K. Wrenn wrote her first story at 8 years old while sitting on the scuffed wooden floor of her childhood bedroom. Then and there, she fell in love with ripe words, rich metaphors, and complex characters. An award-winning professor, researcher, and writer, she spent decades authoring dozens of scholarly articles and nonfiction essays about women's lives, losses, and loves. Secretly, though, as she worked her ways up the academic ranks, she continued writing novels. She weaves her love of and admiration for women into all her works, fiction and nonfiction, and is especially enraptured by the courage and fortitude women display when facing difficult times.

Ana is rooted in the mountains of Southern Appalachia, USA, where she writes in a house atop a hill, surrounded by weeping hemlocks, towering poplars, draping rhododendrons, and whining dogs and cats adopted from her local shelter. She is a member of the Golden Crown Literary Society, Tennessee Mountain Writers Association, and Women's Fiction Writers Association. *Strange Attractors* is her debut novel.

CONNECT WITH ANA
Website: www.anakwrenn.com
Twitter: @AnaKWrenn1
E-Mail: anakwrenn@gmail.com

Acknowledgments

Truly, writers do not write in solitude. We are surrounded by those who guide us and who sometimes save us from getting lost.

First, I acknowledge David and Mom. You helped me stay on my path, whether it was choked with new ideas or dry from an extended drought. I'm at a loss for how to express my appreciation for all the ways you add to my life. Thank you for championing me when I had a nascent dream and could not always map my way from dream to reality. You comforted me after each failure, each rejection. Then you encouraged me to keep on keeping on. Thank you. I love and cherish you both.

Second, Cary (though you should never come second): we have been together for years, even when apart. Across the miles, we are threaded, and you'll see our connection woven throughout this story. Thank you for your love and support all these decades. During my life journey, I recite your mantras to keep me motivated and grounded. I appreciate your willingness to read one of the earliest drafts of this book and giving me your insights. My deepest love to you, My Cary, my Lifey.

Third, I must acknowledge the work of my editors. Lori Ann Manis, you read my work before anyone else did, but your keen insight helped me find my way to lusher, more fecund worlds. You are my sister. You are my editor. You are my friend. Thank you, dear Sis.

Then there are those who enter the editing process at later stages. Jeni Chappelle, you helped me see what else could be done to make this book thrive. Thank you for your pointed questions and comments.

Lee Winter, you are one of the best editors I have ever worked with, and I've worked with many. I was intimidated as hell when I found out you were going to be my editor, but I am grateful that you stepped into that role for my debut novel. You pushed and prodded, inspiring me to rethink how to execute my vision. Somehow you were persuasive, compassionate, and funny as hell all at the same time. I found myself killing many of my most precious darlings, grumbling under my breath as I did so. Time and again, though, I came to realize that your suggestions transformed my story in unexpected ways.

Thank you, Jawahara and Kelly Heard, for beta reading my book at some of its most vulnerable stages. Jawahara, you are one of my oldest and dearest friends, and I was comforted by your guidance, which inspired me to make final changes before releasing this book to a larger world. You figured out how to tell me to tend to a section with more care, and you did it in a way that made my soul sing. You will always be my writer whisperer. Thanks, Sis.

Kelly, I trust you in ways that continue to surprise me, and I'm so grateful that I listened to my instincts and asked you to join my writing journey. With compassion and grace, you provided insights into my words and worlds, and you're a damn fine writer too.

Writers nurture the worlds we create, and it looks like solitary work, but it isn't. Shannon Kirk, thank you for your books. They inspired me, and your DMs kept me going.

Cam, thank you for being my patient guide through the world of technology and for cocreating and writing for *Old Gods of Appalachia*, my favorite podcast! You are Goddess Sent.

My extended family of choice has always been there in some form. Katie, I deeply appreciate your willingness to help plan the book birthday for my debut novel; you are compassionate, patient, and kind and honor me with your friendship. And thank you, Bekah and Hannah, for your input and advice. Jamie, thank you for cheering me on during phone calls and meals together. Tee, Matt, Amber, and Wesley, thanks for inspiring me and championing me, even when you had no clue what I was doing on weekends and during work "breaks." Thank you, Dylan and Tyler, for your patience and for feeding me after I had spent long hours on my laptop. To my broader family, I love you all.

Writers need to find their packs when traveling across the hostile terrain of publishing. For me, the Golden Crown Literary Society and Women's Fiction Writers Association (shout out to you, Leslie Kain!) provide safe, nurturing communities for authors to connect and continue developing their voices.

And of course, a huge thank you to Astrid Ohletz and the entire pack at Ylva for giving this professor and researcher a chance to fulfill a lifelong dream.

Dad, I miss you. And see, I didn't give up. Thanks for the years of mentoring me as a writer.

Also, I must acknowledge the various ways that Samuel Taylor Coleridge's *The Rime of the Ancient Mariner* captured my heart and imagination, something that readers familiar with the epic poem may discover in this story in the various quotes and "eggs" waiting to be cracked open.

Strange Attractors
© 2022 by Ana K. Wrenn

ISBN: 978-3-96324-669-2

Available in e-book and paperback formats.

Published by Ylva Publishing, legal entity of Ylva Verlag, e.Kfr.

Ylva Verlag, e.Kfr.
Owner: Astrid Ohletz
Am Kirschgarten 2
65830 Kriftel
Germany

www.ylva-publishing.com

First edition: 2022

Credits
Edited by Lee Winter and Julie Klein
Cover Design and Print Layout by Streetlight Graphics